BEAU TANCREDE;

OR,

THE MARRIAGE VERDICT

BY

ALEXANDER DUMAS.

Fredonia Books
Amsterdams. The Netherlands

Beau Tancrede: The Marriage Veredict

by
Alexander Dumas

ISBN: 1-58963-406-3

Copyright © 2001 by Fredonia Books

Reprinted from the 1888 edition

Fredonia Books
Amsterdam, The Netherlands
http://www.fredoniabooks.com

In order to make original editions of historical works available to scholars at an economical price, this facsimile of the original edition of 1888 is reproduced from the best available copy and has been digitally enhanced to improve legibility, but the text remains unaltered to retain historical authenticity.

BEAU TANCREDE.

CHAPTER I.

THE nobility of France has been cut up by three men: Louis the Eleventh, Richelieu, and Robespierre. Louis the Eleventh overthrew the great vassals; Richelieu decimated the great lords; and Robespierre annihilated the aristocracy.

The first prepared the way for sole monarchy; the second for absolute monarchy; the third for constitutional monarchy.

But as the events we are about to relate occurred between the years 1708 and 1716, we shall leave to the historian the appreciation, under their social relations, of the acts of the butcher king, and the deeds and crimes of a guillotining tribunal, to take a rapid survey of the condition of Paris and the provinces twenty years after the death of Richelieu; that is to say, at the commencement of the eighteenth century.

When we say Paris, we mean Versailles; for at this date there was no Paris, strictly speaking; Louis the Eleventh having never forgiven the offense it had committed against his august person, in ejecting him, when a child, from its walls, during the stormy days of the Fronde. And as, when enjoying the full plenitude of his power, he took the same pleasure in revenging himself upon things as upon men, he, in opposition to the capital, created Versailles, "that unworthy favorite," as it was then called; "the gigantic folly," as it ever will be called, to punish the old Louvre for its former rebellion, by withdrawing from it the sunshine of his royal presence.

Versailles, from the day Louis the Fourteenth transferred his residence thither, was the center of light, the luminous focus of the kingdom; the torch at which all the gilded butterflies, called courtiers, burned their wings; the sun

which rose upon a world not less resplendent than others,
and which increased in power and splendor in proportion to
its progress. Louis the Fourteenth adopted a double sun
as a device for his arms.

Thus the intensity of light concentrated upon Versailles
left the rest of the kingdom in comparative obscurity and
gloom. Everything that did not gravitate around this cen-
tral sun appeared to belong to the system of some inferior
planet, to some unknown nebulæ, scarcely worth the notice,
still less the study, of the political astronomers of the day.
Therefore, it happened that for the period of seventy-three
years that the reign of Louis the Fourteenth lasted the history of Versailles is, almost without exaggeration, the history of all France.

The result of this state of things is that in this splendid
gallery which the "Memoirs" of the time have opened to
our curiosity we see only great fortunes and notable dis-
graces and ruin. We trace the rise to prosperity of Lou-
vois, Villars, Argenson, and Colbert, and watch the decline
and fall of Rohan, Richelieu, Lauzan, and Guise. But as
to the brave and loyal provincial nobility that once formed
the strength of the monarchy, which, with Duguesclin,
chased the Black Prince from Guyenne, and, with Joan of
Arc, drove Henry the Sixth from France, it no longer existed, or, rather, being so far removed from the center of
action, it gave no signs of life and might be said to have
ceased to exist.

The fact is that far from the sun, and consequently from
the light, this rusticated nobility vegetated in obscurity and
was forgotten.

Had we the power to choose, we should select our hero
from among the gay courtiers who, as Saint Simon has
shown us, assisted regularly every night and morning in the
king's bed-chamber, uneasy if the royal eyebrow was elevated beyond its ordinary level, intoxicated by a royal smile,
or dying with grief at a harsh word dropped from regal
lips.

But we write a true and faithful history, and must take
our hero as we find him. It may possibly happen that,
strictly following his checkered career, we may be compelled, when he quits his provincial obscurity, to accompany him for a moment to the circle of light which Versailles, even at this period of decline, still diffused around.

But for the present, we must beg the reader to quit Versailles, which the presence of Mme. de Maintenon had for some time rendered a very dull and gloomy place of residence. He must accompany us some sixty leagues beyond Paris, to the left bank of the Loire, the environs of the city of Loches, to a beautiful plain situated between the Indre and the Char, intersected with woods and groves, pompously styled forests, and with ponds aggrandized with the title of lakes.

This plain was a complete nest of gentlefolks, where resided what was left of the great families from which Louis the Eleventh had lopped the feet, and whom Richelieu had decapitated. What with their dilapidated châteaux, their confiscated estates, and the curtailed privileges, all these brave rustics, noble as Charlemagne, were as poor as Job.

They were highwaymen under Louis the Eleventh and Philip Augustus, chiefs of partisans under Philippe le Bel and Charles the Fifth, captains under Francis the First and Henry the Second, and ended by becoming ensigns or sergeants under Henry the Fourth and Louis the Thirteenth; at last, finding no means of employing the swords of their ancestors in the lowest ranks of the army, the rust of which had nearly effaced the gilt, they had reverted to the primitive times we read of in Scripture, and, like Nimrod, had become great hunters. As we have endeavored to show, they were the descendants of the oldest, the noblest, and the richest families of France, but we must also, in candor say, they had in every respect greatly deteriorated.

The large land-owners had gradually drawn nigh to Versailles; and old Touraine, with its splendid castles, had emigrated, goods and chattels, to the environs of Chartres and of Maintenon. Loches, sharing in the general decay, had ceased to be a royal city; and the poor country squires inhabiting a rich, quiet, but abandoned territory, had, after making some noise in disputing the last days of the suzerainty against silence and oblivion, felt the veil of obscurity gradually fall upon their heads.

This state of things was quietly acquiesced in; for there was no escape from it. The consequence was, that at this epoch there existed throughout the province a silent reaction against the government of the great king. The gentry, whose pride was wounded by the opposition movement alluded to, supplied the place of what they had lost by names that reminded them of their former greatness. Thus they continued to call their houses castles; their external walls ramparts, the muddy brook a moat; they had a court of honor, but it was the only one to the house; there was a *salle d'armes,* but it did duty as a dairy or granary; their chapel was the nearest village church, often an hour's walk through the fields.

But pride apart, and ignoring the relation existing between things and their names, all these homes might have been quiet nests of happiness if their inhabitants had not thought themselves humiliated by admitting they could by any possibility be happy. Their vanity, it is true, was concealed by their discontent; too poor to go to Versailles, they loudly proclaimed that they despised the court. They pretended they were constantly invited thither, and that they as steadily refused to go. Now, as they all repeated the same story, they were compelled to pretend mutually that they believed each other. But, strange to say, this powerful little opposition was never heard beyond the limits of the province, and for the fifty or sixty years it had existed, transmitted from father to son, it had never reached the ears of the king.

In this little corner of the globe, which formed part of the garden of France, a gentleman was considered opulent with an income of two thousand crowns a year. Very few of them could command this coveted sum. This community of martyrs enjoyed an income averaging from twenty-five hundred to three thousand francs a year. And some of them were reduced to a hundred and fifty or two hundred pistoles a year, but still found means, notwithstanding the straitness of their incomes, to figure to advantage with their families at the meetings of the neighboring gentry.

All these noble lords, or rather their ancestors, formerly enjoyed extensive rights and privileges, which, one by one, had fallen into abeyance; but which enabled them, while reperusing their cha ters and deciphering their parchments, to experience a certain amount of pride, which they turned to the best account. A certain farmer of Baron Agenor Palamede d'Anguilhem's was one day greatly excited at hearing his lord and master, while hunting a wolf, say in a very loud voice:

" The Anguilhems, by a charter of the thirteenth cent-

ury, have once a year, while hunting, the privilege of
warming their feet in the entrails of one of their vassals cut
open by their trenchant squire."

It is scarcely necessary to remark that the worthy gentleman never felt so cold in his feet as to find it necessary
to have recourse to this strange method of warming them.

As the name of the Baron d'Anguilhem has dropped
from our pen, we will profit by the occasion to say who and
what he was.

The Baron Agenor Palamede d'Anguilhem was one of
those suzerain land-owners whose fortunes we have just
figured up, and whose privileges we enumerated.   He resided in a castle in the upper part of the valley, and was
proprietor of sixty sheep and six cows; his wool brought
him in two hundred francs a year, his flax three hundred,
making altogether a revenue of five hundred francs a year,
which he generously handed over to the Baroness d'Anguilhem for pin-money and the support of a son, her only
child.

Madame the Baroness Cornelia Athenias d'Anguilhem
possessed only six dresses, but they were, if not of the most
perfect elegance, at least of great beauty.   One dated from
her wedding-day, the other from the christening of her son,
who was styled baronet by courtesy, although in the aristocratic hierarchy he only had a right to the title of chevalier,
which we shall give him purely and simply, as we have not,
like those about him, any motives for flattery.   As to the
other four dresses, they were of more recent date, and were
modern in style, but, notwithstanding their comparative
freshness, they had seen at least two lustra.

The baronet, or rather the Chevalier Roger Tancrede
d'Anguilhem, presumptive heir to the domains of D'Anguilhem, Pintard, and Guerite, that is to say, sixty acres of
arable land and twenty acres of woodland, together with a
field planted with cabbages, was just entering his fifteenth
year.   He was a fine boy for his age, who could beat a hare
at running, and was as good a shot as his father's gamekeeper; he could hit nineteen partridges out of twenty, and
could ride the most restive horse in the country, without
bridle or saddle, and for ten leagues round enjoyed the reputation of being a veritable centaur.   From the time that he
was five years of age, his father, the baron, had daily put a
small-sword into his hands, and for an hour or two at a

time practiced him in the art of self-defense. The baron
enjoyed the reputation of being one of the best swordsmen
in the province, and this reputation fully protected him
from the painful necessity of drawing his sword in earnest.

These lessons in swordsmanship repeated daily for ten
years had not failed in their effect. From time to time the
smaller weapon was changed for a longer and stronger. His
arm became as firm and rigid as a bar of iron. The youth
could stand half the day on his guard, as immovable as a
statue, the weight of his body resting on his left leg, his
sword sustained on a level with his right breast in conformity with the first principles extant at that time, which
have never been superseded.

Beside these acquired advantages, the young chevalier
possessed certain natural gifts, such as a fine head of flaxen
hair, a straight figure of five feet five inches in height,
which promised to become taller; a pair of blue eyes,
which shone with a free and open expression; two plump
rosy cheeks upon which a light down was deigning to appear, and an admirably turned leg. The ladies of his
neighborhood, availing themselves of the privilege his extreme youth allowed, called him, almost always with a
smile, either their "pretty Roger" or their "pretty Tancrede," according as their romantic imaginations dwelt
upon the conquering hero of Sicily, or upon the lover of
Clorinda.

So much for the physical—let us now turn to the moral.
This essential feature in the education of the man destined
to the honor of sustaining and perpetuating the name of
D'Anguilhem had, from the hour when by the goodness of
God they were favored with a son, been the supreme duty
and pleasure of the baroness. Mme. d'Anguilhem had
imparted to her child all she knew of reading, writing,
and arithmetic. The curate of the neighboring village had
taught him to decline nouns and conjugate verbs, but
there his knowledge ended, and he avowed with a candor
that did more honor to his integrities than to his abilities,
that he could no longer act in the capacity of preceptor
after the youth had attained the seventh year of his age.

The baron and baroness were then much embarrassed as
to the means by which the education of their son should be
continued. At his tender age they could not think of parting with him. Fortunately, the difficulty was solved by

the assistance of a friend, who recommended a certain Abbe Dubois, who having just completed the education of one of the richest heirs of Loches, was in quest of a new pupil. This was just the thing for the baron and baroness. The references and recommendations of the Abbe Dubois were found perfectly satisfactory, and he was forthwith duly installed at the chateau with a salary of one hundred and fifty francs a year, besides his board and lodging, with the pompous title of Preceptor to the Chevalier d'Anguilhem.

We must now say a few words concerning the chateau inhabited by the four personages we have passed in review, one of whom, we may say in confidence to our readers, is destined to become the principal hero of this history.

The chateau was not exactly a castle, neither was it merely a house. It was a structure that occupied a middle place between the two, but which might easily have been taken for a farm, and a very pretty farm too. Out of respect to the worthy occupants we shall adopt this last appellation. This farm then consisted of eight rooms on the ground-floor. There was the dairy dignified by the title of *salle d'armes;* a dining-room; a drawing-room adorned with three ancestral portraits, and a modern one representing a naval officer wearing the uniform of a captain. We shall have occasion to recur to this portrait. There was a guard-room without guards, but ornamented with five armories, which in the time of the guards were filled with arms, though now occupied with more useful weapons, such as fowling-pieces, bill-hooks, fishing-tackle, etc. This guard-room was now used as a common sitting-room. There were four bed-chambers. The kitchen, and its underground dependencies, cellars, vaults, etc., ran under the whole length and breadth of the house. At one of the four angles of the building there rose a tower, about fifty feet high, called the Guerite. The Baron Agenor d'Anguilhem slept in this tower, and it was upon this feature in particular that he supported his pretensions in calling his house by the pompous name of castle. This name, however, either through custom or courtesy, is generally bestowed upon such residences in the country, and it would be bad taste in us to question the title.

This castle was not the richest in that quarter. The Baron d'Anguilhem drew from his tenants who farmed his territory, the sum of 200 francs annually. Now as in the

country the income of each is well known to all his neighbors, it was necessary to acknowledge that his fortune was
small, on lie. The baron lied without remorse. He pretended that he enjoyed a pension of a hundred louis a year
from the War Office, and another hundred from the king's
private purse. We do not go so far as to say that he positively asserted this himself, but he caused the report to be
set afloat, and did not contradict it. But he was in just the
same predicament as the malcontents we have before mentioned. Nobody was duped by these imaginary two hundred louis of income, therefore the Chevalier Tancrede did
not pass in the country for a very grand personage.

This, as may readily be imagined, did not disturb the
equanimity of our young gentleman. He was stout and
strong. If he had no horses of his own, he rode those of
his neighbors. His hunting ground was magnificent. For
by an agreement tacitly entered into by these worthy gentlemen, each of them, too restrained if limited to the bound-
aries of his own estates, could hunt over those of all his
neighbors. This explains what is said in Cornelius Nepos,
that having no wants, he did not perceive he was poor.

What, in fact, did he require? He had a tutor whom he
did not exactly detest, but whom, nevertheless, he regarded
as an unnecessary superfluity. Upon returning from the
chase, thanks to the maternal thoughtfulness of the baroness, an ample dinner always awaited him, the remains of
which he bestowed upon his dogs. After this he retired to
rest, and refreshed himself with unmeasured slumbers.
Whenever Tancrede quitted the castle, either on horseback
or on foot, walking arm in arm with the Abbe Dubois, or
with his gun over his shoulder, the peasants at work in the
fields saluted him respectfully, and the young gentlemen
his neighbors shook hands with him. That is all the power
to which a simple heart and philosophic mind can aspire.

When company was expected at the castle, Tancrede
went to work just like the two servants that composed the
domestic establishment. He cleaned the massive old family
plate, and assisted the baroness in kneading her pastry,
which, like a *chatelaine* of the olden time she desdained
not to make with her own hands. He was then entrusted
with the special care and cleaning of several tuna vases,
which had been in the possession of the family for three
generations. But when the guests arrived Tancrede donned

his best suit, which was some two or three years old, combed out his fine curling locks, and offered his hand to the ladies.

CHAPTER II.

THE baron and baroness often thought of the future of their darling boy, and frequently passed in review all the different pursuits that seemed opened to him. The father was in favor of a military career; but the baroness remarked to her husband that he would have to condescend to inscribe the name of Anguilhem in the lowest ranks of the army, and there was nothing to hope for in that quarter, if he was not rich enough to buy a colonelcy in some favored regiment. There had been, it is true, some exceptional cases, where, for instance, the king had removed all obstacles, by bestowing a commission upon some aspiring scion of decayed nobility, and even added to it a purse of a hundred thousand crowns. But Louis the Fourteenth had performed so many acts of this kind, that he found it necessary to curtail his liberality, reserving it for very special candidates for the royal favor.

Now there was no particular reason why the king should deviate from this sage resolution in favor of the Chevalier Tancrede, as the baroness explained to her husband, whenever he referred to this subject in conversation on the future prospects of their son. But what the baroness thought and whispered to herself, was, that she did not wish her darling boy to share the fate of the last of the Anguilhems who served in the army, for, as common soldiers, one was killed by a thrust from a pike in Flanders, and another by a musket-ball on the banks of the Rhine. A most vulgar style of dying, quite unworthy the son of a nobleman.

Despairing of success in this direction, the baron next supposed a government appointment, in the treasury department, for instance. Finance, even at this period, had opened a career to high-born youth which it would not be derogatory to enter upon. But here again was an insuperable obstacle. It would cost twice as much for bribes and fees to obtain such an appointment as to purchase a commission in the army. The only reward a soldier could reckon upon was wounds and glory, but the gold that passed through the hands of a financier generally stuck to his fingers, and found its way into his pockets. It is not surprising, therefore, that there was much competition for situations of this class, but they could only be obtained by the favorites of a Maintenon, a Father Lachaise, or a M. du Maine.

Now the Baron d'Anguilhem, brave and loyal country gentleman as he was, heartily execrated political old women, Jesuits, and bastards. Therefore he had not much chance as a courtier in the quarter where a financial post could be secured for his son; and the baroness herself, much as she desired to see her son occupy a position in which his life would not be endangered, was reluctantly compelled to admit, with a sigh, that it would be a gratuitous folly to look for success in this direction.

The baron then fell back upon a project he had long indulged in secret. This was that his son should enter the navy. This opened a noble career, in every respect worthy of a gentleman. Louis the Fourteenth had made France a maritime power that could cope with England and Holland, and counterbalance their influence. These rival queens of the sea were seeking to weaken each other's power, while Louis sought to aggrandize his navy at the expense of both. But here the poor baron encountered the strongest opposition from his wife. If she trembled for the life of her son as a soldier, she had still more reason to tremble for him as a sailor, who had to contend daily not only against the power of man, but also against the caprice of the elements. Once only in their lives had the baron and baroness visited a sea-port, and that was during their honey-moon.

They were at Brest, and made an excursion by pleasure-boat. Overtaken by a sudden squall, their frail bark was on the point of foundering, and they regained the shore by what appeared little less than a miracle.

After this misadventure the baroness exchanged the steady nerves of a country lady for those of a Parisian marchioness The mere mention of the word "sea" was sufficient to excite fainting or hysterics. She constantly pictured to herself a stormy sea, in which her darling chevalier, menaced with thunder and lightning, the sport of the wind and waves, expected every moment to be ingulfed in the fathomless abyss; of the dangers of which, with respect to her son, she had been forewarned by a rustic seer. Whenever with

cautious circumlocution the baron approached this subject,
a storm, invoked by the baroness, soon made its appearance. She would inquire of the baron, in the shrillest of
voices, if it was his intention to recompense the exemplary
conduct she had ever manifested toward him, by sacrificing
her only child.

Then the baron, good worthy man, would sigh profoundly and murmur:

"Madame, Madame Cornelia, you are not worthy of the
name you bear."

To which the baroness would reply:

"Sir, we do not live in the times of the Gracchi: and I
am not a Roman matron."

In truth, the poor lady was nothing more nor less than a
good tender mother and an excellent wife, not very interesting perhaps to philosophers, but very acceptable in the
eyes of Heaven.

The future of Tancrede thus continued to be a matter
upon which no decision could be arrived at. Meantime
they continued to give him, as a patrimony, the best education in their power, although they could see in the future
nothing better for him than the career of a country gentleman with an income of 400 crowns a year. This was but a
poor and dismal prospect.

However, behind these dark clouds that obscured the
glory of the house of Anguilhem, there shone a bright particular star, whose occasional glimpses excited and sustained the feeble hopes of the family. This guiding star was a
heritage; possible, if not probable. It consisted in the fortune of a certain second cousin, a retired navy captain, a
sort of sea-wolf, who had fought under the famous Jean
Bart—his name was Viscount de Bouzenois.

It was the portrait of this hero that adorned the walls of
the drawing-room of the castle, among those of the found-
ers of the family.

Sometimes, though very seldom, the conversation turned
upon this illustrious contemporary, who had come to add
the splendor of his renown to the picturesque chronicle of
by-gone times. But he was spoken of with singular reserve. Although his fortune was considerable, their hope
of inheriting it was so precarious, that to build any expectations upon it was like building castles in the air, mere
chimeras and dreams. This, however, did not prevent the

baron saying, with some degree of pride, "We have a relation at Versailles, Monsieur de Bouzenois, captain in his Majesty's navy." Then extending his hand in the direction of the picture, he would add: "There is his portrait in full uniform."

Now all the ideas of the navy that had occurred to the Baron d'Anguilhem were excited by the constant sight of this portrait, and the hopes and expectations raised by the original. The baron reasoned with himself in this fashion—

"At all events, the Viscount de Bouzenois is my second cousin. I am the only relation he has left, and if he dies intestate, I must of a surety inherit his property. If I ask the favor of his interest for my son, he can not well refuse me; the recommendation of the captain of a frigate must carry some weight, and doubtless open a career in the navy to my son; and once this career is entered upon, who could tell where the Chevalier Trancrede would stop?"

The ideas the baron indulged in were strengthened by the eccentric life led by the Viscount de Bouzenois. The most romantic stories were circulated as to the origin of this fortune, so colossal that it baffled all calculation, and dazzled the imagination of every member of the family. But there was some truth at the bottom of all the fiction, which may be briefly stated as follows.

Viscount de Bouzenois entered on board the French frigate "Thetis" when sixteen years of age. He gained glory and fame in fighting both English and Dutch. During the second war with Flanders, he had fitted out as a privateer, the brig "Marsouin," and attacked English merchantmen returning from India, and the Dutch company's vessels returning richly laden from Batavia, from both of whom he took valuable prizes. These, together with what he derived from his position as captain of the "Thetis," established the foundation of his fortune. Peace proclaimed, and M. le Viscomte de Bouzenois recompensed for his loyal and valuable services, was next appointed governor of a little colony the French possessed on the coast of Malabar.

The custom of *suttee* prevailed in full vigor in that country at the date of the viscount's arrival. Thanks to the humane influence of the English it has since fallen into disuse.

It happened one day that one of the richest and most

powerful Malabar chiefs took his departure from this world, leaving behind him a young and handsome widow, who, according to custom, announced her intention of immolating herself on the funeral pile of her husband.

M. de Bouzenois was at that date a handsome young man of thirty; the widow was not yet twenty, and as beautiful as a houri. He had often dined at the chief's table, and envied him the possession of such a domestic treasure, but he had never broken the tenth commandment. When the news of the widow's intention reached the viscount's ears, his chivalric feeling was roused, and he determined, at all risks, to prevent so horrible a sacrifice. He hastened to the house of the deceased chief, and there found the widow clothed in her best robes, perfumed with the most costly cosmetics, and preparing for her death as other women prepare for a ball.

The viscount explained to the lovely widow the object of his visit, and assured her that it would be a crime for so charming a creature wantonly to sacrifice her life, when a single glance of her eyes or a smile from her lips had the power of making others happy. He reminded her that she was a mother before she became a widow, and that she owed more to a living son than to a dead husband. He exerted all his eloquence, tenderness, and gallantry; he even became pathetic, but all in vain: the widow was inflexible in her resolution. She admitted that, being so young, she would quit life with some regret. But it was evident to the viscount that it was less for love to the dead than deference to the prejudices of the living, that she was induced to sacrifice herself. She felt that she would be forever dishonored if she neglected the commands of Vishnu, Siva, and Brahma, and make her weakness an excuse for deviating from the general custom. But the viscount could plainly see that the poor widow had no very great enthusiasm for the flames, but sacrificed herself because she thought she must do it, as it was expected of her. And in every country on the face of the globe women too often blindly follow the fashion, however painful or ridiculous it may be.

Seeing he could make no impression on the widow, the viscount quietly resolved to take the matter into his own hands. He let things take their usual course. The preparations for the ceremony were completed. The moment ar-

rived when the widow took farewell of her friends previous
to mounting the funeral pyre, around which the viscount
had placed a troop of his soldiers, ostensibly as a guard of
honor.   The critical moment had arrived; he drew his
sword: this was the signal for his men, part of whom quickly
scattered the straw, fagots, and other combustibles, while
the others covered the retreat of the captain as he forcibly
carried off the widow to his government residence.   How
the viscount succeeded in persuading this Malabar Venus
we are not informed; but this much we know, that the
widow not only renounced the funeral pile, but became
quite reconciled to life.

A year afterward the viscount married the widow, both
agreeing that in the event of death, the survivor should inherit all the property they each possessed individually.   As
the widow died first the viscount found himself in possession
of a fortune equal to that of a nabob.

Thus it appeared, in case the Viscount de Bouzenois died
intestate, his whole fortune would revert to the Anguilhems, his nearest relations; the son of the Malabar chief
being, in all probability, disinherited by his mother's marriage settlement.

Still this probability was subject to too many chances to
allow the family to make much calculation on the future of
the Chevalier Tancrede.

During the long winter evenings, when the gentlemen of
the neighborhood of the Castle of Anguilhem assembled
round the fireside, and talked of the exploits of their relations, or of the noble feats of their allies, M. de Chemille,
who had a great uncle in the camp, discoursed on cavalry;
M. de Bigarou, who was cousin to the great Vauban, talked
of sieges; M. Gantry, who had a paymaster for a brother-
in-law, spoke of finance; while the Abbe Dubois discoursed
on church matters.

The Baron Agenor-Palamede d'Anguilhem, by virtue of
his relationship with the Viscount de Bouzenois, represented
the navy in this congress where every branch of the state
had its representative.   The heroic and gallant adventures
of the captain of the frigate "Thetis" could not fail to reflect some of their glory and splendor upon his relations at
Loches.   Glory is not a very productive appanage, it is
true, but, in the absence of everything else, it is better than
nothing.

CHAPTER III.

THUS tranquilly passed away the days, and the nights also, of this amiable family, without anything occurring to determine the future career of their son and heir. He, meanwhile, had attained his fifteenth year, and took things as they came. Hunting and sporting was the chief business of his life; he worked when he could find a few spare minutes, pretending that the open air was most favorable to the development of his ideas; but when he was in the open air he generally whistled for want of thought.

Besides, young Tancrede, who was the terror of the hares and rabbits of his father's estate, had never once thought of making love, even to a pretty shepherdess. He inherited, it is true, a great fund of sensibility from his mother, but nothing had yet occurred to develop the germ of it. Plenty of exercise, a few romances, and almost no opportunity of falling in love—such was the sum and substance of his monotonous existence.

But at length an opportunity presented itself. We will relate how the Chevalier Tancrede hastened to avail himself of it.

One Easter Sunday the baron and baroness gave a grand supper. Easter was, at that period in history, the customary period of family *réunions*, and all the nobility of the neighborhood, for six leagues round, were invited to the Castle of Anguilhem. The Chevalier Tancrede, after rendering his accustomed service to his mother, performed a rather remarkable toilet, and at length made his appearance in the drawing-room, where all the guests had already assembled.

The conversation turned upon timber cutting, upon the last harvest, and upon the coming hunt, and as these subjects possessed an absorbing interest for country gentlemen, they paid no attention to the non-arrival of one of the invited. This expected guest was none other than the Viscount Beuzerie, whose extreme punctuality had become proverbial.

The cards of invitation specified that supper would be

served at half past seven precisely. The clock struck eight.
still no Beuzerie.

The guests' appetites now began to grow rebellious, and
they inquired of each other, in whispers, what could be the
cause of the delay. They had observed that the baron
constantly turned his eyes to the clock with an expression
that showed considerable anxiety. At intervals of a quarter
of an hour a messenger from the cook knocked at the drawing-room to inquire if supper might be served. To her the
baroness replied loud enough to be heard by all the company—"A little patience, Catherine, Monsieur de Beuzerie
will not be long now before he arrives."

The clock on the mantel-piece chimed a quarter past
eight. The anxiety that prevailed was marked by universal
silence. It was evident some accident must have happened
to delay M. de Beuzerie's arrival. The Baroness d'Anguilhem began to express her uneasiness for the welfare of the
viscountess, to whom she was warmly attached, and for
Mlle. Constance, her daughter, who had left her convent to
spend Easter week at home, and was invited, with her respected parents, to the Anguilhem supper.

The baron could endure his suspense and his hunger no
longer. He commanded his son, the Chevalier Tancrede,
to saddle his steed Christopher and go in search of Viscount
Beuzerie. If he returned in half an hour without meeting
him on the road, supper should then be served, happen
what might.

Tancrede accepted his mission without a murmur. He
was one of those lively youths to whom nothing comes amiss,
and who was always ready for any adventure. He quickly
buttoned a pair of gaiters over his silk stockings, saddled
Christopher, a pony of some three years old, leaped on his
back, gathered the reins, and taking a branch of holly to
serve both as whip and spur, he soon roused the quiet
creature into a gallop.

The weather was all that a poet could desire. A full moon
sailed through a sky covered with large cottony clouds, a
sharp breeze whispered through the still leafless branches,
the night-birds screamed. All this would have enchanted
Rene, Hamlet, or Werther, but Tancrede was insensible to
these nocturnal enchantments. Tancrede was hungry, and
when hungry nothing in nature or art appeared worthy
of his consideration but a well-furnished table. Heed

less of nature's poetical attractions, he galloped along, inwardly cursing all unpunctual gentlemen, calculating that the ragouts would be as tough as leather, and the joints burned to a cinder; throwing all the blame upon Mlle. de Beuzerie, who, he considered, was the cause of the delay by taking too much time over her toilet.

Thinking of these things, the youthful messenger plied his holly branch more and more vigorously, to the great astonishment of Christopher, who galloped at the top of his speed, his nostrils fuming like those of the enchanted steed of the lover of Leonora.

But though Tancrede continued to advance on the road to the residence of De Beuzerie, still he saw nothing move but the clouds across the face of the moon, which for the moment shrouded the road in darkness. From time to time he stopped to listen, but could hear nothing except the whistling of the wind among the trees. At length he turned his head toward home again, and sighed when he saw through the branches the windows of Anguilhem brilliantly illuminated. At this sight, he felt inclined to turn his steed's head and say, on his return, that he could see nothing of what he went in quest of. But he reflected that it could not be more than ten minutes since he set out, and he had received orders to proceed for a quarter of an hour.

Taking courage, he applied his whip to Christopher, who again struck into a gallop. Suddenly, it appeared to him that he heard a cry of distress at a distance of some hundred paces: at this sound his steed stopped of its own accord, snuffing up the air through its dilated nostrils. The chevalier looked cautiously around him. He found himself on a narrow pathway, in a marshy hollow. The cry was doleful, the night was darkening, and Tancrede trembled.

Yet to the credit of the heir of D'Anguilhem, we must affirm that the sentiment of fear experienced by the chevalier was of very brief duration, and ceased the moment he reflected that he might be able to assist some one in distress. He again pushed Christopher vigorously forward, shouting at the top of his voice:

"Hilloh, ho! where are you? who calls?"

"Here! here!" said a voice much nearer than before, and which now seemed to issue from the depths of the earth.

"Where is *here?*" cried Tancrede, still advancing.

"On the left of the road, in the marsh, here, just un-
derneath where you are standing."

Tancrede stopped Christopher, and endeavored to penetrate the darkness occasioned by the clouds obscuring the
light of the moon. He thought he could discover something moving about fifteen feet below where he stood.

"Is that you, Monsieur de Beuzerie?" he inquired.

"Yes, oh yes, it is I, my dear chevalier," replied the
voice. "Take us out of this for Heaven's sake; our coach
has slipped off the road, and slided down here into the
mud."

"Help! Monsieur Tancrede," cried a lady's voice.

"Help!" echoed the voice of a girl.

"Ah! poor Monsieur de Beuzerie," cried the chevalier,
"wait a minute, and I will see what I can do for you."

Tancrede leaped quickly from horseback. He could
hear a frightful noise below in the marsh. One of the
horses was stamping furiously, splashing the water in which
it was ingulfed. The old coach, as M. de Beuzerie had
stated, had slipped off the road, and landed at the
bottom of the marsh quite flat; but from the thickness of
the body, and the softness of the mud, the fall had not
proved serious to any one.

Mme. de Beuzerie found it convenient at first, to
faint, but at the sound of Tancrede's voice she revived.
As to her daughter Constance, she had endured the shock
with the greatest fortitude. M. de Beuzerie, finding he had
sustained no injury, had no fear except for his wife and
daughter.

The Chevalier Tancrede wisely concluded that there was
no time to lose; so, sliding down the bank, he found himself on the top of the coach. He then called the coachman
to assist him; but he called in vain, for that worthy functionary had departed in search of assistance in the neighborhood. The young chevalier then resolved to release,
unaided, monsieur, madame, and mademoiselle from their
difficulty. The merit would be greater. He began, therefore, by opening the door of the coach, and first released
Mlle. Constance, who was sustained by Mme. de Beuzerie
as the child is sustained by its mother in pictures representing the Deluge. Tancrede lifted mademoiselle up to the
meadow bank with as much ease as if she were a bird.
Next in turn was the viscountess, and here a more difficult

task presented itself. Madame was what they call in the country " a fine woman "—that is to say, a good, motherly looking dame, about five feet one inch in height, plump as a partridge, and weighing about ten stone; but, gathering all his strength, the chevalier, with the assistance of the baron, who lifted her from below, drew madame up, and in a few minutes succeeded in placing her in safety beside her daughter.

There now remained only M. de Beuzerie, who was far from presenting the same difficulties as his wife. He was a thin, meager old gentleman, still lively and vigorous. He was out of the coach in an instant, and, without assistance from Tancrede, leaped to the bank, where he found his family anxiously awaiting him.

Tancrede, who had nothing more to do on the coach, immediately followed M. de Beuzerie, with whom he exchanged formal salutations, while the two ladies overwhelmed him with courtesies and thanks.

Meanwhile the coachman had not returned. Tancrede, whose stomach became more and more rebellious, began to grow very impatient, and proposed that they should not wait for the coachman, who, in all probability, would return alone, but rather set themselves to work to release the horse from the coach. In a moment the horse found himself in the meadow, at about ten paces from his owners.

The only question now to be mooted was how to reach the castle. The way that appeared easiest at first sight became complicated, as we shall see. There were two steeds, and four persons to be transported. As for the coach, that was out of the question; it would require the aid of seven or eight persons to set it on its wheels again. The viscount's horse was covered with mud. Tancrede proposed to M. de Beuzerie, to lead Christopher by the bridle, while the viscountess and her daughter rode on his back. But as Christopher, warmed by his hard galloping, neighed and stamped loudly, the ladies became timid, and politely declined the chevalier's proposal.

Our hero next proposed to mount Christopher with Mme. de Beuzerie, while the viscount mounted his own horse with his daughter. But, as we have remarked, the other horse was covered with mud and the viscountess whispered to her husband, that if he adopted this advice, Constance would spoil her new dress. This proposal was therefore rejected like the former.

Finally, it was decided that Mme. de Beuzerie, having less to risk in her dress than her daughter, should mount the coach-horse with her husband, transferring Christopher's saddle to the horse's back, while the Chevalier Tancrede, who was a squire of great prowess, should mount Christopher's bare back, and support Mlle. Constance *eu croupe*.

They proceeded to put this project into execution, with some slight modifications. M. de Beuzerie mounted first, then Tancrede assisted madame, and placed her majestically behind her husband. Thus far all went marvelously well. But, arrived at this point, a little difficulty stood in the way of the execution of the rest of the project.

If the Chevalier Tancrede mounted Christopher first, there was no one to assist Mlle. Constance up. While, on the other hand, if the chevalier placed Mlle. Constance first *en croupe*, how was he to mount, unless he performed some extraordinary gymnastic feat. They sought everywhere for a bank or trunk of a tree, but in vain. At last Tancrede, whose ingenuity was stimulated by the pangs of hunger, bethought him of an expedient. This was for mademoiselle to mount first, while he would ride *en croupe*, holding her in his arms, instead of being held by her. This posture doubtless had its inconveniences, and the viscount and his lady raised their eyebrows when it was proposed; but the viscountess, putting her mouth to her husband's ear, whispered:—

"What is it to be done, my dear? I see no help for it; besides, they are only children."

"Mount, then, as you will," said M. de Beuzerie, "we must lose no more time in discussion."

"Mademoiselle," said Tancrede, "will you permit me?"

And he lifted her up like a feather, and was soon seated *en croupe* behind her.

Timid Mlle. Constance uttered a little scream, a very faint one it is true, to which the viscount, full of paternal anxiety, responded with "What's the matter?"

"Nothing, sir, nothing," replied the chevalier. "When I mounted, mademoiselle was near falling off; but now I hold her in my arms, and there is no danger."

"In your arms?" murmured the viscount. "In your arms? *morbleu!*"

"Hush, my dear," whispered the viscountess, "you put wrong notions into the children's heads."

"Do not say anything more," said the viscount, putting his horse to the trot, while Christopher followed behind.

But we must hasten to remark, that the fears of the viscount were not groundless. For, scarcely had the chevalier felt Mlle. Constance leaning against him than his heart began to beat in a fashion it had never done before. The young lady too, fresh from a convent, mounted now for the first time on a horse, trembled with fear. And whether it was that she experienced a new pleasure, or that in her primitive innocence and simplicity, fear overcame conventionality, she pressed the hand of the young man against her breast, and, turning her head from time to time toward him, cried:

"Oh! Monsieur le Chevalier, hold me tighter, tighter still! Oh! Monsieur le Chevalier, I am so frightened, I shall fall!"

And every time she turned her head, her blonde curls brushed the young man's forehead, her beautiful eyes met his, her fresh breath mingled with his own, so that poor Tancrede soon forgot his hunger, and began to wish that the journey might last forever. So strongly did he feel a strange delight, an unknown happiness, a transcendent bliss, spread its influence over his whole frame, while his bosom swelled, and every branch of the trees that brushed against him, and every ray of the moonbeams whispered to his soul, "Tancrede, is not this happiness?"

Yes! the chevalier was happy, and without knowing why. Mademoiselle was happy too. Mingled with her fears there was a charming trait of gentleness, of which she made no account; for she thought to herself that she had never trembled so agreeably before, and that fear was a feeling full of delightful emotions, a thing till then but imperfectly known, and, like all such things, greatly calumniated. It was while enjoying this happiness, so ill defined by the head, but so profoundly appreciated by the heart, that the young couple arrived at the Castle of Anguilhem: their horses' footsteps had been heard by all the guests. Every one hastened to the door, and the viscount, viscountess. Mlle. Constance. and Tancrede were received like sovereigns returning to their states, for whom the royal residence is illuminated.

The baron gave his arm to the viscountess, who, availing herself of this support, came safely to the ground. The viscount descended solemnly, in measured time, like a good squire. The chevalier made but one bound, took Mlle. Constance by her two hands, and, lifting her from the horse as if she had been a feather, deposited her on the ground so gently, that no one could tell when her two little feet reached the earth. It was then that Tancrede, for the first time, saw the face of Mlle. Constance by the light of the torches. How shall we describe her? Two ravishing blue eyes, blonde curls, that seemed like skeins of silk; a mouth like a cherry, a neck like a swan, the figure of a sylph. This was what Mlle. de Beuzerie was like. A burning cloud appeared to flush across Tancrede's eyes, and it seemed to him that he must die with joy.

He followed without daring to offer her his hand. Mlle. Constance had made a very pretty little courtesy to her cavalier, blushing meanwhile, and then hastened to join her mother. But, strange to tell, Tancrede's heart, so lately swelling with joy, now felt a sudden contraction. It seemed to him as if he was separated from the fair girl. And Tancrede, the young man whose strong appetite was proverbial—poor Tancrede—sat himself down to table without any appetite.

But a great triumph awaited our hero. The guests, impelled by hunger, crowded hastily into the dining-hall. As soon as the first course was removed, the conversation began to flow, and a host of questions were addressed to the young chevalier by those who were curious to learn what caused the delay of Viscount de Beuzerie; and they particularly wished to know how it happened that this worthy gentleman commenced his journey in a coach and finished it on horseback.

Then M. de Beuzerie related the adventure in all its details, declaring that he and his family owed their lives to the chevalier, praised his skill, and exalted the devotion which, notwithstanding his youth, he had so strongly exhibited. Mme. de Beuzerie echoed and confirmed the praises of her husband. Mlle. Constance said nothing, but blushed prodigiously, and cast furtive glances toward Tancrede. The chevalier, who never for a moment ceased gazing upon her face, remarked her blushes, and put his own interpretation on her glances; and, without knowing why, he felt that these blushes and glances did him a great deal of good. No other topic of conversation engaged the guests during supper; and during the dessert, Tancrede was looked upon by all the company as the liberator of the family in general, and as the savior of Mlle. Constance in particular.

Mlle. Constance and the Chevalier Tancrede were then toasted with all the honors, according to the custom of those good old times of politeness and heartiness. Indeed, it seemed that at this period of our history every one endeavored to render the world agreeable and pleasing to the novices who were just putting their feet on the threshold of society. The women flirted with the scholar while still under the hands of his tutor. The men sought to captivate the heiresses, still captives behind the railings of their convents. On coming out of the parlor or the college, the young men discoursed of love, and the young girls listened to them.

M. d'Anguilhem was delighted to the bottom of his heart at the importance his son had acquired by his adventure in the marsh. In all his plans for the future, the baron sought an establishment for his son; and Mlle. Constance, who, upon the death of her parents, would inherit a fortune of six thousand francs a year, would not be a very bad match for the chevalier. By purchasing three or four leagues of marsh that lay between Beuzerie and Auguilhem, the two estates might be united into one; and if two or three little groves, scattered here and there on the road, belonging to some poor proprietors, who would sell them for a trifle, were added, then it would form one of the most important baronies in Touraine. Thus the children born of this marriage would possess both hill and valley, as their ancestors had done in the palmy days of their greatest prosperity. This would be very fine! splendid! magnificent! the thoughts of it made the worthy baron very gay during supper, and at the dessert he treated the company to a song.

But it was quite another affair with the Viscount de Beuzerie, who, as if he had divined the ambitious projects of the baron, held himself at table with an air of great dignity, and became more and more formal as the supper drew

to a close, making a sign to his wife to keep on the defen
sive, a maneuver which the vicountess accomplished, it must
be confessed, with a conjugal intelligence worthy of all
praise.   Still more, as the two young people sat beside each
other, and instead of eating their supper like children of
twelve and fifteen, whispered low, like two lovers, M. and
Mme. de Beuzerie cast angry glances upon their daughter,
two thirds of which passed unnoticed by Constance, so entirely was she occupied with her companion; but the last
third at length caught her attention, and put the young
lady into a terrible state of agitation; the more terrible inasmuch as she was totally ignorant of the cause of the anger
her parents appeared to exhibit toward her.

As soon as the company rose from table, Mme. de Beuzerie took her daughter by the hand and placed her beside
her while M. de Beuzerie, after declaring his intention of
returning home the same evening, went out to learn news
of his shipwrecked coach.

M. de Beuzerie returned in despair; the coachman made
his appearance in a state of helpless drunkenness, and the
coach still occupied its delicate bed at the bottom of the
marsh.   Then, as politeness naturally required, the baron
and baroness offered their neighbors a bed-chamber in the
castle; the best was at their service.   But at this proposal,
in which there was really nothing unusual, M. de Beuzerie
made such a start of indignant surprise, that the baron was
very glad to turn the discourse upon some other topic.   Next
he ventured to propose putting the viscount's horse to his
own chaise, in which the family party, as they appeared to
wish it so ardently, could regain their home the same
night.   Next day the baron would have the coach landed
from the marsh, which Christopher should draw to Beuzerie and bring back the chaise.   This proposal was eagerly
accepted by the viscount and viscountess, to the great grief
and despair of Mlle. Constance and Chevalier Tancrede.
She ventured one little glance through her tears, and
heaved a gentle sigh, which fortunately was not observed
by her inexorable parents.   In a quarter of an hour after
this resolution was taken, the horse and chaise were pronounced as ready.

They must go.   The poor children who had met for the
first time within the two previous hours felt as if they had
known each other from infancy.   The baron shook hands

with the viscount; the baroness and Mme. de **Beuzerie** embraced. Constance made a pretty courtesy to all the company, and threw a tender glance at Tancrede. Then all three got into the chaise; the horse started off, the sound of the wheels grew fainter and fainter, and then was lost altogether.

Tancrede did not return to the supper-room with the rest of the company. He remained on the door-step, and ran from there to the door of the court-yard, where he remained fixed and immovable, his eyes following the chaise until it was lost in the darkness of night, and then he continued to gaze upon the vacant spot where it had disappeared. Doubtless he would have remained there all night, if his reverie had not been disturbed by some one placing a hand on his shoulder. It was his tutor, the Abbe Dubois, who came to tell him that his protracted absence from the drawing-room would be regarded by those who remained as a breach of good manners. Tancrede let two big tears fall furtively from his eyes, and then followed his tutor into the castle.

CHAPTER IV.

HAPPILY for the chevalier, the vigils at the Easter-tide were not very long. At midnight the company broke up, and departed to their respective homes, some on horseback, others on foot. One or two, whose homes lay very distant, accepted the hospitality offered by the baron, and retired to the apartments he had prepared for them.

Tancrede, before retiring to his chamber, went, as was his habit, to embrace his father and mother, who regarded him with a significant smile. Then he made an obeisance to the abbe, and retired, not to sleep—for which he had no desire, it had gone to keep company with his appetite—but to think upon Mlle. de Beuzerie.

It was the first time that the young chevalier had thought of anything more serious than a hunting party, or a fencing match; or of some excuse by which he could avoid translating his Sallust or his Virgil.

He was now profoundly sad. He fully understood that the precipitate departure of the viscount had no other object than the removal of Constance; but he had read in the eyes of the fair girl that she would have preferred staying where she was, which in some measure consoled **him**. Besides, there is in the first griefs of an early passion something which oppresses the heart so sweetly that we accept it as preferable to the state of indifference which it has displaced. What we desire beyond everything is not exactly to be happy, for we do not quite understand what happiness is, but it is rather not to return to the arid desert from which we have escaped: it is to repose under the foliage of the green trees, to bask in the sunbeams, amid flowers whose enervating perfumes lap the senses in forgetfulness; their thorns have already pricked our fingers, but we gather them with all our strength, and inhale the perfume at all risks; what we desire is the tempest rather than the calm, pain rather than joy.

At length Tancrede fell into a feverish and troubled sleep, which, however, did not prevent him waking at daybreak, fresh and lively. Besides, he had formed a little project of his own, which was to take Christopher with the coach, under pretext of asking, in the name of his father and mother, news of the family De Beuzerie, to whom, considering the lateness of the hour at which they had quitted the castle, it was feared some accident might have happened. Besides, he had a first idea which rendered the second quite natural, that of giving the coachman a crown to pretend sickness, and declare he had not strength sufficient to hold the reins.

The chevalier, who knew where the coach was, set out, accompanied by the gamekeeper, the stable-boy, the gardener, and some laborers, by whose united efforts the coach was replaced on the highway. Fortunately, the strength of the massive old coach had kept it whole, and once on the road again there was no difficulty in wheeling it to Beuzerie. As for Christopher, stimulated by the reiterated blows of his young master's whip, he set off at a brisk trot, frisking and neighing in token that he could not understand the new style of treatment he was subjected to since the previous evening.

But in proportion as Tancrede approached nearer to Beuzerie, his instigations with respect to Christopher were less pressing, and the intelligent animal, profiting by this intermission of blows, passed from a gallop to a full trot, and finally subsided into a walk. In fact this affair, which had at first appeared very simple to the young man, merely returning the viscount's coach and fetching away the chaise, appeared to him now as a piece of mendacious audacity. He called to mind the severe countenance of M. de Beuzerie, his contracted brows, his sharp voice, and, more than all, his precipitate departure, and he asked himself, whether he who had shown so much haste to quit the Castle of Anguilhem, would exhibit any very great pleasure in seeing the heir of this castle in that of Beuzerie. All these reflections contributed very little to give the chevalier much assurance. Among the many good qualities with which heaven had endowed him, he had not received that happy boldness which almost always insures success. He had, therefore, ceased to push Christopher on very briskly, and had the animal stopped altogether, or turned his bridle, it is possible his master would not have mustered sufficient courage to push him on his right road again. Fortunately this did not happen. Christopher was an honest creature, quite incapable of such an action. He did not like to be foundered, but when left to himself, put a provincial conscience on the matter, which could be fully relied upon. Tancrede continued, therefore, to advance at his usual pace toward Beuzerie, and soon perceived the two slate-roofed turrets of the little chateau, which elevated their weather-cocks above the trees in the park.

The chevalier still advanced, but it must be admitted that instead of leading Christopher, it was Christopher who led him. He had approached near the reception gate when, casually looking up at the turrets, he saw a pretty little head covered with light, curling hair, and a pair of bright blue eyes which looked eagerly around. The hand that accompanied this fair head was busily engaged in waving a handkerchief, in token that the visitor was recognized. At the sight of this vision Tancrede stopped Christopher, and the innocent youths began to exchange all the signs of natural tenderness which their hearts could suggest.

This pantomime continued for some minutes, and would probably have continued till the evening, if Tancrede had not seen another person appear behind Constance. This untimely intruder was no less a personage than Mme. de Beuzerie, who, passing along the corridor, saw her daughter, whose chamber-door was open, making extraordinary signals from her window. She had some curiosity to know to whom these signals were addressed, and gliding softly into her daughter's chamber, looked over her shoulder, and saw the chevalier eagerly responding to her daughter. Mme. de Beuzerie, who on the previous evening had blamed her husband for so quickly taking alarm, and quitting the Castle of Anguilhem at so early an hour, now began to believe that the viscount was in the right, and not quite so foolish as she had at first imagined him.

Tancrede finding himself discovered, saluted madame, and giving Christopher the whip, soon found himself in the court-yard of the Château de Beuzerie.

The first person who perceived Tancrede was the viscount, who had just returned from his customary morning walk in the park. The chevalier thought that the time had now arrived when he would have to pay for his audacity. He alighted from his steed, and advancing toward M. de Beuzerie, informed him with an air very deliberate for a man who was only serving his apprenticeship to deceit, that his coachman was taken very ill, and that he had therefore taken upon himself the responsibility of bringing back the coach to Beuzerie, fearing the viscount might require it. He stated also that he was instructed by the baron and baroness, his respected parents, to inquire if the viscount and viscountess had arrived home without further accident.

Although the viscount readily divined the real motives of the chevalier's visit, he was obliged to accept these plausible pretenses for what they appeared. He therefore feigned to believe all he heard, and politely inquired after the health of the baron and baroness. It was dinner-time, and the servant coming to announce that the repast would be served as soon as monsieur was ready, the viscount stretched his courtesy so far as to invite Tancrede to partake of it— an offer that we need not say was eagerly accepted.

The viscount thought this a good opportunity of putting the correctness of his surmises to the proof. He felt that some allowance must be made for the exciting circumstances under which the young people met on the previous evening; he could now submit them to a fresh scrutiny. Alas! these poor, tender young hearts knew not how to feign. Constance, upon entering the dining-room, blushed as a girl of fifteen blushes, and Tancrede became as pale as a youth of eighteen becomes on such occasions. M. de Beuzerie remarked the opposite effect the meeting produced upon the two young people, and attributed it to the same cause in both, and his suspicions were soon fully confirmed.

During the repast Constance and Tancrede committed themselves again and again. This time M. de Beuzerie did not frown as he had done the previous evening, but took no notice whatever, contenting himself with making signals to his wife, which were intended to say, "Am I the visionary you say I was? Is it not plain enough now?" In fact it was so very clear, that, when dinner was over, M. de Beuzerie, in order to put a stop to Tancrede's further visits to the chateau, quietly remarked, in the course of conversation, that Constance would return to her convent that same evening. At this news Constance uttered a faint scream, and the chevalier became very pale, and, thinking something had happened to her, rushed to her side. But the viscount taking him gently by the arm, quietly observed that Mme. de Beuzerie was there, and that if her daughter required any assistance she was the proper person to give it.

But Constance had not arrived at the fainting age. As yet she was too natural for that; she contented herself, therefore, with shedding a flood of tears, which Tancrede perceiving, he had considerable difficulty in restraining his own. Besides, these signs of uncontrollable grief brought fresh misfortune upon the young people. Constance was ordered to her own room, to which she retired sobbing, after making a courtesy to Tancrede. who responded by a pitiful face and a low bow. After this, seeing there was nothing further for him to do at the chateau, the chevalier announced to the viscount that he would now have the honor of wishing him good-day.

The viscount had anticipated this precipitate departure, for upon stepping into the court-yard Tancrede found Christopher ready harnessed to the chaise. He saluted the viscount, who returned his salute with a hearty shake of the hands, sent his compliments to the baron and baroness, and wound up his civilities by wishing him a pleasant journey home.

We may reasonably suppose that Tancrede did not pass under the little window of the turret without raising his eyes to it. He was well rewarded. It fortunately happened that Mme. de Beuzerie supposed that Tancrede was still at the dinner-table, and had left her daughter alone in her

2

chamber. Constance, as soon as she found herself at liberty, ran to the window just at the moment the chevalier was passing. To the great astonishment of the chevalier, her face was radiant with joy. He inquired of Constance what made her look so pleased, when she held up a pencil and a piece of paper. By this Tancrede understood that she was going to write her answer, and he waited. In a few seconds both paper and pencil fell at his feet.

Picking them up in great haste, he read as follows:

" Mamma, who loves me dearly, assures me that it was only to prevent your coming here again that they said before you I was to return to my convent this evening. The truth is, I shall not go till next Sunday.

"CONSTANCE."

Tancrede understood that the pencil was thrown to him to write a reply. Tearing a piece off the paper, he wrote:

" Take a walk in the park to-morrow, near the summer-house. I shall climb over the wall. We will then consider how we can contrive to meet each other. I do not know whether you feel as sad as I do, but this I do know, that I shall die if I am separated from you.

"TANCREDE."

He folded a stone up in this note, which, we must admit, was rather precocious for a lover of fifteen, and with the *adresse* of a school-boy threw it in at the window where Constance was standing. She caught it in her hands, disappeared for a moment, then returned to the window, and nodded her head to signify that she would be at the rendezvous. To remain any longer in this place would have been the height of imprudence; therefore Tancrede, his heart overflowing with joy, interrupted the meditations of Christopher by a fresh application of the whip. Three hours afterward the young chevalier arrived at Anguilhem.

Tancrede was in that delightful state of enchantment, peculiar to young lovers; his heart overflowing with generosity; his eyes sparkling with happiness; every word, look, and gesture betokening the lover. Perceiving this, the baron and baroness exchanged smiles. Never had Tancrede appeared so busy and bustling; he dusted the china, cleaned the plate and his father's gun, and explained to the

Abbe Dubois, his tutor, the touching episode of Dido and Æneas.

The day appeared very long to the chevalier. He knew not how to kill the time: he ran here and there, up and down, in and out; compared all the clocks in the house, hurried supper, as if he were dying with hunger, and when he sat himself down to the table could not eat a morsel; and with his eyes wider open than ever, retired to his chamber upon the pretense of being sleepy.

But it is very well understood that it was not to sleep that Tancrede withdrew to his room. He went to tell his tale of love to the moon, the stars, the flowers, and the zephyrs. He opened his window, and the monologue commenced.

Tancrede passed a happy night.

At day-break he arose; no one was yet stirring. He awoke a servant and told him that he was going to make an excursion to Saint Hippolyte. That place was in just the opposite direction to Beuzerie. Poor fellow! he felt that he must deceive everybody, even a servant! Having taken this precaution, which proved, at least, that he did not lack discretion, he at once proceeded to saddle Christopher, and galloped off. This time the poor animal did not attempt to rebel. To make sure, Tancrede had provided himself with a pair of spurs and a whip. Christopher, who had felt the spurs and seen the whip, immediately understood, with his accustomed sagacity, that if he attempted any resistance he was sure to get the worst of it.

Upon rising to breakfast, the baron was informed by the servant that his son had gone to Saint Hippolyte. Of course he did not believe a word of it, nor did the baroness.

The Abbe Dubois, who had sought his pupil everywhere since he arose, came at eleven o'clock to inquire of his parents what had become of him. The baron and baroness greeted the tutor with a malicious smile, and, M. d'Anguilhem, putting his hand on the shoulder of the poor abbe, whispered in his ears:

"Ah! sir, sir, you have made a very bad subject of your pupil."

The baron never lost sight of his dearest project, the union of the houses of Anguilhem and Beuzerie. The baroness confessed that Constance was a charming girl, and that she would be happy to call her daughter.

"At all events," remarked the Abbe Dubois, "I hope

the marriage will not take place until my pupil has completed his studies!" The baron and baroness laughed a little at each other, and much at the abbe. It appeared quite ridiculous to speak of such projects between a boy of fifteen and a girl of twelve. The baron changed the subject by observing:

"Time is master of everything. Let matters take their own course. We will talk about something else." And then spoke of M. de Bouzenois.

The morning passed away without Tancrede making his appearance. But at two in the afternoon, just as they were sitting down to dinner, he entered the dining-room. He looked quite crestfallen, and his eyes were red with weeping. The baron exchanged glances with the baroness as much as to say, "The coach he rides in does not go upon wheels."

The chevalier seated himself at table, but eat nothing—a sure sign that things went wrong with him. After dinner he seated himself beside his mother, arranged the thirty volumes that composed his private library, and followed the baron when he took his walk in the garden, observing all the while a strict silence, which was only broken to complain of a bad headache, and to ask permission to retire to bed early, a request it was thought best to comply with without remark.

Tancrede forgot, when in his room, that it was situated just over his mother's bed-chamber, where his every movement could be heard. All night long he paced up and down his chamber, like a man with the toothache. Nothing was lost upon the baron and baroness. "Surely there is the devil to pay," said the baron, "and the Beuzeries have defeated us."

When the baron arose next morning he proceeded directly to the stable. There was Christopher, gnawing his manger. Next he proceeded to the kitchen. The three fowling-pieces were in their usual places above the mantelpiece. Tancrede had not gone out; he was still sleeping. At his age, whatever may be our troubles, nature will not be cheated. We must eat and sleep.

The chevalier slept until the clock striking nine awoke him. He went down to breakfast with pale cheeks and swollen eyes. Poor boy! Yet he had slept two hours longer than he had done the previous day. There is a considerable difference between the sleeplessness of joy and the sleeplessness of grief.

But Tancrede eat his breakfast; and while he was eating it, the door opened, and the *valet de chambre* of M. de Beuzerie made his appearance, bearing a letter in his hand. The chevalier, recognizing Comtois, blushed and grew pale alternately. Then, seeing him approach his father, he rose from the table, and went and locked himself in his chamber.

The Baron d'Anguilhem, in spite of his pretensions to philosophy, trembled as he opened this dispatch from Beuzerie, the contents of which he pretty well guessed. Besides, Comtois had assumed a grave and consequential air, which betokened no good. We can always guess the nature of the message by the demeanor of the messenger. However, the baron withdrew his eyes from the face of Comtois, and turned them upon the viscount's letter, and read as follows:

"My dear Sir and Neighbor,—This is to wish you the enjoyment of every blessing you can desire, and to offer our very humble compliments to yourself and to madame the baroness. We are constrained to address you a few words respecting Monsieur Tancrede, your son, whom I surprised yesterday, in a secluded portion of our park, on his knees before our daughter, Mademoiselle Constance de Beuzerie, whose hand he kissed with an ardor quite unusual for a youth of fifteen years. You may readily imagine, dear sir and neighbor, how painful it is to us to have to reproach the son of those we love so well, and to be put in fear for our dear daughter, who is doubtless honored by his suit. But it appears to us that he is rather precocious (seeing that she is not yet thirteen years of age), and very inconsiderate also, in not first asking our consent. We regret being obliged to say to Monsieur le Chevalier Tancrede, that we can not allow him to repeat his visit to Beuzerie; and we reckon upon your friendship and good advice to bring him to reason; for our daughter is very ill from the shock he has given to her feelings. But this will not prevent us, seeing the urgency of the case, sending her back to her convent this evening.

"Adieu, dear friend and honored sir: believe in our

sincere desire to please you, and in our very great regret in
being compelled to make these complaints to you.

" DE BEUZERIE.

" 17th April."

The letter almost fell from the baron's hands. He,
however, so far recovered himself as to be able to ring the
bell for a servant, whom he directed to give some refreshment to the valet Comtois, and regale him with the best
the larder afforded.   Then he sat down to reply to the viscount, promising that he would come and make a proper
apology, in the name of the chevalier to the viscount and
Mme. de Beuzerie.

Comtois, mollified by the unexpected courtesy of the
baron, and by the good cheer placed before him, became
communicative, and while drinking his wine, told the cook,
in confidence, that Mlle. Constance appeared to be in great
tribulation, and did nothing but weep all day.   The result
of this communication was, that there was almost as much
grief at Anguilhem as indisposition at Beuzerie.   Tancredo,
in his capacity of only son, was not only adored by the
baron and baroness, but also by the whole establishment,
male and female; and it is very certain, if it had been a time
when such matters as now disturbed the peace of mind of the
young chevalier could have been settled by the lance and
sword, the baron would have experienced no difficulty in
arming his six vassals to go and bring off the young chate-
lain refused to his son.

Comtois took his departure, and the chevalier came down-
stairs.   The baron addressed a few words of reproach to his
son, paternal and mild in their tenor, and reasoned with
him on the precocity of his amorous desires, and upon the
necessity of, at least, finishing his studies before thinking of
marriage.   Then the baroness put in a few words, to the
effect that when the period arrived that the chevalier might
properly undertake matrimony, it would be as well for him
not to look too high in choosing too rich an heiress, a piece
of presumption that might draw upon his parents the humiliation of a refusal.

The chevalier, stung to the quick, replied that they deceived themselves; that he did not love Mlle. Constance at
all; that he had never once thought of marriage; and that
he never for a moment entertained any other desire than to

obey the instructions of his tutor, the Abbe Dubois. That with respect to the fears entertained by his mother of aiming too high, this fear was perfectly chimerical, as he was fully resolved to remain a bachelor. Poor boy! who would have supposed that the greatest peril he had to encounter in life would perhaps arise from polygamy!

The chevalier supported his denial with so much dignity and pride, that his father and mother respected his deceit. Consequently, the baron took him by the hand, and the baroness kissed him, and in obedience to the wish he had expressed, they sent him to his tutor, begging him to construe, not the loves of Dido and Æneas, but an essay on the vanity of riches. As a lover, he had fallen from Mlle. Constance to M. de Beuzerie; and as a scholar, he fell from Virgil to Seneca.

CHAPTER V.

No sooner had the chevalier left the room than the baron proceeded to dress himself in his best, to go and make his promised visit to Beuzerie. He was received by the viscount and vicountess with an air of constraint. They threw their embarrassment upon the preparation they were making for the departure of their daughter to the convent. The baron requested to see Mlle. Constance. This request could not be refused him. Constance made her appearance with eyes red and swollen with weeping, so that M. d'Anguilhem comprehended that, for this once, at least, her departure was not a pretense. The baron then spoke very courteously of the inexcusable folly of the chevalier, and attributed all the irregularities of his conduct to his youth and the thoughtlessness peculiar to his age; adding that the poor boy bitterly repented his conduct, and begged his neighbors, and particularly Mlle. Constance, to forget everything that had happened during the past three days. Upon hearing this, Constance grew very pale, and feeling that she must soon give vent to her grief in sobs, she hastily quitted the room.

The baron fully divined the feelings of the young maiden. She deeply loved the chevalier; he saw into the profoundest depths of the virgin heart of the heiress of Beuzerie. It now remained for him to study the parents in their turn. This was not difficult. The viscount turned the conversation upon a certain Marquis de Croisey, who resided at Loches, with his parents, and who enjoyed an income something like 300 louis a year. For a long time the viscount had entertained projects of an alliance between the two families, and it was said that so much importance would not have attached to what had happened if it were not that it might interfere with the marquis's intentions.

The baron felt that this was a palpable hit, and, as we have shown he was a master in fencing, he made a straight thrust, saying that in making this visit to Benzerie, he only wished to justify his son, for he had always intended that this visit should be the last he would make. It was in vain that he was entreated to be less susceptible; he persisted; excuses were offered, to no purpose; he rose, saying that an Anguilhem was quite as good as a Croisey, and, with the exception of a slight difference in their fortunes, his opinion was that one D'Anguilhem was worth all the Beuzeries in the world.

This opinion, which rather exaggerated the value of the family of Anguilhem, would doubtless have produced a serious collision between those two worthy old gentlemen, both very susceptible upon points of honor, if Mme. de Beuzerie had not come to the rescue. The baron and the viscount contented themselves with saluting each other coldly, and parted completely at variance with each other. The same evening mademoiselle returned to the convent of Chinon, according to the programme.

The Chevalier Tancrede awaited the baron's return with the utmost impatience. For, in the filial respect he entertained for his father, he reckoned much upon him to renew with the Beuzeries the thread of their old friendship, which was now in danger of being broken. But, quite contrary to his hopes, the chevalier saw his father return wearing a more severe countenance than he went out with. He at once concluded he had made bad worse; and, under the pretext that he had much Latin to construe, he went and locked himself in his room to work, as he said, but, in reality, to hide his feelings and conceal his grief.

We have all passed through the early emotions of a first love; we have all recognized by increasing sorrows that we were serving our apprenticeship as men. We have grown many years older in an hour; it was with the poor chevalier as it is with all the world.

He passed the night in pacing up and down his room; and at daybreak, to overcome his mental anguish by physical exertion, he took his gun on his shoulder, loosened his dog Castor, and set out for the chase.

But the chase was only a pretext with which poor Tancrede sought to deceive himself. Without knowing how the thing was done; without being in the least diverted at the sight of a hare, or the flight of a covey of partridges enticing him to cross the hills and valleys; without having the least excuse for making the four or five leagues he had traveled on foot, our sportsman found himself in a warren, situated four or five hundred paces from Beuzerie, on the high road that led to the castle of Loches. Now it happened, by a chance otherwise not very extraordinary, that the Viscount de Beuzerie, doubtless also with a view to distract his mind—for he too had his paternal anxieties, as the chevalier had his amorous vagaries—it happened, as I said, that the Viscount de Beuzerie had come out to shoot a rabbit, and at the turn of the road the two sportsmen found themselves face to face. Both recoiled a step or two upon perceiving each other. Tancrede had a great inclination to take to his heels and run, but he instinctively felt that course would make him appear very ridiculous, and that being surprised, he had better put a bold face on the matter; besides, being in the middle of a warren, he might just as likely be looking for a rabbit as for Mlle. Constance.

There was a moment of first astonishment, during which M. Beuzerie raised his eyebrows, and Tancrede grounded his gun and raised his hat. The viscount was the first to break silence.

"Here again, Chevalier Tancrede?"

"Monsieur le Viscount," replied Tancrede, "it is quite by accident that I am here. My dog pursued a wounded hare, and I followed him, without noticing where he was leading me, until I found myself in this warren."

"And why is your dog in my grounds?" inquired the viscount.

"Why is my dog upon your grounds? Why, I have seen your dogs twenty times in Pintard, which I believe belongs to Anguilhem, and, besides, I have always understood that we both enjoyed the privilege of sporting on each other's grounds."

This was said in a tone of firmness that the viscount did not expect to hear from a youth of fifteen; but Tancrede had his misadventure very much at heart, and felt that he must vent his spleen upon some one. Here he had only the father of Constance, and he bullied the father of Constance. If it had been a mere gamekeeper, he would have thrashed him.

"Doubtless," replied the viscount, a little astonished at this logic, which proved that Tancrede was not easily daunted—"doubtless it was so agreed upon. I know very well that our hunting-grounds were held in common; but after what has occurred, young man, many things are not as they once were. You understand?"

"On your side, perhaps, sir, but not on ours," replied the chevalier. "You are master of your own grounds, Monsieur le Viscount, and can prevent any one you please from hunting over them; but I think I may venture to say, on behalf of my father, that you will always be welcome to enjoy yourself upon ours. Here, Castor, here!"

Saying this, Tancrede politely showed his back to the viscount, who remained perfectly stupefied at the assurance of his young neighbor; but the youth had scarcely taken ten steps before he reflected upon the difference in years between the viscount and himself, and he reproached himself for the lecture he had given him. He turned back, and, approaching the old gentleman, said, politely:

"Monsieur, allow me the honor of being your very humble servant."

He bowed respectfully to the viscount while saying this, and the viscount mechanically returned the salute.

"Diable! Diable!" exclaimed the viscount, as Tancrede went his way; "this young fellow will give us a tangled skein to unravel, or I am much mistaken. Fortunately, Mademoiselle de Beuzerie is on her way to Chinon."

The viscount had forgotten that the superior of the convent of the Augustines at Chinon, whither he had sent his daughter for greater safety, happened to be aunt to the Chevalier d'Anguilhem. Tancrede's memory, however, served him better.

CHAPTER VI.

But Tancrede remembered his aunt, and it was this remembrance solely that prevented him despairing utterly.
He thought also, that if the remembrances of childhood
were not illusory, this good aunt, to whom he had in company with his mother paid several visits, loved him very
much.   She had also visited Anguilhem, where they become better acquainted; but he now felt some remorse at
not having shown her all the affection he began to think
she merited.

He reflected upon a thousand little things, which at the
time appeared to him very tiresome, but which he now
thought he ought to have performed cheerfully.   Among
other claustral distractions, Tancrede had not forgotten
with what repugnance he had, during his visit to Chinon,
been compelled to attend mass and vespers, notwithstanding the angelic voices of the nuns and novices which accompanied the divine service. But see how fickle-minded man is,
and how changeable in his inclinations.   Under present circumstances nothing would be so agreeable to Tancrede as to
attend these services, and endeavor to discover among the
choir of angelic voices that of his beloved Constance. Tancrede had also a vague recollection of a certain window in
his aunt's apartments which overlooked the garden where
the nuns took their walks during the hours of relaxation:
a window to which he could not understand how he had
been so blind—he had scarcely paid any attention; all this
had rushed into the youth's head since he had learned that
to this convent, superintended by his aunt, Mlle. de Beuzerie was banished.   It was only now that the tenderness
of this kind, worthy aunt became evident to him, and he
could not help reproaching himself for so lightly appreciating her good qualities.   He resolved at once to seek an opportunity of amending his fault.   He would pay her a
visit, and devote himself to her as a nephew and a Christian, and regularly attend every religious service during his
stay at the convent.   This visit was at once resolved upon,
but as may be guessed, *in petto*, and without the chevalier
considering it at all necessary to consult any one about it.

Consequently, one fine morning before daylight, Tancrede arose and saddled Christopher. To prevent any uneasiness arising from his protracted absence, he told the stable-boy that he would not return for some days.

The distance between Anguilhem and Chinon is nearly twenty-four leagues. This was a two days' journey for Christopher. In fact, Tancrede slept the same evening at Sainte-Maure, a little town situated about half-way on the road he had to traverse, and next day, at four in the afternoon, he arrived at Chinon.

Although some seven or eight years had elapsed since the chevalier had last visited his aunt, he had not forgotten the road to the convent. He marched straight to the Augustines without finding it necessary to inquire his way of any one, and boldly knocked at the gate. As the convent of the Augustines was kept very strictly, the attendant who came to answer the knock commenced frowning in a very formidable fashion when she saw a fine, handsome youth demanding admittance into the sacred asylum. But when he gave his name, and proclaimed his relationship to the lady superior, the harsh features of the venerable doorkeeper relaxed, and the gate appeared to open of its own accord. Five minutes afterward the Chevalier Tancrede respectfully kissed the plump hand of his good aunt.

She was one of those charming abbesses of whom the aristocratic traditions of the "great age" have preserved to us the portraits; neither too big nor too little; fat and plump; made up of soft words and pious glances; who found means to give to their costume, while strictly observing the rules of the order, a dash of grace and coquetry, a little worldly, it is true, but still not exactly reprehensible. Moreover, she was a younger sister of Mme. Anguilhem, born, like her, of Roche Berthaud, that is to say, issue of one of the oldest and noblest families of Touraine.

The good superior, whose thoughts were always pious and holy, had no suspicion of the motives that brought her nephew to Chinon. She ordered Christopher to be stabled and groomed, and every care to be taken of that excellent beast, whose life, usually so quiet and orderly, had lately become so irregular. As to Tancrede, he was immediately conducted to his apartments and placed under lock and key. Now it happened that the smaller of the two rooms was just the little chamber he coveted, as it overlooked the cloister.

Tancrede's interview with his aunt was of the tenderest description. Three years had passed away since the good lady had seen either the baron or baroness; and during those three years her nephew had grown and altered so much that the venerated superior could scarcely recognize him. She almost withdrew her hand, when, in his delight at finding himself within the walls that inclosed the object of his affections, the chevalier pressed it with too much warmth. But at the first words he spoke of the baron and baroness, announcing that he had come in their name to remove the uncertainty they felt as to the state of her health, and to learn news of their sister and sister-in-law, the good abbess no longer checked her feelings, but took him, big boy that he was, in her arms, and, embracing him, returned, in a very motherly manner, the kiss she had received on her hand.

This was all that Tancrede desired for the moment—he was introduced. He had nothing more to hope for that evening; besides, the dear boy must be greatly fatigued with his journey of four-and-twenty leagues on horseback, and all exertion until the next day was forbidden. A delicate supper was served in his aunt's room—chicken, jellies, pastry, and sweetmeats; after which he was locked in his room, with orders to go instantly to bed and not to wake until the hour for morning prayers.

Tancrede submitted quietly, lest he should excite suspicion. He retired to his bedroom, and heard, with philosophical indifference, the door of his room double-locked upon him. There was the window, he could open that, it is true, and he quickly hastened to it, for it was the hour for recreation. But, unfortunately, a heavy shower of rain was falling, so that the garden, instead of being full of lively girls, was as silent and deserted as a cemetery. As it afforded no shelter from the rain, all the young ladies had flocked to the cloisters.

As long as the rain continued to pour, Tancrede felt convinced that it would be only waste of time to watch for the appearance of any one in the garden. Perhaps, however, if Constance had known that a handsome youth was stationed at the window, with beating heart and eager eyes, watching the flower-beds where she amused herself every day, certainly the rain would not have kept her out of the garden, and, regardless of what damage might accrue to her white frock and satin slippers, she would have felt an imperious necessity for taking fresh air, however moist or unwholesome it might be thought at that hour. But the poor child supposed she was not to see the favored youth until the holidays at least, perhaps not even then, and perhaps never again. Thus thinking, she walked up and down the cloister, leaning on the arm of her companion, sad and weary.

At sunset a crimson sky and purple clouds in the west gave Tancrede hopes of a fine day on the morrow. He was familiar with weather prognostics. Before he had met Constance the only emotion that stirred his heart was that which he experienced the evening before the day appointed for a chase or a hunt, as to whether the morrow would be wet or dry. The celestial barometer he now consulted put his mind quite at ease.

This confidence in the morrow secured him the best night's rest he had enjoyed for the last week past. He slept full of confidence and hope as to the future. For what is the future to a youth of fifteen? The morrow, three or four days, or a week at the most.

In the morning Tancrede was awakened by the singing of the birds in the garden. He rose and dressed himself. He had scarcely completed his toilet before he heard a knock at his door. An aged nun placed his breakfast on the table; it was composed of boiled milk, warm cakes, and freshly-gathered fruit.

Our hero surveyed these delicate articles of diet with something like contempt. He preferred more substantial fare. But as he understood that these were only offered as a stay to his appetite, he inquired when breakfast proper would be served, and was informed after mass. Upon inquiring when mass would be performed, he was told that it commenced at nine and finished at eleven. Upon hearing this he drank his milk to the last drop, and eat every crumb of his cake. He had just finished his repast when he heard the rustling of a dress in the passage, and soon the door of his chamber was opened by his good aunt, who came to inquire how her nephew had passed the night—if his bed was comfortable—if he had slept undisturbed—if he had had pleasant dreams, and so forth.

Tancrede replied to all these questions in a satisfactory manner. Besides, to eyes less anxious than those of his good aunt, his looks, so cheerful and gay, had been sufficient answer. Moreover, he had curled his hair and dressed himself as coquettishly as if he had been a veritable little abbe. The good lady felt quite a pride in her nephew.

But she had not forgotten the infantine freaks he had indulged in some five or six years previously, the dear little fellow, whenever he was required to attend religious service. And she thought she would even now have to employ some circumlocution to reconcile him to the proposal that he should attend mass; but, to her great astonishment, the chevalier promptly replied that since his previous visit he was very much altered with respect to religious matters; that he had reflected a good deal on the subject of devotion, and that he now regarded attendance at religious services as a pleasure as well as a duty, and that he attended mass and vespers every day.

This assertion overwhelmed the superior with delight; she regarded her nephew with a pious tenderness, and declared that from that moment she indulged the hope that some day the family of Anguilhem would exhibit to the world a great saint, as it had already presented great jurists and captains; the nobility of the Anguilhems was both of the robe and the sword.

During this conference the bell for mass sounded. Tancrede had to put in practice the principles he had just confessed to, so he gallantly offered his arm to his aunt, to conduct her to the church. But here our hero deceived himself; the superior gave him to understand that since his last appearance in that place he had grown far too big a boy, and had become much too handsome a young gentleman to allow of his entering the choir with her, and seat himself on the steps as of yore. Now he must simply take his place among the general congregation in the nave; the choir being exclusively reserved for novices, nuns, and boarders.

Tancrede felt that he had no alternative but to submit. Had he made any opposition he would have incurred the risk of betraying the motives which had suddenly rendered him so devout. Bowing his head in token of obedience, he begged his aunt to point out the way he must follow in order to obey the instructions she had given him.

CHAPTER VII.

THE convent chapel was already open to the faithful. As the ladies of this convent were justly regarded as the best voices in the province, divine service in their chapel was always well attended. Tancrede placed himself in the foremost ranks of the congregation, as near as he possibly could to the screen that separated the choir from the nave.

His expectations were not disappointed. Amid all the pure virgin voices that raised their notes to heaven he distinguished one so sweet, thrilling, and inspired, that he never for a moment doubted that it was the voice of Constance. Henceforward his sole idea was to follow this voice in all its modulations, without for a moment losing it amid the voices of her companions. Clinging to this voice, it seemed to him that his soul ascended with it to the celestial regions, where for awhile it joined the heavenly choir, and then descended again to earth, to soothe the woes and miseries of sinful man, rising unceasingly above all terrestrial sounds, like the nocturnal melodies of the Æolian harps, which are supposed to be strains from the concerts of the spirits of the air.

All the time mass continued Tancrede listened in a state of ecstasy. Never had he listened to such delightful sacred music, the most beautiful of all kinds of music. His heart responded to these divine harmonies in emotions of love and piety. Until now he had been ignorant of what devotional feelings were lying dormant in his soul.

Long after the mass was ended he continued kneeling before the railing of the choir. The good superior had kept her eyes upon him during the entire service, and was greatly pleased to see the rapture depicted on her nephew's countenance whenever the chants were resumed. She was impatient for the time to arrive when she could compliment him upon the change that had been worked in his heart, of which she now entertained no doubt, since she had witnessed it with her own eyes. Nor was she astonished when he begged permission to retire to his room for a few moments to overcome the spiritual emotion he experienced. The worthy superior not only gave her assent to this request, but, being carried away by a feeling of admiration excited by his remarkable piety, was on the point of asking the young neophyte for his blessing. Tancrede retired with slow and measured steps to his chamber, but no sooner did he hear the door double locked behind him than he rushed to the window and opened it.

The garden was full of young girls, scattered up and down, who, like bees, ran from flower to flower, and revealing their modest or lofty instincts in making garlands of daisies, violets, or forget-me-nots, or crowns of roses, tulips, or lilies.

Far apart from these groups, flowers amid flowers, strolled arm in arm, two young boarders, whispering together, and every now and then looking around with an uneasy air to be assured their conversation was not heard. One of the two was Constance. Their backs were to the window where Tancrede was watching them as they strolled down a shady walk. When returning, the eyes of Constance were raised raised mechanically to the window. The young girl immediately recognized Tancrede, and could not conceal her surprise, but shrieked aloud with joy.

The chevalier had been seen; that was all he desired. He then hastily withdrew from the window.

The scream uttered by Constance was so piercing that all her young companions hurried around her to learn the cause of it. Constance drooped her head, like a lily on its stem, and in reply to the torrent of questions addressed to her, said she had trodden upon a stone and sprained her ankle.

Some proposed running for the doctor, but Constance assured them she no longer suffered any pain. And as she did not appear to suffer any, her companions gradually quitted her, one by one, to resume their pastime, till at length she was again left alone with her friend.

Constance took this friend into her confidence. The two girls cautiously raised their eyes to the window, and Tancrede soon perceived that there were no secrets between those two pure hearts. He again placed himself at the window, taking care, however, to keep in the shade of the curtains, so that he could see without being easily seen, except by those who knew he was there. Constance rested her hand on the arm of her friend and blushed charmingly, then stooped to gather some pansies, which she made into a bouquet and placed in her bosom. Their violet tints contrasted well with her white dress. Then, after taking a few turns up and down, the two girls retired. A moment afterward Tancrede heard a rustling noise and light steps in the corridor. He rushed to the door of his room, but alas! it was double locked.

Over the door was a window admitting light through his room into the corridor. A pane of glass had been removed to secure ventilation. Through this opening Tancrede saw a bouquet of pansies thrown into his room. He had no doubt it was thrown by the hand of Constance, and was the same he had seen her gather in the garden.

He picked it up with eagerness and delight, and kissed it a thousand times, as he would have done its donor, had she been there. But at this moment he heard the footsteps of his aunt approaching, and hastily concealed the bouquet within his vest. Thinking his religious fit must by this time be over, the amiable superior came to invite him to breakfast, to which welcome invitation he cheerfully responded.

Nothing emboldens a hero so much as success. Tancrede had seen Constance, and she had seen him. He pressed to his heart the bouquet that had rested upon her bosom. This was much more than at first he had dared to hope for or expect; but now he was less satisfied than before. He wished to be near her and speak to her. He looked now for an opportunity, resolved to make the most of it when it occurred. This was soon vouchsafed to him by the good superior herself.

It may readily be supposed that the conversation between his aunt and himself was a perpetual interchange of questions on one side, and responses on the other. At first the questions referred to the baron and baroness, then to their tenants and dependents, then to the estate; from these subjects it passed to their nearer neighbors—those of Senectere, after Senectere to those of Chamille, and after they were passed in review, the transition to Beuzerie was quite natural. Upon hearing this last name, Tancrede took his cue.

"Ah! my dear aunt, that is well thought of; how fortunate that by speaking of the Beuzeries you have reminded me of a commission I had entirely forgotten. Three or four days previously to setting out for Chinon, I was out hunting, when I accidentally met Monsieur de Beuzerie, and as he learned that I was about paying a visit he begged of me to take charge of a letter for his daughter. Now what I have done with this letter, which was put into my hands when I was busy packing, upon my word, I do not know."

"Heaven forbid that you have lost it! The poor child has been very sad and miserable since her return, and this letter would have been a great comfort to her."

"I will go and search my portmanteau for it at once; it must be there, somewhere among my things; but if Mademoiselle de Beuzerie is unhappy, why not give her a doll to play with, for it seems to me she is but a child."

"You shall see, my fine gentleman. You will find yourself mistaken. Six months ago she was, perhaps, only a child, but now Mademoiselle de Beuzerie is a young lady. I do not know what can have happened to her when she went home for the holidays at Easter; but this I must say, she scarcely appears to be the same person."

"But I supped with her a week or so ago at Anguilhem, and I must say, dear aunt, that I saw nothing very extraordinary about her."

"Ah! well, you shall see her, and judge for yourself. Go and look for the letter, and Mademoiselle Constance will be here when you return."

"Gladly," replied Tancrede, stooping over his plate; for he felt the blood mounting to his cheeks, and if his aunt should happen to see his emotion, it would have betrayed him. "Gladly, dear aunt, as soon as we have finished our breakfast."

"Time enough. Take your breakfast comfortably, there is no need to hurry. I am well aware that, at your age, breakfast is a very important affair. But pray be sure to find the letter, for if it is lost, mademoiselle will break her heart, I am sure."

"Oh! it will be found, I have no doubt. I begin to think I put it into the pocket of my coat; if so, it is quite safe."

"I hope so. I shall be delighted. I am so happy when I see my little ones happy about me. I love them so dearly."

"Now, dear aunt, I need not retard the pleasure you anticipate in seeing Mademoiselle de Beuzerie made happy. I have breakfasted, and, with your permission, I will go and look for the letter, while you send for mademoiselle."

Now Tancrede quitted the room with such a careless air, that had the superior been ever so suspicious, her suspicions would have been disarmed before so much apparent candor and truth. But not a shadow of suspicion ever crossed her mind. She was completely duped by the chevalier's precocious hypocrisy and deceit.

Our hero was in no great haste to return, for two reasons. First, he wanted time to write the pretended letter from M. de Beuzerie to his daughter: in the second place, he wished to give Constance leisure to compose herself, and prepare for the interview.

As to what he put into the letter, it is not very difficult to guess; but to those who are dull of comprehension, we may say in confidence that it was filled with the conjugation of the verb *to love* in every mood and tense. In a postscript, he informed Constance of the encounter he had with the viscount, her father, and related word for word what had passed when they met in the warren at Beuzerie. It was important that Constance should know what had happened in this particular, so that she might not be taken by surprise. Upon returning to the breakfast-room, Tancrede found Mlle. de Beuzerie seated near his aunt. Constance, on perceiving him, blushed and grew pale successively: but fortunately she was seated with her back to the window, so that her face being in some measure in the shade, the good superior could see nothing amiss. The chevalier approached the young lady with a deliberate air, and presented her the letter.

"Mademoiselle, I must beg a thousand pardons for neglecting to deliver this letter to you, after being here ever since yesterday evening; but Monsieur de Beuzerie urged me so strongly to deliver this letter to you in person, that I might be able to speak with certainty as to your health, about which he is greatly concerned, that I have begged my dear aunt to speak to you about this little derangement. You will excuse me, I hope?"

Constance murmured a few words of thanks; but as, at the first glance she threw upon the letter, she saw that the superscription was not in the handwriting of her father, she comprehended all; and, instead of opening the letter, she put it into her pocket.

"Ah, well!" said the superior, taking the young girl by the hand, and drawing her to her side, "ah, well! this letter will console you a little, naughty little puss! I know the news: they tell me that since you have returned, you do nothing but sigh and weep."

"But consider, dear aunt," interrupted Tancrede, "that this young lady was very sorry to leave home; and it was very natural that she should shed a few tears; and the convent is not like home, however much you may endeavor to make it so. Is not that true, Mademoiselle Constance? It is not so lively here as at Beuzerie, is it?"

"Come, now," said the abbess, "I will give you a holiday to-day; you shall dine with me and my nephew, my pretty pet, and perhaps that will be more agreeable to you than dining in the refectory with all the house."

"Oh! how kind you are; how delighted I shall be!" exclaimed Constance, unable to control her joy at this unexpected pleasure.

"Mademoiselle," said the chevalier, recognizing the necessity of leaving his aunt no time to analyze the feeling that had excited Constance to the expression of delight which she imprudently allowed to escape her, "Mademoiselle, shall I have the pleasure of being the bearer of a reply to your father's letter? and will you overlook my neglect in delivering his, which I had the honor to bring, on my promising to be more careful with yours?"

"Do you, then, return immediately?" inquired Constance, blushing.

"I am in fear of being summoned away at any moment; I am at the mercy of an exacting tutor: and I admit that every noise I hear, every door that opens, makes me look out for the appearance of my respected abbe. Lose no time, then, I beg, if you wish to profit by the occasion presented to you of sending a reply to your father, who, I am sure, looks for it with much impatience."

"In that case, sir, if our good mother will allow me, I will retire to my room to peruse the letter you have brought me, and write an answer to it."

"Go, dear child, go," said the superior, kissing the young girl on her forehead; "and do not forget that dinner will be ready at two o'clock. I shall let you know when it is served."

"I shall have no occasion to give you that trouble, madame," replied Constance; "I shall have too much pleasure in the company of yourself and nephew, our good country

cousin, not to take care to be punctual to your kind invitation."

Mme. de Beuzerie, now entirely recovered from her first
emotion, made a very pretty and coquettish courtesy, then
left the room, her hand upon the letter, which she held
in her pocket; while Tancrede, watching her every movement, placed his hand on the bouquet, and pressed it to
his heart.

Constance kept her word; she was more than punctual.
At a quarter to two she attended the superior, who was in
conversation with the chevalier. He inquired if she had
finished her letter. Blushing all over, she drew from her
bosom a pretty little letter, addressed to Viscount De Beuzerie, which she handed to Tancrede without power to utter
a word. He, under pretense that he might lose it if he
carried it about with him, went out, as he said, to put it
into his portfolio, but in fact to devour every line of it.

It was one of those charming epistles which only young
hearts can indite; very tender, sincere, and full of vows of
eternal love, born of yesterday, and which they vow shall
end only with death. These protestations covered four
pages, but might have been summed up in three words—*I
love you.*

Tancrede first kissed the envelope, then each page in
succession, then every line on each page, and lastly every
word in each line. His joy resembled a delirium.

Upon returning to the room he found Constance blushing as red as a rose. The two poor children exchanged
looks full of tender meaning and happiness. At this moment the door of the apartment opened, the superior uttered a cry of joy; at this sound the two young people
turned their heads, and tears soon occupied the place of
smiles.

The person whose unexpected appearance had caused the
superior to utter a cry was—the Baroness d'Anguilhem!

The two sisters affectionately embraced each other, while
the poor children hung their heads with an air that proclaimed—"All is lost!" Then Tancrede went toward his
mother, who instead of embracing him, as she had embraced his aunt, gave him only her hand to kiss. As for
Mlle. de Beuzerie, she made a profound reverence to the
baroness, to which the latter responded only by a cold inclination of the head.

The two children trembled from head to foot; but the baroness said nothing, and after exchanging compliments with her sister, she accepted her invitation to take a seat at the table.

Constance would gladly have retired if she dared. At the table she was placed between the baroness and the lady superior, so that all the time the dinner lasted she dared not venture to raise her eyes. More than once Tancrede observed a tear stealing furtively down her cheek, which she quickly wiped with her napkin. As for himself, he blushed and grew pale again twenty times in a minute. He attempted to eat, but his heart was so full, he found it utterly impossible to swallow a bit.

During dinner the baroness related the circumstances that determined her to give her sister a little surprise; and how the baron could not accompany her because he was busy making preparations for a journey he intended to make with the chevalier immediately he returned to Anguilhem. At this news the chevalier pricked up his ears, and the tears of the unhappy Constance flowed so fast, that the napkin was in constant requisition. At length her emotion quite overpowered her, she threw herself back in her chair and sobbed aloud. At this unexpected explosion the good abbess saw only the grief of the young girl, whom she interrogated, we must do her the justice to say, with the tenderness of a mother. But Constance merely replied that she did not know what was the matter with her, she supposed it was what people called *the blues*, and asked permission to retire to her own room.

This permission was readily granted, and Mme. d'Anguilhem expressed no wish for her to remain. Constance therefore retired without a word of comfort from any one; for Tancrede, fascinated by the presence of his mother, dared not utter a word, or even say "Adieu."

When Mlle. de Beuzerie had retired, and the baroness supposed she had reached her chamber, she invited her son to proceed to his room and pack up his portmanteau without the least delay, as the orders of the baron were that he should instantly return to Anguilhem. Tancrede obeyed without uttering a word. Filial respect, at this date, was one of the most precious family virtues, regarded as a sacred duty, especially by the country aristocracy, that key-

stone of nobility. Saluting his mother very humbly he
withdrew to his room.

The two sisters were now alone.

———

CHAPTER VIII.

IT can scarcely be necessary to inform the reader what
was the subject of conversation between the two ladies;
let us remark that at the end of an hour the chevalier was
summoned to their presence. He made his appearance
with his portmanteau in his hand, and quite crestfallen at
his discomfiture.

The superior knew all. She had demanded of Constance
the pretended letter from her father, the viscount, brought
by the chevalier; but Constance had passed her bosom
friend in the corridor, and adroitly slipped this letter, her
dearest treasure, into her hand. Now as no one was aware
of this stratagem, Mlle. de Beuzerie boldly asserted that
she had burned the letter they demanded of her, and that
if they doubted it, they might search her and everything
belonging to her. This was actually done, but with no result.

The baroness had come to Chinon in the chaise, with the
horse of a tenant, and under his protection. Christopher
was now harnessed to the chaise, and they set out, after
very brief adieus, during which the good abbess retained, in
the presence of her nephew, all that severe dignity calculated to express her wounded pride.

No sooner were Mme. d'Anguilhem and her son alone in
the chaise, than seeing the extreme grief of the chevalier, all
rancor fled from her bosom. Women have an instinctive
sympathy for the pains of love, and the severest mother
will become indulgent the moment the fault appears to
proceed from affection. Thus instead of receiving reproaches, as he expected and dreaded, the chevalier was
treated to a series of logical reasonings, first upon his extreme youth (he was scarcely fifteen), then upon the dis-
parity in fortune that existed between the Beuzeries and
the D'Anguilhems; and lastly, upon the understanding entered into for some time past, between the father of Constance and the father of Count de Croisey. But to all these

reasonings Tancrede replied by this *dilemma*, more powerful and stronger than all the reasonings in the world:

"Dear mother, I love Constance, and Constance loves
me, and we are determined to die if we are parted."

During the two days the journey lasted the baroness attacked her son upon all points, but she exhausted all her
logic without being able to obtain any other reply than the
one we have just given.

When the chevalier disappeared from Anguilhem a grand
family council was held, consisting of the baron and baroness and the Abbe Dubois. They were not long in discover-
ing what road the chevalier had taken, nor the object of his
journey to Chinon. The principal question discussed at the
council was, what means should be employed to prevent
this love-chase, which presented so many alarming symptoms of renewal from being continued; for it was greatly to
be feared that some serious collision would take place between the families Beuzerie and Anguilhem, who had always been such excellent neighbors; and it was the desire
and intention of the baron and baroness to maintain, on
their part, these good relations.

The decision this august triumvirate arrived at was that
as soon as the chevalier returned to Anguilhem he should
be sent to the Jesuits' College at Amboise, and there complete his studies.

This decision come to, the baroness lost no time in hastening to Chinon, to bring back her scapegrace son, while the
baron, as Mme. d'Anguilhem had informed Tancrede, made
preparations to conduct, in person, his son to the capital of
the province, for fear that, if intrusted to the care of his
tutor, he would give him the slip on the road.

Upon arriving at Anguilhem, on the second day after his
departure from Chinon, the chevalier found every preparation made for his starting for college within four-and-
twenty hours. It is unnecessary to say that an idea of
rebelling against parental authority never once entered his
mind. In presence of his love, the chevalier felt himself a
young man; but in presence of the baron and baroness he
very quickly perceived that he was still a child.

The journey was very dull. Between the Abbe Dubois,
for whom Tancrede had not a very deep affection, and his
father, who, by the severity of his countenance, instantly
repulsed any expression of tenderness, he felt very ill at

case. Besides, the idea that he, the child of the woods and
fields, and of liberty, should go and pass a whole year in a
sort of prison, with a mob of black-robed gentlemen, who
subjected his whole existence to the rules of their order!
This idea weighed like a punishment greatly dispropor-
tional to the fault he had committed. And to live a whole
year without seeing Constance—an age. Impossible!

It is true that from time to time a project which at
first shocked the chevalier, but which by much thinking
upon he gradually became reconciled to, brought relief to
his tortured mind. It was nothing less than this; that he
would take the little sum of money the baroness gave him
at parting, and another which the baron would doubtless
also give before he left him, and be as economical with these
as possible; then, when he had accumulated two or three
hundred francs, which to the chevalier appeared a fortune,
he would escape from the college, fly to Chinon, scale the
walls of the convent, carry off Mlle. Constance, and marry
her as soon as he could meet with a priest.

Among the five-and-twenty or thirty volumes contained
in the library of Anguilhem, there was a romance entitled
" Astrea," which had been the delight of the baroness in the
days of her youth. This romance set forth a multitude of
cases, wherein kings had carried off shepherdesses, and
queens had married shepherds. Now the chevalier thought
that, however great might be the pecuniary barrier that
separated him from Constance, it was as nothing when
compared to the social distance that separated a powerful
monarch from a humble shepherdess, or a great queen from
a poor shepherd. Besides, there is an age at which we view
life as a romance, and Tancrede had just arrived at this age;
but he was ignorant of the fact that at that age one may
run away but not get married.

It is wonderful to see how, in a situation that appears
desperate, a resolution will be taken quite contrary to common sense, and immediately calm the mind and soothe the
heart. Tancrede fully comprehended that, supposing all
circumstances proved favorable (and they were many) to
the accomplishment of his scheme, yet he must wait a very
long time before he could hope to put it into execution; but
n'importe, however remote it might appear at that moment, days would become weeks, and weeks months, and
the favored hour must eventually arrive. Show to a trav-

eler overcome with fatigue, lost in the darkness of night,
wandering in a forest, ready to sink with weariness and
fatigue—show him a light in the horizon, even if distant
two or three leagues, and the poor wanderer will immediately take courage and walk with as quick and firm a step
as when he started on his journey in the morning.

By the time the chevalier had arrived at Amboise his
courage had somewhat revived, and he entered the college
with greater resignation than his father had anticipated.
This resignation moved the old gentleman, who, it must be
admitted, tenderly loved his son and heir. The result was
that his paternal heart melted, and from this tenderness
there flowed no less a sum than seventy-two francs, in the
shape of three louis d'or, which at the moment of his departure he slipped into his son's hand.

These three louis, added to the other two the baroness
had given him, formed a grand total of five louis, or one
hundred and twenty francs, which was a very respectable
beginning for a young capitalist.

Tancrede fully comprehended that to lull all suspicion he must commence by devoting himself to study
with examplary assiduity. The curriculum of the Jesuits,
it is well known, is most excellent. And, although the
Abbe Dubois was a tutor much above the average of his
order, the worthy fathers, after putting Tancrede under examination, decided that he must immediately be put under
a double course of rhetoric. He received this news, which
extended his sojourn at the college to two years instead of
one, with more calmness than the abbe anticipated; but as
the abbe, less easily blinded than the baron, was always
suspecting his pupil of some roguery concealed under his
apparent resignation, he resolved never to lose sight of him
for a moment.

Tancrede was, however, more than a match for the per-
spicuity and vigilance of the abbe. The chevalier possessed
one of those fertile inventions, upon which it is only necessary to sow the seed for the seed to bear its fruit. He had
nothing to distract his attention from his love but work,
and under pretense of working he would shut himself up
and confer with Constance, and he made rapid progress.
Tender souls are easily excited, so our scholar fell in love
with the Greek and Latin poets; for in the bucolics of Virgil,
and in the idyls of Theocritus, he could always find a dia-

logue between a shepherd and shepherdess, which reminded the scholar of his own condition. It was but a poor consolation, without doubt; but, poor as it was, it made his position more endurable, and enabled him to wait with patience.

The first care of the chevalier was to find out, if, among the students in the college, there were any who came from Chinon. Fortune smiled on him; three of his comrades were born in that city, and their parents resided there still. He attached himself to these students, and to his great delight soon discovered that one of the three, Henry de Narcy, had a sister in the convent of the Augustines. Now as this sister had been three years in the convent, it was very probable that she was attached to Mlle. de Beuzerie, or at least was acquainted with her. Here a means of communication was opened to the disconsolate lovers. Vacation time arrived. As Tancrede had only entered college in the month of June, and as the vacation happened in August, a fear that had more than once presented itself to his mind was realized. On the festival of Notre Dame, he received a letter from the Baron d'Anguilhem, in which that worthy gentleman employed all his logic to convince his son that it would be much better for him to employ his six weeks' holiday in study, and make up for lost time, than to come to Anguilhem. The truth was, that the baron and baroness imposed upon themselves the privation of not seeing their son, lest the proximity of Beuzerie should rekindle in the heart of the chevalier the flame they hoped was quenched, because he never spoke of it. To soften as much as possible this hardship upon our hero, they authorized the Abbe Dubois to make some excursions into the environs of Tours. And as they did not know with what parsimony the chevalier had employed his funds, they instructed the abbe to give to his pupil, from the fund confided to his administration, two louis from the baron and one from the baroness. Now as during the three months he had been a student he had expended only twenty-four francs, he now found himself proprietor of seven louis.

Tancrede had placed himself on a very good understanding with the three young men from Chinon, and more particularly with Henry de Narcy; and at the moment the latter was setting out to go home he unbosomed his secret to him. He told him of his love for Mlle. de Beuzerie, and how he was beloved in return; how he had been brought to the College of Amboise solely because his parents disapproved of his love, which had not met with the approval of the parents of Constance; and lastly, how he was detained at the college during the vacation, lest, during his sojourn at Anguilhem, he might, being so near to Beuzerie, get into trouble.

Henry de Narcy fully appreciated the chevalier's sufferings, and placed himself, with his sister, at the service of his comrade. Communication would be all the more easy, as he had often heard his sister speak of Mlle. de Beuzerie, and always as an intimate friend. In fact, Constance de Beuzerie and Mlle. Henrietta de Narcy were bosom friends; and in the portrait of his sister that Henry showed to Tancrede, the latter recognized the young lady that was in close intercourse with Constance on the day he saw them walking in the garden of the convent, when Constance, upon seeing him, uttered the scream of surprise which she had been obliged to pass off as a cry of pain.

Tancrede sent a letter to Constance by the hands of Henry, which, upon the arrival of the latter at Chinon, would be given to his sister, and by her placed in the hands of Constance. Then Constance could inclose a reply in Henrietta's letter to her brother. In his letter he detailed to Constance his project of escaping from college, of carrying her off from the convent, and marrying her at the first church they found on the road. He knew very well that whatever repugnance might now exist as to the marriage, that once married their parents would not refuse their blessing. Moreover, the letter was full of oaths of eternal fidelity and endless love.

The day of the vacation arrived; the two friends separated; Tancrede commending his interests to Henry, and Henry assuring him that his affair could not be in better hands. The month of September passed away without our hero evincing any impatience. Of all the students he was the only one that remained at college, and he worked in a manner that satisfied the most difficult conditions. The Abbe Dubois did not know what to make of it.

Early in October the students returned; but although Henry was the one Tancrede was most impatient to see, he was the very last to return. It is true that in giving his hand to the chevalier to shake, he held in it a neat little letter.

This little letter consisted only of three lines, but these three lines spoke volumes; here they are:

"I love you as dearly as you say you love me. You offer me your life, I give you mine; take it then, and do with it as you list.   CONSTANCE."

From this it would seem, that in the library at Beuzerie, there was some beautiful romance, calculated, like "Astrea," to form the minds and hearts of young girls.

Thanks to the ingenuity of Henry, everything had gone on admirably. As all the letters written in the convent were naturally submitted to inspection before they were allowed to pass out, Henry, at the time of his departure for Tours, had feigned indisposition. This delay had given the boarders time to return to the convent. In this way Henrietta had contrived to communicate with Constance, and as Henry, when about to depart from Chinon, had paid his sister a visit to bid her adieu, when embracing him, she slipped Constance's little note into his hand.

Our hero was now quite easy. Every effort on his part was sure to be seconded by Constance; his love was fully returned. It is the tenderness and devotion of woman's love that gives it ever a superiority over that of man.

CHAPTER IX.

THE days passed away one by one, while Tancrede, faithful to his system of economy, increased his little treasure by adding to it all the money he received from time to time from his parents. Twice the baron and baroness visited Tours to console their son in his exile, which he endured, it must be admitted, with heroic resignation. During these visits the name of Constance, as if by tacit understanding, was never mentioned; so that, upon their return to Anguilhem the second time, the baron and baroness felt convinced that their son had become quite reasonable on that point.

Thus, at the end of six or eight months, he had silenced all suspicions, and as he now had attained his sixteenth year and had finished his rhetoric, he was given to understand that if he would renounce his follies he might leave the college. On hearing this he promised everything required of him.

Tancrede had revolved in his mind a thousand projects of escape, each one more extravagant than the other. It was not an easy matter for any student to escape, and still less so for Tancrede; for besides the general surveillance of the Jesuit fathers, there was also the particular watchfulness of the Abbe Dubois. At length he hit upon a very simple project, which was the last to be thought of on account of its very simplicity.

Like all the other students who had attained their sixteenth year, or who were in their course of rhetoric and philosophy, he had a room to himself, but in this room the abbe slept, for security's sake. It is true that the abbe once asleep slept heavily, and was not easily awakened, and always gave sonorous tokens by which the profundity of his slumbers could be measured. In fact, to speak plainly, the abbe had the infirmity of snoring.

It was upon this infirmity that our hero built his plan of escape. On the evening appointed for his escape, Tancrede would go to bed first, and leave the abbe to follow. He would carefully notice where the abbe put his clothes, for the abbe and he were about the same height. When the light was extinguished, and the abbe commenced his snoring, he would feel quite sure that his Argus was fast asleep. He would then rise quietly, and put on the abbe's black gown, wig, and cap, and slip out of the room as quietly as possible, carrying his shoes in his hand. In all probability the abbe would, as usual, sleep till six o'clock in the morning, therefore the fugitive would get a six or eight hours' start of his pursuers.

It was necessary to find a pretext to induce the porter to open the gate at such an hour, and one was soon found. Our hero had arranged his escape to take place on the night of Wednesday or Thursday. He had calculated upon making the journey from Amboise to Chinon in three stages, and that, consequently, he would arrive there in the course of Sunday. Once there he would trust to fortune, and be guided by circumstances; only he would present himself as abbe at the gate of the convent, and leave there a letter from Henry to his sister, and by a certain mark on this letter, unintelligible to all the world but Constance, she would recognize that he was at Chinon.

This important Wednesday was a day of exquisite torture to the chevalier, but he had cherished his project too long to falter in the execution of it. He therefore kept his countenance and voice under perfect control: he even managed to write his theme and translation; and at supper he eat heartily, and was as lively as usual. Truly, the chevalier seemed predestined to romantic adventures, and nature had endowed him with all the qualities necessary to aid him in accomplishing them.

At nine o'clock the abbe and the chevalier retired to rest. The abbe placed his clothes on a chair near his bed, and extinguished the light. In a quarter of an hour he was sound asleep.

Tancrede waited for another quarter of an hour to elapse, then slipped out of bed, which, being a very creaking one, was a difficult matter to accomplish silently. At last his feet touched the floor, he leaned against the wall, and rested a moment to discover if he were safe so far. The snoring of the abbe kept time with the pendulum of the clock, sonorous and loud. All went well. Then he cautiously felt his way to the abbe's chair, which, for the time, did duty as a portmanteau for all the preceptoral wardrobe. He carefully removed the clothes to his bed, and began his toilet. He finished it without interruption. Completely transformed into an abbe, he opened the door gently, and put his head out to see if the coast was clear, and then withdrew it again into the chamber in order to assure himself that the preceptor had not been aroused. Satisfied that all was right, he made for the staircase, crossed the court-yard, and boldly knocked at the porter's lodge.

"Who's there?"

"I am the Abbe Dubois, preceptor of the Chevalier d'Anguilhem. Monsieur, the chevalier, is taken very ill, and I want to fetch a doctor."

The porter aroused from his first sleep, put his head out, and, recognizing the abbe's costume, pulled the cord that lifted the bolt of the gate, muttering something which Tancrede did not care to hear, and in an instant he found himself outside.

He took to his heels with all speed, and continued running for about ten minutes, when suddenly he found it necessary to halt. Another step, and he would have been in the River Loire.

Here he took time to consider. He knew that Chinon was nearly twenty-five leagues from Amboise, and that by following the course of the river he would in due time arrive there. But there were two sides to the river, either of which would conduct him to the same point; but one must be preferable to the other. He decided upon taking the right bank, although it lengthened the journey some three or four leagues, but it offered more safety from pursuit. He therefore crossed the bridge, and walked on all night, and at about six o'clock in the morning he found himself at Rouvray. Here fatigue forced him to make a halt. He had accomplished eight leagues already. Stopping at a little road-side inn, he went to bed, giving orders to be called at ten. His intention was to start again immediately after breakfast.

While undressing, Tancrede discovered that besides his own purse, which he had carefully concealed in the lining of his vest, he was in possession of another, the abbe's, which he found in the pocket of his robe. He concluded that this money was what his father had sent to be disbursed on his own account, and therefore he felt no scruples in appropriating it, but rejoiced greatly over this unexpected addition to his treasury, which increased his capital to the extent of nearly a hundred francs. The chevalier felt now as if he could pay his way to the end of the world.

While he was at breakfast, the host entered to inform him that a passenger-boat was going down the river, and that if he preferred that mode of traveling he would engage a passage for him. The idea pleased him very much, seeing that his pursuers would be more likely to lose his traces on the water than on the land. The track made by a boat on the river would be as difficult to find as any of those indicated by King Solomon, of poetic and proverbial memory.

To the host's proposition, Tancrede replied by saying, that if going by the boat should not cause him to lose time, he would be glad to avail himself of that mode of conveyance. The host assured him that, so far from losing time, he would gain it, seeing that he should travel both by day and by night. This assurance decided the chevalier, so he instructed his

3

host to secure him a passage at once, although the boat
would not start for two hours. It is true, that the advantage gained by traveling day and night would more than
compensate for the delay.

As the host was leaving the room, Tancrede called him
back to inquire who was traveling in the boat. He ascertained that there was a company of merchants going to the
fair at Nantes, some soldiers going to join their regiment at
Rennes, and some Parisians traveling for pleasure. He
concluded he had nothing to fear from them; therefore his
original determination was not disturbed by the information he received, and he told his host that the boatman
might reckon him for one.

About noon they made a start. The boat, or rather the
coach, seeing that it was drawn by four stout horses, made
as good progress as could be desired. Therefore the chevalier congratulated himself on having adopted this mode of
conveyance, which promised a nocturnal journey as rapid as
that he could otherwise have accomplished in a day. About
three o'clock, they stopped at Tours to dine, and started
again at five, and until dark proceeded at the usual speed.
Inquiring of the captain what progress he would be able to
make during the night, he received for answer, that they
would arrive at Langeais in time for breakfast. Upon the
strength of this promise, Tancrede wrapped himself in his
cloak, laid himself down on a bench, and went to sleep.

But, notwithstanding all his precautions, he was not
easy in his mind. His sleep was soon troubled by a dream.
He thought he saw in the horizon two horsemen, whom he
recognized as his father and the Abbe Dubois, who, on perceiving the boat, redoubled their speed; while the boat, in
spite of his entreaties to the captain, moved slower and
slower as the horsemen gained upon it. At last they approached so near that he, still dreaming, thought he had
no alternative but to conceal himself in the hold. He
therefore jumped into it, and, hiding between two casks,
awaited the result. In a few moments it appeared to him
that the boat not only moved very slowly, but stopped altogether. Then he heard footsteps approach him, and
then it seemed that a hand seized him by the collar; and
he was a prisoner again. Uttering a loud cry, he awoke.

His first feeling was that of joy, for upon opening his
eyes he quickly perceived that he was still at liberty. But

his dream was not altogether a dream; the boat had stopped, and remained immovably fixed in the middle of the stream. He wished to ascertain from the pilot the cause of this stoppage, but he was asleep at his post, like the rest of the travelers. He hesitated for a moment whether he should awaken the pilot, but the suspense he felt was too great for him to hesitate long. He therefore shook the navigator by the arm, and the latter, grumbling at being awakened out of his sleep, explained that there was nothing the matter, and consequently nothing to be surprised or alarmed at; the boat was merely aground on a sand bank, an accident that occurred two or three times every voyage. After giving this information the pilot leaned his head against the rudder again, and went to sleep.

The Loire at that period was just like what it is at the present day, one of the most capricious rivers in France; one we can never make sure of finding where we leave it. It is like that ancient tyrant who had twelve bed-chambers, and who never slept two successive nights in the same bed.

They were therefore "sanded-up;" and likely to remain so until a rain storm supplied the river with a fresh supply of water. By doubling or trebling the number of horses composing the team, it was just possible they might be able to draw the boat into deep water again. But how obtain the horses?

It is not difficult to imagine what impression this information produced upon our hero. Twenty-four hours elapsed, and he had not yet made more than eighteen leagues; that is to say, scarcely half the distance. Yet critical as he felt his position to be, he could do nothing but exercise his patience. If in the morning the boat was not likely to move, by water or by horses, he would go ashore, either on the right bank or the left, no matter which, and continue his journey on foot.

Having settled this point in his own mind, he attempted to compose himself to sleep again, but found it impossible. Therefore, he lay awake, thinking of Constance, and how he should get to her. This appeared to him a very easy matter. As soon as Constance became aware, through the letter Henry de Narcy sent to his sister of his arrival at Chinon, she would, doubtless, hold herself in readiness for anything that might happen. Then, by means of a ladder, which he would put over the convent wall that formed one side of a deserted street, he would arrive at Constance's window, which looked into the garden. She would descend from her window by means of the ladder, then, they would both scale the wall, and fly to the nearest village, and ask a priest to marry them.

He resolved all this nice little plot over again and again, until day began to dawn. But daylight brought no change in the condition of the boat; the night had passed away without adding a single inch to the depth of the Loire. On the other hand, the captain, seeing the insufficiency of his team of four horses, had sought re-enforcements in a neighboring village, and returned with eight others, which, added to his own four, formed a total of twelve. But in spite of the combined efforts of the poor animals, stimulated by the whip of the conscientious driver, the boat would not move an inch, but remained firmly rooted in the sandy bed of the Loire. Two or three hours were thus wasted in fruitless attempts.

The chevalier endured all the bitterest pangs of the impatient, and could not understand the apathy of his fellow-travelers, who quietly reasoned upon the disaster that so greatly exasperated him. They proposed the most impracticable means of getting out of the predicament, and these exhausted, they quietly resigned themselves to remain where they were, until a miracle from heaven should come to their deliverance. It was very evident that these gentlemen were accustomed to descending the Loire, and familiar with such accidents.

Our hero went in search of the captain, and, having found him, declared to him, that if the boat was not afloat in half an hour, he would jump into the river and swim ashore. The captain was quietly discussing his breakfast, and patiently listened to this address, from beginning to end, he then inquired if the chevalier had paid his passage. Tancrede replied by showing him his ticket. The captain then assured him that he was perfectly at liberty to do as he pleased, and quietly finished his cutlet and bottle.

Tancrede felt a strong inclination to choke the captain, and take command of the boat himself, and was only restrained by reflecting that a homicide might complicate his situation. So he finally concluded to remain where he was and await the result.

He hoped to find other travelers as impatient as himself,

and reckoned upon profiting by their impatience in getting up a little row. He mingled with several groups, but to his astonishment found, that instead of talking about the accident to the boat, they were quietly discussing business matters, politics, the battle of Malplaquet, taxes, and such topics. He very soon perceived that there was nothing to be got from their assistance, so he was beginning to consider how he had best put into execution his threat of swimming ashore, when he saw five or six little boats rowing toward the passenger-boat. Some people from the adjacent country, seeing the boat aground, brought cakes and fruit, and offered them for sale to the travelers, just as the South-Sea Islanders surround ships in the Pacific Ocean.

Tancrede bought the whole cargo of one of the boats, on condition that the owner would immediately row him ashore.

The departure of the little abbe interrupted for a moment the conversation that was going on. Some turned their heads to see him descend the side of the boat, and watched him until he disappeared. But conversation was soon again resumed, and no one seemed to think anything more of the deserter.

The chevalier landed near Luynes. He was anxious to proceed to that town, distant about a quarter of a league from the river's bank, to see if he could hire a horse. But then he thought that would delay him; besides, in hiring a horse, he would have to hire a man with it, and admit him into his confidence. He therefore resolved to continue his journey on foot, and immediately took the road to Langeais, where he arrived at seven o'clock in the evening.

However much he might desire to keep on his way, here he was obliged to stop that night. At least he felt he must halt to sup and rest a little.

To start again on a journey at eight o'clock in the evening, alone and on foot, would expose him to grave suspicion. Besides, our lover had arrived at the place where he must recross the Loire, and proceed through the fields; for if he kept to the road in going from Langeais to Chinon there were ten chances to one that he would be recognized. He had therefore made up his mind to remain that night at the inn, and, to save time, he got the landlord to describe to him the road he must take in the morning. At daybreak he pursued his way. He hoped by brisk walking to reach Chinon about two in the afternoon. He breakfasted at nine at Armentieres, and at noon halted at Saint Benoit, and a little before two o'clock he had the pleasure of seeing the steeples of the much-desired town of Chinon.

This sight, instead of inspiring him with fresh courage, quite damped his ardor. He stopped for a moment, for his legs seemed to give way under him. He pressed his hand to his breast to repress the wild beating of his heart. Ashamed of his weakness, he made an effort to recover his courage, and resumed his journey. In another quarter of an hour he reached Chinon. Then, as it happens to all resolute hearts, the proximity of danger gave him fresh strength and vigor. He proceeded straight to the convent, knocked without hesitation at the gate, and submitted to the careful scrutiny of the attendant with the greatest composure.

"My sister," said he, "I believe you have in your convent Mademoiselle Henrietta de Narcy?"

"Yes, my brother," replied the attendant; "what is your pleasure?"

"I have brought a letter to her from her brother. Will you have the kindness to deliver it to her after it has been submitted to the inspection of your worthy lady superior?"

"Immediately." replied the attendant. "Alas! poor dear girl, this letter will be very welcome to her, for at the present moment she is very unhappy."

"Unhappy! from what cause?" inquired Tancrede anxiously.

"Unhappy at the loss of her dearest friend."

"Her dearest friend," replied Tancrede, with increased trepidation, "lost her dearest friend, did you say?"

"Ah, yes!" replied the attendant, raising her eyes to heaven; "God has given, and God has taken away, but He has done wisely, for she was an angel upon earth, and He has called her home."

"But—but—this best friend," cried Tancrede, wiping the perspiration from his forehead, "if I mistake not, was —was—"

"Was Mademoiselle de Beuzerie," replied the attendant; "did you happen to know her, dear brother?"

"Constance! Constance!" cried the chevalier, "in Heaven's name proceed! what has happened?"

"She died three days ago, and was buried yesterday."

Tancrede uttered a cry of anguish, and staggered like a

man struck by a thunder-bolt. He would have fallen flat on the ground if the Baron d'Anguilhem, who was at this moment about to enter the convent, had not caught him in his arms.

CHAPTER X.

WHEN the chevalier recovered his senses, he found himself in a bedroom at an inn, and the Baron d'Anguilhem watching by his pillow. Upon opening his eyes he looked around him as one who, awaking from an unpleasant dream, endeavors to recover his senses. His memory gradually returned to him. He remembered what had passed at the convent gate; that he had learned from the mouth of the attendant that Constance was dead, and that, shocked by this news, he had fallen into the arms of a man whom he believed he recognized as his father.

For a moment the chevalier tried to doubt his misfortune. But the state in which he found himself, the clothes of his preceptor lying on a chair, and his father weeping at his bedside, all were proofs of his misfortune too strong to admit of doubt or of hope. Turning to the baron, and throwing his arms round his neck, he sobbed:

"I am so unhappy, my dear father."

The baron loved his son, and lavished upon him all the consolation he could think of under the circumstances. He reminded him that he was a man, and as a man born to trouble, which God would give him strength enough to endure. This was very good philosophy, but to all its axioms, sound as they were, Tancrede murmured, as he laid his head on his pillow:

"If my mother was here! Oh, if my mother was here!"

"What would she do for you that I can not do?" inquired the baron.

"Oh! she would weep with me," cried Tancrede, sobbing.

The baron thought that the best thing he could do was to let his son give vent to his sorrow. In a little while the first burst of grief was over, and Tancrede began to speak of Constance. He asked a thousand questions as to her sickness and death. The baron contented himself with replying that he knew no more about her sickness and death than anybody else; she had been taken with the small-pox, and died after six days of great suffering,

The chevalier then declared that he would go to the convent and see her chamber, and the tomb where she was buried; that he would weep in the one and pray at the other.

The baron replied that on the morrow a requiem for the repose of her soul would be sung in the church convent; and that if he would promise to behave like a man, and return the same evening to Anguilhem, he would take him to hear the requiem, and upon quitting the church he should accompany the abbess to the tomb, and afterward to the cell of Constance.

The chevalier promised to behave himself becomingly. As to quitting Chinon, he desired it from the bottom of his heart, for he felt how much, under existing circumstances, he needed a mother's love.

The rest of the day passed tranquilly, but sadly. Tancrede kept his bed, and, from time to time, pretended to sleep. As soon as his father thought he slept, he went out on tip-toe, and the chevalier, finding himself alone, gave himself up to the full indulgence of his grief!

Night came, and, unhappy as he was, he took a little sleep. He dreamed of Constance, and, strange to say, he dreamed of her not as lying pale and dying on her bed, or in her coffin, but he dreamed of her in the full vigor of health, a smile on her lips, love in her eyes, just as she had appeared at Anguilhem, at Beuzerie, and at the convent. When he awoke his heart bounded with joy, for a few minutes he could not realize the extent of his misfortune. But the strange bedroom, the ecclesiastical vestments, the footsteps of his father pacing up and down the adjoining room, and which at every turn seemed to approach the door, reminded him too surely that the death of Constance was not a dream.

At day-break he heard the tolling of the convent bell, announcing that the funeral service would take place that day. Every stroke on the bell, as it swung slow and heavy, struck despair to the heart of the chevalier.

One thing troubled him very much—he had no other clothes than those in which he had fled from Amboise. And he could not attend the requiem for Constance dressed as an abbe. It seemed to him that this grotesque disguise

assorted very ill with his grief. To elope with Constance
in this costume might do very well, but to listen to a funeral service, and weep at her tomb in that costume, would
be a profanation.

The heart has its instinctive delicacy, which never mis-
leads us.

By a singular coincidence, as he was thinking over this
difficulty, the baron entered the chevalier's room, followed
by a servant bearing a complete suit of clothes. Tancrede
thanked his father, and inquired how he had obtained them.
The baron replied that the abbe, upon returning to Anguilhem, had informed the baroness in what disguise her son
had taken flight. And as the baroness naturally concluded
that he had run away only to see Constance, she had immediately forwarded his clothes, fully understanding how
embarrassed he would feel upon arriving at Chinon without
them. One thing alone astonished him—why had not his
mother brought them herself?

The chevalier rose and dressed himself; for mass would
begin at eight o'clock. To the great astonishment of the
baron, Tancrede never spoke a word of Constance. The
poor boy had felt that in all the replies his father had made
to him, there was a coldness and constraint which only
aggravated his grief. The baron, on his side, doubtless in
the fear of awaking the regrets of his son, constantly
avoided the only subject he felt interested in. He did not
understand that in crises of this sort, such as his son was
in, the chief consolation is tears, and that the way to dry
those tears is to speak of what will make them flow.

The baron therefore believed that his son suffered less
affliction, because he no longer wept. Alas! his grief was
all within; his tears dropped one by one upon his heart.

He went out with his father, and they proceeded arm in
arm toward the convent. But upon approaching the gate
where twice before he had presented himself with such delightful emotion, he felt the earth sink from under his feet;
the houses, walls, trees, all seemed falling; he was obliged
to lean heavily upon his father's arm. The baron, on his
part, was deeply moved, and when Tancrede perceived his
father's emotion, he endeavored to master his own.

On arriving at the gate, he recognized the attendant who
had imparted to him the dreadful news. The poor woman,
accustomed as she was to the sight of grief and misery, ap

peared affected herself at the chevalier's pallor, and when the latter in passing slipped a *louis* into her hand, she could no longer restrain her tears.

The chevalier entered the church, where a year before he had listened so eagerly in the hope of recognizing the voice of Constance among all the others. A year, a brief year, had elapsed, and that pure, chaste, thrilling voice was hushed forever on earth. He was about to hear all those other voices, amid which he would vainly listen for that, which at this hour was singing the praises of the Lord in heaven.

The chevalier knelt in the same spot where he had knelt before, and there, for the first time, he felt that sublime need of prayer which we experience in profound grief. There, for the first time, his soul put itself in communication with another world, which we can never see, except through a veil of joy or despair, which we can only comprehend in supreme happiness, or in extreme grief.

During the whole time the service continued, the tears never ceased to flow down the cheeks of the chevalier; but no sob, no sigh, escaped from his bosom. Prayer caused his tears to flow readily, and by their flowing soothed his wounded feelings.

When the mass was finished, the baron conducted his son to the lady-superior. Perhaps the pious lady entertained some rancor in her bosom against her nephew for the trick he had played her, and for the other he had so recently meditated. Perhaps she had promised herself the pleasure of giving him a severe reprimand, for her first aspect was stiff and cold; but no sooner did she hear a trembling voice cry "Ah! my dear aunt, my dear aunt, you have let her die!" than she no longer had the power to contend with the grief so poignant, which manifested itself by so profound an alteration of voice and features. The good superior melted into tears.

Tancrede profited by this exhibition of emotion to remind his father of the promise he had made him to ask permission of his aunt to visit the room lately occupied by Constance. The superior raised some little difficulties, and only gave way after calling a nun and whispering some orders in her ear, which doubtless were instructions for the removal of such objects as might excite his grief still more.

In a few moments all three descended; the corridors were

deserted; it seemed as if death had at one stroke depopulated all the cells; the young girls were in the garden.

The abbess opened the door of Constance's chamber, and, with the baron, was about to follow Tancrede, but he begged permission to remain alone for a moment in the sanctuary of his love. His father and aunt looked at each other, and, doubtless, saw no objection to granting the request, and they made a sign for him to enter.

He entered, and closing the door behind him, proceeded, with his hands piously clasped together, toward the bed where Constance had breathed her last sigh. There was nothing to indicate that death had passed there. The chevalier bent his head upon her pillow and kissed it. It still breathed the sweet and fresh perfume that emanates from youth and health; you might have supposed that she who had quitted it three days ago for the grave, had gone but that morning to run in the garden, or had flown to some green meadow, diapered with bees and butterflies.

The contrast between the place and the scenes that had occurred in it, and of which nothing seemed to preserve the remembrance, broke his heart. This great truth appeared evident to him—that we are destined to pass away from the earth without leaving any other traces of our passage than the memory of those who have loved us; but how long have hearts, the most deeply moved, retained their souvenirs?

Tancrede vowed that the remembrance of Constance should dwell eternally in his heart.

Then he arose and examined one by one, every article of furniture the chamber contained, the images of which he endeavored to impress upon his mind. On the wall, to the left on entering, were a crucifix and a *prie dieu*, with Constance's little missal lying upon it. He knelt before the *prie dieu*, kissed the book, opened it at the place where the marker showed it had been opened for the last time, and read the prayer that Constance had doubtless read also; it was the angelic salutation, the *Ave Maria*, that beautiful and poetic promise of an angel to a virgin, of heaven to earth, of God to man.

Opposite was the fire-place. Upon the mantle-piece bouquets of flowers blossomed in two vases, which, unlike her who had gathered them, had not yet faded away. Between these two vases was a miniature mirror, a little infraction of the rules of the convent, it is true, but which the superior permitted to those of her boarders who had not bidden farewell to the vanities of the world. Tancrede took a pansy from each of the vases, and put his lips to the mirror, which, faithless and treacherous like all the rest, was ready to reflect the image of every new face, without retaining any traces of the angelic countenance which had so often beamed within it.

From the chimney-piece he went to the window. As we have said, this window overlooked the garden, the same one he had seen before. The same young girls were walking in it; but how different from what they were then, happy and gay, but now silent and sad. They no longer sported on the grass, but walked about in scattered groups. Alone, all alone, walked Henrietta de Narcy, the faithful friend of poor Constance.

This last object was, to the poor lover, the most terrible of all. In these youthful hearts and pure souls, the fair unopened pages of the book of life was the exact image of the deceased, whom Tancrede vainly sought around; there was the track that the bird leaves in its passage through the air. At this moment the door of the room was opened. More than half an hour had elapsed since Tancrede had entered the cell of Constance, and, not having seen him come out, his father and aunt feared that some new accident had followed his strong emotions.

Tancrede came out with a broken heart, feeling that he should carry the recollection of this little room with him to the grave. But he assumed a calmness he did not feel; so that when he asked his aunt to show him the tomb of Constance, according to the promise made him by the baron, neither the baron nor the superior made any objection, but both offered to lead him to it. The cemetery of the convent was in the cloisters. Tancrede, therefore, had not a hundred steps to go from the chamber where Constance had lately reposed, to arrive at the tenement where now she slept the sleep of the dead. At the door of the cloister, as at the door of the chamber, he requested to be left alone. Sorrow is sacred. Men are ashamed of their tears. Tancrede entered the little cemetery alone. As in all convents, the cemetery was a square plot of earth, covered with grass, surrounded with arcades supported on columns. The surface was broken with graves, more or less salient, according to the length of time they had been made. By them we are made to feel the march of Time, that great leveler, under whose feet, little by little, the palaces of the living and the tombs of the dead are effaced. He advanced slowly to a newly made grave, covered with a stone, upon which there had not yet been sufficient time to inscribe a name. He had not yet deceived himself; it was evident that this grave dated from the day which had been named to him as the day of Constance's interment. He knelt upon the stone and prayed.

This was his supreme trial. It was prolonged to such a degree that the baron and superior came to seek him. He had bidden farewell to the church wherein Constance had prayed, to the chamber wherein she had lived, and to the grave where she slept, never to wake again in this world. There was nothing left now to detain him at Chinon. He allowed himself to be led away like a child; and, after mechanically taking leave of his aunt, he mounted the chaise in which his father had arrived, not only without any assistance, but without even uttering a word. The journey was more rapid this time than before. The baron changed horses three times on the road, so that there was no delay; and by noon on the next day they were at Anguilhem. During the whole journey Tancrede remained in a state of profound apathy. No tears, no sighs, and almost without feeling. Upon seeing his mother, however, the tears began to flow afresh. But the shock had been too much for him; a fever attacked him during the night, and he was dangerously ill. Now it was that the baroness developed all the devotion of maternal love, of which she had already given so many proofs to her son. As long as Tancrede was ill, she scarcely ever quitted his bedside, but watched by him day and night, always talking to him of Constance, weeping and praying with him, blending her feelings with his, penetrating his most inward feelings, anticipating his every wish, living only for him, having no wish but his. Sometimes, when she thought him sleeping, he detected her regarding him with an expression of the utmost tenderness, in which, as it seemed to him, were mingled remorse and sadness. Twenty times he was on the point of questioning her as to the meaning of the strange expression he read in her eyes; but he had not strength enough to be inquisitive. What was all the world to him? Constance was no more!

His illness continued a long time, and, by degrees, it degenerated into a somber melancholy; more dangerous than the sickness it succeeded, for he reveled in his melancholy, and after submitting to every variety of treatment ordered to cure the sickness of his body, he wanted nothing done to cure the disorder of the mind. His father vainly proposed to him riding, hunting, fencing. All these exercises, of which he had formerly been so passionately fond, now inspired only weariness and disgust. His scholastic labors alone distracted his mind, and one fine day, to the infinite astonishment of both father and mother, he requested to be allowed to return to the Jesuits' College at Amboise.

The baron and baroness, however painful it might be to their feelings to part with their son in his present state of mind and health, could but receive this proposition with joy. It proved that he attached some value to life. For three months he had expressed no desire whatever, therefore his wish met with no opposition.

Accordingly he returned to Amboise, still under the care of his preceptor the Abbe Dubois. This time his father and mother accompanied him. The baroness wishing to recommend her son to the reverend Jesuit fathers herself.

A great disappointment awaited Tancrede. He returned to the college during vacation, and had to await the reopening of the classes to meet his friend Henry de Narcy. But he waited in vain. Henry had finished his course of rhetoric, and as his parents intended him for the bar, they did not consider it necessary that he should go through a course of philosophy. The chevalier found himself completely isolated in his grief.

Then was developed within his heart the religious sentiment of which hitherto we found no trace previous to the event which had probed his heart to the bottom. He passed entire hours in the church, praying until he fell into a kind of ecstasy, which almost always ended in an abundant flow of tears. The reverend fathers soon noticed this propensity, not for the exercises of piety, but for devout reveries. He was not a practical devotee; he even forgot the hours of the services, to which he had always to be called. They understood that a soul exalted like that of their young scholar was accompanied by a fertile mind, and that, in all probability, it would soon recover all the vigor it had temporarily lost, and become an excellent recruit for their order. Then, he was surrounded with every flattery, kindness, and adulation. Religion has its vertigo, which attracts all tender hearts toward it. Since Constance had become an angel in heaven, all Tancrede's thoughts and desires turned heavenward. The rector was an adroit, supple, eloquent man, devoured by a passion for proselyting, which exists nowhere so strongly as in the order founded by Ignatius Loyola. He sent for Tancrede, questioned him as to his feelings, encouraged his tendencies, and worked upon him so much and so well that one fine morning, at the expiration of six months, he informed his preceptor that he had fully made up his mind to become a Jesuit.

As the Abbe Dubois was in holy orders, and as he had counseled that Tancrede should be sent to the college of Amboise he greatly feared that the chevalier's parents would attribute their son's singular resolution to his influence. He therefore wrote immediately to the baron an account of what was happening, and implored him to come, without loss of time, and save his son before the reverend fathers had wholly perverted his mind.

The baron saw at once the danger that threatened his son, and hastened to Amboise.

CHAPTER XI.

THE baron found Tancrede perfectly calm and resolute. Had the project he conceived been the result of exaltation, the baron might have some hope that, as this exaltation calmed down, the project would vanish; but, as that was not the case, the affair looked very serious. And the more so seeing that it happened during the reign of Louis the Fourteenth, or rather of Mme. de Maintenon, when everything turned on religion; when a powerful support was given to the heads of congregations, and to the superiors of convents. In many instances the youth of both sexes, belonging to some of the first families of France, became monks and nuns, in spite of the opposition of their friends. The baron could think of no other means to employ with the chevalier but persuasion.

This he tried, but to all the baron's entreaties Tancrede replied that he obeyed an inward monitor, the voice of his conscience, and that from the moment he had lost the only thing that attached him to life, he felt himself drawn by an irresistible power.

The baron next addressed himself to the father-rector, and begged him to aid in combating the resolution of the chevalier; but the rector replied that he considered it as an offense against Heaven to divert a soul from seeking its salvation; and that all the baron could ask of him was not to urge his pupil in the course which he had entered upon of his own accord; he had already imposed this reserve upon himself, and he should continue to do so.

Three or four days were passed in these fruitless negotiations. At length, toward the evening of the fifth day, a letter arrived from the baroness, who, informed by her husband how matters were proceeding, wrote to the chevalier, begging him, before taking a final resolution, to come and pass a few days at Anguilhem, promising the neophyte that if, after the expiration of a fortnight, he was still in the same mind, he might do as he pleased. This maternal request was so rational that it was immediately acceded to.

Next day, after receiving the blessing of the father-rector, the embryo Jesuit set out for Anguilhem, in company with the baron and the abbe. The two latter cursed in their hearts the fatal day upon which Mlle. de Beuzerie had set foot in Anguilhem. For, ever since that unhappy day, everything had been turned topsy turvy in their usually quiet dwelling; the denizens of which, once the most sedentary in the whole province, now passed almost every hour of their lives in running after each other on the highways.

The baroness renewed all the persuasion her husband had employed upon her son, but her maternal influence had lost its wonted power; she could not overcome his obstinacy. Then his father discoursed most eloquently upon riding, hunting, fencing, and other worldly allurements, to which Tancrede replied, that such profane exercises were quite unsuited for a man who intended to devote himself to the service of the Lord. The result of his steady refusal was to lead the baroness to despair of bringing her son to the ideas befitting a gentleman, such as he formerly entertained, before the fatal event they now deplored had effaced them from his memory.

Twelve days passed away, during which the baroness renewed her efforts, but with the same want of success. At last she appeared to lose hope herself, and the chevalier was delivered from the maternal importunities to which he had always responded with firmness, mingled with respect and veneration. The thirteenth day passed away in sadness, and almost in silence, for as his resolution ever since his arrival at Anguilhem, was the constant theme of conversation, when they did not speak of that, they did not know what else to talk about.

The evening was even more silent and sad than the day, and every one retired at an early hour to bed. Tancrede, as customary, knelt and prayed before a large picture of the Crucifixion which at his last visit, when already occupied with religious ideas, he had caused to be removed into his bed-chamber from an ancient chapel in the chateau, now used as a store-room. Then, while under the influence of one of those fits of ecstasy which sometimes took possession of him after prayer, he went to bed and soon fell into that state of slumber which is neither sleeping nor waking.

In extinguishing his light he had remarked a circumstance due, doubtless, to chance, but which in his pious frame of mind he attributed to one of those special favors which he considered was occasionally granted by Heaven. A moonbeam, passing through an aperture in the upper part of the window-shutter, happened to fall upon and illuminate the picture hanging just opposite the foot of his bed. It was with his eyes fixed on this picture that he, little by little, came out of the religious ecstasy which, as we have stated, degenerated into slumber. Suddenly it appeared to him to move away, and its place became occupied by the figure of a young girl, clothed in a long white robe, with her face veiled. This happened silently and imperceptibly. Then, when the picture had completely disappeared, and the nocturnal ray which had illuminated it now shone on the figure of the young girl and enveloped it in a mysterious light, the veil was slowly raised, and Tancrede, trembling with joy and fear, recognized Constance.

It really was Constance, that lovely girl become an angel of heaven.

The first impulse was to rise from his bed and take her to his arms; but the form made a sign with its hand to indicate to him that he must remain where he was, and, in a voice that caused every nerve to thrill, it spoke as follows.

"Tancrede, Heaven has permitted me to leave my grave, to tell you that the sacrifice you desire to make to my memory is too great. Your destiny is not to bury yourself in a cloister, but to perpetuate the name of your fathers, which dies with you. Renounce, then, the idea you entertain of taking holy orders. I entreat you, and, if I must, I command you. Adieu, Tancrede, remember what I say to you, for what I say is the will of the Lord."

At these words, by a movement, the reverse of that which had brought the pale vision before his eyes, the picture reoccupied the place it had quitted for a moment, and was again in the moonlight.

Tancrede had listened in breathless silence, with haggard eyes, and the perspiration streaming down his face, while the vision remained. Scarcely had it disappeared, when, doubting the evidence of his senses, he sprung from his bed, to satisfy himself by feeling that the picture was still in its place. Nothing was changed. There was the canvas, the frame, the woodwork, and he was satisfied that no one had come in or gone out of the chamber, which was locked on the inside. It was then, really the spirit of Constance that had appeared to him.

We can imagine what sort of a night he passed. So long as darkness prevailed, he entertained no doubt as to the reality of the vision. It was still there, present to his eyes. He could still see the pale and beautiful image of his young friend, he could hear her sweet voice, he felt her extend toward him the hand whose imperative movement had imposed upon him silence and fixity, and, with a gentle motion, had waved him an adieu. But where were the young man's faith and confidence, when the first tints of morning drove from his chamber the solemn and mysterious obscurity of the night? He felt the stones of the fantastic castle, built in a dream, fall one by one, and he passed from a state of profound conviction to that of absolute incredulity.

During the day he was moody; restless, and thoughtful. Many times his mother inquired the cause of the change that had come over him since the previous night. But the only response the baroness could obtain to her inquiries was a fixed and melancholy smile. As to the baron, he had the air of being reconciled to the resolution his son had taken, and of having completely lost all hope of making him relinquish his project.

That day passed away, more diversified than many others

that had preceded it. Tancrede left the castle and walked in the wood that surrounded it. From time to time his countenance became flushed, as if all the blood rushed at once from his heart to his face. Sometimes he started, and seemed to follow with his eyes some fugitive shadow visible to himself alone. Then a deep sigh would escape from his bosom, and tears would flow from his eyes. This was something unusual for him who had not been seen to weep for six months.

He awaited the coming of night with uneasiness mingled with fear. More than once during supper, his mother, who never took her eyes off him, saw him furtively wipe the perspiration from his brow. At the usual hour he begged to be allowed to retire, and proceeded to his chamber.

We have stated how, with the day, doubt, then incredulity, then the certainty that this pretended apparition was only a dream, succeeded each other in his mind. But by a contrary effect, in proportion as night drew on, belief returned to his heart; and when he found himself alone in his chamber, lying in his bed, without light, when he saw the picture again illuminated by the moonbeam, his first conviction returned to him, and he felt that his pretended dream became reality.

For an hour all was silent; no sound of any kind was heard save the pulsation of his heart. He lay with eager eyes fixed upon the picture, but during all this time it never moved, and he again began to doubt. But suddenly it appeared to him that the frame of the picture began to turn, and soon all doubt was removed, for he saw that the picture gradually disappeared, and then the white robe, and soon Constance herself, occupy its place; it was the vision of the previous night renewed.

"Tancrede," said the voice, "you have not believed my words, and I am permitted to come again to repeat them. Abandon your sad resolution, which throws your family into despair; I will not accept the sacrifice you make me. You are destined for the world and not for the cloister; live for the world and be happy."

Then, as if this time the shade of the young girl feared that doubt would efface the impression produced by her presence, she took from her bosom a bouquet of pansies, similar to those which, when living, she had thrown from the corridor of the convent into his chamber: and in the gesture she made with her hand to bid him adieu, she let them fall on the floor of his room.

Tancrede leaped from his bed, but the picture had returned to its place before he could reach it. No trace remained of the apparition of the young girl except the bouquet of pansies, which with a gesture full both of joy and fear, and perhaps even more worldly than devout, the chevalier pressed to his lips.

This time he entertained no doubt; a material proof, visible and palpable, marked the presence of the graceful phantom, and remained in his hands. The young man returned to his bed, pressing the bouquet to his heart, and lay expecting the vision to return. But he waited in vain.

He awoke at day-break. This time, as before, his first impression was that he had had a dream. But here in his hand was the bouquet, faded, but still there. This was better than before; the spirit of Constance, withdrawn from her grave by a miracle of love, had really appeared to him!

The next day had been appointed for his return to Amboise; but would the graceful apparition venture to follow him among that terrible crowd of black-robed men? To go to Amboise! would not that be disobeying the orders that fell from the lips he loved so well?

But how could he retract from a resolution so publicly proclaimed? How, after resisting all the entreaties of his father and mother, could he himself propose to remain longer at Anguilhem? It was impossible; worse than that, it was ridiculous; and he, to his eternal praise be it said, had almost as much self-respect as he had love.

This day was passed under mutual constraint. The baron, as usual, appeared resigned to the separation; but the poor mother could not lose sight of her son: it was evident that the fear of another refusal checked her entreaties. Tancrede, on his part, desired only to be detained, and his wish, as well as his mother's, was brought about by accident. The abbe came in to inquire of his pupil at what hour he would like to set out for Amboise. Tancrede attempted to reply, but could not. The baroness immediately threw herself upon his neck, and asked him if he really meant to abandon his intention. He could no longer control his feelings, but shed tears of grief and joy, and in a submissive voice, full of hypocrisy to us who understand the motive that actuated him, he replied:

"Madame, you are my mother, and it is my duty to obey you. Whatever your wish is, that shall be mine also."

The baroness uttered a cry of joy, and ran through the house telling every one she met that her son was not going away yet, and perhaps would not go at all.

In the evening Tancrede retired to his room at the usual hour: he was anxious to renew the emotions of the previous night; but this time he suffered under a terrible anxiety. The phantom appeared to possess the power of reading his thoughts, for on the previous night it had come to dispel his irresolution. But now that his irresolution was dispelled —now that he had decided to obey the orders given by the shade of Constance, and had promised his mother not to go to Amboise, would not the spirit conclude that its mission was accomplished, and consider it unnecessary to appear to him again? This was perplexing. He had begun to accustom himself to this charming spirit, which, even minus a body, was at least some compensation.

Once locked in his room, he lost no time in seeking his bed and extinguishing the light. But he had to wait longer than before for the moonbeam to arrive at the picture which, every night, became later and later. He lay and watched its progress on the wall until finally it fell on the picture. This moment had been awaited with the utmost impatience. Never did invocation come from the lips of an enchanter with more fervor than the prayer that escaped from his, that Constance might appear at least once more, and the prayer of the chevalier was granted.

Again the picture disappeared, and again the beautiful vision occupied its place. Again he uttered a cry of joy.

"Yes, 'tis I," said the spirit. "*I* have come to bid you farewell! Adieu! then. You have obeyed the will of Heaven. The Lord will reward you. Adieu! adieu!" With these words the spirit disappeared. Tancrede fancied he heard it utter a sob, or at least a sigh, which seemed to him to indicate that their separatoin was as much a source of regret to the dead as to the living.

"Oh! no! no!" cried he, springing from his bed. "Oh, no! do not say farewell. If I thought I should not see you again, Constance, I should go mad."

And he threw himself on his knees before the picture,

extending his hands imploringly toward the image of his Saviour, praying that He, who had himself suffered so much, would take pity on suffering.

But Tancrede invoked only a senseless picture, a dumb canvas. He was alone; the last vibrations of the voice of Constance were silenced—the spirit had disappeared.

He then returned to his bed overwhelmed with grief. He had heard the last adieu of Constance, which he had so much dreaded to hear: this vision was the last; the stone had again closed over the grave: it would never be lifted again.

It seemed to him as if he had lost Constance a second time. For more than an hour he lay in a state of feverish agitation bordering on despair. This farewell thrice repeated, the two last adieus accompanied with sighs and sobs, sounded as a knell in his ears. Without knowing what he said, he involuntarily repeated "Adieu! adieu!"

Suddenly it seemed to him that he could hear the sound of light footsteps and a rustling noise, scarcely audible, such as a sylphide might make in passing among the flowers. It appeared to be on the other side of the wainscoting of the room. He raised himself in bed with bated breath quite bewildered. With his eyes fixed on the picture, now lost in obscurity, he lay trembling and hoping; but through the gloom and darkness he thought he could perceive by a faint glittering in the frame that the picture again moved; soon it became a certainty—Constance appeared again; but this time she remained not stationary as before, but, stepping lightly on to the floor, rushed to the astonished youth, exclaiming—

"Tancrede! Tancrede! I am not dead! Tancrede! I am not the spirit of Constance! I am Constance herself, quick and living!" And at the same moment the chevalier, almost mad with joy and amazement, felt that it really was not a shadow but a substance that he clasped in his arms.

CHAPTER XII.

In a few words Constance apprised Tancrede of everything that had taken place.

The time our fugitive had lost on his journey from Amboise to Chinon, had given the Abbe Dubois time to go to

Anguilhem, and inform the baron and baroness of his new freak. They rightly conjectured that he would shape his course toward Chinon, and they bethought themselves of some means to put an end to his amorous infatuation, which foreboded constant trouble and anxiety to the parents of the two young people. The Abbe Dubois then proposed to the baron the getting up of a pretense that Constance was dead. The baroness, understanding in her mother's heart that this unexpected news would grieve her son, opposed the deceit for a long time, but was at length obliged to yield to her husband's wishes; and the baron went to inform the lady-superior of the plot. It so happened that a nun had died the previous evening, and this gave every facility for executing the scheme.

We have seen the result of their ingenuity.

But they had not calculated upon the intense grief this news would cause to Tancrede, nor the resolution it would lead him to make. Therefore, when the Abbe Dubois sent word that the chevalier intended to become a Jesuit, it threw the baron and baroness into a state of complete despair. As we have seen, the baron immediately started for Amboise, hoping that his paternal influence would bring his son to reason. But from the first conversation he had with him, he felt convinced that his resolution was fixed, and that nothing could alter his determination.

He then wrote to the baroness, informing her of the grievous conclusion he had come to. Inspired by her maternal feelings, the baroness, in her turn, conceived a project. It was to make Constance, whom Tancrede thought dead, a means of inducing him to renounce his foolish project. With this view she went to Beuzerie, and so powerful were her entreaties, that neither the viscount nor the viscountess could resist her tears. They consented to the baroness's wishes, which were, that it be so contrived that Constance should appear as a visitant from the other world, to restore Tancrede to this.

The baroness then wrote to her husband to try and induce Tancrede to come and spend a week at Anguilhem, before finally making up his mind, a request he could not refuse his parents. We have seen how the first twelve days were spent, and how the obstinacy of the chevalier had made the interference of Constance necessary.

Everything thus far has gone according to the wishes of

his parents, and the mechanism, contrived by the cleverest carpenter of Loches, worked to admiration. The baron and baroness had watched the impression produced day by day on the heart of their son by the successive apparitions of Constance, till at length the third settled the matter. Constance slept with her mother in one of the most remote chambers in the castle. With tears in her eyes and despair in her heart, she had bid a final adieu to Tancrede, when, grief outweighing every other consideration, she, in her turn, formed an extreme resolution; and, taking advantage of her mother being fast asleep, she rose again after she had played her part as a spirit, and, dressing herself, left the chamber on tiptoe; and, free from watchers, who had previously dictated her words and restrained her feelings, she glided along the corridors to the spot where she was accustomed to place herself, and, touching the spring, appeared again to Tancrede—no longer as a vision, but as a living reality.

Tancrede was a man of quick resolve. For a moment he was perplexed and bewildered like one rising from the grave, who, upon suddenly opening his eyes, sees the light once more, and returns to life and happiness almost overwhelmed with joy. But, that moment past, he saw that the opportunity he so long sought had unexpectedly arrived, and at once made up his mind not to let it escape.

In a moment he was decided. As to Constance, she had written to her lover, that her destiny was no longer her own, but his; and it was for him to dispose of it as he saw fit. When he proposed to fly immediately to the nearest village where they could be married, she not only made no objection, but assured him she was ready to follow him to the ends of the earth. The chevalier now no longer doubted that he was reaching the climax of his romance.

They descended from the room together, gliding noiselessly along the corridors and down the stairs, like two ghosts, until they reached the court-yard. Tancrede ran to the stable and saddled Christopher, who had had good opportunity of resting after his former fatigue, and, being always quiet and gentle, allowed the saddle to be placed on his back without offering the least resistance. The chevalier then opened the great gate as gently as possible, jumped upon Christopher, directed Constance to a large stone, by standing on which she could mount the pony, and the moment she was securely seated behind him they galloped off.

On they rode for a couple of hours, but as it was in the middle of the month of July, when the days are at their longest, at the expiration of that time the dawn began to appear, and they thought it necessary to stop, as the sight of a young couple galloping along the road at that hour must look suspicious in the eyes of some inquisitive people. Looking around, our hero saw on the right a village, which he knew to be Chapelle-Saint-Hippolyte, and thither they directed their course.

The only knowledge of matrimony Tancrede possessed was gathered from the novels of the day. Now in these novels all forbidden unions were solemnized, unknown to the parents, by some kind-hearted, but reckless village priest, who, following the recommendation given by the Creator to our first parents, to increase and multiply, thought he was following the precepts of Scripture by performing as many marriages as possible. Under this sage impression the chevalier confidently advanced boldly toward the parsonage, and knocked at the door. It was opened by a good-tempered, plump-looking housekeeper, of thirty, or thereabouts. Tancrede asked to speak to the rector.

The rector was preparing for mass, which to our hero appeared an auspicious omen. Briefly explaining the object of his errand, he asked the good priest if he could not marry them instantly. The priest smiled at the young man's haste, and explained to him that there were some preparations to be made, some formalities to be gone through, such as confession; the declaration of the family and Christian names; to swear that they were not related by ties forbidden by the Church, and so forth.

He further explained that going through these formularities would occasion a delay of four-and-twenty hours at least; or, even six-and-thirty; and that, consequently, however willing he might be to tie the nuptial knot, the ceremony could not take place until the morrow or the next day. Meanwhile they might remain at the rectory if they thought proper; Tancrede under his care, and Constance in charge of the housekeeper.

This delay greatly displeased the chevalier. He therefore pressed his suit very warmly, but the rector remained inflexible; and as he declared that none of his fellow-priests would be found more tractable than himself, our hero had to submit. He chose to accept the rector's offer, and remain in his house, as he considered he would be safer there, and less likely to be recognized than if he went to an inn.

The curate then went to perform mass, and as he seemed to share Tancrede's fears, he advised the two children not to show themselves at the door or windows. Upon his return from church, he proceeded to ask them the customary questions. The youth declared his name to be Tancrede d'Anguilhem, and that of his fair companion, Constance de Beuzerie; the former, aged seventeen years and five months; the latter, fifteen years all but a week. Both also swore that they were neither godfather nor godmother, nor relation in any degree whatever.

The rector then ordered them while he went to attend to some urgent private affairs, to prepare themselves for confession, by well examining their consciences.

Upon his return the mutual confession took place. It is as well to say, that it was that of two pure and innocent children, who, in confessing the love that had hitherto made them attempt such foolish projects, had neither of them to blush even for a thought.

With this double confession the rector appeared to be completely reassured, for before it was made he had appeared suspicious and uneasy. Then, under the pretext that it was necessary these two young people should sin neither in thought, word nor deed, during the interval between absolution and the nuptial benediction, he proceeded to shut up the chevalier in his library, and handed Constance over to the care of his housekeeper.

Our hero thought this a very strange way of getting married, and could not conceal his chagrin and disappointment. At dinner, however, the two young people met again. Tancrede then asked the rector if he thought he should be able to marry them next day; to which the worthy man replied, that he saw nothing to prevent him, provided no obstacle arose in the meantime. This assurance somewhat eased the chevalier's mind, so that after dinner he retired to the library with a lighter heart. He there found a bed, which had been prepared for him while at table.

Supper-time arrived. As at dinner, the young people met again. Tancrede was very happy after the miracle of

Constance's resuscitation, and he thought separation no longer possible. Constance was timid and bashful, but joy shone through her half-closed eyelids, and happiness was in every word that fell from her lips.

After supper the rector prayed for all, and then they each retired to their respective pillows.

The chevalier could not sleep, he therefore tried to read; but how could he do so when his heart was full of his own thoughts, which were more soft, tender, and harmonious than any the world could offer. Nevertheless, he managed to read that charming story of the loves of Jacob and Rachel, but he found that Rachel was nothing compared with Constance, and he decided that to deserve Constance he would have endured many more trials than Jacob suffered.

However, dreaming was one way of making the time pass quickly. Eleven o'clock struck, and at each slow and solemn tone, Tancrede trembled to think that in eight hours he would be the happy husband of Constance. This delightful idea accompanied him to his bed, and even in his sleep. He dreamed that the morning had come, that the priest was waiting only for him. At that moment it really seemed to him that through his closed eyelids he could see daylight, and that several persons were walking and talking loudly near him. This sensation became so real that he awoke, and upon opening his eyes he found himself face to face with his father.

At this sight such despair was pictured in his face, that although the baron had determined to reprimand his fugitive son very severely, he could not now find it in his heart to do so; and seeing the sufferings of a man already in this poor child's heart, he contented himself with holding out his hand to him, exclaiming but one word:

"Courage!"

Perhaps Tancrede would have resented reproaches; but he could not resist indulgence. He threw himself into the baron's arms, asking if he were going to part Constance and him again. The baron looked fixedly at him, and, seeing anxiety pictured on every feature, said to him:

"Listen! My first word was 'Courage,' my second is 'Hope.'"

"Oh, father, father, I have already been so cruelly deceived that I no longer dare to hope!"

"But at the time we deceived you we were poor, whilst now—"

"Now, father? Are we become rich, then?"

"Perhaps."

"Perhaps, perhaps! What mean you, father? How can our fortune have so changed in one day?"

"Our cousin, the Viscount de Bouzenois, is dead. We received the intelligence only this morning."

"Dead! and made us his heirs?"

"If he had done so, I should not have said ' perhaps ' we are rich. I should have said *we are* rich. The viscount died *intestate !*"

"*Intestate*, father?"

"Yes, *intestate.*"

The baron pronounced this word with so much emphasis that the chevalier understood that it was a word of great importance.

"What will be the consequence?" asked the young man, in a timid voice, not yet perceiving how the death of M. de Bouzenois could affect himself and Constance.

"It happens, sir," replied the baron, "that the succession is left open, and our right is disputed by a son of his wife's by her first husband, who pretends that his mother bestowed her property on the Baron de Bouzenois, solely on condition that it should revert to her son at her death."

"Well, father, go on!"

"Well, we must go to law, and contest our claim. Monsieur Coquenard, my attorney, writes me word that if we pursue our cause vigorously and promptly we must gain it, and if we gain—"

"*If* we gain. Well, father, go on."

"If we gain, my boy, we shall have an income of 75,000 a year, and then Monsieur de Beuzerie will be only too glad to pay court to us, and we shall look down upon him, and then we shall be making a sacrifice for—"

"Oh! father, father! what hopes you give me! Do you think—do you believe—"

"I know what I think, I know what I believe. Our good rector, of whom you made a confidant—sent a messenger to Beuzerie and to Anguilhem at the same time, so that I overtook the viscount about three leagues from this place, flying to seek his daughter, as I was hastening after you. He was quite furious at what had happened, saying that his daughter's reputation was ruined, and, but as soon as I hinted to him that Monsieur de Bouzenois had gone and left all his baggage behind, and read to him Monsieur Coquenard's letter, he cooled down amazingly, and became 'unco' civil,' and even admitted, that after the scandal that your running away with his daughter had caused in the neighborhood, he clearly foresaw that his projected marriage with the Marquis de Croisey must be given up."

"Oh! father, father! did he tell you that?"

"You will understand, sir, that this was an appeal to my honor."

"And what did you say in reply, father?"

"I replied, that among gentlemen a title was only a title, that the name was everything; and that it was well known throughout the province the D'Anguilhems, although only barons, dated from the first crusade, while the grandfather of the Marquis de Croisey had all the difficulty in the world, at the commencement of the reign of our great king, to prove his title to enter the stables of his majesty. And further, that if a Baroness d'Anguilhem were presented at court, she would certainly take precedence of the Marchioness de Croisey."

"And what did he say?"

"He gave me his hand and said, 'That is true, baron; we must speak on that matter again.'"

"Oh, father, you make me well again. And Constance! where is my Constance?"

"Constance is in her father's care, as you are in mine. Constance will return to Beuzerie as you will return to Anguilhem. To-morrow I must go and make another apology for you to the viscount, and during my visit I may find an opportunity of speaking again on the subject."

"Do, father, exalt my love for Constance; say I adore her; say I can not live without her; say if they part us we shall both die of grief; say—"

"I shall say that you will probably very soon have an income of seventy-five thousand a year, and take my word for it that he will appreciate my argument much better than he would yours."

"Say what you please, my dear father, but get the viscount to promise—"

"As for that, leave it to me; for be assured I know better than you do how he will take me."

"And—and—"

"And what? my son."

"And Constance; shall I not see her?"

"Here? It is quite impossible. You can not see Mademoiselle de Beuzerie now, but only in her paternal home, and with the permission of her parents."

"And do you think I shall be able to obtain their consent?"

"In three or four days, I hope."

"Three or four days! ah! that is a very long time."

"Not so long as when you did not expect ever to see her again, I should think."

"Then I wished to become a Jesuit."

"Yes, yes, sir. I remember it very well. You have a lot of ingenious ideas of one sort or another. You are a man of infinite resource. We shall have to give your imagination some employment."

"For what, father?"

"We must tell you that at Anguilhem."

And without the chevalier's being able to get any light on the subject hinted at by the baron, of which it appeared he must be the mainspring, they both mounted their horses and took the road to Anguilhem.

The baron alone took leave of the good rector. The chevalier begged to be excused the honor of bidding *him* farewell.

CHAPTER XIII.

THIS was the third time that Tancrede returned to Anguilhem with defeated projects; but this time he did not return entirely without hope. Although profoundly ignorant of worldly matters, he perfectly understood the change that the death of M. de Bouzenois would effect in his position, supposing even, as his father said, the succession was disputed, and subject to the glorious uncertainty of the law.

Upon arriving at the castle, his hopes increased, for the baroness, who watched the baron and her son at the window of the tower, from whence the country for miles round was visible, came down when she saw them approach, and welcomed them with a face radiant with smiles. Tancrede spurred his steed toward her, leaped from his saddle, and threw himself into her arms, murmuring:

"And have you hope too, dear mother? Oh! do not deceive me. Do not trifle with me!"

"Yes, my child; yes, dear boy, all goes well."

In fact, the baroness, as well as her husband, had perceived a great metamorphosis. When, on the morning of Tancrede's escapade, the viscountess, who had accompanied Constance to Anguilhem, discovered the flight of her daughter, she was furious. In the midst of this irruption of maternal wrath, M. Coquenard's letter arrived, announcing the death of M. de Bouzenois. The perusal of this letter calmed the viscountess as if by enchantment, and she incontinently forgot part of her grief to take a share in the joyful news her neighbors had received.

Finally, when the messenger of the rector of Chapelle-Saint-Hippolyte arrived breathless at the castle, announcing that the fugitives were at the rectory, it was with something like a feeling of regret that the viscountess learned that, owing to the scruples of the rector, the two children were not married. But as she was ignorant that the same message had been dispatched both to the baron and to her husband, and as she wished to announce to the viscount both the flight and the event which had converted this flight almost into an honor, she had her horse put to the chaise, and set off for Beuzerie. In bidding adieu to the baroness, however, she dropped a few words which clearly hinted that a visit from her to Beuzerie would not only be well received, but even, under existing circumstances, be regarded by the viscountess as indispensable.

Thus, the presages on the part of the viscountess appeared to be as favorable as on the part of the viscount. As for Constance, the chevalier had his own reasons for concluding her views to be favorable to his cause.

It was therefore arranged, in a general council, at which the Abbe Dubois assisted (his office was becoming a sinecure), that the baron should go next day and pay a visit to Beuzerie, and talk over the marriage, or say nothing, according to circumstances; but the general opinion was, in which even the abbe coincided, that he must speak of marriage at all events.

This eventful day, so eagerly desired by Tancrede, dawned at last. He rose at six, and called his father. But the baron was too strict an observer of etiquette to think of presenting himself at Beuzerie before noon-day. There was therefore nothing left for our lover but to practice patience, so he went and bestowed his tediousness upon his mother, by talking of Constance.

When two o'clock arrived, he could contain his impatience no longer, so he threw his game-bag over his shoulder, took his gun and dog, and started in search of a hare or a pheasant, on the road to Beuzerie. When about half-way, he perceived the baron approach at full gallop. This he thought a good omen.

In a couple of strides, the chevalier was at the horse's head.

The news was good; everything was arranged, according to the baron's wishes, at least, if not to the lovers'.

Tancrede's choice was tacitly acquiesced in by the viscount and viscountess.

The Anguilhems were invited to visit their good neighbors at Beuzerie on the morrow. This was to be merely a complimentary visit, no question or discussion on personal matters was to be raised. The viscount, prudent man, did not wish his new projects to be suspected. Then next day, or the day after, Tancrede was to set off for Paris, to watch his lawsuit in person, upon the result of which depended the final consent of the viscount. This resolution possessed the double advantage of putting matters into the hands of those who had the greatest interest in the issue, and of keeping Constance for at least a year away from Tancrede; for at this date law traveled very slowly. In the meanwhile, Constance was to return to the convent until she had completed her sixteenth year, and the chevalier his nineteenth. This was the marriageable age in the provinces a century or so ago.

In these arrangements there was much that our hero considered agreeable, and some things that he did not. He would have preferred marrying first, and setting off to Paris afterward. This appeared to him to be much more logical and reasonable. The baron had the greatest difficulty in the world to convince him that the thing was impossible, since the marriage could only follow his gaining the law-suit. This argument was so clearly established that the chevalier was forced to submit, and had nearly made up his mind to fall into the new arrangement when, at about half a league from Anguilhem, they encountered the baroness, who, accompanied by the abbe, had come to meet the baron and her son.

Then the plan proposed by the viscount was detailed anew by the baron, and, to the infinite despair of Tancrede, generally approved of. The poor chevalier was compelled to submit. It was then arranged that they should pay their visit to Beuzerie next day, and as there was no time to be lost, that the chevalier should start for Paris in three days.

Nevertheless, it must be said that our hero grumbled at fate. After seeing Constance positively refused to him, after believing her dead, and resolving to become a Jesuit, he still found her faithful; and as in all probability fortune and happiness would both knock at his door at the same time, he had only a short time to wait to become both a rich lord and a happy husband. In this double idea he had a source of true consolation; besides, in weighing it in the balance of his reason, he began to see the future a little more under *coleur de rose* than he had done when the baron first spoke to him; so he gradually forgot his departnre in thinking of his return.

At all times the word PARIS has had a magical sound in the ears of a provincial. Paris is the goal which all young and active imaginations strive to attain. To the libertine, Paris means pleasure; to the ambitious, Paris is synonymous with glory; for speculators and adventurers, Paris is fortune. This word Paris had very frequently been pronounced in Tancrede's ears, yet he had never given any attention to it, for he never expected anything could happen to him in life to draw him thither. But suddenly an event occurs which renders a journey to Paris not only agreeable but indispensible. The word Paris now sounded upon his ear accompanied with the musical ringing of money; perhaps the most agreeable music in the world, even to the most disinterested. In brief, that same evening, when he retired to his pillow, he avowed in confidence to himself, that since he was absolutely compelled to separate from Constance for a certain space of time, it was much better to spend this time in Paris than anywhere else.

Next day, the baron and his son donned their best clothes, and the baroness put on the best among her six robes. At

ten o'clock all three mounted the chaise and took the road
to Beuzerie.

Matters passed off as it had been previously arranged between the baron and the viscount they should, that is to
say, in strict conformity with the rules of etiquette bordering on royal models.

No notice whatever was taken of what had occurred between the two young people. Tancrede and Constance
saluted each other as formally as if they had now met for the
first time. The baron officially notified M. and Mme. de
Beuzerie of the death of M. de Bouzenois, chevalier of the
order of Saint Louis, the ex-captain in his majesty's navy;
received the condolences of the viscount and viscountess,
and announced that the succession was disputed, and that
his right was now undergoing examination before the law
courts, and that his son, the chevalier, was about to proceed to Paris to watch the proceedings.

Then the viscount and viscountess wished the chevalier
success in his cause, and dwelt emphatically upon the pleasure this success would afford them. They then observed
that their beloved daughter, still too young to think of an
establishment of her own, was about to return to the Convent of Chinon, where she would remain until she arrived
at a marriageable age.

These official communications mutually exchanged, the
baron, baroness, and chevalier rose; then gravely saluting
the viscount and viscountess, remounted their chaise and
returned to Anguilhem.

That evening and the next day were occupied in making
preparations for the chevalier's journey. In the evening
the baron, in a serious tone, begged Tancrede to come to
his chamber with him. Comprehending that this was to
receive the paternal instructions, he respectfully presented
himself before the baron, who received him standing. The
baroness was seated; but Tancrede perceived that she had
been weeping, and that she was obliged to collect all her
strength to master her feelings, and dry her tears.

The chevalier advanced slowly, and when within two
paces of his father he bowed respectfully.

"My son," said the baron, "you are about to enter a
new world, of which, thus far, you have had no idea.
Above all things, guard your honor. The honor of a gentleman is like the reputation of a woman; a stain upon it

can never be effaced. Above all things, I repeat it, keep strict watch over your honor.

"You will make the acquaintance of young men like yourself. I shall not say nobler than you (because all gentlemen stand upon an equality), but more fortunate. You will find them addicted to gambling. Never play if you can possibly avoid it. You are not rich enough to lose, nor poor enough to wish to gain. In any case, if you have the misfortune to play and lose, sell your last coat to pay your debt. Every debt is sacred; but a debt of honor doubly so.

"The baroness and I have calculated that a hundred louis will be sufficient to cover all your expenses for a year, and here is a purse containing half that sum. They are old coins, for they are our savings during the last fifteen years. Young and active as you are, you will hasten to the court; salute the judges, and make powerful friends, and, I hope, meet with success. Fortune favors the young and brave.

"Every week you will receive from us a detailed letter, to which you will reply by details equally exact; so that if you gain your suit you will have been the architect of your own fortune. Then, your cause gained, if you marry Constance, as I have no doubt you will, and as this marriage will make you happy, you will owe your happiness to no one but yourself, which, as things go in this world, is surely something to be proud of.

"You will take Christopher: he is a good creature, used to hard work; of a good color, which would have been still better if you had not overridden him sometimes. He was shod yesterday; in passing through Saint Aignan, get his tail cut to the present fashion. There is a good saddle and bridle, and you will find my traveling pistols in the holsters.

"Now, my son, you have lately given us a good deal of trouble. Both your mother and myself forgive you. I have myself caused you some pain, in that affair of the death in the convent, which I doubt if I had any right to do. It was a piece of deceit, made with good intentions, but a deceit is always a deceit, and I ask pardon of heaven for it."

"Oh, father, father," cried Tancrede, no longer able to restrain his tears.

"I did not tell that to pain you," replied the baron, mistaking the feeling which had wrung this exclamation from his son. "You possess a brave and generous heart, but you are wrong-headed. Your greatest enemy is yourself. This is all I have to say. So now," continued the baron, deeply moved, "receive our blessing."

Tancrede fell upon his knees, and the baron, with a gesture full of paternal dignity and tenderness, raising his eyes to heaven, laid his hands upon his son's head. When he arose he threw himself into his mother's arms.

"Dear boy," said the baroness, "go to your room. I judge by my own feelings that you want to weep. Make yourself happy. I will add a postscript to the letters your father will write to you."

He embraced his mother again, who, without speaking, readily responded to the most secret thoughts of her son. Then, kissing the hand his father extended to him, he retired to his chamber, where he spent half the night in weeping.

He rose early the next morning, and put on his traveling suit. He found the baron already up, making every preparation necessary for his departure. Christopher was at the door, saddled and bridled, with a well-furnished portmanteau strapped on his back. The chevalier was deeply moved on perceiving that his father's eyes were as red with weeping as his own.

Breakfast was served, but no one could touch it. All were weeping, or struggling to suppress their grief. The baron felt that the sooner this painful situation was put an end to, the better for all parties. Tancrede rose from the table, and, approaching his preceptor, asked his pardon for all the trouble and anxiety he had given him. The poor abbe, egotistical as he was under the ordinary circumstances of life, in a trembling voice accorded the pardon demanded by his pupil for the thousand and one peccadilloes he had committed, and gave him his blessing. The chevalier left the breakfast-room, giving his arm to his mother, his hand in his father's. At the door he found all the domestics assembled; tears were in their eyes, for at Anguilhem he was idolized by every one. He embraced them all as friends, at which they wept still more.

Castor saw what was going on, and seemed to comprehend it. He struggled with his chain, and set up a lamentable howl. His master went to comfort him; the poor animal put his paws on the chevalier's shoulders and rubbed his head against his master's breast; and in this way he bade farewell, after the manner of faithful dogs.

The baron and baroness accompanied their son nearly a quarter of a league on his way, and at parting Tancrede threw himself into the arms of the baron.

Then came the poor mother's turn. She could not bear to part with her child, and she cursed from the bottom of her heart the unfortunate inheritance that deprived her of her son. The abbe had ascended to the top of the tower, where he could watch the progress of his late pupil; seeing the critical moment had arrived, he waved his last adieu with his handkerchief.

The baron took his son by the hand and led him to his horse.

"Courage, my son! Remember, you are eighteen years of age. Show yourself a man."

The chevalier mounted Christopher, who seemed to partake of the general grief. But the baroness ran again toward her son with extended arms. He seized her hands and covered them with kisses. It required all the baron's strength and remonstrance to put an end to these embracings, which threatened to be interminable.

"Away, both, I desire you," cried the baron.

Tancrede obeyed; but had not proceeded a hundred steps before he again halted, and turned his head to look at his mother. Seeing her weeping in the arms of the baron, he retraced his steps, and embraced her again. Shaking his father by the hand once more, he put spurs to his horse, and galloped off. In five minutes he was out of sight.

He now felt that there was still another farewell to make. He could not go without seeing Constance again. He had spoken in her presence of the day fixed for his departure, and he had hoped that she would understand that, although Beuzerie was not exactly in his road, he would contrive to make a detour that should include it. He spurred Christopher vigorously on, and soon had the happiness of seeing the turrets of the chateau before him.

He continued to approach, but looked cautiously around him, with a timidity which the former prohibitions of the viscount and viscountess had left on his mind. At a turn on the road, he saw a glimpse of a white robe through the trees; he advanced nearer, and saw Constance, who, with a book in her hand, which she only pretended to read, was seated on a mossy bank.

In an instant he was at her feet.

"Is that you, Tancrede? I was waiting for you."

"And I, Constance, was sure of meeting you."

"You are going, then?"

"I must, as you well know; our happiness depends on it."

"Yes, Tancrede, yes; my mother has told me everything. Our marriage is arranged to take place upon your return. It appears you are going to be rich. I am so happy. I shall owe everything to you."

"You are an angel, Constance. I dare not reckon upon future happiness, for I am always in fear that I shall lose you."

"It is much more likely that I shall lose you, for you are going to Paris; and, amid the gayeties and attractions of that dangerous place, you will have no time to think of me."

"I forget you, Constance! Oh, never! never! If I have nothing more to fear on that score than you have, I am sure of my happiness."

"And what have you to fear on my part, dear Tancrede?"

"What I fear, Constance, is this: I am afraid of losing my suit and the inheritance; and then the viscount, your father, will retract his promise to me, and marry you to the Marquis de Croisey."

"I will never marry any one but you, Tancrede. If I can not be yours, no one else shall have me."

"Swear to me, then, Constance, that you will never marry until I release you from your oath myself."

"I swear it!"

"That you will believe nothing that you hear about me only what I say myself, or write to you in my own hand?"

"I swear it!"

"And I too; I swear too—"

Tancrede had no time to finish his vow, for at this moment he was interrupted by the report of a gun close by, and he could plainly hear the voice of the viscount calling his dogs.

"My father!" cried Constance, in terror. "Save yourself! fly!"

Tancrede kissed the trembling girl, and whispered an

adieu, leaped upon Christopher, and put him to the gallop.
When he turned his head, Constance had disappeared.

He then reflected that Constance only was bound by oath
to be faithful, and that he had had no time to promise anything. But as he possessed a sound conscience, he now
uttered the vow he had left unfinished, and felt as strictly
bound by it, as if it had been made in the presence of Constance.

Poor Tancrede!

Poor Constance!

CHAPTER XIV.

IT took the chevalier eleven days to travel from D'Anguilhem to Paris. In passing through Saint-Aignan, in compliance with the recommendation of his father, he took
Christopher to the principal veterinary surgeon establishment, to have him polished up, and his mane and tail cut
in the newest fashion. At Orleans he bought a traveling
cloak, and put a new ribbon to his hat. At Versailles he
had a great mind to stop and see the court, but upon comparing his equipage with those of the courtiers he met,
he felt ashamed of his own, and kept on his way; so that he
arrived at Paris without halting, except to eat and sleep,
and allow Christopher to rest; but this steady progress did
not prevent him, as we have said, from taking eleven days
to perform the journey.

The chevalier entered Paris by Chaillot. This entrance
to the capital was far from being, at that period, as inviting in its aspect as it is now; so that our hero was not
greatly enamored of what he saw, but at the entrance of
the great city kept a very respectable reserve. He, however, stopped to admire the fine prison that stands near the
convent of Filles-Sainte-Marie, which, at first, he took for
a palace. Then he proceeded along the quay of Saint-
Savonnerie, and entered the Cours-la-Reine. Then, it
must be admitted, his astonishment commenced. There
was the Louvre before him, and the resplendent dome of
the Invalids on his right. As it was a fine summer's day,
a crowd of carriages full of gay lords and ladies, dressed in
the height of fashion, followed the road to the left. He
soon found himself in the midst of that vast marble work-
shop where Louis the Fourteenth was having carved the

statues he bequeathed to France, and which, extending
along the street of La Bonne Morue, covered the space now
occupied by the Place de la Concorde. God forgive those
who have substituted iron and stone for the bronze and
marble that covered it at that epoch.

Upon arriving at this marble magazine, he found it
formed an obstacle to his progress. Embarrassed to know
whether he should turn to the right or to the left, he asked
his way of a workman.

"Sir, although your horse looks a good strong creature,
it is easy to see he is worn out. Don't go along the quay,
for the road is very bad; but pass along by the Porte Saint-
Honore, leaving the Filles de la Conception and the Luxembourg on your left, and you will come to the Place
Louis le Grand: you will easily recognize it. It is a large
square in the middle of which stands a statue of the king
on horseback. It is a good neighborhood, where you have
your choice of hotels."

The chevalier followed the advice and the road. He
soon arrived at the Place Louis le Grand, but dared not
venture to halt at such a fine place. He proceeded a few
steps further, and, perceiving a modest-looking hotel, which
appeared in consonance with the state of his purse, he
stopped. It was the sign of the Golden Candlestick.

The chevalier passed under the gate-way with a very resolute air for a provincial, and handed Christopher over to
the care of an hostler. After partaking of some refreshment
he mounted to a little room on the fifth story, and, as he
was very much fatigued, he threw himself on the bed and
slept soundly until next morning.

In the morning his first business was to go and present a
letter of introduction to a certain Marquis de Crette, which
the baron had obtained from M. d'Orquinon, his neighbor.
But upon going to the window the chevalier remarked that
there was a wonderful difference between his outward appearance and that of the gentlemen he saw pass by in
coaches and on horseback. Although he dressed inferior
to none when in the country, he now blushed at the sorry
figure he made in the gay capital. He therefore set out in
search of a second-hand clothes-shop, and bought a coat,
"better than new," a tolerable vest, some stockings, and a
sword. These put on, the country squire was immediately
transformed into a city gentleman; and, aided by a good

personal appearance and address, he was now presentable
in any *salon* in Paris, notwithstanding his sky-blue coat was
adorned with an apple-green shoulder-knot—a combination
of colors which might appear rather bold, but which was
doubtless due to the amorous fantasy of its original owner.

As soon as he was equipped in his new costume, the
chevalier thought he would first study the effect his appearance created upon matter less noble than the Marquis de
Crette, and the society our *débutant* might calculate upon
finding about him. So to make his experiment *in animâ
vili*, he called first upon M. Coquenard, his father's attorney, Rue de Mouton, near the Place de Greve.

Tancrede, as we have said, was a handsome fellow, and
although a provincial, felt himself none the less a gentleman. It was easy to recognize the effects of country air
upon his fine figure and robust hands; but he had a well-
turned leg, and sometimes his eye flashed fire through its
timidity. Only his sword troubled him very much, for it
would go between his legs, and make him very uncomfortable. He had never worn a sword at D'Anguilhem, and he
had not yet learned the proper way to buckle it on. He
could not get along at all in walking through the streets,
everybody appeared to knock against him, and he seemed
to be in everybody's way; he was not yet aware that he
should make the vulgar give way, and yield the wall to his
superiors; so that he was nearly knocked down by a chair-
man, while he jostled against a gentleman of quality. But
his air of utter astonishment saved him from the resentment
of the latter, while his vigorus arm protected him from the
abuse of the former. He was nearly five feet ten in height,
an altitude calculated to inspire respect in any part of the
world.

M. Coquenard received his client very graciously, and as
he was just sitting down to discuss the qualities of a hare ra-
gout, of very inviting aspect, supported by a pigeon-pie that
emitted a most appetizing savor. Tancrede, without ceremony, accepted the attorney's invitation to take a share in
the repast, and seated himself at the table. After a mutual
exchange of compliments, they opened a chapter on business. M. Coquenard approached the matter in hand very
cautiously, and with some circumlocution, in order to soften
as much as possible the blow he knew he would have to
inflict.

The pursuit of the inheritance that had brought the chevalier to Paris, as M. Coquenard said, was one of the most difficult and uncertain cases he had ever undertaken. That the Baron d'Anguilhem, in accepting the responsibility of heir, had made himself liable for the debts of the deceased, amounting to some twenty thousand francs.

Tancrede was quite staggered at this first installment of law.

But this was not all. M. Coquenard proceeded to explain how, in eight days only, the expenses of the preliminary proceedings had amounted to nine hundred francs.

At this second dose, the chevalier grew pale, and lost his appetite. For, at the bottom of all, besides the money lost there lay the great question of all to him, the eventuality of marrying or not marrying Constance. To the praise and credit of our hero it must be said that, although he had been twelve days absent from Mlle. de Beuzerie, he had not even been home-sick; still, from the evening he arrived in the capital, the image of Constance was as fresh in his memory as if he had only that moment taken leave of her.

There was, however, an end of dinner when he heard this communication from the man of law. His appetite was gone for that day at least.

Laden with this dismal news, Tancrede returned to his hotel, but it must be admitted with a less confident air than he wore upon leaving it.

In obedience to the promise he had made to his father, the chevalier sat down to write to him an account of his safe arrival in Paris, of his interview with Coquenard, and the sad intelligence he had received from the worthy attorney. He concluded his epistle by saying that he would go immediately to the Marquis de Crette, and deliver to him the letter of introduction he had received from M. d'Orquinon.

His letter written and dispatched to the post, the chevalier carefully examined his personal appearance at the mirror. He changed his cravat, drew on his ruffles, and wended his way, not without a slight palpitation of the heart, to the residence of the Marquis de Crette, situated in the Faubourg Saint-Germain.

The cause of the chevalier's nervous excitement arose from his expecting to find a grave, severe, starched old gentleman, like M. de Beuzerie, a style for which he had an especial aversion. He also expected to meet a querulous, asthmatic old lady, with a shrill voice, deaf, and perhaps half blind, with a dozen insolent valets in attendance. There was one redeeming feature to be reckoned upon by the chevalier, which was, that old gentlemen, even at Paris, are always a little provincial.

But upon entering the residence of the marquis, he found things just the reverse of what he had anticipated. In the court-yard he saw some half-dozen race-horses equipped in the newest style, and attended by as many grooms in different liveries, but all brilliant and gay, so much so that he concluded that both grooms and horses belonged to men of rank, perfectly *au courant* with the elegancies of the day. This sight made him much more uncomfortable than the two old family portraits he had been painting mentally.

At the door of the house stood an herculean Swiss, with a three-cornered hat upon his head, a large knot upon his shoulder, while with his gold-headed cane he warned off, with a most aristocratic gesture, the dogs and beggars that hovered around.

But when he perceived Tancrede, he lifted his hat respectfully from his head, with that instinct which indicates to a flunky that he has to do with a gentleman, and politely tendered his services. Tancrede replied that he wished to speak with the Marquis de Crette. The Swiss then called one of the grooms, who was in attendance upon the horses, and this worthy, upon receiving his instructions, made a signal to a great bedizened flunky, who introduced the chevalier into an elegant *salon*, which looked out upon a garden.

A moment afterward six young gentlemen, all glitter, noise, and mirth, descended the great staircase, half a dozen steps at a time. One of the number bent his steps toward the *salon*, while the five others scattered themselves in the court-yard, and each approached the horse he was about to ride.

"Who wants me?" inquired the gentleman, as he approached the *salon* in which the chevalier was sitting.

"Monsieur le Chevalier d'Anguilhem," replied a valet in attendance.

"The Chevalier d'Anguilhem?—D'Anguilhem?" replied

the young gentleman, as if endeavoring to recall the name;
"I do not know such a person."

"That is true, sir," said Tancrede, approaching the
the door; "I beg a thousand pardons for having selected
so inopportune a moment, when you are just about going
out with your friends, but I will call another time, if you
will do me the honor of informing me when it will be most
convenient and agreeable to you to receive me."

This was said with a little awkwardness, but at the
same time with such an air of dignity, that the Marquis de
Crette became at once interested in his unknown visitor.

"Not at all, sir," he replied. "I am quite as much at
your service now as ever; may I ask what has obtained me
the honor of this visit?"

"Monsieur le Marquis," replied the chevalier, "I present myself under the auspices of Monsieur d'Orquinon,
your friend I believe, and I beg to present this letter of
introduction from him."

"I have not the honor of a personal acquaintance with
Monsieur d'Orquinon," replied the marquis, "but he was,
I remember, one of the most intimate friends of my poor
father, whom I have heard speak of him many times."

"So, so," said Tancrede to himself, "the marquis loves
his father; he will not laugh at me."

While the Marquis de Crette unsealed and read the letter,
Tancrede made a careful examination of his person.

He was a fine, elegant man of about three- or four-and-
twenty, small, but perfectly well-made, a model of elegance;
as his speech, gesture, and air might have served as a model
of *bon ton*—a last remnant of the old aristocracy, with the
perfume of the new, which was soon afterward hatched under the reign of the regent.

When he had finished perusing the letter he looked at the
chevalier, and thus addressed him—

"Alas! monsieur, this letter was addressed to the Marquis de Crette, my father, whom we had the misfortune to
lose last year; but I perceive by this that the intelligence of
that event has not yet reached the provinces."

Tancrede blushed; this word *province* made his proud
blood rush to his cheeks.

"And yet," continued the marquis, "we sent a letter
announcing the sad events to Monsieur d'Orquinon, but the

letter you have done me the honor to bring proves that the death of Monsieur de Crette is not known down there."

Tancrede blushed more than before. *Down there* seemed to be at the Antipodes.

"*N'importe*," remarked the marquis, doubless perceiving the young man's embarrassment. "*N'importe*, Monsieur d'Anguilhem, the son replaces the father with our family and friends, and as you have been so good as to come and see us, be welcome, and command my services in anything you require."

"Monsieur le Marquis," replied the chevalier, "you are very kind. I am only a poor provincial, very ridiculous, I feel, and perhaps very tiresome also, for I have never quitted D'Anguilhem; but I assure you I shall never cease to remember the gracious reception you have accorded me."

"There, now you overwhelm me, monsieur," replied the marquis, saluting Tancrede with a cordiality that penetrated the depths of his heart. Then turning to his friends, who were talking near him: "Gentlemen," said he, "allow me the honor of introducing to you, Monsieur le Chevalier d'Anguilhem, who is recommended to our consideration by one of the most faithful friends of my father."

The young gentlemen approached to salute Tancrede. He returned the salute with graceful dignity.

"We were just starting for Saint Germain, chevalier," said the marquis; "are you free from engagement this morning? If you are, and think you will find our company agreeable to you, we shall feel honored and delighted with yours."

"But it seems to me," said Tancrede, "that you are going to ride."

"Ah! I understand," replied the marquis, "you have come in your carriage, therefore have no saddle horse with you."

"My horse is at the hotel," replied Tancrede, smiling, "but I must avow, in all humility, that he would make but a very poor figure beside these. I should not like my poor Christopher to intrude in such a noble stud."

"What?" said the marquis to himself, jesting at his own expense; "aha! this young gentleman is not so countryfied as he looks." Raising his voice, he said:

"There is a way of arranging that. There is a horse in the stable that we seldom ride, because he is very difficult to manage; you shall take my horse and I will ride Marl-borough. Besides, you know, gentlemen," said the mar-quis, laughing, "I have to take my revenge on Marl-borough for trying his best to fling me off yesterday."

"But," replied Tancrede, hurriedly, "I beg you will not alter your arrangements on my account."

The marquis, misunderstanding his meaning, approached nearer to him, and said, in a low voice:

"But you ride, do you not?"

"Very little, Monsieur le Marquis, but you have misun-derstood my remark. What I wished to say was, that you should ride your ordinary horse, and allow me to ride Marlborough."

"Ah, ha," said the marquis, laughing, "you will soon find you have caught a Tartar."

"As you wish, gentlemen," said Tancrede. "I am only a poor ignorant countryman. I am very fond of riding; and whether it is that I know horses so well, or that they know me, I do not pretend to decide; but I can always manage to keep in the saddle, however vicious the brute may be. But do not trouble yourselves about me. If my society will not be more disagreeable to you than it has been, and you still desire my company, why, then, be pleased to have Marlborough saddled."

"My dear chevalier," replied the marquis, "we shall feel honored."

"Boisjoli, here, saddle Marlborough."

The groom went toward the stables, grinning and wink-ing to his companions, as much as to say, now we shall have some sport.

"But," said the marquis, "you have come in silk stock-ings and shoes, and you can not ride without boots and spurs."

"I can go to my hotel and put them on."

"Where is that?"

"Rue Saint Honore."

"No, that will take you too long. Rameau d'Or," cried the marquis to another groom, "run to my boot-maker's, and tell him to come here at once, and bring with him half a dozen pairs of boots. Quick!"

The groom disappeared.

"Now, my dear chevalier," said the marquis, "you must at least know where we are taking you. We are going to make a bachelors' party at Saint-Germain. You have come just in the nick of time, and I presume you will not be unwilling, while at Paris, to see what is to be seen; as, when your education is finished, you will go away carrying off your millions. For you must know, gentlemen," continued the marquis, turning to his companions, "that Monsieur d'Anguilhem comes to Paris to receive a little legacy of fifteen hundred thousand francs."

"The deuce!" cried the young gentlemen, in chorus; "accept our very hearty compliments and good wishes, Monsieur d'Anguilhem."

"Believe me, Monsieur le Chevalier," said one of the young gentlemen, with that prompt familiarity peculiar to sporting gentlemen, "we will break off a little corner of your plum before you carry it off into the country; we will show you how to spend it."

"Ah! by Jove, chevalier," cried the marquis, "you may believe in D'Herbigny; he is past master in these matters. He has already devoured two uncles and an aunt."

"But pray," said another, "who is the unfortunate defunct who has left a million and a half?"

"My cousin, the Viscount de Bouzenois," replied Tancrede.

"In that case, my dear chevalier, let us shake hands," said another, "for we are both nearly related to that gentleman. I relieved him of his last sweetheart."

"Your inheritance is worth more than mine," said Tancrede, extending his hand.

"Ah, ah!" cried the marquis, "not so bad, by my faith. What do you say, Treville?"

"I?" said Treville. "I say that Monsieur d'Anguilhem refutes the proverb, 'Stupid as a millionaire.' He will be rich and witty; *Gaudeant bene nati.*"

"Amen," said the marquis. "Chevalier, here are your boots."

Tancrede and the boot-maker were ushered into a dressing-room.

"Well, gentleman," said the marquis, "what do you think of that for a provincial? he will not prove so tedious as we feared at first."

In the course of five minutes the chevalier reappeared, booted and spurred in a style calculated to make any other

horse than Marlborough tremble. Upon arriving at the
stable, a groom handed him a riding-whip. The young
gentleman mounted their horses, and Boisjoli brought out
Marlborough.

He was a beautiful brown bay, with a finely curved neck.
His nostrils distended with pride. His eyes flashed fire, and
the veins of his head and legs displayed his noble blood.
Tancrede regarded him with the eye of a connoisseur, and
soon recognized that he had a worthy adversary to contend
with, and neglected none of the precautions required in
similar cases. He took the bridle and rested firmly in the
stirrups. When he felt himself fairly in the saddle, he made
a sign for Boisjoli to let go. This was the moment for
which Marlborough had waited. No sooner did he feel himself free than he commenced to rear and caper, then to kick,
and executed every sort of maneuver by which he usually
succeeded in unseating his cavalier. But this time he had
met with his match. Tancrede quietly allowed him to play
off all his tricks, and contented himself with so accommodating his movements as to make it appear that horse and
rider were one, like a centaur. When he thought the time
had come that he ought to put a stop to the freaks and caprices the animal indulged in, he began to make him feel
his knees so strongly and so well, that Marlborough quickly
understood that matters were going very badly for him.
Then he redoubled his efforts, but in vain. He had found
his match. After a desperate struggle for about ten minutes, Marlborough gave in, quite beaten. Tancrede then
amused himself by making him execute some clever maneuvers, such as traveling round in a circle, curvetting,
prancing, etc., so that one would have thought him a well-
trained circus horse.

The young gentlemen at first watched this performance
with the greatest curiosity, afterward with admiration and
delight. The Marquis de Crette especially was proud of
the triumph of his friend; and when Master Marlborough
had calmed down a little, he approached nearer to the
chevalier to compliment him, in which he was joined by a
chorus of praises from the rest of the party.

They set out for Saint-Germain. All along the road the
conversation was upon the *ennui* into which the rigor of
Mme. de Maintenon and the austerities of Louis the
Fourteenth had plunged France. These young gentlemen

all wished the widow of Scarron at the devil: "the old woman," as they unceremoniously called her.

Then Pere la Chaise and his august penitents came in for a share of ridicule; it was he who had begun to get around the Duke of Orleans and raise an opposition against the old *regime;* but at present this party was very feeble, and as he was not very welcome at Versailles, it was a little hazardous for any one to admit that he belonged to it. Our hero, who had been brought up amid the provincial nobility, who formed as we have already remarked, a systematic opposition, felt quite at home, and made himself a very agreeable member of the party in the concert of maledictions bestowed upon the royal favorite; he even enriched the conversation with some rude songs composed on the directress of Saint-Cyr and upon Father la Chaise, by some clever wits of the neighborhood of Loches. He thought himself remarkable audacious, when in fact he was only a little lively.

But what Tancrede particularly admired amid all this amusement was, the fashion in which his companions wore their frills, laces, and ruffles, the great superiority of the cut of their coats, and the marvelous beauty of the cloth, the colors of which blended so harmoniously together, as to make him almost despair of ever being able to squeeze his body in so tightly, and at the same time wear his clothes with as much ease. In spite of the naïve admiration which he took no pains to conceal, there was not a single remark directed against himself, and he was so grateful for it that he became quite humble, and took every opportunity of showing his humility. But he no sooner opened his mouth to deprecate his costume and provincial manners, than some one among the young gentlemen interrupted him. His heart overflowed with gratitude.

Arrived at Saint-Germain, they ordered dinner, but as it would not be ready for an hour, M. de Crette proposed a game at brelau. Tancrede trembled at hearing this proposition.

"Alas!" thought he; "these gentlemen will play for at least three or four pistoles." Poor Tancrede!

He looked timidly at his host, who immediately comprehended his perplexity.

"Gentlemen," said the marquis; "perhaps the Chevalier d'Anguilhem does not understand our game: stakes only

twenty louis, so that he may have time to learn without
ruining himself."

At this gallant announcement, a cold perspiration bedewed the forehead of the chevalier.

"The half of what I possess," said he to himself.   "I
am a ruined man!"   In a moment he understood all the
vanity of human wishes.   Anguilhem, Guerite, Pintade,
the savings of half a century hoarded in his father's strong
box, all might be devoured in an hour at brelau, and by
gentlemen who gambled very little; surely, he thought,
such a pursuit could not add much to the dignity of a gentleman.

M. de Crette perceived that Tancrede was desirous of
speaking with him in private; so while the table was being
made ready for the game, he stepped carelessly into an adjoining apartment.   Tancrede followed him.

"On my honor, marquis," said our hero, with that
frankness which had at once conciliated the good feelings
of his new companions, "I do not misrepresent matters
when I tell you that my father is not rich.   He has given
me very little money for my journey, and I am afraid—"

"Of losing it?"

"No, but of losing too much."

"Bah!   Don't think of such things here.   One of the
first qualifications of a gentleman is that of being a good
gambler."

"Yes; but to be a good player, he must not lose more
than he has got."

"Why not?"

"But the money?"

"The money, he can always find that, if not in his own
pockets, at least in those of his friends."

"Excuse me, marquis, but I am not a pickpocket."

"You are a child, though, my chevalier; we do not
steal, not we: we play on credit.   Why, I do not suppose
we could show a hundred louis among the whole of us; but
at the bottom of our purse is our *word*, chevalier, and the
word of a gentleman is as good as a bank-note.   Besides,
when honorable men like us play together the winnings
balance the losses.   We play against each other all the year
through, gaining and losing prodigious sums; and on the
31st of December we balance our accounts, and the most
unlucky has seldom more than a hundred pistoles to pay.

Play, then, fearlessly, lose cheerfully; I shall keep my eye on you."

"I shall do everything in my power to deserve your kind favor," said Tancrede, smiling.

"Then return to the table immediately, I hear the money chinking."

The marquis and the chevalier returned to the room where the table was ready and the game made. D'Anguilhem lost twenty louis in three throws. During this half hour all the anguish of fear racked the heart of the chevalier. But although the muscles of his temples quivered a little, his smile never faded for a moment. The marquis made a fresh game.

The chevalier drew another twenty louis from his purse.

After five throws, the chevalier had regained his twenty louis, and forty more. He then began to play in earnest.

"Our friend D'Anguilhem is a real sharper," said the Marquis de Crette, pushing him fifty louis as his share of the winnings. "He has come to Paris to receive 1,500,000 francs, and not content with that he wants to carry off all our cash also."

Tancrede understood his lesson; thanking his friend with a smile, he sat himself down to play as freely as when he had lost.

He was now in the vein; in ten minutes he was in possession of 300 louis.

We must confess that if his terror had been profound, his joy was delirious. Dinner was announced as ready. D'Anguilhem inwardly thanked fortune, which had given him this opportunity of making his fortune. Crette saw the smile of satisfaction that passed over his face imperceptible as it was. "Chevalier," said the marquis, "you would make us believe that it is your winnings that make you so merry and happy, but that is sheer modesty on your part. I understand you better than to believe it; I will bet that if you venture your 300 louis against D'Herbigny, that he will lose 400 on the first *vingt-et-un* you can show." Saying this, he winked at the chevalier. Tancrede understood that he must behave like a gentleman, and sacrifice his newly acquired fortune with a good grace. He suppressed a sigh and replied—

"You are quite in the right, marquis. I will stake my 300 louis against Monsieur d'Herbigny's 300."

"Done," said D'Herbigny.

They took the cards. Tancrede turned up twenty-nine, D'Herbigny thirty. Our hero colored a little, that was all.

"There's your 300 louis, viscount," said he, smiling.

"You are a capital player, Monsieur d'Anguilhem," said D'Herbigny, inclining his head.

"My compliments to you, chevalier," said the Count de Chastellux; "you play like a prince."

"My compliments to you," said the Baron de Treville.

"My compliments to you," said each of the company.

Crette took Tancrede by the hand, and pressed it warmly, and putting his mouth to his ear, he whispered:

"We know a man by the way he plays his cards and handles his sword. Always act as you have done to-day, and in three months you will be an accomplished cavalier."

I get plenty of praise, if nothing else, thought Tancrede, rising from the table, and it appears I have done something very fine; but in his progress from the gambling-table to the dinner-table he heaved a tremendous sigh. The dinner was exceedingly lively. The Marquis de Crette and his companions drank freely; but in this respect they were but as children compared with their provincial guest. The chevalier found, in good earnest, that the glasses were very small and the wine very weak.

"*Sacre*," said D'Herbigny, "you are as fine a player as cavalier, and drink as well as you play. It appears to me they understand a thing or two at Anguilhem."

Tancrede was delighted to find himself not only equal, but also superior in many things to these miracles of elegance.

The conversation during dinner was upon sporting, love, and dueling. On the first two points the chevalier had a good many stories to relate, although his amours were not of the same sort as those of his friends. But upon the last chapter he could boast neither of his prowess nor of his triumphs. He had never seen fire, never had had the slightest duel. This was very humiliating, and made him figure as a very dissatified auditor.

During dessert, another company arrived. Those who composed it were as noisy at their arrival, as the Marquis de Crette and his companions were at the end of their dinner.

"Hallo! see, we are going to have the Kollinskis," said

the Marquis de Crette, with an air of dissatisfaction which did not escape Tancrede's notice.

The chevalier looked toward the window, and perceived four gentlemen approaching, two of whom, superbly dressed in a foreign costume, made a great uproar at the door of the hotel.

They were two Hungarian gentlemen, dressed so richly as to appear extravagant. Their luxury was insulting, even in that luxurious age.

The marquis's party relapsed into a state of silence, as if they were afraid of encouraging the least familiarity in the new-comers.

Tancrede whispered in the ear of the marquis:

"Who are these Kollinskis?"

"Two Hungarian noblemen, who are living here after the fashion of their own country," replied the marquis, "in bullying innkeepers, beating the servants, and insulting everybody they meet; very good sport if dueling was not prohibited and so cruelly punished. Brave, however. I have nothing to say against them on that score."

Our hero profited by the explanation. The Kollinskis entered the large room of the inn, and saluted courteously all the company; but no sooner were the first compliments exchanged, than the Marquis de Crette rose from the table. His example was followed by all his friends. He paid the innkeeper and went out, followed by Tancrede and his other companions.

While descending the staircase, the chevalier heard shouts of laughter proceeding from the Kollinskis, and the words *apple-green* knot struck his ear several times. Now, Tancrede wore, as we have said, an apple-green knot upon his shoulder. It was an ornament in very bad taste, especially upon a sky-blue coat. Tancrede was not aware of this in the morning, although he fully understood it before evening. He was, therefore, very indignant against the jeerers; and detested them from the bottom of his heart. He felt that he looked ridiculous in their eyes.

M. de Crette on his part, had not lost a word of their raillery, for, in mounting his horse, he said:

"*Mon Dieu!* those Kollinskis are very insolent and provoking."

Tancrede guessed that the jeers of the Kollinskis were well understood by his companions, and he suffered cruelly in consequence; but as no remark was made upon the subject, he was obliged to suppress his indignation.

Upon their arrival in Paris, Tancrede thanked the marquis very warmly for his kind attentions, asked permission of all the gentlemen present to visit them, and accepted an offer they made him to make one of a party at tennis on the morrow.

"Take off your apple-green," said the marquis to him, in a whisper, at parting, "and take a poppy-colored one; that is the fashionable color."

The chevalier would have preferred receiving a thrust from a dagger than this delicate hint from his new friend.

"Certainly, I am insulted," he thought, "and I have not demanded satisfaction. Am I, then, become a coward?"

CHAPTER XV.

THIS idea prevented Tancrede from getting a wink of sleep all night. He viewed his adventure in a hundred different ways. He raised a thousand arguments in its favor; but the result of all was, that he had been jeered at, and had suffered in consequence. The remembrance of it would darken all the days of his existence, otherwise so happy. This, added to what Coquenard had told him respecting his lawsuit, was not calculated to lull him to sleep; so, after dozing an hour or two, he got up again in a very bad humor.

But as he had learned the evening before the supreme importance attached to wearing an elegant coat, as soon as he had taken his chocolate he sent for a fashionable tailor, and ordered him to have a complete suit ready by ten o'clock, made in the highest style of fashion.

At ten o'clock the tailor returned with a coat of shot taffety, with silver lace trimmings; a vest of gray silk, embroidered with the same, and breeches to match the coat. The rest of the costume was made up of a cravat of Malines lace, embroidered stockings, and new-buckled shoes, together with a new richly mounted sword.

He candidly confessed to his tailor his fears as to being able to wear all these fine things in a becoming manner. The tailor was an accomplished artist, and could impart the most valuable advice. Tancrede, who wished to put it into immediate execution, walked, turned, and twisted before his learned professor, who finally declared that he was perfectly satisfied with the style in which the chevalier stroked his chin and placed his hat under his left arm. He then paid the tailor and dismissed him, already a little distracted from the gloomy ideas that had tormented him all night. He set out with a light step for the Rue de Vaugirard, where the game of tennis was to be played.

One thing only was wanting to complete his satisfaction, which was, that he could be seen by Constance in his new clothes. This feeling increased greatly when he perceived the great sensation his appearance produced upon everybody he met—a sensation exhibited by everybody turning round to look at him, and watching him until he was out of sight. In fact, no one could understand where a fine young gentleman, who appeared to be on such good terms with himself, was going at ten o'clock in the morning, dressed as if for a wedding.

Tancrede was the first to arrive at the rendezvous. The markers made him a profound reverence upon entering, which he accepted as a good omen. This was the first time that he had seen a game of tennis played. He expected to have found himself in a Louvre; he was in a cockloft, or something very much like it. Profiting by the opportunity his very exact punctuality afforded him, he asked from the markers some theoretical instructions upon the nature of the game, and took some practical lessons also. He had a quick intelligence, and immediately comprehended the part he had to play; and, as he had a good eye and steady hand, he threw very straight for a beginner.

While this was going on his new friends arrived. The astonishment of the chevalier was great when he saw them in their dressing-gowns. Alas! the poor chevalier had much to learn before he could become a Parisian.

The Marquis de Crette perceived his astonishment.

"We live in the neighborhood," said he; "why did you come here without us?"

"I," said Tancrede, "have some visits to make when I leave you, so that I have dressed myself beforehand."

"You had better have come *en déshabille*," said the marquis. "You will be obliged to go home when you leave here; this costume will inconvenience you very much."

"I do not think I can make one of your party," replied

our hero, biting his lips, "for I do not understand the game, and—"

"Ah, well!" said the marquis, "we shall go and play a little to get breath, and give you some idea of things; then we will make our party."

At this moment a sound of bad augury was heard in the anteroom. Many voices were heard, among which Tancrede fancied he could recognize the one that had jeered at him the day before on account of his apple green. The chevalier felt a presentiment.

Almost immediately afterward the Kollinski party entered with their companions. A cold perspiration bedewed Tancrede's forehead.

"Make haste," said the marquis; "let us take our places, where we can dispute with these bravoes, whose turn it will be to begin."

The marquis took off his morning-gown, his friends did the same; the chevalier, on his part, laid aside his coat, vest, and sword.

The party made their arrangements.

Tancrede commenced by making some of those blunders inseparable from the apprenticeship to so difficult a game, amid the general mirth of all who stood looking on. But little by little his play became better. Generally all manly exercises suited him marvelously well. He was quite apt at matters requiring strength and address. The vigor of his wrist soon excited the admiration of his new friends; his balls whistled like cannon-balls, and it required some one very clever to *tierce* against him.

The young gentlemen amused themselves very much in watching the resources of his strong nature display themselves so impromptu. They were profuse in their praises and compliments.

The gallery did not appear to enjoy the game so much. The Kollinskis had come to play a game also, and found that the party of the Marquis de Crette occupied the place a little too long for their taste. So, by the way of amusing themselves, while the younger Kollinski laughed with his usual impertinence, his brother commenced throwing the balls into the pocket.

This happened to the Marquis de Crette's side, who found it particularly disagreeable.

As the marquis grew more and more impatient, he paid

less attention to the game, so that he began to lose.   He
was a good player when he lost through his own fault or
through that of his friends, and he was easily irritated when
he lost through the fault of others, especially if they were
persons he did not like.   Upon another ball being pocketed
by Kollinski the marquis lost all patience.

"*Parbleu*, sir," said he turning toward the pocketer,
"you pocket my balls and make me lose.   That may,
probably, amuse you, but it does not at all amuse me."

"Then, marquis, I will pocket those of this gentleman,"
said the Hungarian, passing over to the side of Tancrede.

Our hero threw an inquiring glance at the Marquis de
Crette, to which the marquis responded by a significant expression.

"Do so, if the gentleman will permit you," said the
Marquis de Crette.

"Ah! but I shall not permit it," said Tancrede, with a
slight palpitation of the heart, while stepping nearer to
M. Kollinski.

"Stop," said the Hungarian, "this is the fellow with
the apple-green knot; and pray where is your apple-green
knot, my fine fellow?"

"Monsieur d'Anguilhem has no longer got his apple-
green knot, it is true," said the Marquis de Crette, "but
he has got a new sword."

These words acted like a spark applied to a barrel of gun-
powder.

Tancrede advanced toward M. Kollinski, and saluted
him gravely.

"Yes, sir, a new sword, which I shall have the honor of
passing through your body, if agreeable to you."

A shout of laughter greeted the singular provocation from
the chevalier.   M. Kollinski wished to reply in his usual
noisy manner, but the Viscount d'Herbigny stepped forward, with his finger on his lips.

"Gentlemen," said he, "consider where you are, I pray
you.   Not here, for the world.   We shall meet again."

The Hungarians saluted, then retired to the end of the
room, and amused themselves with laughing loudly together.

"Ah well," said the marquis, in a low voice, to Tancrede,
who, after the blood had left his face, looked very pale.
"How are you, chevalier; they say you are not well?"

"No, sir, I am only a little excited."

"Will this emotion prevent you from fighting if we had need of a fourth?"

"Prevent me from fighting! me?" replied our hero, who remembered his father's instructions; "I will fight ten times, if need be, and against ten persons, if you think proper. But something has got hold of me now, stronger than myself, and I tremble; it is anger, I think."

The marquis smiled at the naiveté with which the chevalier translated his sensations.

"Can you fence?" he asked.

"Yes, a little."

"Who was your master?"

"My father taught me."

"The devil! You know something, I'll warrant."

"I think I can defend myself."

"If you can use your sword as well as you can manage a horse!"

"But I hope I can do both equally well."

"Truly."

"I have never fought except with foils."

"So that you do not know how you will fight, when you are on the ground?"

"I know that I shall fight and that's enough, and without budging an inch, I promise you."

"Ah, if you promise it," said the marquis, "I shall make myself quite easy."

"I promise you."

"Very good."

The marquis resumed his morning-gown, adjusted his cravat, and went in search of the two Hungarians, who were seated on a bench at the other end of the room, with two of their friends. They rose at his approach.

These noisy gentlemen exchanged the usual compliments. The Kollinskis had become perfectly polite. That was easily accounted for; they were going to fight.

They made a rendezvous for four o'clock, and arranged to meet behind the convent of the Filles du Saint Sacrement.

Our four young gentlemen returned to the house of the arquis de Crette.

"My faith, gentlemen, this is an ugly business," said the marquis, upon re-entering the *salon*. He threw himself on a couch, and motioned his companions to do the same.

"How is that?" asked D'Herbigny.

"Why, my dear viscount, the Kollinskis actually wish to fight four to four."

"Well, are we not four?" said Treville.

"Doubtless," said the marquis; "but being only the second day we have been together, I should wish to take the chevalier out of this scrape."

"And why me, rather than another?" asked Tancrede.

"Because, my dear chevalier, a first affair is — a first affair."

"Ah, that's it, is it?" replied the chevalier. "But have you Parisians by chance found a way of beginning with the second?"

"No, not yet, that's true," said Crette, laughing.

"In that case, sir, make use of me, I beg of you," replied the chevalier; "and if it is only to give a good thrust with my sword, I can do that as well as another."

"Chevalier, if you return," said Crette, "you will be my friend. But do not deceive yourself. The Kollinskis are distinguished duelists; they fight with rapiers of the time of Charles the Ninth."

"Well, marquis, as you please; they will endeavor to do their best, I have no doubt."

"Be it so, then; but you are forewarned. There is still time for you to retire honorably, chevalier, and in case you do, we shall have recourse to Clos-Renaud, who is a good swordsman."

"You will vex me very much, if you repeat what you say, marquis. I am at your service, and at the Hungarians' also."

"Well, gentlemen, this afternoon at four o'clock," said Crette. "We must make our wills, for in all probability that will be necessary. Come with me, my friend, and I will give you a good sword; the one you have got is merely a pretty toy."

The marquis took leave of his companions, and led Tancrete into a kind of armory, where he had a collection of swords of all sizes, with hilts adapted to different hands.

The chevalier made his choice like a connoisseur. He took a neat weapon, neither too long nor too short, nor too heavy nor too light; a blade as sharp as a needle.

The marquis watched his guest's choice with the closest attention. "Ah," said he, "I perceive you possess very good taste. Throw your sword in a corner, it is good for nothing, and put this in its place."

"This afternoon, at four, behind the convent of Filles du Saint Sacrement. You know where?"

"Perfectly."

"Wait for me. I shall call for you as I pass along. But no; come here in a couple of hours, and we shall eat something together."

"You are very kind, marquis."

When he returned to his hotel, and had locked himself in his chamber, he made some very gloomy reflections. That word *will*, which had dropped as it were by accident from the Marquis de Crette, kept running in his head.

"By Heaven," said he, "it will be a very absurd thing if I have come from Loches to Paris merely to be killed!"

Upon this the chevalier rested his elbow on the table, and leaning his head upon his hand, began thinking of Constance, of his mother, and of the baron; of his happy home, the happiness of which he appreciated only when removed from it. Then he wrote a few lines to Constance and to his father and mother, weeping very naïvely in proportion as he wrote.

He wept so much, that he ended by not weeping at all. Besides, it was a splendid day: the sun darted his rays through the window, and a million of atoms played in his beams. Death is less hideous in fine weather. It is remarked that there are many more duels in August than in December.

Tancrede held up his head, took the marquis's sword out of its scabbard. In his strong hand it was as light as a feather. He made a few passes against the wall to satisfy himself that he was up to the mark, for it was nearly eighteen months since he had touched a foil.

At two o'clock he proceeded to the residence of the marquis. Crette was in the armory with D'Herbigny and Treville.

A table was laid. Upon it there was some cutlets, a tart, and only two bottles of wine.

At the sight of this, the chevalier declared, that having only had some chocolate at nine in the morning, he was literally dying with hunger. The other three young men joined in chorus.

They were as merry over their repast as if they were going to the opera upon quitting the table. Only from time to time the chevalier felt a nervous twitching near his heart; but it was only a passing twinge, and had not the effect of making the smile quit his lips.

They remained an hour at table; but not a glass of wine more than the two bottles was drunk. At dessert the four friends embraced each other.

"Hark ye, chevalier," said D'Herbigny, who was considered the best swordsman among the gentlemen who composed the society of the Marquis de Crette, "it was easy to see yesterday, when you mounted Marlborough, and to-day when you were playing tennis, that you have a leg of iron and an arm of steel. Flog this obnoxious Kollinski, for I fully believe he will be your man; and it is quite natural it should, as it was you who had the gallantry to offer to put your sword through his body. He is a fencer; a maker of feints."

"At my second duel," replied the chevalier, "perhaps I shall flinch; for, as my father always told me, to flinch is not to flee; but at the first I shall not budge a single step; and to make sure of it, look out for a wall against which I can place my back."

"Then he will pin you against the wall, as they do butterflies in a cabinet. No bragging, my friend. Consider that when he has finished you he will fall foul of our backs."

"I shall give him enough to do to mind his own business. He will have no chance of interfering with your little affairs," said Tancrede.

"Amen!" replied D'Herbigny.

"Amen!" repeated Crette and Treville.

All three took their swords; the chevalier had not laid his aside. They then got into the coach.

When they arrived at the corner of the convent of Filles du Saint Sacrement, Crette pulled the check-string. The coachman stopped, and a little jockey jumped down and opened the door.

"Wait here, Basque," said the marquis, "and observe carefully what happens; we shall probably have more need of the coach to return in than we had for it to bring us here."

The four gentlemen descended from the coach.

"Well, Tancrede," said the marquis, "how do you find yourself?"

"I? I find myself very well indeed, I thank you; and to honor the company in which I find myself, I would fight with the devil himself, if he were here."

A second coach, containing the four adversaries of our young gentlemen, now arrived. They got out: there were the two Kollinskis, Count Gorkaun, a Saxon, and an officer in the lancers named Bardane.

They approached the Marquis de Crette, and saluted him.

It turned out with respect to our hero, as D'Herbigny had foreseen. Kollinski the elder particularly desired to fight with Tancrede, and Tancrede was equally anxious to have him for his opponent. The discussion was very brief.

The rest of the game was arranged as follows:

The Marquis de Crette had the younger Kollinski for a partner; D'Herbigny accommodated himself with M. Bardane, and Treville with the Saxon.

They put themselves on their guard, and as at every moment they were liable to be disturbed, they immediately crossed swords.

The Marquis de Crette received a thrust through the wrist.

D'Herbigny killed M. de Bardane, and Treville was killed by the Count du Gorkaun.

As to the chevalier, he wielded his sword with great skill, as he had promised; he never retreated a step. But he threw himself three times upon his adversary. The first time, with a straight thrust, he wounded him in the cheek; the second, with a thrust, he pierced him in the throat; and in the third, he sent his sword through his chest.

M. Kollinski the elder fell to the ground.

"*Peste!*" said the marquis, who was seated on the grass; "what a ram that great boy is; he would knock down a wall."

Upon seeing his brother fall, the younger Kollinski rushed at Tancrede; but D'Herbigny stopped his progress.

"One moment, sir," said D'Herbigny to the Hungarian.

"It is I, if you please, who will have the honor of accommodating you in the same fashion as my friend D'Anguilhem has accommodated your brother."

And with this he put the chevalier aside, who persisted, pretending that as he had begun with the family, he ought to continue with it; but he had not time to continue the discussion.

The Saxon came to him.

"Pardon, my dear sir," said he, "if I give your big arm no rest."

"It does not require any," replied Tancrede, putting himself on his guard.

"Quick, quick, gentlemen!" cried Crette, "for I see Basque making a sign that some one is coming."

"Now, then, I am ready."

In an instant his sword was deep in the shoulder of the Count de Gorkaun."

"Monsieur," said he, gravely, to Tancrede, "I thank you; and if ever you come to Dresden, I shall be delighted to see you."

"Monsieur," replied our hero, sensible of the compliment, "you may be certain that my first visit shall be to you."

The two adversaries saluted each other.

Meanwhile Kollinski the younger and D'Herbigny were busily engaged. D'Herbigny pierced Kollinski in the hips, and Kollinski scratched D'Herbigny's thigh.

At a signal from the M. de Crette, the coach drove up. Basque and the coachman of M. Kollinski put M. de Bardane and the Viscount de Treville face to face, to make it appear they had killed each other. They put the elder Kollinski, who was not yet quite dead, into the coach; his brother and the Saxon got in beside him; and the coach set off at a gallop. On the other side Crette, D'Herbigny, and Tancrede stepped gayly into their coach, and their horses carried them off.

"My dear chevalier," said the marquis, "I request the honor of your friendship, and I offer you very sincerely mine."

"You overwhelm me," replied the chevalier.

"Tancrede, Tancrede," said the marquis, "you know very well that I have forbidden you to make use of that word. *Sacre Dieu!* how my wrist pains me!"

" Poor Treville," said D'Herbigny, " and I owe him two hundred pistoles!"

"What do you wish for, my friend?" said the marquis " the account is settled."

All three returned to the residence of the Marquis de Crette, which D'Herbigny and Tancrede did not quit until night.

CHAPTER XVI.

ALL these adventures had passed with the swiftness of a dream.

Tancrede had found just time to live, but scarcely had he found leisure to perceive how he lived. With respect to this phenomenon, he consulted the activity of the Marquis de Crette, who replied:

"My dear friend, this is how we live in Paris. This evening we shall have no *soirée;* at least, I shall not, for my wound will prevent me going out. But as for you, Paris is wide. You have two very sound wrists; you can therefore pass your time agreeably from now till midnight."

"No, I thank you," said the chevalier. "I am not disinclined to return to my hotel; but, from the road I am pursuing, and with the examples I have under my eyes, ı hope that in the course of a week I shall be a perfect cavalier."

"I can easily believe it, since these two days you are scarcely recognizable; but there is something more pressing than the dinners at Saint-Germain, or the tennis-parties in the Rue de Vaugirard, and the promenades behind the convent of the Filles du Saint Sacrement: that is, your lawsuit. And I advise you to pay attention to it."

"I intend to do so," said D'Anguilhem, "and to-morrow I shall begin."

"You know, my friend, that my coach and a horse are at your disposal; only let me know in the morning which you desire, and at what hour, and either will be at your service."

"And do you think I shall gain my suit?" said Tancrede.

"Ah! my friend, you ask me much more than I can reply to. If you ask me if you can master Bucephalus, I shall answer yes! If you ask me if you can spit Berthelot

and Boisrobert, our two principal masters-at-arms, I shall
reply, very possibly. But, my dear friend, we can not
soften down a judge as we can a horse, or as you kill a
man. There are counselors, ushers, attorneys, presidents,
both of fine and of recovery, a mob of square-caps, a hell
of black-robed rascals. You must first learn the names of
all these sly dogs, and endeavor to bribe the one with fair
words, and the other with money."

"As for the fair words, all very well," said Tancrede,
"I am quite at home there. I studied rhetoric under the
Abbe Dubois, who is a master in the art; and my philosophy
under the Jesuits at Amboise. But as for money, that is
quite another thing. My father gave me fifty louis, to last
me six months, and during the two days I have been in
Paris I have already got rid of twenty pistoles."

"Well, well. But my dear friend, I have already told
you, that among gentlemen there need be no anxiety on
that head. Use my purse. I have 60,000 a year, and if it
were not for my steward, I should be puzzled sometimes to
pay for a dinner. Help yourself, my friend, help yourself;
you can repay me when you become a millionaire."

"But what if I lose my suit," said Tancrede.

"Well, suppose you do, chevalier, you will not be hanged
for that. We shall take what money you have left. We
shall go and take a seat at a gaming-table; you can not
always lose; fortune owes you a good turn, and she will
give it to you."

"That is all very uncertain and precarious, my dear
marquis, and I must confess to you that I do not see the
future under *coleur de rose.*"

"Ah, yes, that is very true. You grumble! What do
you say to Bardane and Treville, if you are not contented?
Apropos, my dear friend, if you are questioned as to them,
do not fail to say that they quarreled over a game at tennis, and fought and killed each other. It any very inquisitive fellow asks you where you got your information,
say I have told you."

"Very good," said Tancrede, withdrawing.

"One word more; send to-morrow morning to Monsieur
Kollinski, and inquire whether he be alive or dead. You
are bound to do that. If he is dead, all is over. If not,
send every day until he be either dead or recovered. Did
you not also give the Saxon a scratch?"

"I believe I put my sword through his shoulder."

"Oh! you think so.   Well, kill two birds with one stone, and send to inquire about him at the same time."

"But their addresses?"

"Petitpas will bring them to you to-morrow morning."

"And who is Petitpas?"

"He is my courier."

"Good-night, marquis."

"Thank you for your wish, but I doubt it.   My wrist is very painful.   That animal Kollinski could not hit me anywhere else.   What brutes these Hungarians are. *Allons.* Good-night, my dear friend; you know what you have had to reckon upon to-day; a chance between life and death."

While returning to his hotel, Tancrede reflected that he had that day probably killed a man, or at least greatly injured him; and he was astonished to find that he experienced so little remorse, notwithstanding that the commandments of God and the Church ordered him to love his neighbor as himself.

Still more, in seeing M. Kollinski fall wounded, so far from feeling any regret, he experienced a most intense delight; so true it is that a sense of self-perservation supersedes every other feeling and consideration.

But there was one thing that reassured Tancrede when he began to have a bad opinion of himself, which was, that there had scarcely been a thought between the two friends of poor Treville, who was killed, except that D'Herbigny remembered himself that he was indebted to the deceased in 100 louis, a circumstance which, in all probability, he would have found it convenient to forget had Treville lived.

And yet Crette and D'Herbigny had been intimate friends with Treville for ten or twelve years.

But on the other hand, doubtless Treville had a father, a mother, and a mistress, to whom his death would prove a source of great grief.   The chevalier shuddered when he remembered that he possessed all these ties, and that it might have so happened that at this very moment when he was engaged in philosophical reflections, he himself might have been where Treville now was, lying dead in a ditch.

This idea made the chevalier quicken his pace, for he was impatient to write to Anguilhem, and send to the place

that contained all he so dearly loved the feelings with
which his heart now overflowed.

Tancrede wrote both to his father and mother: he felt so
happy that his joy knew no bounds. It is a fine thing to
feel oneself alive after passing so near the jaws of death,
and when the pride of triumph is joined to the feeling of
preservation. Then something more aided in reassuring
him. He would never, in future, experience that palpitation at the heart which is the indecision of the brave. He
knew his strength, and he had made others feel it.

He entreated his mother not to forget that, next to the
love he entertained for her and his father, his heart was
wholly given to Mlle. Constance de Beuzerie. He begged
her to have it made known in the country, that, admitted
to a close intimacy with the Marquis de Crette, he had already put things in good train at Paris. Then he described
the sights he had seen, the manners, customs and fashions,
hinted a few words on his increasing reputation, and that
the other fifty louis, if sent immediately, would arrive none
too soon. Lastly came a postscript of a page and a half
for Constance.

In his letter to the baron—for the chevalier now regarded it as sacrilege to confound affairs of the heart with money
matters—in his letter to his father he explained, at length,
the apprehensions of M. Coquenard. He described the
critical position in which the little fortune of the Angul-
hems was placed by the exactions of the lawsuit, but that,
convinced in his own mind that nothing could resist his
claim to the property, and that he must gain his suit, he
presumed that the attorney had exaggerated the difficulties
of the case, in order to gain more credit for his success in
conducting it.

The postscript of this letter was devoted to Christopher,
who was faring sumptuously and idly in the stable of the
Golden Candlestick.

However, the cause that had brought the chevalier to
Paris would intrude itself. M. de Bouzenois had died of
an attack of apoplexy, without signifying his intentions
with regard to the disposal of his property, either by words
or in writing; for the worthy captain fully believed that
he had ten or a dozen good years to live. His residence,
situated in the Place Louis le Grand, had suddenly become
deserted. The son of the Malabar widow presented himself

there, as if entitled to take possession; but as he could show no title or claim, everything was put under royal seal, and the property sequestered.

Tancrede promised to himself, as soon as he could find a moment to spare, that he would pay a visit to the late Viscount de Bouzenois' residence, and take, at least, an outside survey of what he hoped was his own property. He took that opportunity on the morning he left his cards for M. Kollinski, who resided in the Rue des Capucins, and for Count de Gorkaun, who lodged near the Ferme des Mathurins, both near the Place Louis le Grand.

He found the doors and windows hermetically closed. It was a beautiful large house, worth at least 300,000 francs, an enormous sum in those days. He remarked a stone escutcheon, upon which were engraved the arms of the deceased, and upon which he promised to engrave his own as soon as the successful termination of his suit permitted this little indulgence of vanity. He passed round and round the house, to view it from all points and under the most varied aspects, and while so occupied he perceived a gentleman who had arrived on the spot about the same time as himself, and apparently upon the same errand. Observing his maneuvers, Tancrede concluded he would submit him to a close scrutiny.

He was a man to whom it was scarcely possible to assign any particular age; he might be something under forty, but certainly more than twenty-five. His complexion was of an orange-yellow color, even to what should have been the whites of his eyes. He had small white teeth and jet-black hair. He was dressed very gayly, had two chains to his watch, and several diamond rings upon his fingers. On the opposite side of the street a large gilded coach was waiting, upon the box of which was a coachman of a similar complexion to his master, but yellower; and near the door stood a valet in the costume of a Lascar, who was of a darker complexion even than the coachman.

At the same moment that Tancrede remarked this strange personage, the latter appeared to remark him. They successively viewed each other, then the house, then each other again. Then as the wicket in the great gate was opened to allow a black-coated officer to pass through, both the amateurs rushed forward, and put their heads in with so much precipitation, that they encountered each other like battling-rams.

The chevalier very politely excused himself to the unknown; but the unknown growled out something which Tancrede interpreted to mean—the devil, here is a fellow with a very thick skull. Recovered from the shock, both exclaimed at the same time:

"A very beautiful house, upon my word."

"Is it not, monsieur?" said Tancrede.

"That is my opinion," said the unknown.

"And when the grass is removed from between the stones—"

"When it is newly painted—"

"And when it is enlivened by beautiful horses and carriages—"

"Illuminated at night—"

"I shall have one of the most magnificent mansions in all Paris."

"Pardon me, sir," said the unknown, "you mean to say that *I* shall have one of the most magnificent mansions in Paris."

"No, I did not speak for you, I spoke for myself."

"But who are you, then?"

"I am the cousin of Monsieur de Bouzenois."

"And I am his step-son, sir."

"What, are you the Malay?"

"And you the provincial?"

"Sir," said Tancrede, "that term is not polite; I have come from the country it is true, but for all that I am no provincial. I am the friend of the Marquis de Crette, of the Viscount d'Herbigny, of the Chevalier de Clos-Renaud, and yesterday I hit three times with my sword a Hungarian, who is a head taller than you."

"Well, sir, and what am I to understand by that?"

"That is as much as to say, sir," replied the chevalier, "that since I have been so fortunate as to meet you, I shall take advantage of the opportunity in making you a little proposition."

"Of accommodation?"

"Yes, sir, a compromise."

"What is it? Speak?"

"It is this: That you take a little turn with me behind the convent of the Filles du Saint Sacrement, for, as man's judgment is always doubtful and his decisions uncertain, let us settle our claims, as the old chivalry did, by an appeal to arms and to the judgment of Heaven."

"Then you propose a duel?" cried the Malay, changing from a deep orange to a pale lemon color.

"If you kill me," said Tancrede, "this house is yours without dispute; if I kill you, there will be no lawsuit."

"Your very humble servant," said the Malay, stepping into his coach, "I am sure of gaining my lawsuit, but I am not so sure that I can give you a quietus with my sword; we will therefore still leave the matter to the judgment of men."

The coach started off at a gallop.

The chevalier then proceeded to leave his card at M. Kollinski's, who was not yet dead, and another with Count Gorkaun, who was as well as could be expected.

CHAPTER XVII.

TANCREDE next proceeded to call upon the Marquis de Crette, and related to him an account of his interview with the Malay.

The marquis still suffered very much from the wound in his wrist; but this had not prevented him from making two or three morning calls, so that he might undeceive those who might have heard that he had been fighting and had got dangerously wounded. This precaution was not altogether useless, for the duel had caused much talk. But as the dead preserve the profoundest silence, and as no one had yet been arrested, no one was compromised. There was nothing, therefore, to prevent the marquis from attending to the chevalier's lawsuit, and of making his visits with him.

There were three chief judges and a judge advocate.

The chevalier and the marquis commenced by visiting the judges.

These worthies were three originals, each with a decided taste for a different animal; the one petted a cat; another a monkey; and the third a parrot. The chevalier made himself very amiable with the judges, and the marquis was very attentive to the animals; but the moment either of them made the slightest allusion to the lawsuit, the judges gave these ingenious gentlemen to understand that it would be more agreeable to discourse upon other business. As to the judge advocate, he was such an austere puritan, that he positively declined to receive them.

"Plague!" said the marquis to the chevalier, "this appears to me a bad omen."

Nevertheless, one fine morning they learned that the cause was put down for a hearing. It had taken no less than two months to prepare the briefs, complete the inventories; and examine the titles of the respective parties. During this time Tancrede had considered whether it would not be better to come to some understanding with the Malay, and compromise with him. But the marquis was opposed to opening any such negotiation as that; for the Malay proclaimed everywhere that his success was certain, and that he had furnished the court with a deed, so authenticated, that Messieurs D'Anguilhem would suffer a shameful defeat in all their claims.

Meanwhile, matters proceeded with their accustomed slowness. Justice is not only blind, but halt. The chevalier experienced a most bitter disgust for every road that led to the Palais de Justice and the Sainte Chapelle. But yet he found himself in the environs once in every week at least, in his coach, or rather, in that of the Marquis de Crette. This was generally the day after he had received his weekly letter from the baron.

If he had not been in some measure the guest of the Marquis de Crette, if he had not found there at the same time friend, banker, and counselor, he would probably have asked mercy of the Malay, who was so well supplied with the sinews of war.

But it was the "authentic document" that troubled Tancrede's mind most. As to the Baron of d'Anguilhem, who saw a fresh subject for uneasiness in every new letter he received from his son, he could not sleep. "Endeavor," said he, "to discover what this document is; whether it be a will, a deed of gift, or a substitution."

Tancrede sought, but could not find.

He assembled his council, composed of the Marquis de Crette, D'Herbigny, Clos-Renaud, and Chastellux, to consider what was best to be done.

There was a certain M. Velliere, clever at abstracting all sorts of things, such as bringing concealed papers to light, gauging safety chests, and even stealing deeds and titles if he were well paid to do it. In this case, however, it was understood that stealing the document put in by the adverse party was not to be thought of for a moment. But it was thought a copy might be obtained for Tancrede's counsel. Yet this proposition was rejected by the council of gentlemen as dishonorable.

One day D'Herbigny believed he had found a means of smoothing matters a little. In passing the gate of La Conference, he recognized, by the description Tancrede had given him, the Malay, seated in his coach with a woman who had formerly been a mistress of the viscount's, and who was at the present time, as it appeared, on the best terms with the chevalier's adversary. As a true friend, D'Herbigny believed that the moment had arrived for terminating the lawsuit which disturbed the peace and jeopardized the fortune of the Anguilhems.

He made a sign to the coachman to stop, and impudently approached the door, looking very hard at the lady, who belonged to the Comedie Francaise; her name was Mademoiselle Poussette.

Mademoiselle Poussette, who recognized in D'Herbigny an old lover that she was still very fond of, smiled tenderly upon him.

"*Pardieu!* monsieur and madame," said D'Herbigny, "what say you to we three taking a nice little supper together to-night? I think we can amuse ourselves—"

"I do not know you," said the Malay, sharply, his eye becoming very yellow; "and I do not sup with strangers."

"But I am no stranger to madame, and I am sure she will tell you I am very good company. Poussette, my dear, I beg you will do me the pleasure of introducing me to monsieur—"

"I present to you Monsieur Viscount D'Herbigny," said Poussette, laughing at the impertinence of her old lover.

"Oh! D'Herbigny! D'Herbigny!" said the Malay, "I remember that name. You are a friend of the little D'Anguilhem, and you come to pick a German quarrel with me in order to get the inheritance of Monsieur de Bouzenois. My lawyer has informed me of this possibility."

"I have the honor of being one of the friends of Monsieur d'Anguilhem, who, by the bye, is a head taller than you or I. But you do me a mortal injury to suppose me capable of any such intention. Therefore, monsieur, I hold you for a very rude savage, and I beg you to say at what time and place my seconds may confer with yours."

"Good! you are all trying for the same thing, only you take different roads; it is always a duel you want to entangle me in. Now let me gain my cause, and then we shall see."

This conclusion appeared so ridiculous to D'Herbigny, that he burst out laughing.

"*Pardieu!*" said he to the Malay. "You are a very droll fellow, and I shall be delighted to sup with you; nothing would please me better than to cultivate your acquaintance. If you are so agreeable now, you must be charming when you are drunk."

"Another trick of Anguilhem's! you want to poison me," said the Malay.

"Ah! you are a baboon!" said Mademoiselle Poussette, "and I will not remain another minute in your coach. Open the door, D'Herbigny! I will sup with you, I will."

D'Herbingy quickly opened the door, and Mademoiselle de Poussette stepped on to the pavement; then, after taking leave of the nabob—the one by a slight inclination of her head, the other by a low bow—they walked off arm in arm.

Then mademoiselle related to him that this man was the most ridiculous person she had ever seen; that he spoke of nothing but his inheritance, and fancied he saw in every one who approached him an emissary of the chevalier; and this very day he had asked the lieutenant of police for an escort, but could not obtain one.

To D'Herbingy things looked serious; and next morning he went to the Marquis de Crette, and related what he had heard. The marquis concluded that the Malay had already spent much money, and had, in all probability, the support of the secretary of the admiralty, where Monsieur de Bouzenois had very good connections.

Tancrede, in his last letter, communicated these disa greeable facts to his father. Day by day the symptoms became more and more alarming. Soon the rumor spread abroad that the Malay had shown the three judges the precious document, and that the three judges had assured him he would gain his cause.

This news was like a thunderbolt among the D'Anguilhem party. The little council of friends now regarded the matter as desperate. They began, therefore, to consider how they should find the money necessary to pay the enormous expenses of the suit, and the damages which would be required by the step-son of M. de Bouzenois. They estimated the expenses at 16,000 francs; besides, Coquenard claimed for his costs 4000 francs. Then the sojourn of Tancrede had cost, including the advances made to him by his friends, nearly 5000 francs. The suit lost, all the baron's little property was gone; and the sad day was fast approaching when the dismal truth must be unveiled.

The Marquis de Crette was a true friend to the chevalier under these trying circumstances. He offered him 6000 crowns, to be repaid when convenient. Tancrede replied that neither he nor his father would accept of a sum which they knew at the time they had no means of repaying. He declared that he would sustain the blow on his own resources; and if he lost his cause, he would enlist in one of the regiments going to Flanders.

D'Herbigny, on his side, did all that he could. By his influence with Mlle. Poussette, he obtained from her a promise that when she returned to the Malay she would satisfy herself as to the existence of the precious document, and of its contents also; and if it did exist, upon what grounds the Malay supported his pretensions.

On his part, the chevalier had found his advocates, Branchu and Verniquet, and begged them to omit nothing in their plea. But, in spite of all the pride natural to practitioners, they shook their heads, and complained that they were engaged in a very poor case. Tancrede pressed them, and they admitted that the three judges with whom they had conferred about the case had given them no hopes. They advised the chevalier to visit them again, and vigorously caress the cat, monkey and parrot, which formed the delight of these respectable jurisconsuls. But this was like the advice physicians give to their patients when they recommend them to take the waters, so as not to be reproached with any negligence. If they had known, they said, that the opposite party was in possession of a title like that they heard of, nothing in the world would have induced them to take charge of this case. Tancrede, who could not, nor dared not, promise them mountains of gold, bowed his head before these dismal forebodings; and as he was only his father's agent, he faithfully transmitted to him everything that was unpleasant in the reports of the advocates.

But it was in his letter to the baroness that all his despair found vent. To her he not only deplored the loss of the cause, and, consequently, the loss of his fortune, but also— the cruelest loss of all—the loss of Constance. For amid all his dinners, duels, parties, sports, and visits, be it said to the praise of the chevalier, never was the image of Mlle. de Beuzerie absent from his heart.

He communicated to Crette the advice his advocates had given him to make another and last attempt on the virtue of the judges. He filled his pockets with giblets for the cat, with almonds for the monkey, and macaroons for the parrot; but so far from appreciating his polite attentions, the cat scratched him, the monkey grinned at him, and the parrot called him a "rascal."

"You are a ruined man," said the marquis to the chevalier, upon quitting the house of the third judge; "you will lose your cause, and have to pay all the expenses."

That evening the conduct of the judges and their respective animals was explained to Tancrede and his friends by Mlle. Poussette. As the judges were men of probity, they had no desire to receive bribes. But the Malay had given a bag of 2000 pistoles to the cat, a donation of 10,000 crowns to the monkey, and settled a pension of 3000 francs on the parrot.

As to the judge advocate, every attempt upon his virtue had failed. His door was as firmly closed against the Malay as against the chevalier, and he was not known to possess any animal, wild or domestic, to which could be offered purses of gold, donations, or annuities.

Tancrede and the marquis made another forlorn attack upon him, but with no better success than at the first.

Master Bouteau, the judge advocate, was a man of inflexible integrity.

It may easily be imagined that all these profound disappointments, following each other in quick succession, had, notwithstanding his happy disposition and cheerful temper, gradually led the chevalier into a state of settled melancholy. The prospect of the utter ruin of his family, of the loss of Constance, whom he had recovered only to be sep-

arated from her a second time more cruelly than at first,
and of service as a simple volunteer in the army, was certainly very desperate. Thus the chevalier mourned, and
would not be comforted. He refused to go to the parties
his friends had arranged for the purpose of distracting his
mind, and passed all his time in his room at the Golden
Candlestick, in writing letters to his mother, or in making
elegies on Constance. For we must add that, as a last
misfortune, with melancholy there came a taste for writing
poetry.

CHAPTER XVIII.

ONE morning, as Tancrede was admiring himself in a
little mirror, examining the ravages grief had produced,
and repeating the lines of a verse of very bad poetry, upon
Mlle. Constance, he heard distinctly three loud knocks
upon his door.

"Come in," said D'Anguilhem.

The door was slowly opened by the person who had
knocked, and he came in.

He was a man whose face bore a most marvelous resemblance to the physiognomy of a fox. He was evidently
a myrmidon of the law, one of the vermin who prowl and
prey in the purlieus of law-courts. During the four months
that Tancrede had frequented the hall of the *Pas Perdus*,
he had learned to recognize this class, and his fingers itched
to wring their necks whenever he encountered them. The
visitor had red hair, smoothed down over his forehead. He
had a large black mole on each cheek, his eyes were irides-
cent, like opals. Between his teeth a great vacuum was
visible, and his nose and chin were in close proximity to
each other.

"Good," said the chevalier to himself. "Some new
adventure is about to befall me. If I have to pay in advance, my last pistole and I must soon part company. No
matter, let us put a good face on the matter."

And he quietly awaited the initiative from the worthy
with the black warts and firm step.

The unknown bowed almost to the ground.

"Have I the honor," said he, "of addressing Monsieur
Tancrede, Chevalier d'Anguilhem, Lord of Anguilhem,
Guerite, Pintade, and other places?"

Tancrede, for a moment, thought he really was lord and master of all these places, and could not easily undeceive himself. Somewhat astonished at the preamble, he replied, in a firm tone:

"Yes, monsieur, I am that person."

"Have you any one concealed behind your bed, or under it?"

"No one, that I am aware of," replied he; "and permit me to remark that your question appears to me a very singular one."

"Yet a very natural one, you must admit. I might have disturbed you with a mistress or friend. Such a fine-looking fellow can want for neither one nor other, I am sure. You might have had with you a mistress or a friend, as I was saying, and in order to receive me more at your ease, you may have concealed them where I said."

"I was alone, monsieur, and there is no person in this room besides ourselves."

"Will you permit me to satisfy myself on that score?"

"*Parbleu*, monsieur, it is very strange you will not take my word!"

"Oh, I believe what you say, of course, Monsieur le Chevalier," said the unknown, looking under the bed, "I believe you, because I know you to be a gentleman and a man of honor. But without your knowledge, or permission, some inquisitive person may have slipped in unperceived—"

And the unknown opened a cupboard, and put his head in to examine it.

"Good," he said, "there is no one here."

"What devil has sent me this original?" the chevalier asked himself.

"And the walls? are they pretty thick?"

"You had better measure them yourself," said D'Anguilhem, "for you really begin to make me very impatient."

"Do not excite yourself, monsieur—do not excite yourself. I very humbly ask your pardon for requiring all these precautions. but you will soon understand that they are not altogether unnecessary."

"Go on, then, sir, go on, look wherever you please, under the bed, in the bed, behind the bed, in the cupboard, behind the curtains; and if you want the keys of my secretaire, say so, and you can have them."

The unknown availed himself of the permission, and

looked everywhere; threw a glance at the wardrobe to see if it was large enough to contain a man, and was apparently satisfied with the inspection, for when the chevalier was about to hand him the keys, he politely declined them.

"Now, Monsieur le Chevalier," said the unknown, "now that I am quite satisfied that we are alone, I crave the honor that you will pay close attention to what I say, for I wish to speak with you on a matter of the greatest importance."

"Good or bad?"

"As you choose; it will be just which you choose to make it." And he went to the chamber door, and locked and bolted it.

The chevalier threw a glance at the sofa, where his sword was lying, for he began to think, as the Malay did, that this was a messenger of evil dispatched by the opposite party.

The unknown interpreted this glance, and attempted to measure Tancrede by a smile and a gesture, at the same time helping himself to a chair, which he placed beside the sofa where the chevalier was seated. Tancrede, by an involuntary movement, changed his position on the sofa.

The unknown remarked this second movement, as he had done the first, and put on a hideous smile, as much as to say, " Yes, yes, I see you have not much confidence in me —but wait awhile."

Our hero did wait. The unknown looked around, as if the assurance that he was still alone with the chevalier did not satisfy him, and stretching out his neck, threw these words, as it were, into Tancrede's ear:

"Monsieur, have you any objection to getting married?"

Tancrede looked steadily at his interlocutor, who, believing him to be a little deaf, repeated the question in a louder tone.

"Married?" repeated the chevalier, stupefied.

"Married!" replied the unknown, with the same hideous smile.

"But what sort of a marriage?" asked Tancrede.

"How? what sort of a marriage? why, a real marriage."

"I do not understand," said Tancrede; "but proceed."

"Then," said the unknown, "I must put the question in another fashion."

"Put it, sir."

"Have you any desire to gain your lawsuit?"

"Whew! Have I not? Can I desire anything better?"

"Good," said the unknown. "Then we are likely to understand each other."

"We understand!" said the chevalier, drawing a little nearer to the stranger.

"Very well, my gentleman, I am the man that can gain it for you! Your suit, ha, hah! Your suit, ha, hah!"

The chevalier drew nearer to the unknown, and, in his enthusiasm, was ready to throw his arms round his hideous neck; but a sudden thought made him pause.

Poor human nature, which believes it has its sympathies and its antipathies, when it has only its interests at heart.

"Gain my suit!" said Tancrede. "Then you must be the devil himself."

"Perhaps I am; you will see by and by."

"What must be done to get it?" asked Tancrede.

"Oh, *mon Dieu,* almost nothing."

"But what?"

"You must marry, that's all."

Tancrede looked at the unknown a second time, but more scrutinizingly than before, and began to think he was dealing with a lunatic or a fool.

"Provided he does not become furious, the thing is very amusing," said the chevalier to himself. Then, as the silence was not broken, Tancrede being satisfied with talking to himself, and as this was not satisfactory to the unknown, he resumed the discourse.

"Well?"

"And you say then—"

"You will have to marry, I said, Monsieur D'Anguilhem."

"I marry, I?"

"You, yourself. Understand that another will not do so well."

"You joke! but proceed."

"If I had the honor of being better known to you," said the marriage-broker, "you would never suspect me of joking."

"Then the matter is really serious?"

"Very serious, very serious indeed: and I must beg of you to consider it from that point of view."

"So I must marry?"

"Must I repeat it? Yes!"

"And whom?" asked Tancrede, with an effort.

"Ah! whom?" echoed the unknown, with his frightful smile. "Ah! whom? There is a very important word required to fill up that gap."

"Doubtless, but whom?" replied Tancrede. "Do not think, sir, that I am going to buy 'a pig in a poke,' as they say at Loches."

"But, Monsieur D'Anguilhem, that is just what you will have to do, when you marry."

"Are you quite sure you are in your senses?" asked Tancrede.

"What if I am sure?"

"It is, that in the contrary case, as the joke may be carried on too long, I must inform you that I am rather pressed for time. I have an engagement, and I wish to finish this game we are playing as quickly as possible."

"It is by no means a game, monsieur," replied the unknown, with a serious air; "or if it is a game, your future fortune is staked upon it, and you may gain 1,500,000 francs."

"Then," replied Tancrede, "for God's sake explain yourself clearly, and without further preface."

"Are you already in love with any one?" inquired the unknown, fixing his little opaline eyes upon him with a scrutinizing glance. The chevalier shuddered involuntarily, for the glance seemed to penetrate his inmost thoughts.

"As for that," said he, blushing prodigiously, "excuse me, sir, from replying."

"I will respect your secret, sir, since you ask it. I shall then have the right of asking you to respect mine."

"But you! That is quite another thing," cried the chevalier.

"How is it quite another thing?"

"You ought to tell me, especially to one who—"

"On the contrary, Monsieur le Chevalier, you are the last person to whom I ought to tell it; but I can not prevent you from guessing it."

"Ah, that is very good; thanks for the permission, sir; unfortunately, I am not very clever at guessing riddles."

"In that case it is a study you will have to make, for I can only repeat what I have already said to you."

"Sir," said Tancrede, rising, "you understand—"

"Yes, sir, I understand that you are a very disinterested person," said the unknown, rising also, "and that it matters very little to you whether you gain your suit or lose it. A mere trifle, after all, for a gentleman like you, is a sum of 1,500,000 francs, more or less."

"Pshaw!" said Tancrede, "bagatelle! No, sir, I can not treat the matter as you do; but, to be candid, I can not marry thus—the absurdity—"

"Sir, sir," said the unknown, with an air of profound commiseration for Tancrede's ignorance, "I tell you, you do not know what you refuse."

"But, monsieur, in case I consent to enter upon a negotiation, must I go on with it?"

"A negotiation of this kind, once entered upon, must be carried to a proper conclusion."

"Then it is a positive engagement you now ask of me?"

"Positive."

"That I engage to marry—"

"A name, in blank."

"That would not be common sense."

"Still allow—"

"Never, sir, never."

"Is that your determination?"

"Final and supreme."

"Reflect once more."

"I have reflected, or rather, I never can reflect upon such an absurdity. I marry, without knowing who—without having seen my intended—without having spoken to her—without knowing whether she be young or old—fair or plain—stupid or sensible. Why, my good sir, you must be out of your mind."

"And your lawsuit?" said the unknown, taking up his hat. This ill-looking fellow had so much assurance that Tancrede was disconcerted. He walked with heavy strides from the alcove to the windows, from the door to the cupboard, and then returned to the sofa, and threw himself down upon it, and furtively glanced at his interlocutor, who, with the most natural air possible, quietly stroked his chin.

"But, sir," said the chevalier, who was the first to break silence, "will you not really give me some information?"

"I would gladly, if I dare, on my honor, but I am expressly forbidden to do so."

"Tell me, only, if the young person—hem!" said Tancrede, interrupting himself—" is she young, though?"

The unknown continued stroking his chin, without uttering a word.

" See now! Is she fair or dark?"

No answer.

" But surely I may be permitted to inquire if my intended is a maid—or widow."

Not a word from the unknown.

" Ah!" said Tancrede, striking his forehead, " on my word, I shall go mad!"

"I shall leave you now, till to-morrow, sir, to reflect upon my proposal," said the stranger.

" And to-morrow?" inquired the chevalier.

" To-morrow I shall return at the same hour I come to-day."

" Alone?"

" No! I shall bring with me the promise of marriage."

" The promise of marriage!" cried Tancrede, growing pale.

" Oh! that binds nobody," said the unknown, " you sign only when you please to do so. Rest easy, my gentleman," he added, laughing with his usual grimace, " we shall not force you to do anything against your will."

This said, the mysterious unknown bowed more respectfully than he had done upon entering the room, and departed.

For a long time after he had gone, Tancrede sat, horrified, with his moist brow resting on his trembling hands.

CHAPTER XIX.

TANCREDE remained for some time stupefied by the weight of the blow that had fallen upon him, but, at length, collecting all his energy, he rose, took up his hat, and hastened to his greatest support—his only resource—the Marquis de Crette.

Fortunately the marquis was at home.

" What is the matter, chevalier? Have you lost your cause?"

The chevalier's dejected appearance warranted the marquis in asking this question.

"No! thank God, not yet," said Tancrede; "it will not be decided for three days to come, and in three days, and then—"

"And then—?" repeated the marquis.

"And then I have some hope of gaining it," said the chevalier, sighing deeply.

"It seems to me you need not sigh so deeply at such a prospect."

"No doubt it appears so to you who do not know the conditions."

"Ah! are there conditions?"

"Alas!" said our hero, throwing himself into the arms of his friend.

"Speak! What are they? You alarm me, chevalier."

The chevalier then related to the marquis his singular interview with the mysterious stranger. Crette listened to the recital with the greatest attention. When the chevalier had concluded, he said:

"This is really something very strange. It must be some bastard of Bouzenois that they wish to establish in a good position, or, perhaps, *mon Dieu*—my poor friend!"

"Perhaps what?" cried Tancrede, paling before the presentiment of the marquis.

"Or, perhaps, it is the old widow herself who wants another husband."

The chevalier trembled like an aspen; but a moment's thought reassured him.

"Impossible," said he, "she is dead."

"Then it is not very probable you have anything to dread from her."

"I am not quite so sure of that," said the youth. "I have seen people who were thought dead revive again."

"Oh, *mon Dieu!*" cried the marquis.

"But I believe," said Tancrede, "it is not she in this case."

"Then we must look in some other direction. Perhaps it is a trick of your adversary. What say you?"

"I have thought of that; but what interest can Monsienr Afghano have in getting me married and taking his inheritance?"

"We can not tell; do you still hesitate?"

"Yes, certainly; but my hesitation will not gain me a day. To-morrow I must give my answer. Yes or no."

"Consult your father."

"But my father is fifty-five leagues away from here. Then I must confess to you, marquis, I can not marry in this fashion. I love, I idolize a young lady of my country. An angel, who is attached to me by as strong an affection as I feel for her, and who will die if I marry another."

"Do you believe that?" said Crette, with an air of doubt.

"I am sure of it. She has given me her word."

"To die?"

"No, but to live only for me."

Then Tancrede related to the marquis all his adventures with Constance, but without pronouncing her name.

"Follow your inclinations, my friend; then you will have no reproaches to cast upon yourself; if you love made-moiselle better—Would it be impertinent in me to ask her name?"

"Not at all! It is Constance de Beuzerie."

"The little one promised—*diable!*"

"You ask then?"

"I ask if you love Mademoiselle de Beuzerie better than an income of sixty thousand a year?"

"If I was alone I should love her better than my fortune, better than my life; better than anything; but it happens that I have a father and mother who adore me, and who will be ruined if I refuse."

"You are right," said Crette. "Your duty stands before your inclination, that, my friend, you fully understand; it is an act of conscience that alone can determine you."

The answer was a profound sigh.

The marquis became pensive and thoughtful, and continued so for some time; when suddenly he startled our hero by seizing him by the hand.

"You are a man thrice lost," said he. "I can guess from whence this strange proposal of marriage has proceeded."

"Bah!" cried Tancrede, in terror.

"The gentleman with the moles is some judge, some assessor, or other legal functionary, who has a humpbacked daughter he wishes to dispose of to the best advantage."

"Marquis, do not tell me of such things, I pray you. It makes my flesh creep."

"We must tell the truth to our friends, you know. Besides," continued the marquis, "speak of it to your father, and ask his advice; but as for me, I have no doubt of it."

"There is yet another thing—" replied the victim, in a dolorous voice. "It may be that one of those legal gentleman we have spoken of has a daughter who—"

"I may think, but I must not say what I think. Which of the two deformities do you prefer? For my part, I must say I should prefer the incurable deformity."

"It is a horrible alternative," cried Tancrede, furiously.

"Nevertheless you must choose," said the marquis; "there is no medium. You must either lose your suit, or jump into the abyss with your eyes shut."

"Horrible! most horrible."

"My poor friend," said Crette, as the painful situation of the chevalier moved him to tears. "You are in a trap; —but you must not despair before the second visit of your unknown. Take advantage of the opportunity you will have with this devil of a man; turn, and turn him again, on all sides, ask all sorts of questions, exact what you require. If he refuses you, refuse him. I will conceal myself at the door. I will follow the demon, even to the gates of Hades, and we shall at least have the satisfaction of revenging ourselves. I will respond to your wishes."

"Yes! but I shall lose my cause."

"But, my dear friend, you can not have everything!" As nothing that the chevalier and marquis could advance would let much light on the matter, the former returned to his hotel, and sat down to write to his father; but he soon recollected that a letter was five days in going to Loches and five in returning, which would make ten days, supposing the baron to reply by return of post. Now the judgment in his suit would be given in three days; so that it was physically impossible to receive an answer from Anguilhem in time. The poor boy would have still· required a powerful impulse from his father to take any steps in the matter.

He remained, then, dependent on his own resources, weeping bitter tears, and tearing the hair from his head, despairing of the future, and calling upon Constance and the scenes of his youth, Pintade, Guerite, Garenne, and every place where he had been happy.

He reproached himself with his folly in admiring the profound words of the marquis, when the latter listened to the pastoral amours of Tancrede at Beuzerie, of the apparition of Constance in the bed-chamber, and their flight to La Chapelle Saint Hippolyte.

"How very simple you were, D'Anguilhem!—very natural, my pretty! My poor friend, you were very foolish!"

And Tancrede repeated, "Oh, yes, I was very simple, very natural, very foolish."

We see that his residence in Paris began to operate beneficially upon him.

But there stood grim necessity, stretching forth its iron hand. Every minute was worth a day, and every day had the importance of a year. On the morrow, the mysterious unknown, inexorable as time, punctual as death, would knock at his door, and—

The night was passed in seeking a means of escape out of his critical position; but it is scarcely necessary to say that he found none.

The day came, and he awaited his visitor armed with a host of new proposals and an arsenal of insidious questions.

The stranger did not keep him waiting. He came at the appointed hour, to the minute, even to the second. Tancrede, who kept his ear at the key-hole of his door, heard the sound of his footsteps as he ascended the staircase. Then he stopped before the door, knocked three times, and at the words, "Come in," pronounced in a trembling voice, the door opened, and the fatal messenger entered more humble, more obsequious, and more amiable than the day before.

With a glance he surveyed the chamber.

"Are we alone?"

"Search!" said D'Anguilhem.

The unknown renewed his search with the same scrutiny as the day before. This finished, he approached his victim, who, seated on a chair, pale as death, awaited his doom.

"Well! Monsieur le Chevalier, have you considered?"

"More than that," said our hero; "I have guessed; therefore let us speak freely, and terminate this suspense."

"That is my most earnest wish, sir," replied the unknown, bowing.

"You are sent by some one who has a daughter he wishes to get rid of."

"Get rid of? that is a very harsh expression, monsieur."

"Do not cavil at a word. Unfortunately, I am only too sure that it is true."

"Nevertheless, I hope to rectify your opinion."

"Now, this father is one of my judges, is he not?" said Tancrede, looking steadily into the opaline eyes of the unknown.

The unknown looked with much astonishment, mingled with admiration.

"My faith, yes, sir," said he; "you have guessed aright."

"Ah! I was sure of it," said the youth, with a triumphant air.

"Well, go on! what does that knowledge lead you to?"

"It leads me to be sure that I shall lose my cause if I do not marry."

"And to the certainty that you will gain it if you do."

"That is very sad," said our lover.

"Ah, sir," said the unknown, "you are wrong to grumble. You are on the high-road to fortune. Keep on, chevalier, keep on; I can say no more."

"Yes, and I, a gentleman by honor, upon which he has nothing to say. I shall have married the daughter of the man who has sold justice."

"Oh! you view things under a most deplorable aspect, Monsieur d'Anguilhem," replied the unknown; "and, as this way of looking at them is absurd, allow me to apply that expression. A man who has good credit in the world, obliges his friends, and the law of gratitude, which is the law of noble hearts, being established, his friends in their turn oblige him in exchange for his good offices."

"Yes, I understand that very well, but the lady—"

"Well, the lady?"

"Is she unmarried?"

The unknown laughed.

"Or a widow?"

The unknown laughed still louder.

"The devil," cried the chevalier. "I believe you are mocking me!"

"God forbid, chevalier. I only laughed at your apprehensions."

"Which are quite unfounded, perhaps," replied D'Anguilhem; "while you compel me to buy a cat in a bag."

"Your surprise will be all the greater, Monsieur d'Anguilhem."

" Ah! I will endeavor to content myself with that, sir, only let me see the lady—the young person—my intended —the lady in question—"

"Impossible!"

" Then the father! let me see the father—that is surely not asking too much—hem?"

"On the contrary, monsieur, it is asking everything. When you have seen the father, you will know in twenty-four hours who the daughter is."

"Stop! you will make me mad," said D'Anguilhem.

" Look you here, Monsieur le Chevalier," replied the unknown in his blandest tone, " do not excite yourself in this manner; the thing is not to be despised, believe me, and you will repent of having made any difficulty, for in giving way to all these little considerations, which it pains me to see have an absurd influence upon you, you will lose a fortune of 1,500,000 francs, and a suit involving some thirty or forty thousand; while, by marrying, you make sure of a million and a half, besides furniture worth 60,-000; diamonds, jewels, worth more than a hundred and fifty thousand, without reckoning the ready money in the cash-box, which is very heavy, I assure you. I felt the weight of it when I put on the seals."

" Ah! tell me—just one more question."

" Put it, sir, put it, and if I can answer it, I will."

" How happens it, sir," said Tancrede, " that my future father-in-law has not offered his daughter to Monsieur Afghano, my adversary?"

" Because he felt it his duty to give you the preference."

"I am much obliged to him."

"Then, again, the Malay is ugly, and you are quite handsome. Then, perhaps, your adversary may be a very great man in his own country, but here his nobility is not recognized; besides, the name of D'Anguilhem sounds much better in the ear of a Frenchman than the harsh, savage word Afghano. Madame Afghano! Madame Afghano—you understand? Think of announcing that title at court; but notwithstanding all that, if you refuse to-day—"

" Well, if I refuse to-day, what then?"

"I shall call upon Monsieur Afghano to-morrow."

" But the father desires a position for his daughter."

"She has arrived at the age when she ought to have one."

"Oh! yes! I believe it. I had better go hang myself."

"Monsieur, I repeat to you, you have no occasion to do anything so foolish. You talk like a child. You will get 1,500,000 francs, they will be put into your hands, and remove you from this miserable little room to a palace; and you think hanging preferable. Really you are to be pitied."

"Well, well! let us come to terms, monsieur," said D'Anguilhem. "He who sent you, will he take one hundred, two hundred, three hundred thousand francs? I will yield them, offer them, I give them to him."

"What you propose is not common sense, chevalier; this hundred thousand francs you offer are already required of you; they are the dowry of your future wife, which you must pay yourself."

"What? my wife's dowry?"

"Yes; by marrying the girl, you pay for her with 100,000 crowns; that is very natural, it seems to me, when your father-in-law that is to be gains for you 1,500,000."

"You said girl, sir," cried the chevalier. "You said *girl!* ah, you said *girl!* the lady *is* young, then?"

"Happy, too happy D'Anguilhem. Accept! I say to you, accept!"

"Listen. You know me. I begin to see daylight. There is nothing mysterious in me, and I throw the cards on the table."

"Well, play your game to the end, and play it well."

"I seek nothing better; but I must have a mark of your confidence, a proof of your influence," said Tancrede.

"What is it?"

"Have the judgment, which is to be given the day after to-morrow, postponed for ten days; and in change for this favor, I will give you my word upon two conditions."

"What are they?"

"The lady will not be counterfeited: and will not have, or rather she will have—"

"I understand, chevalier."

"Well!" said Tancrede.

"Agreed."

"How, agreed? You tell me that—"

"Yes." said the unknown.

"In that case you have my word."

"In ten days, then?"

"In ten days," replied the chevalier.

"I will be here on the morning judgment is given."

"I shall expect you."

"All in good time, chevalier, all in good time. Ah! you are born under a lucky star, Monsieur d'Anguilhem!" The unknown took up his hat, and went out, saluting the chevalier more humbly than ever.

Five minutes afterward he returned in a state of great excitement.

"Monsieur," said he, "perhaps you thought a bold stroke would save you, and that is why you placed your friend, the Marquis de Crette, in ambush at twenty paces off your hotel; there he is in his coach. Do not deny it, I recognize his livery and his arms. But you are very foolish. You ought to know yourself better. The delay granted is a pledge for you as well as for me. If in the interval anything betrays our projects, if anything whatever transpires, if any proceeding on your part gives us umbrage, I, the sole witness, mark that, the only witness, will deny everything, and you will lose your cause with shame."

Tancrede was terrified at this new threat, which his secret intentions had deservedly drawn upon him. For, as we have said, he plotted with the marquis to discover the mystery, and throw upon his persecutors a little of the annoyance they had put upon him. Now, seeing himself discovered, he was quite disconcerted.

"What can I do to satisfy you, sir?" inquired he of the unknown.

"Go out first, sir," replied the latter; "and when I have seen you go away with the marquis I shall go my own way."

Tancrede took up his hat sorrowfully, and obeyed, the mysterious unknown following slowly behind him. He found Crette in his coach, and informed him they were discovered. They ordered the coachman to drive to the Luxembourg, where they stayed conversing some time.

Meanwhile the mysterious visitor regained his residence unobserved.

"Nothing more can be done," said the marquis to the chevalier, "except to consider how you will amuse yourself and distract your mind for the next ten days, to soften the blow which you can not avoid. After all, my dear chevalier, consider the thing as done, and that you have married badly. Besides, you may easily console yourself if you look about you, and observe by how many strange family circles you are surrounded."

"Yes, but these wives have entered their circles by the front door, while I am going to be dragged down the chimney. What will all our friends think?"

"They need know nothing but what you choose to tell them—need they? Well. It is probable that the father-in-law will not boast much of the novel method he has invented of lighting the nuptial torch!"

"Alas! have you not yourself told me more than once that all Paris would know of it?"

"Nearly all; but we can disguise the truth a little. Remember what the Jesuits taught you at Amboise; and as you have studied philosophy, why not be a philosopher?"

"Ah, marquis, it is very easy for you to say that. But say, marquis, tell me frankly, would you marry? Say—"

"I, the Marquis de Crette, possessing sixty thousand a year, as I do, without the property of my mother—no! I avow it, I would not marry this girl without seeing her. But—but if I were Tancrede d'Anguilhem, who, in case of refusal, must die of hunger, I would marry Alecto herself; but as to living with her afterward, fighting and quarreling, I should give my horse the reins."

"You speak candidly?"

"On the word of a gentleman."

"But consider that I am in love," said Tancrede.

"That is a folly at all times; but now it is something worse: it is a misfortune!"

"Remember, I shall lose Constance."

"Bah! you know there are only a few mountains between you, and some fine day, you and Mademoiselle Constance will meet again under better circumstances."

"She will suspect the truth."

"You can give a very satisfactory explanation to her."

"She will, perhaps, curse me."

"In that case the wrong will be on her side; she will show herself unreasonable."

"She will not believe that I have any excuse for my infidelity,"

"You can say that your father has done it all, and she will think it is a revenge he has taken against De Beuzerie."

"But perhaps she will marry in her turn."

"So much the better for you if she does, my friend; so much the better for you. You will not then have on your conscience the remorse of having helped her to become an old maid. Then, when you are both married, you will each soon forget your childish romance. You will visit her at her country-house. You will hunt and shoot with her husband; you will invite him to dine with you, and while he will compliment your wife, you will compliment his. You will always have the advantage of him, for you will be sure that his wife loves you—"

"Ah! my dear Crette, if Madame de Maintenon were to hear you!"

"She would think herself forty years younger, that's all, my dear chevalier."

The two friends rose, and separated to their respective engagements.

CHAPTER XX.

THE chevalier and the marquis passed three whole days in running about. The valets were sifted, the *concierges* were spoken to, even the clerks themselves opened their teeth, according as the two friends employed adroit schemes and ingenious devices to discover what they wished to know.

But the result of all their inquiries was, that they found twelve judges and sixteen counselors were provided with daughters to marry, so that after all their trouble they were no wiser than when they first set out.

To some of these damsels the chevalier had a great repugnance, seeing that they were not rose-buds.

One had been surprised at night in a half-ruined cloister, behind the Rue Saint Benoit.

Another had made a journey to Picardy, without the company of either father, mother, aunt or governess; and there was a rumor that her companion in flight was a young musketeer, "her cousin."

A third had been recognized at Marly, quitting the notorious Veau Dore, in a hackney coach, at one o'clock in the morning.

However, there was nothing to show that Tancrede's in-tended was one of these three damsels, at the same time, there was no proof that she was not. It resulted from this unsatisfactory state of things, that our hero was plunged into the profoundest perplexity. Meanwhile, he was grati-fied to find that, in compliance with the desire he had ex-pressed to the mysterious unknown, the judgment was actually postponed ten days. This appeared to him a strik-ing evidence of the good faith of his persecutors, as well as of their influence in the court of justice.

On the ninth day after he had written to Anguilhem, that is to say, on the eve of the day upon which the judg-ment was to be rendered, he received a reply.

The baron had spared neither ink nor paper, for the let-ter filled eight large pages.

He informed the chevalier that he would himself have come to Paris, if the want of money had not kept him at home. He deplored the fatal necessity which oppressed his beloved son, and left him, in this instance, absolutely free to act according to the dictates of his heart, and the conclusions of his judgment. This appeared to Tancrede a trait of the most exquisite paternal delicacy, which, amid a thousand sobs, made him adopt the cruel resolution of giving up Constance, and securing the happiness of his parents.

"Do not be influenced by the thought of us," said the baron, in this model letter. "You are young, and have many years to live; do not imbitter your existence to soothe the rest of our brief term. This lawsuit will have ruined us; but that is of no consequence, as we are accustomed to privations. Besides, you have health, strength, good abil-ities, and influential friends, who will obtain lucrative em-ployment for you, by which you may soothe our last days, which can not, in the course of nature, be very distant."

Tancrede could read no further. He wiped away his tears and respectfully kissed the letter, and when the mys-terious visitor arrived—

"Monsieur," said the chevalier, "I am ready. What must I sign?"

"This," said the messenger; and he drew from his pocket a paper covered with writing.

"Good," said Tancrede, and he signed without reading it.

"*Pardieu,*" said the stranger, "you are a loyal gentle-man; and if you had some difficulty to decide, you act boldly when your mind is made up. Your generous indifference has done you no harm; now read it."

The chevalier read it with horrible anguish; trembling at every line lest he might encounter the name of one of the three notorious girls, but he had the happiness of seeing a name entirely unknown to him.

The paper was a deed binding him to marry Mme. Christine Sylvandire Bouteau, only daughter of Master Jean Amedee Bouteau, judge advocate, and king's counsel; and a gift to the said Christine Sylvandire Bouteau of a dowry of one hundred thousand crowns, upon the day when the most noble and honorable Seigneur Tancrede d'Anguilhem gained his suit against M. d'Afghano, step-son of the Viscount de Bouzenois.

Master Jean Amedee Bouteau was that austere judge advocate, who would neither receive Tancrede nor Afghano: he who had neither cat, monkey, nor parrot to whom they could offer neither purses, diamonds, nor annuities. But he had a daughter to marry.

"Is she very ugly, monsieur?" asked our hero.

"I have orders to answer none of your questions, Monsieur le Chevalier; make your toilet and follow me to the court, and hear the judgment which will be delivered in a couple of hours. After that, I shall have the honor of conducting you to Monsieur Bouteau, your father-in-law."

"What to do?" said the victim, with a gesture of fear, which prevented him from comprehending the incongruity of the question.

"In the first place, to return him thanks for giving you possession of a fortune of upward of a million and a half; and in the second place, to be introduced to your intended."

Tancrede felt his legs tremble under him.

"Quick, quick!" said the unknown. "I see very plainly you want to be alone, to dress yourself. You can go to the court your way, and I will go mine."

This time the mysterious gentleman went out very cavalierly; and Tancrede remarked the difference.

"That is always the way," said he, "he has got all he wanted, and now I may go to the—"

Then, as he had been advised by Master Bouteau's envoy, he proceeded to dress himself in his best.

But he felt heart-sick. He detested his future wife before seeing her, he was sure he should hate her. At the same time, by a touch of vanity, inherent to the heart of man, he was anxious that at the first interview he should not make a bad impression.

He put on a black velvet coat trimmed with gold, a white satin vest, richly embroidered; having meanwhile dispatched a messenger to the Marquis de Crette, who soon arrived in his most magnificent equipage.

Behind this coach came those of D'Herbigny, of Chastellux, and of Clos-Renaud. Mlle. Poussette followed last of all in a hackney coach.

The marquis went up alone to our hero's chamber.

As soon as he entered, Tancrede set up a wail of lamentation, crying—

"Alas! Alas! Alas!"

"It appears, then, that the sacrifice is made," said Crette.

"Done and finished. I have signed the bond. Poor Constance!"

"And—have you any further information as to your future?" inquired the marquis, hesitatingly.

"Her name is Sylvandire."

"The deuce it is, and a very charming name it is. That is something to begin with. But that is only a Christian name. What is the name of her family?"

"Bouteau. Mademoiselle Bouteau."

"Bouteau? Why that is the name of our judge advocate. It is *his* daughter, then?"

"The same. Alas! she is some little monster whom they have concealed from everybody, and which they now unkennel for my especial benefit."

"Say rather in favor of your barony. I have met this Master Bouteau before."

"And pray what sort of a man may my father-in-law be?"

"A Jew grafted on an Arab, and immensely rich, as you may be sure from his pedigree."

"And with all his riches, he is compelled to employ these means to get rid of his daughter. Ah, my friend, it is only filial devotion—"

"Your misfortunes, my dear chevalier, are greater than

those of any other man I ever knew. But you must not stop to mourn now, but come with me to the court. If your wife should prove quite intolerable, you must confine her, with her servants, to one wing of your mansion, and give her a hundred thousand for her support. You may be compelled to marry, but not to live with her. She will have to bear your name, which may not be very agreeable to you, but that is a trifle after all; and with the fourteen hundred thousand francs you will have left, you surely may contrive to make yourself comfortable, and perhaps happy. You have carefully read the agreement, it does not bind you to—"

"No."

"Well then, my dear friend, what have you got to complain of. Come along, let us get into the coach."

Crette carried off D'Anguilhem; at the doors of their coaches he saluted in succession D'Herbigny, Clos-Renaud, Chastellux, and Mlle. Poussette. He then got into the marquis's coach, and drove to the court.

Upon their arrival they found a great crowd assembled. The Malay wished to be present at the *denouement* of the drama. It was supposed that he had expended 50,000 francs in making himself agreeable to the judges. He had so confident an air, that Tancrede was ready to faint at the sight of him, and even the marquis turned pale.

The judges were in the ante-chamber deliberating.

At the expiration of an hour spent in deliberation, the court resumed its sitting. Our hero recognized the three judges and trembled. Behind them came, modestly, the judge advocate.

"What is the name of the judge advocate?" inquired he of a by-stander.

"Master Bouteau," replied his neighbor, "a very worthy man."

Tancrede endeavored to read something in the face of Master Bouteau, but he found it impossible.

The judges took their places with that grave imperturbable air peculiar to judges; their eyes wandered over the court, but fixed upon nothing.

Master Bouteau unfolded a paper.

"Courage," said Crette, in the ear of the chevalier, "that is our father-in-law."

"I know it."

Master Bouteau hemmed, coughed, and read as follows—

"Considering that Monsieur Afghano, *alias* ' the Malay,' can not supply the document which he ought to present to the court, and that there exists no authentic proof of his right to the succession; considering that Monsieur le Baron Tancrede Palamede d'Anguilhem, represented by his son Tancrede d'Anguilhem, is the nearest relation to the deceased, and that he has exhibited his titles fully establishing his relationship—

"It is therefore decreed by this court that Monsieur Tancrede Palamede D'Anguilhem do enter immediately into the full possession of the inheritance of the late Viscount de Bouzenois, comprising residences, furniture, and everything belonging to the said deceased, as he is justly entitled to do.

"Monsier Afghano is hereby condemned to pay all the expenses of this suit."

Master Bouteau pronounced this judgment without once looking at Tancrede, who remained seated on a bench.

The Marquis de Crette took his friend by the arm and whispered in his ear:

"D'Anguilhem, your father-in-law is a great man!"

"Yes, but wait a minute," said our hero, "the Malay is going to produce his precious document."

"He would not have waited till this time," replied Crette. "Make yourself quite easy. If he has not produced it before now, he never will; be sure of that. Besides, the judgment is given."

In fact the Malay produced no document at all, as he had boasted he could. Upon hearing the decision of the court he hung down his head, and appeared quite stupefied. In a few moments he raised it again, with an air of audacity, and, in a voice that could be heard not only by the judges, but also by the whole assembly, he said:

"My mother might have done better than to give everything to that wretch Bouzenois. This shows the folly of enriching those we love."

Tancrede felt the blood mount to his cheeks, and immediately moved toward the Malay to avenge the memory of the relation whose heir he had become.

"Are you mad?" said Crette, holding him back. "Let the wretch howl while they crucify him. Do not begin your new career by showing contempt of court. Your name is not Bouzenois, but D'Anguilhem, and, *pardieu*, the advocates have proved it."

At this moment the Malay directed his steps toward the group of friends. Tancrede believed he was about being attacked, and made ready to receive him. But the Malay passed by very near to them, scowling, but that was all; saying, as he passed, loud enough to be heard by every one:

"It was mean of you to betray me, Mademoiselle Poussette; but no matter. I have still a hundred thousand a year to spend."

"Take my compliments," said our hero; "for, sir, everybody will admit that it is a great deal more than you deserve."

"Come, come," said Crette, impatiently, "do not get into a quarrel with the fellow; he is nothing to you, after he has paid his costs. Let us go home and enjoy ourselves."

"Alas, Crette," replied D'Anguilhem, "you forget that I must now go and see my intended."

Now he had pronounced these words in a less sorrowful tone than he had spoken of that subject before. He thought of the pride of his father, of the joy of his mother, upon finding themselves so prodigiously rich. And the poor chevalier was so dutiful a son that he quite forgot to take into calculation how Constance would take the news.

We soon become accustomed to prosperity. Tancrede left the court with an air of consequential importance that would have done credit to a millionaire by birth.

Crette put the chevalier into his coach to go and pay the visit to Master Bouteau; then he took leave of his friend, reminding him that supper would be ready at eight o'clock.

Tancrede, upon turning his head, perceived the mysterious visitor, standing a few paces off, as if waiting for him.

"Master Bouteau," said he, "has left the court and gone home. Will Monsieur le Baron pay his respects to him now?"

"If convenient, my dear sir, I will. I am most anxious to do so."

"Good! Are you satisfied now, chevalier?"

"Thus far, I am. You have kept your word, it is true; but there are yet two other conditions to be fulfilled."

"And they will be complied with, sir, as exactly, let us hope, as the first has been."

"Do me the pleasure to get into my coach, sir, and let us go at once."

The unknown stepping in, placed himself on the front seat, notwithstanding Tancrede's entreaties that he would place himself beside him.

They soon arrived at the Rue Planche Mibray; and entering a house, ascended to the third story.

Master Bouteau was seated in his library. He was a little man, with an immense forehead, small eyes, concealed behind his spectacles, thick bushy eyebrows, a mouth imperceptibly lost in the folds of his cheek: in fact, an exceedingly ugly father-in-law. But as he was not the person Tancrede was engaged to marry, the chevalier saluted him warmly, and opened his mouth to return him thanks.

"Do not thank me, sir," said Master Bouteau. "You are under no obligations to me. You had a very good case: besides, I have followed the dictates of my conscience; and my colleagues, although a little prejudiced against you, soon yielded to my feeble arguments in favor of justice."

Tancrede saluted Master Bouteau a second time. The latter did not appear to examine the chevalier very closely: he was a man who seemed able to comprehend everything at a glance; still, in returning his salute, he peered at him from behind his spectacles. This examination finished, he turned toward a screen that stood behind him, and said in quite a natural, easy voice:

"My daughter, come and pay your respects to my client, Monsieur le Chevalier Tancrede d'Anguilhem."

Tancrede felt the earth sinking beneath his feet; a cold perspiration burst upon his forehead; his heart ceased to beat; a sense of suffocation came over him. He fixed his haggard eyes upon the corner of the screen, when lo!—

A most charming girl made her appearance.

Tall, of graceful figure, flexible, beautifully proportioned, black eyes veiled by long eyelashes, long curling hair which fell in thick masses upon her shoulders, white as ivory. Such was Sylvandire, who in her eighteenth year might be accepted as a prodigy of beauty.

At the sight of this rare vision our hero lost all presence of mind. He stood petrified with astonishment, without even saluting her. With fixed eyes and distended mouth he stood like the statue of Apollo about to speak.

"My child," continued the judge-advocate, taking Sylvandire by the hand, "this is Monsieur le Chevalier Tancrede d'Anguilhem, who has come to ask the honor of your hand in marriage."

Sylvandire raised her large black eyes, and threw a glance upon Tancrede that penetrated his very soul.

"I am lost," said he to himself; "such a beautiful creature must have already been loved by some one; certainly she can not have been kept in a glass case."

"Will you permit Monsieur le Chevalier d'Anguilhem to pay his addresses to you?" continued Master Bouteau.

Sylvandire looked again at the chevalier with a glance in which astonishment, fear, and passionate languor were singularly blended, but uttered not a word.

"Silence gives consent, Monsieur le Chevalier," observed Master Bouteau. "You must understand that Mademoiselle Sylvandire is my only daughter, and brings to her husband a dowry of 300,000 francs."

Sylvandire took his father's hand and pressed it in token of gratitude.

"*Pardieu!*" said Tancrede to himself; "he might as well give her six hundred thousand, as for what the money costs him. But no matter, I must still thank him, although he is so modest."

"And when shall the wedding take place, Monsieur le Chevalier?" asked Master Bouteau.

"It is for the lady to name the day, and if she will consent—"

Sylvandire again inclined her head without speaking.

"She is dumb," explained our hero, believing he had found the dreaded infirmity, and incapable of concealing the new fear that now seized upon him.

Sylvandire uttered a loud laugh upon hearing Tancrede's exclamation.

"No, sir, I am not dumb, thank God."

"Perhaps she is only stupid," thought the chevalier. "Yet such a pair of eyes never belonged to a fool. Impossible!"

But as this interview was embarrassing to all present, the judge advocate made a signal from the corner of his eye to

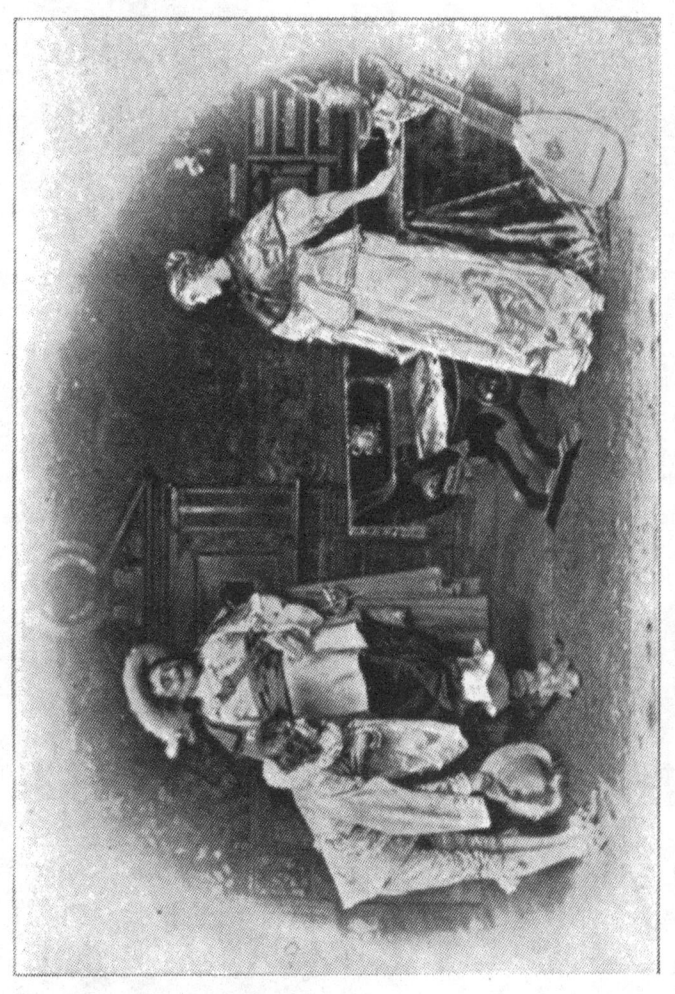

his daughter, who made her reverence, and was about to leave the room.

"How is this, mademoiselle?" cried Tancrede; "are you going without telling me when you will deign to—"

"I leave you to settle that with my father, monsieur," replied Sylvandire; "although a man of the law, he does not like to have business remain long on his hands. Whatever he does will be well done."

"Ah!" said he to himself, "I have again deceived myself. She? she is no fool; she is not stupid."

The bewildered chevalier wandered from one surmise to another. He was determined to find something wrong with his intended, but as yet found no clew to what that blemish was.

Sylvandire retired, leaving him alone with his future father-in-law.

The marriage was fixed to take place in fifteen days.

The arrangements made, Tancrede took leave of Master Bouteau, and descended the staircase with a much lighter step than he had mounted it.

At the street door he found his mysterious visitor.

"Well, sir," said the latter, "are you satisfied?"

"So well satisfied, monsieur," replied our hero, "that if the last condition is kept as faithfully as the first two, there are 1,000 louis for yourself, my good fellow."

"Then I can reckon that I have got them," said the unknown, bowing to the ground.

Tancrede heard this remark, and jumped into the coach without putting his foot on the step.

"Home, to the marquis!" cried he to Basque, in a voice in which nothing of his past fears could be detected.

CHAPTER XXI.

THERE was a large party at the marquis's.

Tancrede entered the drawing-room, beaming with delight and happiness. He was overwhelmed with congratulations and compliments.

The marquis waited until the storm of pretty phrases was over, then, taking his hand, he stepped with him into a boudoir.

"Well, my friend, the intended?"

"Charming!"

"As pretty as Constance?"

"Alas! much prettier!"

"Then what the deuce troubles you now?"

"Ah! my friend," murmured our hero heaving a profound sigh, "I was quite sure that Constance—"

"Ah, yes, I understand," said the marquis; "but what would you have, my dear friend? it may chance to be so. You ask too much. Consider yourself very happy, my friend, and be content. As for the rest, who knows? everything that has happened to you is so extraordinary!"

"Oh no, my friend, you can not persuade me that there is not a serpent concealed under all these roses. But as you wish, marquis. The die is cast, and then I have reflected that the bravest man in the world might be deceived in the situation in which I find myself. To know nothing of the past conduct of my wife! ah, well, I must be contented to watch her carefully for the future."

"All in good time. Come, be as I like to see you. Return to the drawing-room, put on a cheerful face. I will amuse the company. Happy millionaire!"

They sat down to supper. The plate-glass and wax-candles were resplendent. At this sight, Tancrede reflected that he, a few hours before a poor gentleman without fortune, could on the morrow, if he chose, receive a brilliant company in his own house, and display as much magnificence as was now shown in his honor.

"My dear friends," said the marquis, rising, "you are aware that we have met together this evening to celebrate the success of our young friend, the Chevalier d'Anguilhem, in gaining a suit which secures to him an income of 65,000 a year."

"It is to you I owe that happiness," said our hero, saluting the marquis.

"Then here's the health of the Chevalier d'Anguilhem and his 65,000 a year," cried all the guests.

"Wait a minute," cried the marquis, "and you shall drink two healths together, unless you prefer to drink them separately."

"Whose is the other?" asked D'Herbigny and Clos-Renaud, both in a breath.

"You must know," said the marquis, "that our friend D'Anguilhem has suddenly fallen in love, but you can not guess upon what delicate morsel the dainty gentleman has fallen."

"Upon a nun of Saint-Cyr, dowried by Madame de Maintenon?" said Chastellux.

"Upon a palatine princess?" said Clos-Renacd.

"Upon a daughter of the royal blood?" inquired D'Herbigny.

"Oh, yes! very likely, D'Anguilhem is noble enough for that, and he thinks as seriously. Upon a limb of the law, gentlemen."

"Pooh! pooh!" exclaimed several voices.

"Ah, chevalier," said D'Herbigny, "you can stoop lower than that. You can marry a lady of the Comedie Française, or a ballet-girl."

"Listen, gentlemen," said the marquis. "she is beautiful as Venus, and has a fortune of 600,000 francs."

"The deuce, chevalier; we make our compliments to you," cried the young gentlemen around the table.

"Upon which the chevalier will fix his residence in Paris; establish himself at the late residence of De Bouzenois, where he will give parties and suppers, but such suppers as ours will appear like those of a country inn by comparison."

"In that case, long live the chevalier and his lady!" cried D'Herbigny, raising his glass.

The company repeated this toast with acclamations.

"Now," continued the viscount, putting his glass on the table, "since you have started that game, my dear D'Anguilhem, perhaps you can find me a daughter of some colleague of your father-in-law, some pretty little she-lawyer. I will take her with 500,000."

"Then, here's to the future wedded happiness of Viscount D'Herbigny," said the Chevalier d'Anguilhem, raising his glass,

While the guests were drinking this toast, Tancrede turned quickly to the marquis, and took him by the hand.

"Thanks, marquis," said he. "You are good and kind, as ever."

In fact, Crette had saved his friend from all ridicule with regard to his marriage. It is also true, that Mlle. Bouteau's dowry of six hundred thousand had produced a magical effect.

The supper passed off so merrily, that D'Anguilhem

paid no heed to the march of time. It was two hours past
midnight before he quitted the marquis. They appointed
to meet at eleven o'clock in the morning, as the chevalier
wished the marquis to accompany him in his visit to the
late residence of De Bouzenois.

At the appointed hour the marquis called upon Tancrede,
and they then proceeded together to the Place Louis le Grand.
This time the doors of the great entrance opened before the
chevalier. The officers in the court had been waiting for
an hour to remove the seals.

Everything the mysterious stranger had told D'Anguilhem
proved scrupulously true and exact. The cash-box was
full and heavy. The cases were crammed with jewels.
The collection of cut stones, cameos, and coins, was truly
magnificent.

Tancrede was completely dazzled at the sight of so much
wealth and riches. He, who had arrived in Paris with fifty
louis, never supposed there was so much gold in the world
as he now saw. He wished to repay at once the eight or
ten thousand francs he owed to the Marquis de Crette, but
the marquis gave him to understand that he was in too
great haste, and that he would send Basque some fine morning for that trifle.

From among the heaps of diamonds and precious stones
Tancrede proceeded to make a choice selection to send to
his mother. Perhaps, in so doing, he also thought he
would like to do the same for Constance. For, although
he never uttered her name, Crette fully understood, from
the sighs that involuntarily escaped him, he had not completely forgotten her.

De Bouzenois's late mansion, although very sumptuous,
had not been arranged with much taste. It was therefore
necessary to refit it, and the marquis took charge of the
matter He sent for his upholsterer, and gave him eight
days to complete his task. The upholsterer replied that it
was impossible to complete so important an undertaking
in so short a time. Crette contented himself with replying:
" You will be paid the day after your work is finished."

On the seventh day the house was entirely refurnished.

Tancrede gratified his ambition; and the escutcheon of
the arms of De Bouzenois gave place to those of D'Anguilhem.

Meanwhile he sent his mother the best coach he could find

in the establishment. Rameau d'Or took it to her with post-horses.

As Rameau d'Or was a man to be depended upon, Tancrede informed him that the box under the seat of the coach contained a thousand louis. He gave him the key, with a caution to keep his eye upon the money-box.

Tancrede sent, at the same time, letters to his father and mother, inviting them to come and take possession of their property. He sent them an account of all he had been obliged to expend, even to the last sou. He added, by way of postscript, that his intended was, by a most unexpected piece of good luck, beautiful, well educated, and apparently very intelligent.

When the baron and baroness learned that their daughter-in-law was free from objections, their joy was extreme. Besides, the baron immediately declared that he would bestow upon his son fifty thousand francs a year, and keep the rest himself to spend at Anguilhem.

"Only," added he, after some consideration, "we may, perhaps, buy a house at Loches, where we can receive company in winter."

The rumor of the success of D'Anguilhem's lawsuit, and of the marriage that followed it, of course soon reached Beuzerie.

The viscount and viscountess, who, in consenting to the marriage of their daughter with Tancrede, had always retained their old grudge against the D'Anguilhems, hastened to communicate the news to their daughter; but Constance received it only with a smile, and would not believe a word that was said.

"Has he sent me a letter?" she inquired.

"No."

"He told me not to believe anything unless it came from his own mouth, or was written in his own hand."

"So that—?"

"I believe in nothing but his love."

The viscount and viscountess insisted as much as they could, but all in vain. Constance required to see, to believe.

The baron, before setting out, was obliged to pay a visit to his neighbors, and explain to them the cruel necessity that compelled his son to break his engagement. The viscount listened very quietly to his discourse from beginning to end, then he requested his wife to fetch Constance. Constance came, and M. de Beuzerie begged the baron to repeat, in the presence of his daughter, what he had told him respecting his son's marriage. The baron repeated the story word for word. Constance shook her head with a smile full of the divine confidence of love; then, when the baron had finished, she said:

"Has Tancrede sent you a letter for me?"

"No!" replied the baron; "he must have felt embarrassed by his position, and would not dare to admit to you that any necessity could have forced him to be unfaithful to you."

"Then, in that case, I see you wish to deceive me; he has told me never to believe anything I should hear about him that came not from his own lips, or that he did not write with his own hand."

"So that—?" repeated M. de Beuzerie.

"I shall still believe in his love for me," replied Constance.

They could get no other answer from the devoted girl, who, moreover, appeared to think no more of the rumor, which, however, soon spread throughout the province.

The departure of the baron and baroness in a chaise and four, preceded by a courier, was an event that became a theme of conversation for ten leagues round Anguilhem during more than a week. It was confidently believed that Tancrede had found sacks full of diamonds, and a mine full of gold in his cellar.

Meanwhile the chevalier was engaged in courting his intended bride, but he found her placed under the strictest surveillance. Master Bouteau never quitted his daughter for an instant, a paternal watchfulness that gave our hero much uneasiness. Every day he went to spend an hour with Sylvandire, and the young lady, to the great astonishment of her future husband, displayed a most cultivated mind and lively natural wit, so that he was never tired of listening to her wit or admiring her beauty.

All the customary preliminary formalities were gone through, and now they only waited the arrival of Tancrede's parents to proceed with the marriage ceremony.

This arrival was too pompous a spectacle for us to attempt to give any idea of it to the reader. M. and Mme. d'An-

guilhem had had the sense to wait until they arrived in the
capital before renewing their wardrobe.

Therefore they were able to appear at the wedding dressed in the latest court fashion; and as both were of the old
stock of nobility, and had that air of dignity which two
revolutions could not succeed in effacing from true gentlefolks, they were worthy representatives.

But the nephews and cousins from the plain, and the
second cousins from Saintonge and Perigord, produced a
marked sensation; they arrived in their felts and doub-
lets, and trussed breeches and embroidered mantles of the
time of Louis the Thirteenth. They looked like a collection
of family portraits that had stepped out of their frames.

Tancrede, who dreaded ridicule more than anything,
chose to be married at Saint Roch in the evening, and de-
ferred the wedding repast until all his relations, loaded
with presents, had departed in the coaches that brought
them. The baron and baroness covered their daughter-in-
law with caresses, who smiled tenderly upon her husband,
and responded admirably to their favors.

The chevalier thanked the Marquis de Crette for all the
sevices he had rendered him, and for all the honor he had
done him, and promised to write to the marquis respecting
the matter that had troubled him very much, and which
now troubled him more than ever.

The happy pair set out for a little estate, situated at
Champigny, where M. de Bouzenois had for some time resided.

The wedding over, the baron and baroness were impatient
to return to Anguilhem, and restore the pristine integrity
of their escutcheon, which looked so time and weather-worn,
over the carriage-entrance to their castle.

On the day succeeding the departure of our hero and his
bride for Champigny, the Marquis de Crette received at the
hands of an extraordinary courier the following brief epistle
from the chevalier:

"MY DEAR MARQUIS,—I am the happiest of men!
Have the kindness, my dear friend, to obtain from Monsieur
Bouteau the address of his mysterious envoy, and to remit
to the latter a thousand louis on my behalf. Yours as ever,
                    "THE CHEVALIER D'ANGUILHEM.
    "To the Marquis de Crette."

CHAPTER XXII.

TANCREDE had to quiet his conscience with respect to Mlle. Constance de Beuzerie; and he proceeded with that difficult task in the following manner.

As nothing weakened love so much as possession, so nothing sustained it like hope; but hope once lost, the strongest love declines, if it be not extinguished by an imperative necessity. Thus, as soon as he understood that he must no longer think of his old chimeras, and found himself face to face with one of the most bewitching realities the world contained, he sighed and wept, but at last ended by putting his resolution into execution, and even with a very good grace.

He therefore took advantage of his mother's return to Anguilhem, to write a very tender letter to Constance. He informed her, that one of those cruel necessities which sometimes gentlemen encounter to prove their courage had fallen upon him, and that in sacrificing himself to the welfare and happiness of his family, he must renounce forever the hope or prospect of being happy himself. He entreated Constance to pardon and to forget him. But in concluding, he vowed to his love, that in spite of the inflexible law to which he was compelled to submit at that moment, he should continue to love her to the last moment of his life.

By this, Constance was liberated from her vow, and being free, could marry when she chose.

At the time Tancrede wrote this letter to Constance, the substance of which we have just given, he had not yet had occasion to write to the Marquis de Crette that letter, the contents of which we gave at the end of the preceding chapter. He still mistrusted Sylvandire, and thought that, probably deceived by his wife beforehand, he would take care always to have the best of it in any conjugal dispute that might arise, if ever the two rivals should communicate with each other, and if the one should show to the other the letter she had received.

Tancrede was profoundly moved while composing the elegiac lines we have quoted, and his eyes were still wet when he carried the letter containing them to the Baroness d'Anguilhem. The worthy lady, who still believed in eternal loves, even when these loves were crossed by insurmountable obstacles, was desirous of referring the matter to her husband, and particularly when the chevalier requested her to take the letter to Mlle. de Beuzerie herself, and if possible deliver it into her own hands.

M. d'Anguilhem was much embarrassed at this proposal. To fail in fulfilling the wishes of his son was, in his opinion, to betray his duty; and it must be admitted that during the last four months Tancrede had greatly increased in paternal estimation. From the manner in which his son had conducted himself in the capital, the baron now respected him as much as he loved him.

On the other hand, to convey to Constance a letter doubtless full of vows of eternal love was perhaps the way to rekindle the fires which he was sure, if let alone, would become extinguished of themselves. This was probably encouraging culpable designs, and would perhaps foment a rebellion at the Beuzerie fireside.

Now the baron had no knowledge of what the letter contained, else he would rather have thrown it behind the fire than have taken it, so far would he carry delicacy in such matters. The baroness could give him no information, only, knowing the unchangeable love that her son had vowed to Constance, it might be supposed that the letter would contain terrible complaints against fate and bitter recriminations against fortune. The result was, that the baron, after having turned the epistle over and over in every direction, sagely concluded that the best thing he could do would be not to give the letter to Mlle. de Beuzerie at all; and to make sure that this resolution should not be easily shaken, he put the amorous epistle into a box, and double-locked it.

The putting this resolution into effect troubled the Baron d'Anguilhem's mind for some time, but he reconciled himself to it by degrees in thinking that chance and accident sometimes effected much good in the world.

The consequence was, that Mlle. de Beuzerie, never receiving the letter that set her free from her vows, would never believe what was said to her about the chevalier's marriage. She replied to all the assurances of her father and mother by saying:

"I would rather die than believe it of him."

During all this time Tancrede, believing Constance was

restored to liberty, was quite easy in his mind, and we may
even add (if we were not afraid we should give our readers
a bad opinion of our hero), that he was very happy.

I believe that no marriage ever existed, even if it were
between a tigress and a panther, that could pretend to enjoy a peace of fifteen days after the marriage-day.

Besides the perfect beauty of Sylvandire, which Tancrede
particularly appreciated, Sylvandire appeared fascinating
by her naiveté, grace, and virtue. Her husband had questioned her in every way. He had employed his logic and
rhetoric to entrap her into contradictions, but upon no
point could he surprise Sylvandire in a falsehood.

Therefore he was still perplexed to know why Master
Bouteau had thought it necessary to take so many precautions, so much care, and so much pains to place such a
valuable treasure in a good position, while it appeared to
Tancrede that she could, at any time, have commanded any
position she chose to set her mind upon.

"How did you pass your time at your father's, dearest?"
inquired he, in one of his fits of perplexity.

"Very wearily," replied Sylvandire.

"But did you see no company?"

"Oh, as for that, there came some old judges, old counselors, old advocates, all tiresome old men, whose conversation I could take no interest in."

"Was that all?"

"Ah! yes, no one else, I assure you."

Thus Tancrede, after dreading some deformity, infirmity,
or other defect, disabused of these fears, now conjured up
others. He made up his mind that his wife must have some
concealed vice.

"Perhaps she is a glutton," he thought. This, according to Saint Simon, was a vice of the age.

Then he set to work to provoke her appetite by the aid
of the most exquisite wines that M. de Bouzenois had kept
in his cellars for more than twenty years. But Sylvandire,
after tasting the finest Tokay, and the most exquisite Con-
stantia, made a face that strongly expressed her disgust,
and returned to her decanter of pure fresh water, the only
beverage that appeared agreeable to her.

One day, after having taken a thimbleful of Syracuse,
a the pressing entreaty of her husband, the blood rushed
to her head, and she was very much indisposed for the re-

mainder of the evening. She therefore announced her determination of never, from that time, even putting her lips to any kind of wine.

"My wife is certainly not fond of the pleasures of the table," thought our hero; "I must look for some other vice, for surely she must have one."

"Ah! I have it," said he to himself, "my wife is a gambler." So in the evening he placed a rouleau of gold before her, and placed the cards in her hands; but Sylvandire knew not how to play any game whatever. She laughed like a mad person when she gained, and pouted when she lost.

"My wife is not a gambler, it is true," said he, "but perhaps she is avaricious."

Next morning he took his wife out in his coach, after well supplying her with gold, and called upon some of the most fashionable milliners and dress-makers in Paris. Sylvandire laid out 300 louis in bonnets, dresses, laces, but cheapened nothing.

"*Diable!*" said her husband, "she must be extravagant."

But one day, when he made, purposely, a slight objection to a piece of English lace she had paid ten louis more for than it was worth, Sylvandire thanked him for pointing it out to her, and begged that in future he would regulate her expenses himself.

"Worse and worse," thought Tancrede, "there must be something still more serious in the background."

Then he set himself to watch if there were any of those dangerous creatures called cousins hovering about the conjugal home. But not the feather of a lover, as Mme. Scudery said—not even the nose of a gallant, as Moliere has said—showed itself in the neighborhood of Champigny.

"Most decidedly I possess a treasure," said the chevalier, in terror. "I must have been born under some benign constellation, which modern astronomers have not yet discovered."

Still it was true, or appeared to be true.

To say that Sylvandire had an intense love for her husband, is more than we dare venture to affirm. Perhaps Sylvandire did not love him at all, and in the eyes of poor Tancrede this absence of love appeared a virtue. "But is she not one of those pretended indifferent ones, who wake up suddenly, like a volcano? Is she not like the sun con-cealed behind clouds of rain and hail?"

Master Bouteau paid a visit to his children at Cham-pigny.

Our hero, who loved his parents, and wrote to them twice a week, observed that Sylvandire behaved very coolly to this good father of hers, who had done so much for her. He reflected for two or three days upon this coldness, and as he was in the humor for finding good reasons for everything, he ended by concluding that the love Sylvan-dire had for himself extinguished all other loves. It will be seen that he was already very far advanced in the study of his character of husband; for, from a pessimist, he had become an optimist.

Tancrede was very friendly with Master Bouteau, and Master Bouteau was very friendly with his son-in-law. Only the one had a motive, the other had none. The latter wished to bring Master Bouteau to a point, and when arrived there to probe it to the bottom. One day, after an excellent country dinner, which was prolonged until seven o'clock in the evening, our hero fancied the auspicious moment had arrived.

"Look here, Master Bouteau," said he, drawing his father-in-law into the recess of a window, "I wish you to be frank with me, as you can now have no fear of my escaping you. Tell me, what thus far I have not been able to discover myself, I must confess—tell me, I say, what are Sylvandire's defects; for you must have had some cogent reasons for marrying her in the strange manner you did."

"I wish to answer you candidly, my son. In the first place, as you may perceive," said the good old gentleman, whose tongue was let loose by the fine Muscat he had drunk, "I have saved in the dowry of Sylvandire 100,000 crowns."

"I know the figure," replied Tancrede.

"Dowry, besides," continued the father-in-law, "which you will receive when I am dead and gone, revised and aug-mented. And as I was sure that my daughter could ex-pect to marry only one of those country gentlemen who have to depend upon their swords for their fortune, or one of those merchants who are ruined unless they are saved by a woman's fortune—"

"You know, then, the amount of Monsieur de Bouzenois's fortune?"

"To the last farthing, my son; I have estimated it, and verified it myself."

"But was there not some gentleman of your acquaintance worth more than I?"

"Doubtless, but not one who had a lawsuit that tied him to me, hands and feet. Fortunes of 1,500,000 francs are rare. Besides, I had always said that I would endow my daughter with the first important affair that came into my hands. To accept of a bribe, as your three judges have done, is to rob both justice and the suitor at the same time. But, on the other hand, to give to this suitor, who owes to you his fortune, to give him a charming girl into the bargain, is at the same time, at least I think so, to perform a duty and to render a service."

"Always the same story," thought Tancrede; "the plea is very reasonable, and I believe very correct."

"So," said he, "so, my very dear sir, you were not at all embarrassed with Sylvandire?"

"Oh, dear no, not in the least, if it were not that she found it very dull with me, and that, as she has a very decided character—"

"Ah! my wife has a very decided character?"

"A little strong-minded, my son: and, therefore, as she had a most decided character, I trembled every moment lest she should commit some folly. She is a girl of very active mind, and needs distraction."

"She is fond of pleasure, then?" said Tancrede.

"I can not say whether she is or not, as I have never provided her with any; but from what I know of her character, I should say she has no particular aversion for amusement or diversion."

"My dear sir, you believe, do you not, that I desire to make Sylvandire happy?"

"I have not the least doubt of it whatever, my son. Everything you say or do convinces me you desire it."

"Well, then, to accomplish this aim, if I were to consult you as to her tastes and inclinations, what advice would you give me?"

"I should say—have confidence in her—"

"Ah, truly, so much the better," interrupted the chevalier.

"Have confidence in her, as I was saying, but—hem. never lose sight of her."

"*Diable!*" exclaimed Tancrede, greatly dissatisfied with this conclusion.

Next day Master Bouteau returned to Paris, leaving his son-in-law greatly perplexed, and deeply pondering over their conversation of the preceding evening.

In fact he was so very happy, that he felt it impossible his happiness could last; so he tormented himself in every possible manner to find a way of putting an end to it.

It is a strange thing, this heart of man; we do not speak of that of woman, of which we know nothing, except by sympathy. It is a strange thing, this heart of man, as we were saying, and it is difficult to understand what a strange assortment of loves it contains. Certainly our hero had loved Constance very much, even to that degree that, if he had heard she was going to be married, it would have plunged him into despair. Well, he loved Sylvandire also, but with quite another sort of love, it is true. He loved Constance as he loved a beautiful flower, to admire its purity, to inhale its perfume, to preserve it in a corner of the garden of his heart, concealed from every eye, far from every tumult.

He loved Sylvandire as we love a beautiful diamond, for its brilliancy, which we desire should dazzle every eye, and excite the envy of the most ambitious.

The love Tancrede felt for Constance was celestial and pure; that which he experienced for Sylvandire was of the earth, earthy, and consumed all the feelings of his soul.

Perhaps the reason he was so happy, and so much dreaded any change in his position, consisted in this, that the one kind of love was the completion of the other.

CHAPTER XXIII.

HAPPINESS still continued to shed its rosy beams over the days of Tancrede's wedded life, and he might have continued happy, had he not tormented himself about the remark his father-in-law made respecting Sylvandire. He therefore resolved to break up the monotonous calm, which seemed as affected as it was profound with Sylvandire, and proposed something to his wife that would bring about some change.

We must say that he was wrong. He should have let well alone. To know how to enjoy the happiness of the present hour, and to leave to Providence the happiness of the future, is one of the first precepts of human wisdom, but it is one of those that is least observed. Question three fourths of the men who are unhappy, and, if candid, they will admit that they sought their first misfortune, as Diogenes sought an honest man, with a lantern.

In fact, one fine morning our hero lighted *his* lantern, and went to look for Sylvandire.

"My dearest love," said he to her, "I have to announce to you some news which I am sure will delight you very much; for, doubtless since I find myself very happy, you find yourself very happy also?"

"Certainly I do," replied Sylvandire, giving him a searching look, which was not entirely exempt from uneasiness.

"This happiness springs from our love, Sylvandire, and without doubt you like to meditate on your love, as I do."

Sylvandire remained silent.

"Now," continued Tancrede, "as we *both* love" (he emphasized *both*) "to be let alone, and away from the world—"

Sylvandire pricked up her ears, as a horse who hears the whip.

"We will sell our house at Paris, pack up our furniture, and go and live, if you please, at Anguilhem, where Master Bouteau will do us the pleasure of coming to pass his vacations."

"And why go and bury ourselves in the country?" asked Sylvandire, resolutely.

"To live *en famille*."

"Your family is not my family," replied Sylvandire; "and with the exception of one month which my father will come to spend with us, he will remain the rest of the year at Paris."

"Yes, without doubt, my love, you are right. But between you and me, Sylvandire, I do not believe you care the least bit in the world to live with Master Bouteau."

"Sir, you deceive yourself. I love my father very much; and if I did not, I should not desire to bury myself in exile."

"Do you call it exile, a residence anywhere in my company? Oh! Sylvandire, the expression is a little harsh."

"But, my love," replied Sylvandire, "are we not rich enough to live in Paris, and even to live magnificently?"

This was said in a very mild tone, for the young wife dared not venture to advance very far in a first discussion.

"That is true," replied Tancrede; "I only wished to know if you cared more for Paris than you do for me. You have transfixed me at the first blow, thank you."

"Oh no, no! not at all. You are entirely mistaken," cried Sylvandire, with warmth, immediately Tancrede had committed the imprudence of letting her see that his re- solution was only a feint. "Not at all, my love. I will live wherever you wish to live, dearest; provided I am near you, I can make up my mind to live anywhere."

She was very sure that after saying this, she would soon find herself in Paris.

"Yes," said her husband; "but you would prefer, would you not, that we should return to the capital, and spend the winter there?"

"You are quite wrong, my love, to think that. I have no preference for one place more than another, and I wish only for what you wish."

What could he reply to so submissive a wife, but to an- ticipate what he considered to be her desire?

He therefore gave orders for immediate preparations to be made for their departuae; and they returned to Paris.

The chevalier had few acquaintances except his old friends. Sylvandire had none at all; for she could not call acquaintances the judges, counselors and advocates who fre- quented her father's house. Tancrede contented himself with writing to Crette, D'Herbigny, Clos-Renaud, and Chastellux, that he had returned to Paris, that he dined every day at two o'clock, and received company in the evening at eight.

Mme. d'Anguilhem did the honors of the house to per- fection, and was generally considered a very charming person.

The first evening they received visitors, the Marquis de Crette took Tancrede aside, and having led him into the re- cess of a window, he said:

"My dear chevalier, as I do not wish ever to be excluded from your house—"

"Excluded from my house?" interrupted Tancrede, "what mean you?"

"My friend, replied the marquis, "you are young, and do not understand the ways of the world. Your heart is pure, and your mind is unperverted. Now learn this, to begin with: the friends of the wife are almost always the friends of the husband; but the friends of the husband are rarely those of the wife."

"How is that?"

"How is that? It would take a very long time to explain to you how it so happens; when I have leisure, I will write it out for you in two or three volumes. I wish to say this, then: I will allow you to believe everything that is said against me, except one thing, which is—that I come here to make love to your wife. You know me well, my dear friend. I give you my word of honor as a gentleman, that your wife will always be as sacred in my eyes as if she were my sister."

"And never will you be treated by me otherwise than as a brother," replied our hero; "never will you be excluded from my house, except when you choose to exclude yourself. Perish wife, perish fortune, rather than friendship like ours."

"So be it," replied Crette.

The marquis showed himself very assiduous at the chevalier's; but he had the delicacy never to arrive there alone, but to visit at the hour when everybody else visited. Then, almost always he went out with the escort of the friends he had brought with him. Faithful to his promise, he paid court only to the husband; and this was the cause of Mme. d'Anguilhem's taking a dislike to him, and next, hating him as if he had been an enemy.

In a short time, the Hotel de Bouzenois, no become the Hotel d'Anguilhem, was the resort of very good society. Sylvandire, beautiful and agreeable, attracted the gallants, as honey attracts flies. But Crette firm at his post with D'Herbigny and Clos-Renaud, chased away these flies with his jests and pleasantries, and had the hearty approval of his host. Thus six months passed away without the envious being in the least degree able to heap any scandal upon her name.

Mme. d'Anguilhem, however, had a great desire to visit Versailles, and to this end had turned her batteries toward devotion. But the marquis and his friends were dead set against the *old woman*, as they called Mme. de Maintenon; against *the Jesuit* as they called Pere Letellier; agrinst the *lumber,* as they called the courtiers; and against the *old machine,* as they called Louis the Fourteenth.

In that, as in everything, Tancrede partook of the opinion of his friends. And as Sylvandire insisted upon receiving a more religious sort of company, he replied that he did not reckon upon making his house a monastery, and that if the abbes made their appearance, he would bring in, by way of contrast to their black coats, some musketeers of all colors.

There was a great difference, as may be perceived, between the Tancrede of Paris and the Tancrede of Amboise; between the husband of Sylvandire and the lover of Constance; between the libertine revolting against the cassock and the student who wished to become a Jesuit.

Sylvandire, who felt herself the weaker vessel, was obliged to submit. At about this period, Master Bouteau became candidate for the office of president. The chevalier mentioned his father-in-law's desire to his friend Crette. The marquis, with his customary kindness, exerted all the influence he possessed among his friends to secure Master Bouteau the appointment. But from the cool reception he met with in various quarters, be became satisfied that if he depended entirely on hia own influence he would not succeed.

Some one spoke to Master Bouteau of a certain Marquis de Royancourt as a person of great influence at court. He was very liberal with his masses, and a great favorite of Mme. de Maintenon's. Master Bouteau remembered that, three or four years previously, this same Marquis de Royancourt had brought a suit before the tribunal of which he was judge advocate, a suit which he had gained for the marquis.

Master Bouteau therefore paid a visit to M. de Royancourt, who received him very graciously. He reminded him of the circumstances of the suit, which the marquis had not forgotten.

Now, as Master Bouteau thought that the infuence of a pretty woman would do no harm to his affair, he asked permission of Tancrede to be allowed to introduce M. de Royancourt to himself and wife; to which proposition his son-in-law, having no suspicion, made no objection.

The Marquis de Royancourt was, therefore, duly presented to our hero, to whom he paid a thousand unmeaning compliments, and to Sylvandire, who modestly cast down her eyes.

Tancrede rendered himself as agreeable as possible to M. de Royancourt, partly from courtesy, and partly because he preferred being on good terms with him than not, seeing that he was a powerful favorite, and admitted to the sober suppers of Mme. de Maintenon, and was enthroned in the ante-chamber of the Pere Letellier.

On the day succeeding the Marquis de Royancourt's first visit, Master Bouteau was named president.

It was very natural that a man to whom they owed such obligations should be received with every consideration by the D'Anguilhems, especially by madame, for her father's sake. Therefore, on his second visit, the marquis was received with more cordiality than at the first.

M. de Royancourt observed to the Chevalier d'Anguilhem, that he was astonished that a man like him, young, rich, and with good parts, did not seek to obtain a post at the court or in the army. He tendered his services, and begged that he would name any appointment he would desire to fill.

Tancrede, who had always possessed an ambition to appear at court, replied only by thanking the marquis warmly for his kind offer. The offer appeared very generous and kind to the chevalier, and he told De Crette so; but De Crette had a great antipathy against the new-comer, and shook his head.

But, as we have said, there was dissension between the two friends; De Crette looked upon the Marquis de Royancourt with a suspicious eye. He knew full well how devious were the ways of the bigoted courtiers, who had placed themselves, like distinguishers, upon all the bright joys which had extinguished the first two thirds of the reign of the great king.

Sylvandire, on her part, entreated her husband to accept the offers of service of this favorite of Mme. de Maintenon.

"We shall be received at Versailles," said she, "perhaps we may even obtain apartments there."

"Why do that?" asked Crette; "is it not much better to be master in one's own house, as Tancrede is, than to obey the peevish caprices of a weak old king, who is always out of temper, and whom no one can answer, not even

Madame de Maintenon.   As to the apartments—you have
here a beautiful house of your own.   I can assure you
there is no such accommodation to be had at Versailles.
Then, again, if they should give D'Anguilhem a commission in the army, what would become of him?   Although
he is as brave as Alexander, Hannibal, or Cæsar, D'Anguilhem does not appear to me to have the slightest taste
or talent for war.   I held a commission once upon a time;
well, I liked it so well that I sold it.   I shall return to active service when Madame de Maintenon is no longer minister of war."

"You, sir," replied Sylvandire, sharply, "you have exhausted all your pleasures and honors, and I can fully understand why you talk in this strain.   But Monsieur D'Anguilhem and I are novices, and have some curiosity to see
the world."

Upon hearing this, Crette looked at the chevalier with an
inquiring eye, and the chevalier responded by a negative
gesture.   Sylvandire, finding herself beaten, went in search
of her father, and sent Master Bouteau to the charge.

Master Bouteau supported M. de Royancourt.

It happened that one day during fast, a Wednesday, I
believe, that M. de Royancourt, who pretended to fast four
days in the week, eating only fish, reproached the chevalier
—politely, it is true, but very severely, nevertheless—for
paying so little attention to the commandments of the
church.

Crette and his friends waited to see what reply D'Anguilhem would make to this important personage, but they had
to wait a long time.   At length Tancrede replied, but less
sharply than the ill-timed rebuke of the marquis seemed to
deserve.

"Ah! ah!" said the marquis, in a low voice, to his friend,
"I see how it is; the marquis is going up, we are going
down."

In fact, M. de Royancourt had made himself quite at home
at D'Anguilhem's.   He came there with a great retinue,
with his splendid horses, and his insolent servants.   Sylvandire learned from him all the news of the court, at which
she intensely desired to be introduced, but which was closed
against her, like one of the enchanted gardens of the
"Arabian Nights," watched over by a jealous dragon.

The dragon that kept her from entering the enchanted

garden was the Marquis de Crette, so she hated him desperately.

Tancrede, too, began to open his eyes, and could see things were not as they once were in this house; the intruder made him feel very impatient and uncomfortable.

"This Royancourt troubles me greatly," said he to his friend, one morning; "he took my wife and father-in-law, yesterday, to the Jesuit De Letellier."

"Well, make haste and get yourself out of all this," said Crette, who was upon the most intimate footing with D'Anguilhem. "Carry Sylvandire to Touraine; leave me full powers, and make yourself easy while you are away. I will clear your house of all the vermin."

"*Parbleu!*" said Tancrede, "that is a good idea."

He immediately made preparations for his departure, but without saying anything about it to any one.

Only two hours before the time at which his traveling carriage was ordered to be ready, he informed Sylvandire that he was going to take her into the country.

Sylvandire was thunder-struck at this piece of audacity, of which she did not believe her husband capable. She wished to discuss his resolution, but he remained firm. Then she wept, but still he remained unmoved by her tears. The moment of departure arrived, and he made her set out, without bidding farewell to Master Bouteau or M. de Royancourt.

"Oh! this is monstrous," said Sylvandire, upon getting into the coach.

"But," replied the chevalier, in taking his place near her, "but, my love, you assured me you would be happy with me anywhere, and why do you object to go with me now? what have you to complain of?"

"Sir," replied Sylvandire, "you might, at least, have allowed me to take leave of my father and my friends."

"Impossible! dear angel; I only thought of coming away at the moment I named to you."

"Are you going to stay long in the country? for I must tell you at once, I hate your provincials and their formalities."

"There is nothing that will compel us to remain there forever. We shall remain just as long as it is agreeable to both of us."

Meanwhile the postilion flogged his horses into a smart gallop, and left Paris far behind them.

At the fourth relay they stopped to sup. Sylvandire requested permission to write to her father, to which her spouse made no objection.

Sylvandire then wrote a letter. Tancrede had sufficient delicacy not to seek to know what it contained. But, this letter finished, he saw that Sylvandire continued writing others. This made him suspicious. But what he dreaded most was the first family jar, especially if serious in its tone. He had learned that the conjugal lake, once troubled, never entirely regained its primitive purity.

Arrived at Chartres, Sylvandire requested to be allowed to stop and attend service at the cathedral. It will be remembered that ever since M. de Royancourt had made his appearance at the house of the D'Anguilhems, Sylvandire had been seized with a strong fit of piety. Therefore, her request to go to the cathedral did not surprise our hero in the least. He thought that, during the two or three hours she would be there, he would amuse himself by taking a horse and riding over to the country-house of his friend D'Herbigny, a few miles distant from Chartres.

Sylvandire betook herself to the cathedral, and Tancrede trotted off toward the residence of the viscount. He remained there three hours; but, as he was less intimate with D'Herbigny than with the Marquis de Crette, he merely informed him that he was going on a pleasure excursion to Touraine.

Upon his return to the hotel, he learned that Sylvandire had not come back from the cathedral. He waited impatiently for an hour, and, as she did not make her appearance, he went to the cathedral in search of her; but he found the cathedral quite empty. He therefore hurried back to the hotel, and sought an interview with the landlord. From him he ascertained that Sylvandire had set out some hours before, in a post-chaise and four, accompanied by her maid.

Tancrede was greatly astonished at this intelligence, and had some difficulty in concealing his agitation from the host. He preserved sufficient presence of mind, however, to say to him:

"Did she want for anything?"

"No, sir, madame appeared quite satisfied."

" Very good," replied our hero, retiring to his room, his
heart ready to burst with indignation.

He entered the room lately occupied by his wife. Upon
the toilet-table, which had not been disturbed, he found a
letter addressed to himself. It was in Sylvandire's handwriting, and written in a very bold hand. He tore it open
and read as follows:

" MONSIEUR,—You thought it your duty to bring me
away at two hours' notice—I, who am a woman, and who,
by virtue of that title, believe I have my privileges and
rights, as well as you have yours, I return to Paris, and
you will know of it two hours after I have gone.

" SYLVANDIRE.

" P.S. —You may continue on your journey, or return.
It will make no difference to me. You know I have a
home and a father in Paris. "

" She mocks me," said the enraged husband; " but she
shall pay dearly for it. Ah, Crette, you were quite right,
I am no longer master. But wait awhile, and we shall
see."

———

CHAPTER XXIV.

THIS affair was a great shock to Tancrede, and the more
painful inasmuch as it happened to a man who was just
entering upon life, with all its hopes centered in the future.
His heart had already been torn by suffering, and his happiness had been too brief in its duration to have satisfied
him.

Rage, shame, and jealousy at the same time took possession of his heart.

He told Breton, his *valet de chambre,* to order three post-
horses to be saddled immediately, and as soon as they were
brought to the door he mounted one, Breton another, and
the postilion the third, and all three set off at full gallop
on the road to Paris.

Motion is one of the irresistible wants of troubled minds.
The gallop of the horse that carries us to some real or
apprehended misfortune, or even sometimes to revenge, is
a kind of physical balm to the wounds of the heart. We
see the road disappear and the trees fly past: we feel rush-

ing on, and drawing near; we arrive. A thousand feverish visions pass before our eyes. A thousand projects, each more wild and senseless than another, rush into the brain and bewilder it. The swifter the horse flies, the more we spur it. We are pursued by a demon, who continually shouts in our ears, "Quicker! quicker! quicker!"

Tancrede made the journey to Paris in five hours, without stopping to rest for a moment, except to change horses; but still no Sylvandire appeared on the road. Breton, his valet, was overcome with fatigue, but our hero felt none.

When Tancrede entered the court-yard of his mansion he found that Sylvandire had arrived an hour and a half before him. He hastened to the drawing-room just as he was, booted, spurred, and covered with dust, and with his riding-whip in his hand. There he found Sylvandire already dressed in evening costume, reclining gracefully upon a couch, talking with M. de Royancourt and three or four of his friends, whom he had introduced at the Hotel D'Anguilhem.

The sight of so much audacity confounded the chevalier. He felt paralyzed, and leaned against the door for support, pale as death.

"Here's Fontaine's fable realized," thought he. "There are four of them: well, I will bring Crette and two friends, then we can take a little turn behind the convent of Saint Sacrement."

But upon Tancrede's making his appearance in the drawing-room, M. de Royancourt and his companions rose and approached him, paying him as much polite attention as if he had been a clodhopper whom they wished to insult without further delay. Besides, Tancrede felt instinctively that this opportunity must happen some day or other.

As for Sylvandire, she contented herself with merely waving her hand; then, with a slight coquettish shake of the head, "What?" said she; "you make your appearance in my drawing-room in that condition? Oh, what a bad husband you are; it seems to me that I am entitled to a little more respect. You surely could have changed your traveling costume before making your appearance here. Had not you better go and do it now, my dear?"

Tancrede was quite upset at this coolness. He felt a great inclination to apply his whip to the backs of all present, and clear the house of these vermin; but only the fear of scandal restrained him.

"You are right, madame," replied he; "but as you knew I was coming, I expected to have found you a little more alone."

He said this, looking very hard at M. de Royancourt, to let him understand that this admonition was especially addressed to him.

As gentlemen, the three friends of M. de Royancourt understood that the time had arrived when they must raise the siege. They withdrew immediately. M. de Royancourt remained behind a few moments; then rising, he saluted Sylvandire and Tancrede, and made good his retreat, which he had delayed only to exhibit a tacit protest against the husband's orders.

"And in this, sir," said Sylvandire, when M. de Royancourt had retired, "is this the way you drive all my friends away?"

"What do you mean by *my friends?*" said the chevalier; "it seems to me it would be more becoming in you to say *our* friends."

"*My* friends or *our* friends, it is of little consequence. I shall not dispute with you about a word; but understand, once for all, I intend to invite and receive here whomsoever I think proper."

"And I shall put out every one whose presence I do not approve of."

"You are a—"

"Finish, madame."

"A country gentleman."

"And you are a very insignificant little limb of the law."

"Do you think to frighten me, sir?"

"Fear or no fear, you will return with me immediately to Anguilhem; only you do not return so quickly from this second expedition as you did from the first."

"You talk in this style because you think I have no one to take my part," said Sylvandire, breaking out of all bounds; "but I can tell you, sir, you deceive yourself; and you will find, I promise you, some one who will make you repent your proceedings."

"Ah! perhaps your friend the Marquis de Royancourt," cried Tancrede, exasperated. "You mean your fine Marquis de Royancourt, I suppose, madame? Well, well! In

an hour from this time, your Marquis de Royancourt will
receive some news from me, and *pardieu*, if, as I believe I
perceived just now, that he will understand neither my
looks nor my words, I hope I shall succeed in making him
comprehend my actions."

Sylvandire quickly understood her husband's meaning.
She had heard of the Kollinski affair, which had made considerable noise in the world.   Besides, she had often heard
De Crette and D'Herbigny speaking in glowing terms of
the skill and courage of her husband, and she was in great
terror at his significant threat.   Rushing after him as he
quitted the room, she overtook him just as he had put his
foot on the staircase leading to his chamber, where he was
about proceeding to change his costume; for he was one of
those men who fully comprehend that when we propose to
do an enemy the honor of cutting his throat, we must make
this proposition in a velvet coat, laces and ruffles.

But Sylvandire wished above all things to avoid scandal,
for she had great designs upon M. de Royancourt.   She
cowered, then, as we have said, beneath the threat of Tancrede, and endeavored to calm his anger by her tears.   Sylvandire weeping! his heart was not formed of iron.   In this
struggle, where he ought to have at least gained the field
of battle, he lost all!

The same evening, M. de Royancourt was seen playing
tric-trac in the drawing-room with Master Bouteau, and
Sylvandire looked on smilingly.

On that same evening, too, the Marquis de Crette, having
heard of the sudden return of his friend, called to pay him
a visit, but Sylvandire had given her orders, and the marquis was informed at the gate that monsieur and madame
had indeed returned, but that they did not receive company
that evening.

Next day the marquis wrote to Tancrede that he never
would set foot in his house again, seeing that he had been
refused admittance at his door, while he had seen the
coach of M. de Royancourt waiting in the court-yard.

He added that there was an end forever to their friendship.

Tancrede, in despair, ran to Crette and found him deeply
offended.   He had not much difficulty in persuading the
marquis that he was altogether innocent of the affair; that
he knew of no such order being given.   But Crette could

easily perceive where the truth lay, and he would allow himself to be reconciled only on one condition.

"Listen, chevalier," said the marquis: "this denial was an insult, an insult from your people, and which, consequently, in the eyes of the world, comes from you. You must therefore make me a reparation. Some day when my coach is standing at your door, let Monsieur de Royancourt receive the same denial of your being at home that I received. On this condition I will forget what has passed, and never speak of it again."

The chevalier promised that what he desired should be done.

He then returned home, and informed his wife of the engagement he had entered into with his friend.

Sylvandire laughed.

But he was not in a laughing humor, and insisted upon it very earnestly, and pronounced for the first time that terrible phrase, which a woman never forgets, and of which a husband always repents—

"You shall!"

Then a terrible quarrel ensued. Sylvandire showed herself what she really was, a true despot; and there was between them a long interchange between "You shall," and "I won't."

"Well, madame, if you will not," said Tancrede, at length, who expected to triumph by a reproach, so terrible to the ears of an honest woman, "if you will not, I shall conclude that you have very improper feelings for Monsieur de Royancourt."

"Believe whatever you please," replied Sylvandire.

"If Monsieur de Royancourt does not keep away from this house, madame, I shall; but take care, madame; I may never return."

"As you please, sir; the world is wide, you are young, and travel will improve you."

"I will go at once, madame, if you provoke me!"

"Go, sir, I shall not hinder you," replied Sylvandire.

Tancrede had made a false step; he was aware of it, but it was too late. Instead of disputing with his wife, he should have left his orders with the porter, and there would have been an end of the matter.

But he had raised an argument, and the demon of feminine cunning had prevailed over his naive anger.

"Well, you are still there!" said Sylvandire, upon seeing that he stood stupefied at so much audacity.

Tancrede made three steps toward this shameless woman, but a feeling of self-respect restrained him.

"Breton," said he, to his *valet de chambre*, "have my portmanteau and the chaise ready in an hour."

Then he went out of the drawing-room, without Sylvandire taking a step, or saying a word to retain him.

The hour passed away. It was certainly one of the most agitated and painful hours in the life of our hero. At the slightest noise he trembled and listened, for he expected every moment to see his wife repenting in her heart, with tears in her eyes, and a prayer on her lips, come and ask his forgiveness. He would have given the best ten years of his life for Sylvandire to have done so. But he would rather have sacrificed his whole life than have taken one step toward her. In such a case he had but one virtue, obstinacy. It is a good thing to have a strong head when the heart is weak.

The hour had at length elapsed, amid the anguish of a tortured heart, impossible to describe. Tancrede took his hat, and went down into the *salon*.

Sylvandire was alone, working upon her embroidery.

"Then the thing is decided, I suppose?" said she, in a tone as careless and indifferent as if he had been merely going to take a walk before dinner. "You are going to leave us?"

"Yes, madame!" replied her husband, astonished at her coolness, "and I have the honor to bid you farewell!"

"And when do you expect to return?"

"I shall have the honor of sending you word."

"Adieu, chevalier!"

"Adieu, madame."

He refused to take the hand Sylvandire extended toward him, and hurriedly descended the stairs, jumped into his chaise, and said aloud:

"Stop at the Marquis de Crette's."

He had the satisfaction of hearing Sylvandire close the window of the *salon* with great noise. She had watched him go off, and was enraged at the sound of the word Crette.

The Marquis de Crette sincerely pitied his friend, and endeavored to sympathize with him.

The chevalier wished to go and seek out M. de Royancourt, and provoke a quarrel with him, but Crette restrained him from that foolish project.

"My dear friend," he said, "your position is a false one. You must have patience. Watch your wife and the marquis, get proofs, and then, supported by these proofs, appeal to Monsieur de Royancourt. But you have seen nothing, you know nothing. You received this man at your house yesterday: has anything happened to reproach him with since yesterday? He has done nothing, because he has not been near you. Monsieur de Royancourt will reply that he does not know what you mean; that you are a visionary; and everybody will say that you are in the wrong, and I among the first."

"What do you advise me to do, then?"

"Why, go! as you have said you intend taking a journey. Go to Italy, Germany, England, anywhere; take a *danseuse*. or anything to distract your mind."

"I detest women."

"Yes, we know that, but there is nothing so consoling in love as caprice. Why, only eight days ago, without pretty little Poussette, I should have blown my brains out, or turned Trappist. Try it."

"No, I must go, I must quit Paris. If I remain in it, I shall go mad."

"Why not go and take a journey to Anguilhem?"

"What excuse can I make for the absence of my wife?"

"Bah! Do you think Mademoiselle Constance will ask you for one?"

"Constance has forgotten me, as she ought, by this time; Constance, doubtless; is married. Ah! Constance, Constance, what a difference between you and Sylvandire!"

"Yes! my friend, you are right. Nothing less resembles one woman than another woman. Ah, well! go to England; you may learn some useful lessons there in the method of reducing the sex to obedience; our neighbors across the Channel are extremely well-informed on that subject."

"I shall be very glad to follow their counsel. Ah! Crette, Crette, my heart is torn into a thousand pieces—"

Crette embraced his friend, but made no attempt to console him: he knew full well that for such wounds as he suffered from, there is no medicine like time.

Tancrede set out for England, where he remained three

months. During that brief period he had the singular
good fortune of seeing two discontented husbands lead their
wives, with halters round their necks, to Smithfield Market.

Being young and rather good-looking, one sold for six
guineas, and the other for seven.

"*Pardieu!*" said Tancrede, when he witnessed the
transfer, "I would sell mine for nothing, and give something to boot."

Unfortunately, our hero being a Frenchman, did not enjoy an Englishman's privileges.

At the end of three months he began to wish to return
to France. As he was perfectly free, and as there was
nothing to oppose his inclination, he set out at once for
Dover, where he embarked. Twelve hours afterward he
landed at Calais, after a very rough passage, during which
he had been seasick. Upon landing, the first person he
met was M. Crette's valet, Basque, who was proceeding to
embark in the packet from which Tancrede had just landed.

"Why, Basque!" said he, "what the devil are you doing
here?"

"Ah! Monsieur le Chevalier," replied Basque, "how
fortunate that I should meet you. I was going to England
in search of you."

"What for, Basque?"

"To deliver you a letter from my master. But pray
speak low, if you please, sir, else I am afraid they will
overhear us."

"And what if they do, I should like to know? Who are
they that listen?"

"Everybody, sir, everybody. You do not know what
has happened yonder?"

"Yonder—where?"

"In Paris."

"I have heard of nothing that has happened there the
last three months."

"Ah! then my master was examined yesterday, and
threatened with the Bastile!"

"What! Crette threatened with the Bastile!"

"Yes, sir, it is as I have said."

"And for what?"

"Because he challenged Monsieur de Royancourt to fight
a duel, and he would not."

"You say you have a letter for me?"

"Yes, sir."

"Which will give me all the particulars?"

"Probably."

"Then give it to me."

"Ah, sir, that is not so very easy, as it is sewn in the lining of my vest; but if you will accompany me to the hotel—"

"But why all these precautions?"

"You will probably know as soon as you have read the letter from my master. When Monsieur le Marquis saw the police enter the house, he suspected something, and immediately wrote this letter for Monsieur le Chevalier, and ordered me to conceal it. Then he said to me, 'Go, Basque, and find out the Chevalier d'Anguilhem.' I started immediately, and here I am."

"Then come to the hotel without delay, my friend, for I am very anxious to see this letter."

They both quickly proceeded to the hotel; upon arriving there they ascended to an upper room, and locked themselves in.

"The chevalier will excuse my taking off my vest before him," said Basque, "but I can not get at the letter if I do not."

"Go on," said Tancrede, "and be as quick as you can."

Basque ripped open the lining of his vest and took out a letter, which he handed to the chevalier, who opened it with avidity, and read as follows:

"MY DEAR CHEVALIER,—This is the fourth letter I have written to you. Doubtless the other three have been intercepted. Your wife has disappeared, and in spite of every search I have made, I can not discover where she is. Yesterday morning I met Monsieur de Royancourt upon the Cours-la-Reine, and as I had no doubt that he was concerned in the disappearance of Sylvandire, I told him plainly he was a scoundrel, and put my hand to my sword; but I was mistaken. To my great astonishment Monsieur de Royancourt pretended he did not hear me. At the same moment I perceived some police coming toward me, and D'Herbigny drew me away. Yesterday evening I sent him a challenge by Clos-Renaud and Chastellux, but he would not receive them: I shall probably be arrested this morning. I send Basque to you; if he be so fortunate as to find you, lose not a moment in returning to Paris, and clearing up all this affair."

"Yes, yes!" cried Tancrede, "I will return to Paris."

He immediately ordered post-horses, with the firm resolution, since his wife's imprudent conduct had supplied him the excuse, of killing the whole gang, Monsieur de Royancourt and his friends, were they a hundred—were they a thousand! His excitement was aggravated not a little by the rapidity with which he performed his journey.

Arrived at the Cours-la-Reine, as the chevalier was about to enter Paris, a police officer stopped the chaise, and saluted by bowing to the ground. Our hero at first felt disposed to run him through with his sword, and begin his intended butchery with him. But the officer retreated three paces, and taking out a paper from his pocket, he said:

"In the king's name, Monsieur le Chevalier d'Anguilhem, I demand your sword."

Now, as it was a very serious matter to kill a policeman, the chevalier looked at him twice, and at the second glance he drew his sword from its scabbard.

An hour afterward the chevalier was incarcerated in the prison of For-l'Eveque.

CHAPTER XXV.

WHEN a man is thunder-struck he neither sighs nor groans; on the contrary, he remains senseless, stupefied, motionless.

But under this seeming apathy nature continues to act; the relations between the senses and the organs of life, interrupted for a moment, become re-established, and feeling returns to him when he has recovered sufficient strength to understand his position and endure it.

Tancrede entered his prison in the condition of a man thunder-struck. He had not informed Basque of his resolution to return instanter to Paris; on the contrary, he had recommended him to go to bed, which suggestion he was very glad to avail himself of; and as soon as the poor fellow fell asleep, the chevalier jumped upon a post-horse and set out full speed for Paris.

He did not wish that Basque should accompany him, because, in the first place, he was worn out with fatigue; and, in the second, for fear of compromising Crette. He took the precaution of burning the marquis's letter as soon as he had perused it, in order that it might not be said that the marquis was in any way responsible for Tancrede's proceedings. What Basque had told him ran in his head; and he was fully satisfied that all the harpies of Master Voyer d'Argenson were at his heels.

When within ten leagues of Paris he took a post-chaise. He had traveled fifty leagues in fifteen hours, and was quite overcome with fatigue. When seated in the chaise he began to recover his spirits, but as yet he knew nothing. The first inkling he got as to the true state of things was in being arrested.

This abrupt interruption to his thoughts and plans quite overwhelmed him.

"Ah! I am arrested! I am arrested!" and he kept repeating these words all the way to prison.

Every time he repeated these words the officer bowed to him with the greatest courtesy, but said nothing.

The chaise entered the court-yard of the prison, and the chevalier alighted. A man in a black velvet coat with gilt buttons presented himself, and called to an officer to take M. d'Anguilhem to his apartment. Then, in a subdued voice he read the warrant of arrest, which one of the police had written while in the chaise, without even the prisoner having perceived it. Then he said:

"Very good." And made a sign to an officer to conduct the Chevalier d'Anguilhem to the chamber appropriated to him.

Tancrede followed his guide without saying a word.

If, at this moment he had been shown a scaffold covered with black cloth, with the ax and block; and if a sign had been made to him to kneel before the block and bow his head to receive the mortal blow, he would have obeyed mechanically, without the least hesitation or resistance. The adventures that succeeded each other all appeared to him to be so intimately connected, that he felt he must submit to the result without inquiring the reasons. But he went on mechanically, bowing submissively to his absurd destiny; as in a dream one conceives and accomplishes without hesitation, the most absurd follies.

Thus it was that he passed, almost unconsciously, through a dark staircase into a large gallery, and from that proceeded up a circular staircase, a great many stories; then passed through another gallery, and from this gallery through a kind of loft, and from that into a dark, but clean little chamber.

The door was closed behind him, the bolts rattled, and at this sound he recovered his senses.

He found himself seated upon a stool. He raised his head, looked around him, got up, and made the circuit of his chamber, which did not take him very long.

Then, by an instinct stronger than any other feeling, he stopped before a narrow loop-hole of a window, double-barred, through which a little light and air penetrated.

Light! air!! life!!!

Poor Tancrede, that robust country gentleman, accustomed to take so much of the vital fluid into his capacious lungs when he hunted in the woods and fields of Anguilhem, was now reduced to breathe the air through a crevice, and with less light than was admitted into Christopher's stable.

The window was so narrow that he could not pass his head through it; the walls were immensely thick, and the opening was doubly barred, at a distance of about a foot apart. At the extremity of the opening the prisoner could perceive the sky, but nothing between, neither roofs, steeples, nor trees.

The situation Tancrede found himself in was very dismal, and the more so as, in thinking over all the misfortunes that might possibly happen to him, in order to prepare himself beforehand, the idea of imprisonment had never occured to him; so that, of all misfortunes, this was the one he was the least prepared to encounter.

He seated himself again on the stool to reflect, and looking at the old worm-eaten table, loosely covered with faded tapestry, he rose and went to bed, which he found very hard. Then he returned to the stool, and, once more seating himself upon it, gave way to the gloomiest reflections.

When a man has nothing to do but think, it is difficult to say whither his thoughts will wander. Those of our hero wandered everywhere, and compassed every kind of probability; but the one he most dwelt upon was, that he was the victim of some mistake.

He was in prison, however, and of that there could not be a shadow of doubt. But who had put him in prison, and for what? That was the problem he set himself at work to resolve.

"Perhaps," he thought, "my father has conspired against the king, and they think I am his agent, and have been to England to league with the enemy." Although M. le Baron d'Anguilhem was infinitely less dissatisfied with the government of King Louis the Fourteenth, since he had become heir to M. de Bouzenois, his son, who had often heard him complain of Mme. de Maintenon and Father Letellier, did not consider his supposition at all absurd. So for a time it very nearly satisfied him.

"I can prove," he said to himself, "what I have been doing for the last three months in England, and that I have come direct from that country; that for the last eighteen months I have not been to Anguilhem, and that I have not seen my father for a year. In the face of such proofs my innocence must be evident, and I shall be immediately released." For the space of half an hour he was very tranquil.

"Ah, yes," said he, at the expiration of the half hour, "but if they should suspect that I have been to England to contrive with the Prince of Orange, who has vowed an eternal hatred to Louis the Fourteenth! If they take it into their heads that I went to England to forment rebellion! Ah! then I am lost." And for the next half hour he was plunged into the depths of despair.

But, after all, said he, at the expiration of this second half hour, "may it not be something connected with Crette's affair?"

Yet he could not make up his mind to believe that Crette had been arrested on account of his affair with M. de Royancourt, or rather, he could not believe that it was only on that account.

"Crette," said he, "has the reputation of being an enemy of the *old woman's,* which, in fact, he is, and consequently it is likely he will be disgraced. This Royancourt must hate him dreadfully. The king is very severe upon duelists. Perhaps he shut his eyes to our affair with the Kollinskis, and our heads were spared for the want of the necessary proofs to convict us. But now, upon the slightest provocation from Crette, they recognize it as a second offense. Yes—but I am innocent of all that, for I was in London while the marquis challenged Monsieur de Royancourt in Paris."

Next, he thought of—his wife!

"She has disappeared! Perhaps they think I have made away with her."

Recollecting this, he could think of nothing but of his wife's strange conduct toward him; and the more he thought of it the more enraged he became. For he, it is easy to perceive, was as jealous as a tiger; and, it must be admitted, that Sylvandire had given him some little cause for jealousy.

The hour at which prisoners were allowed to walk in the open air had now arrived, and he went to enjoy his two hours of comparative liberty.

He met, upon the platform, eight prisoners, eight companions in misfortune; all the eight with very different faces and costumes.

We might almost read upon their faces and clothes the date of their incarceration.

"What is the news from Paris, monsieur?" cried all the eight voices together.

"Why, gentlemen," replied the chevalier, "they say that I am arrested; but as that event occurred some five or six hours ago, perhaps they have forgotten it, and are now occupying their minds with something else."

"Oh, you are arrested?"

"*Parbleu!* You can see that clear enough. You are not here for your pleasure, are you?"

"No! certainly not."

"No, no more am I."

"But why were you arrested?"

"Well, I have been puzzling my brains all this morning to find out a reason for being arrested, and if you compel me to give you one, you will put me to a great deal of trouble."

"But do you not know why you were arrested?"

"No; do you?"

"No."

"Nor you?"

"No."

"Nor you, either?"

"Nor I. either."

Tancrede put this question to his eight fellow-prisoners in their turn, and received the same reply from each.

Of these eight captives, not one knew the cause of his imprisonment, and yet one of them had been imprisoned ten years.

He was the most calm and resigned.

Our hero shuddered. He had not yet passed as many hours in the prison as his companions had passed years. And yet he had already found the time hang heavily upon his hands.

"I am surely a dead man," thought he.

But, as we always hope that our fate will not be as bad as the fate of others, Tancrede inquired of his companions if it were not possible to speak to any of the authorities.

"You can have the governor visit you whenever you request it," they replied.

"What! can I see the governor?"

"Without doubt."

"By merely asking?"

"Simply by requesting to see him."

"Then I shall ask to see him this evening. Gentlemen, I bid you farewell."

"Farewell! what do you mean?"

"Yes, farewell! for, in all probability, I shall not have the honor of seeing you again."

"How is that?"

"Because, if I see the governor this evening, I shall probably be set free to-morrow."

"Poor fellow," murmured the prisoners, shaking their heads mournfully.

Neither their exclamations nor gestures prevented Tancrede from returning joyfully to his chamber.

Dinner was brought to him, and he ate, very heartily, his majesty's bread and vegetables.

When the jailer came to remove the fragments of his meal, Tancrede begged him to say to the governor that he had a great desire to speak with him.

"It is too late this evening," replied the jailer, "but without doubt, monsieur, the governor will come to you to-morrow."

"Are you sure of it, my friend?"

"Quite sure."

"To-morrow, then," said the chevalier, consoling himself with the thought that a night soon passes away.

He then seated himself on his stool to watch the departure of the last rays of day, through the bars of his window.

While seated there, looking at the sky, and lost in reflection, he thought he heard the noise of something moving in his chamber.

He looked down upon the floor of the room, and saw a mouse nibbling at the crumbs that had fallen under the table:

Tancrede had a great dislike for mice; therefore, he took his hat and threw it with all his force at the poor little animal, which scampered off in great terror, and escaped by a hole under the door, making good its retreat to the adjoining chamber, where, in all probability, it had established its domicile.

For awhile he was greatly disturbed at the idea of these animals making him a visit during the night. So long as a ray of light came into his chamber he sat with his eyes fixed upon the hole. Then, when it had become dark, he took a cork that had been left on his table, and stopped the hole with it. He then felt more at his ease.

During the night he woke up three or four times, and jumped out of bed, believing he felt the little feet of his abhorrence running over his face and hands; but each time he found that, besides himself, there was no living creature in the chamber.

But it was very different in the adjoining chamber, which seemed to be the rendezvous for all the rats, mice, and cats in the building.

Notwithstanding the uproar, our captive slept well. He had hope.

Next day at noon, an hour that seemed to him long of coming, he heard a very unusual noise in the passage to his chamber. Soldiers presented arms, footsteps approached the door, a key turned in the lock, the door opened, and the governor entered.

He was a stiff, formal, dry-looking personage, with lack-luster eyes, who scarcely opened his lips when he spoke. He carried his hat in his hand, doubtless to spare himself the embarrassment of removing it to a prisoner.

"Monsieur le Governor," said our hero, hastening towards him, "I am the Chevalier d'Anguilhem."

"I know it, sir," replied the governor, scarcely opening his lips.

"You know it?" asked our hero, in astonishment.

The governor bowed.

"Ah! then, since you know who I am, Monsieur le Governor, I shall desire—"

"Have you any complaint to make against the *régime* of your prison, Monsieur le Chevalier?"

"No, not at present, monsieur; I have scarcely had time to know exactly what it is; but I desire to know—"

"Do you want for anything, Monsieur le Chevalier?"

"Nothing at present; but I desire to know—"

"Have any of the attendants been rude to you, or neglected to attend upon you, Monsieur le Chevalier?"

"No, sir! on the contrary, I have been surprised at their attention and politeness."

"In that case, Monsieur le Chevalier, as you have nothing whatever to complain of, allow me to retire."

"Pardon, sir, pardon. I have to complain of being in prison."

"I have nothing to do with that," replied the governor.

"But I wish to know why I am here?"

"You ought to know much better than I, Monsieur le Chevalier."

"Better than you—why so?"

"Because it concerns you most. I had the honor of informing you that I had nothing to do with it, and I can attend only to what strictly concerns my duty."

"But you must know—"

"I know nothing, sir."

"But you can guess—"

"I guess nothing, sir; the king sends me a prisoner, I enter his name in a book, provide him an apartment, and see that he wants for nothing while he is in my custody. Such is my duty, and I discharge it with scrupulous care."

"But the king is deceived."

"The king is never deceived."

"But the king may wrong me."

"The king is never wrong."

"But I swear I have done nothing."

"Monsieur, permit me to decline hearing you any further."

"I protest, sir, that I am innocent."

"Monsieur, allow me to retire."

"But tell me, at least, if I shall remain here long; yes, or no. I beg you will, sir."

"So long as it pleases the king, monsieur."

"Ah! stop. You will drive me mad," cried the chevalier.

The governor saluted him, and went out, his hat in his hand, followed by his guards.

This time it appeared to the captive that the door closed upon him with a sinister sound. It seemed to him that from this moment only he became a prisoner. He sunk upon his stool, then fixed his eyes gloomily on the door, and quite overcome, melted into tears.

He thought of his parents, of his friends, of God.

Then all the accounts he had ever heard of captivity, more terrible at that epoch than any other in history, rushed into his mind. Bassompierre imprisoned for ten years in the Bastile; Lauzon thirteen years' captivity at Pignerol; Fouquet, living or dead, no one knew which; he saw pass before him one after another. All those gentlemen, carried off at night from their homes, disappeared, no one knew whither. Matthioli, the Iron Mask, and his fellow-prisoner, even, who had been in that place ten years.

It is true all these prisoners had committed some offense. Bassompierre had aimed to overthrow Richelieu; Lauzan had compromised a granddaughter of Henry the Fourth; Fouquet had presumed to rival Louis the Fourteenth in luxury; Matthioli had betrayed a state secret; the Iron Mask was a political riddle. But as for Tancrede, he had ransacked his memory, carefully reviewed the past, scrutinized every day of his life, but could remember no crime, no fault, no imprudence with which he could reproach himself. The whole world knew what were the faults of those whose names occurred to his mind.

But yet everybody did not know what that man had done with whom he had spoken the previous day, whose name even they did not know, although he had been a prisoner there ten years.

Ten years!

Ah! but this man had perhaps no parents to solicit his pardon, no friends in the good graces of the ministry. This man was, doubtless, some obscure individual.

But if so obscure and insignificant, why kept ten years in

a state prison? This idea tormented our hero for an hour or two. Then he undertook to supply himself with good reasons for concluding that his entire innocence must be made apparent, and gradually all his gloomy ideas vanished.

The hour for the daily promenade arrived, and he went out into the air, as on the preceding day.

He was conducted to the esplanade, as before, where he found his eight companions of the previous day.

He approached the one who had been there ten years, and asked him his name.

"Count Olibarus," was his reply.

Tancrede tried if he could remember this name, but it was perfectly unknown to him.

"And what brought you here? Now, count, between you and me, tell me what it was."

"I can only repeat, sir, what I said to you yesterday, that I do not know."

"You do not know?"

"No, sir!"

"But," said Tancrede, lowering his voice, "during the ten years you have been a prisoner, have you never attempted to save yourself?"

The Count Olibarus looked fixedly, for a moment, then turned his back upon him, without replying. He took him for a spy.

"Pardieu!" said our hero to himself, "it seems to me, that if I had been here ten years I should have tried to escape ten times during that period."

But, stop!

"I'll not remain here ten years without trying to escape."

Upon making this conclusion, Tancrede approached his companions, but they all avoided him as if he had had the plague.

The Count Olibarus had imparted his suspicions to them, and the communication had borne its fruits.

He could not get the other prisoners to exchange a word with him, which put him into a very bad humor, and strengthened him in the decision he had mentally arrived at, that of quitting For-l'Eveque as soon as possible.

He resolved from this moment to give the king just eight days to repair the injustice he committed against him; and if, at the expiration of these eight days the injustice was not repaired, to concentrate all his strength and faculties upon one point—Escape!

CHAPTER XXVI.

UNDER similar but less important circumstances, we have already seen how the chevalier went to work. His resolution once taken, the reader knows with what pertinacity he would set about accomplishing it.

The eight days passed away, during which he would have felt himself deficient in the confidence he owed to his majesty, if he had given the least thought to a project which would be executed only in the event of his being forgotten.

A thousand ideas presented themselves to his mind respecting his flight, but he bravely repulsed them. During these eight days he did not vex himself much, although his fellow-prisoners would have nothing to say to him when he appeared on the esplanade. Hope was ever present to his mind, and every time his door opened he expected that the king, repenting of his error, had sent to rectify it.

Probably the king had something else to do besides repent. Therefore he did not repent, and the eight days passed away without the error committed against the chevalier being repaired.

The last minute of the last hour of the last day expired. Then Tancrede recurred seriously to his project.

He commenced by examining his prison:

Item:—An oak door, three inches in thickness.

Item:—A double-barred window.

Item:—Walls four feet thick.

Here were some difficulties to overcome.

He shook the door.

The rattling of two locks and as many bolts, in the solitude of his chamber, was the only response.

He shook the bars of his window.

They were firmly fixed in the thickness of the walls.

He sounded the walls.

Everywhere he knocked they gave a dull, flat sound, indicating that they were perfectly compact.

He would have required a crow-bar to remove his door.

He would have required a file to cut through the bars of his window.

He would have required a pick-ax to have made a hole in the wall of his chamber.

But these useful articles are not usually supplied to prisoners.

Our hero, however, had the natural ingenuity of a man brought up in the country, and accustomed to depend on his own resources for a thousand expedients that happen to embarrass progress. And he had a prisoner's patience, which during hours, days, and even years, pursues the single and fixed idea of a prisoner—deliverance!

He had examined the interior, he next examined the exterior.

He took his promenade daily, as usual.

In quitting his cell, he had to pass through the large room adjoining it, where every night the mice, rats, and cats held their noisy sports.

It was a kind of store-room, the window of which was not barred. He had once asked permission of his jailer to look out of this window, so as to discover what it overlooked. This store-room was occupied with old mattresses, counterpanes, serge curtains, trunks, and such lumber. It looked like a broker's shop.

It is easy to understand that the mice, rats, and cats were quite at their ease in such a place.

He then proceeded along the gallery. This gallery was closed by two doors; one shut in the chamber adjoining his, the other the winding staircase that led up to the platform.

These two doors were carefully barred, and a sentinel walked up and down the intervening space.

This time he did not even attempt to enter into conversation with his companions in captivity. He had his fixed idea, which spoke to him, and to which he replied. The two hours were passed by Tancrede in awaiting the moment of his return to prison. It was idle to think of escaping from the platform, as there were two doors to force, and a sentinel to elude.

All his hopes were centered upon the chamber which served as a store-room. So, in returning to his own room, he examined it as carefully as circumstances permitted. From the noise he heard through the window, he knew it overlooked the street. There was a sufficient quantity of old sheets and counterpanes to form a long rope.

Every chance, therefore, was centered upon this store-room.

The prisoner returned to his chamber; the door was closed upon him, and double-locked and barred.

His thoughts now fixed themselves upon one point, viz., that escape, if it were possible at all, could only be by means of the store-room. Tancrede was, therefore, separated from liberty only by a door.

But such a door!

An oaken door of three inches in thickness, fixed in a stone wall! Not a screw or nail in it was on the side of Tancrede's cell. All the iron-work was on the other side; so that if he had possessed the means of cutting the screws or drawing the nails, they would have been of no use to him.

The jailer brought his supper. When his door opened, he very carefully glanced through it, and he could hear the noise of the itinerate merchants in the streets.

Having partaken of his supper, he threw himself on his bed.

Then he heard a slight noise; he stretched his neck, and perceived the little mouse, encouraged by the silence that prevailed, venture out to devour the new crumbs that had fallen beneath the table.

This time our hero was astonished to find that he did not experience his usual repugnance to the mousy race. This little animal, which came to visit a prisoner and seek to live upon his superfluity, already inspired him with more interest than disgust. Besides, he began to feel weary, and this little visitor promised amusement.

Moreover, in his pride he wished to address a few words of encouragement to his visitor, convinced that the mouse only awaited a few words of invitation to run to him, full of gratitude for the honor done to him. But quite the contrary; the mouse, which had only returned into the chamber under the conviction that its enemy was not there, no sooner heard Tancrede's voice than it disappeared like lightning.

Our hero, after murmuring against the injustice of man, now murmured at the ingratitude of mice.

When night came, he undressed himself and went to bed. As it was contrary to the rules to allow lights to the prisoners, they had to go to bed with the sun.

Unluckily for the chevalier, since his departure from Anguilhem, he had lost his habit of going to bed early. On the contrary, during his sojourn in Paris, he had contracted the habit of sitting up late—it was during the fashion of the *petits soupers*, and Tancrede could seldom find his way to bed before two in the morning. While at Anguilhem, he usually retired to rest at eight o'clock in the evening, after a hard day's hunting or other rude exercise. Then physical lassitude soon induced sleep.

But in prison it was quite another thing; the vital energy which coursed through his veins had no outlet for escape. The blood mounted to the head of the prisoner; his pulse beat as if he had been in a fever. He closed his eyes, but fell into that state which is neither sleeping nor waking, but dozing, during which the most extraordinary visions passed before his eyes. He passed part of the night very restlessly, tossing and turning in his bed; but about two in the morning he fell into a sound sleep, during which he had some incoherent dreams. He thought he was endowed with wings like a bird, by means of which he escaped through the window of his prison. Next he was a mouse, and escaped by creeping under the door of his prison. But at the moment he had reached the gutters or gained the free air, his feet or wings suddenly failed him, and he felt himself falling, and falling; but before he reached the ground he awoke in a cold perspiration, his breast heaving and throbbing with a mortal terror.

He could not go to sleep again, but lay awake till daylight.

As soon as he saw the first rays of the sun he jumped from his bed. He immediately commenced turning round and round his cell, as a bear travels round his cage, examining the walls and floor, but always finishing with pausing before the door.

That cursed door, over which ought to have been written Dante's inscription for the gates of hell:

" Abandon hope all ye who enter here."

Yet it was through this door he must pass—there was no other way.

In the morning Tancrede's breakfast was brought as usual. He eat with avidity.

He threw the crumbs near the door, and then went and seated himself on his stool in the opposite corner.

In consequence of taking these precautions he had the satisfaction of seeing, in the course of half an hour, the sharp nose of his neighbor protruding through the hole.

Notwithstanding the impunity with which it had over run the chamber on the previous day, the little animal hesitated a long time before he would venture further in. He withdrew his nose, then protruded it again, crept in a little way, then suddenly retreated, till at last, attracted by the crumbs scattered on the floor, and encouraged by the immobility of the occupant, it darted into the chamber, then suddenly stopped, as if alarmed at its own boldness. But soon, encouraged by its safety, began to eat the crumbs with antics and gambols so amusing, that our hero could never have believed, had he not witnessed them, a mouse could have been so entertaining.

Tancrede, who had remained as immovable as a statue, was unfortunately seized with a cramp in his left leg, and was obliged to change his position. In so doing, the little noise he made was sufficient to alarm his visitor, who quickly made off to his hole under the door. Tancrede reflected that there were two ways by which he could pass in and out as the mouse did. He must either make himself as small as the hole, or make the hole as large as himself.

It was evident to him that only one of these two projects could be entertained.

"By what means can I make the hole larger?" And he replied to himself, "By two means."

By iron, and—

By fire.

To obtain any iron instrument was impossible.

To procure fire was exceedingly difficult.

"I must procure fire," thought he.

Unfortunately, he had no excuse for complaining of cold. It was the middle of summer, and he felt that he should not have patience to wait till winter. Besides, the governor might take it into his head to change his lodging.

He then set his wits to work to consider how he should procure fire. By evening he had matured a plan.

At nine o'clock the sentinel on duty in the gallery heard groans; he listened at both ends of the gallery, and satisfied himself that the groans came from our hero's chamber.

At ten o'clock, when the relief came round, the sentinel informed his officer of what he had heard. The officer went to the door and satisfied himself as to the truth of the sentinel's report. He could hear sighs and groans proceeding from Tancrede's chamber.

The jailer was summoned.

He came, and on opening the door, found our hero stretched upon his bed, complaining of violent pains in his stomach. The physician of the prison was called and prescribed for him.

Next day the chevalier kept his bed, still complaining of the burning pains. At two o'clock he partook of a small quantity of soup sent to him from the governor's table. But the soup was no sooner swallowed than the groaning commenced anew; the physician was sent for, and when he appeared, Tancrede declared that he was being poisoned.

The physician immediately administered suitable antidotes; but, as he had surmised, he found nothing poisonous in the food supplied.

Still he persisted in considering himself as the victim of poison, and declared that from this moment he would rather die of hunger than partake of any food he did not prepare himself.

For the remainder of the day he kept his word; he left his supper untasted, and next morning the jailer removed his breakfast intact as he had left it.

At the usual hour for promenade, he requested to be allowed to go out, but was informed that the hour had been changed.

The governor was afraid that when Tancrede should meet his fellow-prisoners on the platform, he would complain to them of having been poisoned, and that they might believe him.

It was not until five o'clock that he was allowed to go out and take the air on the platform. He had eaten nothing since noon the previous day; he was pale, and appeared to be suffering very much. He could not stand; they were therefore obliged to bring him a seat; and he sat all the time he remained on the platform.

When he reached the store-room, on his way back to his chamber, he became so ill and faint that he asked in a feeble voice for air, and was led to the window.

He put his head out of the window, and saw that it over-

looked the quay named Vallee de Misere. It was at least
sixty feet from the window to the ground; and as all the
other windows of the lower stories were secured with iron
bars, he saw beneath him a perfect forest of railings and
chevaux de frise, with the sharp ends pointing toward him.

At this sight he shuddered; his keeper naturally concluded his sufferings to be the cause of this emotion. He
nevertheless determined that he would make his escape
from that window.

After returning to his chamber, he persisted in refusing
all kinds of nourishment, and still continued to affirm that
he was certain a plot was laid to poison him. He declared
again and again that he would rather die with hunger than
by poison.

An accusation of this kind was too serious a matter not
to give the governor great anxiety. So next morning he
visited the prisoner at breakfast-time. He found the supper that had been left with him on the previous evening
still untouched. Fifty hours had elapsed since the prisoner
had tasted food.

As may be supposed, Tancrede looked very feeble and
much altered in appearance. The governor protested warmly against his suspicions, and tried every means to restore
his confidence; and even offered to partake in his presence
of everything served to him. But our hero obstinately refused, saying that this demonstration went for nothing, as
it was easy for the governor to take an antidote before eating anything, and so neutralize the effects of the poison.

The governor felt greatly embarrassed. He was not acquainted with the offense for which the Chevalier d'Anguilhem had been committed to prison. It was as likely to
be upon some trifling charge as for a grave offense, and in
either case the king might require his prisoner living, either to punish him or to set him at liberty. He then asked
our hero what he wished done to satisfy him, promising to
comply with every wish, so far as it lay in his power.

Tancrede repeated the request he had already made,
namely, to be allowed to prepare his own food.

Taking everything into consideration, the governor could
see no great harm in complying with his prisoner s request.
As Tancrede was very weak, he sent him two new-laid eggs,
so fresh that they were quite warm, and part of a bottle of
Bordeaux wine.

It is scarcely necessary to say that the prisoner exhibited no very alarming symptoms after partaking of this light repast. But slight as it was, it restored much of the strength he had lost. He was not accustomed to fast, and had suffered seriously from his abstinence, and if the governor had not so obligingly relieved him from his embarrassment he would not perhaps have had the courage to play much longer the farce he had undertaken.

But he had attained his object. A stove, some charcoal, and a pair of bellows were brought to him to cook with; also some plates, saucepans, eggs, vegetables, and butter, with a small keg of water.

The chevalier was a sportsman, and in his long excursions around Anguilhem he had frequently had occasion to cook his own dinner. Therefore he was not the least embarrassed in making use of the utensils they brought him.

Whether it was that long fasting had prepared him to find everything good, or that he had a natural talent for cooking, it is certain he did ample justice to the dinner he had prepared for himself.

During the night that followed this repast no groans disturbed the sentinel, who had received orders to listen attentively. As Tancrede expected that on this night he would be subject to unusual surveillance, he contented himself with sleeping soundly; sounder probably than he had done any night since he had been imprisoned. Next morning the governor came again in person, to satisfy himself as to the state of his prisoner's health. He found him up, and busily engaged in preparing his breakfast. This satisfactory state of affairs precluded the necessity of the worthy governor's making lengthened inquiries. He therefore contented himself with asking after his health, and of receiving his thanks. He then departed with the same vague expression on his countenance, and the same motionless lips that the prisoner had constantly remarked in his host at every visit he had paid him.

At five o'clock Tancrede was taken to the platform for his customary promenade; but the arrangement of not allowing this prisoner to have intercourse with the others remained in force. He therefore walked alone, ruminating upon his project, which he decided to put in execution on the following night.

The rest of the evening and all the following day were

passed without molestation. Nothing occurred to derange
the project he had planned. The omens were neither good
nor bad. There was neither comet nor eclipse, therefore
he never felt the least indecision.

Still, with a beating heart, he saw night approach; but
his emotion arose not from any fear that he experienced on
account of the dangers to which he exposed himself, but
from a dread that some unforseen circumstance might occur
to frustrate his attempt to escape. Nevertheless he supped
at his usual hour, and eat with a good appetite; and when
the customary visit was paid to him at eight o'clock, he was
in bed, and apparently composed for the night.

He had two hours to wait before he could make the least
preparation for his escape. The first relief came round at
ten o'clock, the second at three in the morning. Now it
sometimes happened, though seldom, it is true, yet it had
already occurred twice since he had been in For-l'Eveque,
that the officer in command had ordered the doors of the
cells to be opened, and the walls and bars to be examined,
to assure himself that the prisoners did not meditate any
attempt at escape.

Tancrede could not, therefore, undertake to do anything
before ten o'clock. This precaution was not unnecessary,
and he had acted wisely in waiting. For as soon as he had
counted the striking of ten by the prison clock, he heard
the steps of the patrol enter the gallery; then he heard the
door of the store-room opened, then the door of his chamber. For a moment he feared that his intention had been
discovered, and gave himself up for lost; but upon reflection, he considered that to be impossible, seeing he had
made no preparations that could possibly lead to detection,
and as he had communicated his project to no one, there
was no confidant to betray him. So he put a good face on
the matter, and pretended that he had been awakened out
of a sound sleep.

As our hero had concluded, this late visit was only a pre-
cautionary measure. The officer, after examining the walls,
bars and door, retired, saying, " All's well!"

The prisoner soon leaped from his bed, and rushed to the
door to listen to the retreating footsteps of the guard.
Then, when every noise had died away, and the prison had
resumed its customary calm and silence, he proceeded to
dress himself.

As he had been arrested with only what he stood upright in, and as he had left his portmanteau with Basque, so that his progress to Paris on horseback might not be impeded, he had been obliged, while in prison, to provide himself with linen from the stores of the governor. His stock of shirts and handkerchiefs was consequently very small. He took them out of the chest, and commenced tearing them up into slips, and twisted and knotted them, so as to form a kind of rope-ladder.

Meanwhile he had placed all his charcoal against the door of his cell and lighted it, and by applying the bellows, soon raised a pretty large fire.

He then took the coverlet of the bed, and the sheets and blankets, and tore them up also into slips, and fastened the handkerchiefs and shirts to one end, and measured the whole by using his bed as a measure. He reckoned that his bed was six feet in length, and that he would require at least ten times that length, or sixty feet, to reach the ground. All he could reckon upon having attained was about twenty-five feet.

While he was thus engaged, the charcoal was performing its work. It raised a tremendous smoke, and to avoid being suffocated, he was obliged to draw near to the window, and stand upon the stool to obtain fresh air. The night was very dark, else he would surely have been discovered by the smoke that escaped from his window. Fortunately the wind was high, and the smoke was quickly dispersed.

Eleven o'clock struck, then half past, and the prisoner was still busy. At length, about midnight, the fire had burned a pretty large hole in the door, sufficient, or nearly so, to enable him to pass through. He extinguished the fire with the water in his keg, and by removing the charred portions of the wood he made the aperture still larger; then taking the portion of the rope he had already prepared, he crept through on his back, and in another moment found himself in the store-room.

There he could breathe more freely. He listened attentively, but could hear no sound save the measured tread of the sentinel pacing up and down the gallery beyond.

"All's well," murmured Tancrede.

He groped his way to the place where, in passing, he had

seen the heap of lumber, and contrived to single out some old sheets and counterpanes, which he quickly attached to the other portions he had brought with him, until he concluded he had a sufficient quantity to reach the ground, and accomplish his perilous descent in safety.

The rope prepared, he next sought for some firm support to which he could attach it. But the window had no bar sufficiently strong to which he could intrust his safety. He then remembered that his bed had four upright iron rods for supporting a canopy, which would answer his purpose admirably. He returned to his chamber by the same way he had left it.

Quickly removing one of the four rods from his bedstead, he returned to the store-room, tied one end of the rope to the middle of the rod, and placed the rod across the window, so as to fix it securely; then, recommending his soul to God, and breathing a prayer for his father and mother, he addressed a last sigh to Constance, and prepared for the final plunge. He seated himself on the window-sill, then resting his knees against the outside wall, while tightly embracing his rope, he commenced his fearful descent into the abyss, the very sight of which had made him shudder.

As we have previously stated, the distance from the window to the ground was upward of sixty feet. It required, therefore, besides courage, an unusual amount of strength and skill to render the attempt successful.

Our hero was skillful and strong, cool and collected. He made his descent in measured time, not one movement was more hurried than another. He stopped a moment at every succeeding knot to rest, and making use of his feet to clear the sharp-pointed bars that protected the windows of the rooms he had to pass in his descent. By these he reckoned he had descended three stories, and was already beginning to calculate upon success, when suddenly he felt there was nothing between his knees.

He had arrived at the extremity of the rope!

He tried to find a support for his feet, but could feel none. He looked around, but the night was so dark he could see nothing. All he knew was, that an unfathomed abyss was beneath him.

For a moment he entertained the idea of climbing up the rope again, and adding fresh pieces to it, but he felt that his strength would not hold out. His arms were giving him very much pain; he was seized with terror; a cold perspiration bathed his forehead. There might be twenty feet or more between his feet and the ground. He felt that it had now become a question between fortune and misery; that his life was in the hands of fate. He descended to the very extremity of the rope, made another fruitless attempt to find a resting-place for his feet, and then, murmuring a few words of prayer, abandoned himself to his fate, and let go.

The sentinel on duty in this part of the prison was startled by the sound of a falling body, and a smothered cry of pain, and then a groan. He gave the alarm, and soon a number of soldiers ran to the spot with torches. They found our hero in a fainting state, suspended at the extremity of an iron rail, the point of which had pierced his thigh.

CHAPTER XXVII.

WHEN Tancrede recovered his senses he found himself in an unknown chamber. A physician was seated near him. His bed was better and cleaner than the beds in prisons usually are, so that, for a moment, he fancied he had gained his liberty; but unfortunately for the chevalier, such was not the case. The governor had provided him temporarily with a room in his own house.

The wound he had received in his thigh was serious, but not dangerous. He was very weak from having lost a great quantity of blood. His first idea was to satisfy himself whether he could not profit, even by the accident that had befallen him, to attempt another escape. Under the pretext that he felt faint, and wanted fresh air, he begged the physician to open the window. Like most of the windows of the For-l'Eveque, this one was strongly barred on the outside.

When the physician went out, recommending his patient to go to sleep, Tancrede heard him double lock the door after him. By this he understood that he was still in prison, although in one a little more convenient and elegant, but still a prison.

Next day the governor himself paid him a visit, to ascertain why our hero had made such a desperate attempt to escape. He wished to satisfy himself, he said, that it was neither the diet (although frugal) nor the rules of the prison (although rather strict) that had led him to this dangerous act.

Tancrede replied that it was neither of these; that he understood he fared as well at For-l'Eveque as he could expect at any prison, and that it was only the desire of regaining his liberty, which he denied he had ever forfeited, that led him to this extremity.

The governor begged him to sign a declaration to this effect, which, he said, would justify him in the eyes of the superior authorities; and Tancrede signed it immediately.

In fact, he saw some shadow of hope even in this declaration. The poor boy, in the naïveté of his heart, still believed himself the victim of an error, which, some day or other, would be recognized. Therefore he conceived there was a means of his position being discovered through this declaration, which, in some way or other, would soon bring his name before the authorities.

This simple matter inspired the chevalier with fresh courage. It requires very little to excite hope in the bosoms of those who are in despair.

He waited, therefore, with more tranquility while his wound was healing, than he would have done without this little incident. At the expiration of eight days he was able to rise from his bed, and in a fortnight he was permitted to walk about his chamber.

During this interval the governor had visited him three times, and at each visit Tancrede inquired if his declaration had been placed before the minister of police. To the first two inquiries the governor replied that "he hoped it had," but at the third, he informed the prisoner that, as a recompense for the active watchfulness he had displayed on this occasion, he had been named Chevalier of Saint Louis.

The prisoner warmly congratulated the governor upon the honor the king had shown him; and he felt no doubt that the result of the inquiry into his own accident would be, that he would soon regain his liberty. At times he even ventured to think that his being set at liberty would not fail to be distinguished by some mark of favor from his majesty. In his opinion the king was too just to leave such an act of injustice without reparation. But it is necessary to say that our hero dwelt upon this idea of supreme justice only in those moments of optimism, which he himself regarded as slightly exaggerated the moment they had passed away.

Nevertheless, more than fifteen days had elapsed since his declaration had been submitted to the authorities, and apparently no further notice had been taken of it. The chevalier had become nearly convalescent.

One evening the governor entered his chamber.

"Monsieur le Chevalier d'Anguilhem," said he, in his usual tone, and with his vague, unmeaning glance, in which one could read nothing—

"Monsieur," said he, " get up and put on your clothes."

"Get up, and dress myself?" replied Tancrede.

"Yes, monsieur, we are going to part."

"Ah!" said the prisoner. " I knew very well that some day or other my innocence would be proved."

The governor said nothing.

"Monsieur le governor," said the chevalier, while hurrying on his clothes, "rest assured, that if any inquiries are made of me respecting yourself, I shall have great pleasure, as I told you before, in rendering justice to your good intentions toward me, and in providing for my security."

The governor bowed without replying.

"And if, through my friends, I can serve you in any way, I shall avail myself of the opportunity, not only with eagerness, but with gratitude."

The governor muttered something that was quite unintelligible to our hero.

"But," said Tancrede, "I am still too weak to walk much; will you have the kindness, monsieur le governor, to let one of your people order me a coach?"

"There is one at the door, sir."

"Thank you, very much obliged to you, monsieur le governor. I shall have much pleasure in seeing you again, not here, perhaps, but at my house, the Hôtel D'Anguilhem, Place Louis le Grand, formerly the Hotel De Bouzenois."

The governor again bowed without replying; but as the chevalier was ready he did not pay much attention; he held out his hand to the governor, and, leaning on the arm of a soldier, he went out.

The chevalier proceeded through the hall between a double file of soldiers; at the door he saw a coach waiting; he then turned round to pay his last respects to the governor, but the governor had stayed behind.

The chevalier stepped into the carriage, very briskly for
an invalid, and, as the door was being closed, he ordered
the coachman to drive to the Place Louis le Grand, Hotel
Bouzenois.

He fancied he heard a laugh follow this direction to the
coachman; but he paid no attention to it. He stretched
his wounded leg along the seat, and squeezed himself into
the furthest corner of the coach.

Next moment he saw a musketeer riding on each side of
the coach; this excessive honor on the part of his majesty
in sending him home under a military escort, made him
feel rather uneasy.

Then he observed that, instead of descending the quay
the coach crossed the Cite. That was not at all the way to
the Place Louis le Grand.

He then leaned out of the window, and inquired of one
of the guards " where they were taking him to?" Doubtless the noise of the coach wheels, and the rattling of the
horses' hoofs on the stones prevented him from being
heard; for when he repeated the question he received no
reply.

In the course of fifteen minutes, he thought he could
perceive that they were approaching a large isolated building; he put his head out of the window, fixed his eyes upon
the huge black mass, and, to his great horror, recognized—
the Bastile.

What Tancrede had·taken for an emancipation was only
a translation. The favor the king had conferred upon him
was, taking him from For-l'Eveque to immure him in the
Bastile!

He alighted under the archway, where he was searched,
as was customary with prisoners brought to the Bastile.
Then he was taken across the draw-bridge and led into the
guard-house. He had to·wait there while his room was
being prepared.

Tancrede was perfectly dumbfoundered; he had no power
to speak, scarcely to move. One of the musketeers, who
had accompanied him as a body-guard while in the coach,
gave him his arm as a support while he proceeded to his appointed chamber. He allowed himself to be conducted as
resignedly as if he had been going to the scaffold.

While passing through a corridor darker than the rest,
he felt that his guide wanted to slip something into his

hand. He opened it, and received a small billet. He trembled violently.

"It is from the Marquis de Crette," whispered the musketeer.

Our hero wished to reply; but the musketeer immediately ceded his place to a comrade, and disappeared.

The prisoner had been searched, so that he had nothing to fear on that head. He put his hand into his pocket and let the note fall; then he rested his arm on his new guide. They soon arrived at a staircase. They only ascended two flights; doubtless out of consideration for the prisoner's wounds. Arrived there, first one door was opened; then a second; lastly a third, when our hero found himself in a room, where, by the light of the torch, he perceived something like a bed. Immediately afterward, the door of his room was closed, and he heard the other two doors locked and bolted.

He was again a prisoner.

As he was much fatigued, and as his wound was very painful, he set himself to work to find his bed, and proceeded to that side of the room where he supposed it to be. He soon found it; but on seating himself upon it, he was startled by a voice addressing him.

"Monsieur, may I ask what you want?"

"I beg your pardon," said Tancrede, rising. "I was not aware the bed was occupied."

"It is, as you may perceive; and as I am the first comer, allow me to keep it."

"Certainly," said Tancrede; "it is quite right you should. But, as you are the first comer, you know the house better than I do; have the goodness to inform me if there is a couch, chair, or stool in this place, that I can sit down upon; I have a wound in my thigh, and I feel that I can not stand much longer. I am very faint."

"Feel about, sir; there is, doubtless, a couch or something of the sort put here for you."

The chevalier played at blind-man's-buff with the furniture, and at last put his hands on a couch.

He stretched himself upon it, and began to reflect.

At the first sound of the voice from the bed, he fancied he had heard it before; but he could not remember where. He had a good search in order to apply it to some one of his acquaintance, and, at last, his ideas became very confused. Then he thought the best guide in his search would be to ask his companion in captivity, boldly, who he was.

"Monsieur," said he, "when persons are destined, as we are, to occupy, I fear for some time, the same room, the best thing they can do is to become speedily acquainted, in order to know to whom they have the honor to speak."

"But who are you, yourself?" said the voice.

"I am Tancrede d'Anguilhem, prisoner by mistake," said he, "and it is quite right that I should proclaim myself first. And you, who are you?"

"I, sir? I am Number 158."

"What is Number 158?"

"That is my denominator, which has replaced my name and title. To-morrow you will not be called the Chevalier d'Anguilhem; you will be called Number 159, or 160, or 161."

Tancrede shuddered at the idea of first losing his liberty, and then losing his name; that after being a man he should become merely a number.

"Have you been here so long, then, as to have forgotten your name?"

"But I shall be punished, perhaps, if I remember it."

"The deuce! you are very prudent."

"When you have been here ten years, three months, and five days, under lock and key, it is a virtue, I assure you, that you will be glad to put into practice."

"Ten years!" cried Tancrede, "ten years, three months, and five days; I would rather break my head ten times against the walls."

"Sir," said the voice, "it will be better for you that I should not reply any further to you."

"And why so, if you please?"

"Because our great king, Louis the Fourteenth—whom God preserve!—has the right to call us by what name or number he pleases, and of keeping us in prison as long as he pleases."

"Oh! as for that, I recognize you," replied Tancrede, "you have betrayed yourself by too much prudence. You are Count Olibarus!"

"I am not Count Olibarus," replied the voice; "I am Number 158!"

At this moment a step was heard in the corridor.

"Ah! you have ruined me," cried the poor count, "and for the second time; the first, you spoke to me on the platform of For-l'Eveque, and when you tried to escape they took me for your accomplice, and brought me here. You now speak to me for the second time, and here they come to take me to some dungeon, from which I shall never get out."

They heard the first door open.

"But, sir count—" said our hero.

"Silence, sir! in the name of Heaven, silence! Hold your tongue, not another word. I do not know you. I have never spoken to you. I have never seen you."

Thereupon the Count Olibarus rolled himself up in his bedclothes, and turned his face to the wall.

The unhappy prisoner was deceived in his gloomy predictions. The visit was only to make a bed up for his fellow-prisoner.

This attention afforded the chevalier much pleasure. He would have been for the time satisfied with his position, could he have perused De Crette's note, which he turned over and over in his pocket; but his jailers never left the room for a moment during the whole time they were making the bed, which was, however, not very long; and when they went away they carried their candle with them.

Tancrede believed that he was rid of them, when one returned, and opening the door, said—

"Apropos, the last comer is called Number 169."

"Plague!" said Tancrede to himself. "It appears that between the Count Olibarus and myself, ten lodgers have arrived at his majesty's hotel."

And he went to bed with this consolation on his mind, that if the Bastile went on filling at that rate, they would soon be obliged to put the oldest tenants out-of-doors, or put eight or ten prisoners in each room; which, in the first case, would lead to the accomplishment of his most earnest desires, or, in the second, at least procure him some amusement.

Upon this minimum of comfort he composed himself to sleep, holding the Marquis de Crette's note in his hand, with the intention of reading it by the first ray of daylight that penetrated his prison.

But a man is no surer of himself in misfortune than in happiness. Tancrede slept as well as if ne was in his own

bed, perfectly happy, and did not awake until broad daylight. He had much difficulty in making out where he
was. The sight of Count Olibarus seated on his bed, with
his nightcap on, roused him to a sense of his position; and
in looking around the room, he soon remembered that he
was in the Bastile.

Then all the details of his removal from For l'Eveque
rushed into his mind, and he remembered that a musketeer
had put a note from De Crette into his hands, which he
had not been able to read, that he had gone to sleep with
this note in his hand, and that he had promised to read it
as soon as it became daylight.

He shuddered at the thought of losing this note. He
immediately set himself to work to find it; fortunately, he
soon discovered it under his bolster.

The note read as follows:

"I hear that you are to be transferred from For-l'Eveque to the Bastile, and by means of Clos-Renaud, who is
lieutenant in the gray musketeers, I send you this note.
Your wife has not yet made her appearance; and did I not
think it would drive you to despair, I should say she is no
stranger to your imprisonment. Royancourt is more than
ever in favor, and from the manner in which he replied to
me when I solicited your release, I am convinced the blow
came from him. Moreover, they pretend to have found
some satirical songs against Madame de Maintenon, written
by you, or at least, in your handwriting. Probably one of
those you used to sing to us at Saint Germain. You can
very easily see that no one but your wife could have committed this piece of petty treachery.

"We can do nothing to obtain your release; but try and
escape, and come to me. Two or three disguises are
ready; you will travel night and day, and in four-and-
twenty hours, be in a foreign country and free."

This letter was like a thunder-bolt upon poor Tancrede.
He fully believed his wife culpable; he had not the least
doubt that Sylvandire had betrayed him; but what she had
to do with putting him in For-l'Eveque he could not
imagine. He could not doubt that his arrest had made
some noise, and it was not probable that Sylvandire was
ignorant of it; and if she were not ignorant of it, and was
gone away, why had she not returned to Paris to endeavor

to obtain his liberty? Why had not she applied to Master Bouteau, and to M. de Royancourt for the assistance of their friends? Why had she not solicited a favor rarely, if ever, refused to wives, that of obtaining permission to visit their husbands?—even if this interview must take place in the presence of witnesses.

He could readily believe what Crette said. Besides Crette was not deceived when he predicted the future, and for that reason must be considered correct when he related the past.

Having reduced De Crette's note to fragments, and threw them into the fire-place—for, at the Bastile, the rooms above the first story had fire-places—he arose, and planned the most terrible projects of vengeance against the Marquis de Royancourt and Sylvandire.

But to execute his plans of vengeance he must be free; and Crette had told him he must reckon upon no one but himself, convinced that all efforts on his part would be fruitless. Our hero then began to consider by what means he could escape. He was so near making good his escape from For-l'Eveque, that he could not see why he should not succeed as well at the Bastile.

There was, however, one great obstacle in the way of any attempt at flight; this was the presence of Count Olibarus.

Tancrede reflected several days upon his project; but after all his reflecting, he could decide upon nothing. Meanwhile his companion exhibited more and more caution, avoided all conversation and would reply to him only when he called him by his number.

Three weeks passed away. Number 169 spent his days in meditating plans of evasion, and in cursing the cowardice of his companion in imprisonment, who, immediately Tancrede hinted at the subject, threatened to call the sentinel. Many times he felt a ferocious inclination to strangle him, and say that he had died while in a fit of apoplexy; but fortunately he always checked himself in time, reserving this high-handed measure for the last extremity.

We have already stated that, notwithstanding his many anxieties, he always slept well. He was scarcely twenty-one years of age, and at that age sleep is seldom troubled. Yet it frequently happened that while asleep he heard noises which he took for episodes in his dreams.

As for the count, he seemed still more addicted to sleep

than our hero; for almost always, when he arose, the count was still sound asleep.

One night when Tancrede was in bed, revolving in his mind a new plan, lying motionless with a coverlet over his ears, ruminating all the good and bad chances of his new plan, he thought he heard a singular noise, which he remembered to have heard in his dreams. He immediately began to listen with all his ears, and soon recognized the sound of a file cutting iron, the sound of which came from the side of the room where Count Olibarus slept. Then, without interrupting his breathing, which, on the contrary, he now regulated so as to appear sleeping soundly, he opened one eye and looked toward the window, which, notwithstanding the darkness of the night, always admitted sufficient light to enable the eye to discern an object before it.

At first he could distinguish nothing; but gradually his eye became accustomed to the darkness, and then he could perceive Count Olibarus kneeling on his bed and filing the bars of his window.

If ever our hero had been astonished in his life, it was now. He remained for some moments breathless. The moment the count no longer heard the sound of his respiration he stopped. The chevalier understood he was watched, so he turned over in his bed, yawned and murmured some unmeaning words, like one in a dream, then pretended to sleep again. The count remained some time listening; then, upon the respiration of his companion appearing to be again regular and calm, he resumed his labor.

There was no doubt whatever that Count Olibarus, that nervous, timid, prudent man, was making preparations for escape.

Tancrede immediately made up his mind what to do.

Four o'clock struck. As in all probability the affair could not come off that night, he composed himself to sleep.

Upon waking at his usual hour, he found the count as quietly asleep as usual. Our hero could now understand why he slept so late in the morning. When he awoke Tancrede endeavored to get into conversation with him; but with no better success than on former occasions. The count complained loudly of the misfortune that pursued him, in finding a man like the chevalier so frequently crossing his path and compromising his safety.

In all his complaints there was such an air of good faith, that our hero in looking alternately at the bars and at the count, began to think he had had a dream.

The day passed without Tancrede betraying by a word, look, or gesture, that he had discovered the count's secret. But he awaited the coming of night with impatience.

This time he did not go to sleep. The count was very coy, and kept quite still for a couple of hours, modulating his respiration with that of his companion. At length, convinced that his companion slept, he raised himself upon his knees, and set himself to work, as he had done the previous night, and probably many others.

The chevalier quietly watched him, without disturbing his confidence.

At the expiration of a couple of hours, the count stopped at his labors, and, stepping on to the floor, advanced toward the fire-place, taking with him a stool, upon which he mounted, and then spoke a few words in a low tone, yet not so low but that Tancrede could hear:

"To-morrow all will be ready."

A voice replied a few words, but what they were our hero could not distinguish, as they appeared to be uttered in another chamber. Only he could hear the count's reply:

"Very well; to-morrow."

He listened, and the same voice sounded in the chimney, to which the count replied:

"Say at two o'clock."

Then the count quickly returned the stool to its place, regained his bed, and appeared to go to sleep.

Tancrede, who was quite satisfied with what he knew, went to sleep in earnest, and slept tranquilly.

The next day passed like the preceding, without the count betraying in any manner, by impatience, trepidation, or nervousness, the project he had arranged for the coming night. He was the same mute, trembling coward as ever; so much so that our hero, who, as we have shown, had a certain command over himself, stood in admiration before this master of dissimulation, which chance had presented to him, and who so greatly surpassed himself.

When night came, the two prisoners retired to bed. Each pretended to undress himself, but lay down in his clothes. Soon both began to snore much better than if they had been asleep.

About midnight the count rose in his bed, and began to file the last bar. This occupied him for nearly an hour. Then he left his bed, went toward the chimney, and mounting upon the stool, whispered.

"All's ready."

The voice replied some words our hero could not understand, but which seemed to be in complete harmony with the count's wishes, for he merely replied,

"Very well."

Then he got down from the stool, and returned to his bed.

Half an hour passed away.

Then the count arose, went to listen at the door of the room, and after satisfying himself that the greatest tranquillity prevailed in the place, he remained motionless for a few moments, as if considering; then, with a slow and silent step, the stealthy tread of which his companion could scarcely hear, he approached Tancrede's bedside.

It immediately occurred to our hero that the count was come to assassinate him, to secure his own safety from interference. The chevalier therefore put himself on his guard; for although he had no means of defending himself, he felt he could soon master an old man, who probably had no other weapon than a dirk or a knife. He made himself quite ready to seize the count's arm the moment he should raise it to strike him.

But the count did not raise his arm; he merely touched him on the shoulder with his hand.

At the same moment Tancrede sprung up and stood before the astonished count, who recoiled a step or two.

"Silence!" said the count.

"The more willingly as I know everything, my dear count," replied our hero.

"How's that?"

"For these last three nights past, I have not slept; and as I can not say I saw what you were about, I may say I heard you."

"Then you understand what's going on?"

"Perfectly, and I am ready."

"Dress yourself."

"I am dressed."

"Capital!"

"You see you did me an injustice in not making a confidant of me."

"But you are so young."

"But I have courage and resolution."

"I know it; you have given good proof of it at For-l'Eveque; and for that reason I resolved to wait: for the moment when you would have most need of those two virtues; that moment has arrived; prepare yourself."

"I am ready, what is to be done?"

"I am going to tell you. I have established a communication with two prisoners in the upper chamber; one of them is my friend; and we were going to escape together from For-l'Eveque, when your attempt led to our all being brought to the Bastile. Fortunately we were separated only by a plank; and we contrived to communicate with each other by an opening in the chimney. We have one file between us; each cuts the bars of his own window. Our neighbors will first let down the rope they made with their own sheets and coverlets; we shall add ours to them. They will then draw the whole up and fasten one end to the sound bars of their windows; and as their window is directly over ours, we descend, they from their window, we from ours."

"Excellent!"

"Then you are satisfied with the arrangements?"

"Perfectly. Now, my dear count," said Tancrede, "as we are going to escape together, one word before we start. Tell me candidly, why you are in the Bastile? What's your offense?"

"Do you wish particularly to know?"

"Yes; it will really afford me much pleasure," said our hero. "I shall measure my offense by yours. You have been a prisoner ten years. I shall then be able to reckon how long his majesty intends to keep me in confinement."

"Well! I was so imprudent as to say—"

"You had the imprudence to say—" repeated Tancrede.

"That the king—" continued the count, lowering his voice.

"Well—that the king—"

"Had become so blind—"

"So blind—"

"So blind that he could see only with the spectacles of Madame de Maintenon."

"What!" cried Tancrede, "and ten years for saying
that?"

"Hush!" cried the count.

"You have been in prison ten years for saying that?"

"Ten years, three months, and seven days."

"Ah! *mon Dieu!* in that case I shall be imprisoned all
my life!"

"What have you done, then?"

"I have written two songs about her!"

"And she knows it?"

"It seems that my wife has given up the originals."

"In your writing?"

"In my writing."

"Then, my dear friend, in that case it is very fortunate
for you that you have an opportunity of escaping; or, as
you said, you will be kept here all your life."

"Or for all of theirs," replied the chevalier.

"Which may be a very long while yet," replied the
count. "Egotists live 150 years, like parrots. But silence;
I hear our rope coming down."

The count approached the chimney, and felt for the end
of the rope. The two prisoners then fastened their sheets
and coverlets to it; when this was completed, the prisoners
in the upper story drew it up again.

Proceeding to the window, the count, aided by our hero,
removed the two bars, which were now easily detached,
and made an opening large enough for a man to pass
through.

It was agreed that the count should pass first.

They both stood on the bed and held themselves in readiness.

The heard the friction of the cord as it descended.

Then they could see an opaque body pass down; this was
one of the prisoners from the upper story. He reached the
ground without accident and waited.

The second then passed down, and he also reached the
ground without accident.

Now it became the count's turn, who reached the ground
with the same success. Our hero went down last, and arrived safely among his companions.

At about twenty paces off was a sentinel who walked
slowly along his post, alternately with his face and his back
toward the fugitives. There was no way to flee except by

passing within ten paces of him. They must leap from the rampart into the ditch, cross the ditch by swimming, as cend the opposite slope, and slide down upon the roof of some house of the Faubourg Saint-Antoine, and escape by the gutters and garret-windows. They ran the risk of breaking their necks twenty times.

It was arranged that at the moment the sentinel turned his back, the four fugitives should start, and each take care of himself.

They watched the soldier along his accustomed promenade, till he turned toward the opposite end.

At this moment the four fugitives ran straight for the ditch.

Tancrede heard the " *Qui vive !*" of the sentinel, then he saw a flash, followed by a detonation, felt one of his companions roll between his legs, and at the same time he experienced a sensation similar to that of a violent blow from a whip which struck him in the side. But he kept on and threw himself into the ditch, and was soon gaining the other side of the water.

Meanwhile, he heard a great uproar at the Bastile; lights appeared at the windows, torches were hurried to and fro, and the soldiers cried, " To arms! to arms!"

Our hero swam on, the coolness of the water prevented him feeling any pain: he reached the shore, believing himself only slightly wounded; but no sooner had he put his foot on the slope, than he felt his strength begin to fail him. He gathered all his courage, and, aided by his hands, continued to slide down the grassy bank. But it appeared to him that the sky became the color of blood; he felt a sound of ringing in his ears. He tried to speak, calling mechanically for help, but his voice expired in his throat. Then he beat the air with his hands, made a last effort, in which all his strength became exhausted, and fainted.

CHAPTER XXVIII.

COUNT OLIBARUS was killed, and our hero dangerously wounded. The count was interred as Number 158, and the chevalier was brought back to the Bastile.

But Tancrede was a Hercules; at the expiration of three weeks he was on his legs again; still weak, it is true, but

completely out of danger. These two unsuccessful attempts
had considerably cooled his imagination with regard to attempts at escape, and for a time, at least, he was nearly
cured of his mania for flying.

Of one thing, however, he was not cured, and of which
he promised himself never to be cured: this was his hatred
of Sylvandire, to whom he owed, as Crette informed him,
first his imprisonment, and next his two wounds. It is
true, that Sylvandire, in getting rid of her husband, by
means of For-l'Eveque and the Bastile, so much in vogue
at that date, could never have imagined that he would
have had the bad taste twice to attempt to escape, and that
both these attempts would be attended with such unpleasant consequences. But it was none the less true that Sylvandire was the cause of it all.

Therefore the chevalier promised himself, if ever he
gained his liberty, to take a most bitter revenge. But what
shape should this revenge take? He did not himself yet
know. He only knew that some day or other he would be
revenged.

One evening, after having all day nursed his ideas of revenge, he heard steps in the corridor. It was a very unusual hour for any one to be there. As, during the four
or five months he had been in prison, he had gained some
knowledge of the habits in establishments of this kind, he
had now no doubt that something new was going to happen
to him.

He was not kept long in suspense. The door of his
room opened, and two soldiers placed themselves on either
side of it; they were followed by the governor, who, after
saluting his prisoner, invited him to take what things belonged to him in his room, and follow him. The inven-
tory was soon made, one of the attendants took charge of
the package, and Tancrede followed the governor.

He traversed the corridor that led to the inner court,
then the court next the archway, all lined with a double
file of guards; then arrived outside, he saw a coach.

He was about to undergo another translation.

The chevalier had acquired some doubts as to the quality
of the memory of his most gracious majesty King Louis
the Fourteenth; so on this occasion he did not allow himself to be deceived with the idea that he was going to be
taken to the Place Louis le Grand. Besides, he saw a mus-

keteer placed on each side of the carriage, and a policeman inside. The prisoner bade the governor farewell, and thanked him for the care he had taken of him while suffering from his wound. He then took his seat opposite the police officer. The door of the coach was closed and locked, and they started off in a gallop.

The coach traversed a part of Paris, without our hero being able to discover in what direction he was being taken. It was one of those dark nights usually selected for the removal of prisoners. But he soon felt that the air was cooler and purer than that of the capital, he leaned toward the door of the coach, and perceived he was passing trees and fields; but as he appeared too deeply interested in the sight, the officer addressed him:

"I beg to inform you, my gentleman, that the door of the coach is locked, that two musketeers are riding outside, and that I have a pistol in each pocket; and my orders are to shoot you if you make the slightest attempt to escape. I tell you this because I am an old soldier, and do not wish to assassinate a gentleman without letting him know my reasons for so doing: now you are forewarned, take care of yourself."

Tancrede threw himself back in the coach, heaving a profound sigh. He began to entertain a very deep respect for physical force, which hitherto he had understood to mean "to fight and conquer."

"But where are you taking me to?" said he.

"I am forbidden to tell you," replied his companion. "Be a little reasonable, and do not despond; better times will come. I have accompanied women who showed more fortitude than you do."

"Are you taking me to another prison?" asked our hero.

"Oh! as to that, I may as well tell you as not. You will not believe me, so I shall say, frankly I am."

"To Pignerol? to the Isle of Saint Marguerite?" murmured the chevalier. "Ah! Fouquet. Ah! Lauzun!"

"Hush!" said the officer; "hush! Do not damage your position by speaking of those great gentlemen. Go along quietly, without bothering your head about politics. Look you now, I am a free and easy sort of fellow; and it is very lucky for you that you have not fallen into the hands of some of our fellows, coarse and brutish rascals, who would not open their mouths to you the whole journey. For my

part, I like to take things as they come. I like to talk,
and I find it much pleasanter to laugh with my prisoners
than to cry: ready to show my teeth and claws though, if
they are not pleased with my behavior; but I am proud to
say, I have never had occasion to do that. Now, be a
good boy, like the others, and I promise you the road will
not appear so very long."

"Ah," said our hero, shuddering, "that's it, is it? You
are going to take me to the other end of France. Ah, Matthioli!—oh! Iron Mask!"

"Oh, stop, stop," cried the officer. "Now, on my
word, you are going to make the journey very disagreeable,
while I ask nothing more than to make it pleasant. Courage, now; and put a good face on the matter. I say that,
not that I can see you at present, but because I can guess
you are down in the mouth; and I shall talk to you,
although I am strictly enjoined not to do so."

"And what will you talk about?" asked the prisoner.

"Of things in general, and of your friend Madame de
Maintenon in particular; of the weather, of the rain; anything will be better than sitting here as mute as a couple of
fish."

"But there is only one thing I desire to know—only one
thing upon which I desire to be enlightened."

"What is it, now? say."

"Where are we going?"

"I am ordered not to tell you."

"Ah! you know very well."

"Yes. But I am not forbidden to tell you where we are
not going."

"Oh! then tell me."

"In the first place, let us make some conditions. Promise that you will not attempt to escape, and that you will
not be so melancholy. Ah, me! Dull care would be the
death of me."

"But, on your part," said Tancrede, "give me your
word, as an old soldier, that you will faithfully discharge a
little commission I shall entrust you with."

"I?"

"Yes, you!"

"If you were to offer me a hundred thousand crowns I
would not promise you anything. Consider, my dear sir,
what an absurd thing you ask of me. Why, pray, does his

majesty keep you out of sight, under lock and key, but to prevent you from sending messages? Be reasonable then."

Our hero reflected that he should gain nothing by putting himself in bad humor with his companion, while possibly he might lose a great deal. Escape on the road appeared clearly impossible. Besides, as we have said, he was temporarily cured of his monomania. So, after a momentary silence,

"Ah, well, sir," said he to his traveling companion, "I give you my word as a gentleman, that I will not attempt to escape while I have the honor to be in your company, and that I will make myself as happy as I possibly can."

"That's sensible now, and we shall be sure to have a very pleasant journey. Ask me as many questions as you like, and I will reply to all I can."

"Are we going to the Isles of Sainte Marguerite?"

"No!"

"Are we going to Pignerol?"

"No!"

"Are we going to the Tower of St. John's?"

"No!"

"Are we going to Pierre-en-Scise?"

"You burn."

"To the fortress of Dijon?"

"You burn! You burn!"

"Then we are going to the castle at Chalons?"

Silence, perfect and prolonged.

"You do not answer me!" said Tancrede, impatiently.

"That was not in our agreement," said the officer. "I promised to tell you where we are *not* going; but I told you that I was strictly prohibited from telling you where we *are* going. Suppose I am compromised by my good feeling toward you, and that I am compelled to take an oath that I have not told you you were being taken to Chalons, then I can raise my hand and conscientiously swear that I have never told you so."

"Ah! then, I see, we are going to Chalons," murmured the chevalier with a sigh, at the same time throwing himself back silent and pensive into the corner of the coach.

"Come, come," said his traveling companion, "you are getting into the dumps again; we shall have a very dull journey if you go on in this fashion, and for a couple of

days too. Come now, understand, once for all, I shall not
allow it."

"Will you compel me to be cheerful, then?" said the
prisoner.

"I have your word, sir, and as a man of honor, you
should have pity on a poor police-officer, and keep it. But
do not think I was born to be a policeman; oh, no! not I.
My vocation is to play at Turlupin's in the vaudeville. I
can sing a good song, sir. I can sing some of your songs,
sir—think of that! Ah! you make capital songs, you do!"

"What do you mean?" asked Tancrede.

"Ah! now, don't deny it. Don't be so modest. Why, I
have seen them in your own hand-writing."

"I really do not know what you mean."

"I understand. I understand. I don't ask you to confess. But it is very certain that your vein is the satirical."

"Satirical? Dear me! what next?"

The officer hummed a tune very popular at the time, and
then broke out with the following:

> " ' On dit que c'est la Maintenon
>   Qui renverse le trône,
>   Et que cette vieille guenon
>   Nous réduit à l'aumône.
>   Louis le Grand soutient que non
>   La faridondaine, la faridondon,
>   Et-que tout se règle par lui
>   Biribi,
>   A la façon de Barabri, mon ami,
>   Mon ami.' "

"I never wrote that!" cried the chevalier. "I had the
misfortune to copy it—that's all!"

"And this, too?" said his companion, taking up another
air:

> " ' Tout ce que fait la Maintenon,
>   Ne saurait jamais être bon.
>   Cette vieille sempiternelle,
>   A donné la guerre au Voisin,
>   Et je crois que Polinchinelle,
>   Aura les finances demain.' "

"But I can assure you, I did not write that song either,"
said our hero.

"Good! Let us try another." And the officer commenced a third song:

> " ' Ah! ah! ah! Maintenon,
>   Margoton
>   Dit le bon roi,
>   Laisse-moi
>   Car c'est toi
>   Qui me fera rire
>   Dans la poêle à frire.' "

"But," said Tancrede, "how is it you can sing these songs without being arrested?"

"I sing them to you only, my gentleman; but to no one else. I am not such a fool as to sing them in public, or to leave copies lying about in my handwriting. I thought the verses very good; and the proof of it is, I have not forgotten a word, have I, sir? Hem! It is you, now, is it not? if I am not deceived, you are the author; say, now, are you not?"

"On my honor," said the prisoner, "I protest—"

"Hush! hold your tongue. I had better pretend not to believe it. Oh! no, it is not you—say no more about it."

"Oh! miserable fool that I was, to sing such songs; unfortunate wretch that I am!"

"Quite the contrary; we may sing them; there is no harm in that; but we must sing them in very select society, en tête-à-tête, as we are. But we must not keep copies of them, in our handwriting; that is dangerous, very—especially when we have a wife who wants to get rid of us. Ah! that is too great a temptation for a woman!"

"Ah!" said Tancrede, "then you know of my adventure."

"What adventure?"

"What you just alluded to."

"I did not allude to anything nor to anybody. I said nothing that had any reference to anything in particular. I knew nothing, but

> "On dit que c'est la Maintenon
>   Qui renverse le trône."

Tancrede, quite astonished at the singular situation in which he found himself, began to fear that he was losing his senses in the conflict of ideas which besieged him. He closed his eyes, and leaned his forehead against the sides of the coach, and endeavored to clear his mind of the rubbish that confused it.

The officer passing from one song to another, continued to hum the seditious verses, for which he appeared to have a particular admiration. But as our hero had not slept for three nights, he was quite drowsy, and soon fell into a profound slumber, from which he only awoke late in the morning. He found his companion in his place, quite lively and fresh, who smilingly inquired of the chevalier how he had slept. As for himself, he assured him that relying upon his word of honor, he had passed a very good night.

When they stopped to breakfast, he asked Tancrede if he had any money; but he had not a copper. Everything valuable he possessed had been taken away from him, even his rings, for fear he might corrupt his guards with them, The prisoner, therefore, humbly confessed his poverty.

The officer seemed to be debating in his mind as to what he should do. There appeared to be a struggle going on between the good genius and the evil, till at length the good prevailed.

"Hark you. I could keep fifteen sous out of the two francs the king allows for your breakfast; but you are so agreeable and polite, and you have kept your word; so instead of extorting anything from you, as most of my fraternity would do, I shall add something, and with your permission, if my company is not disagreeable to you, we will take breakfast together."

"With the greatest pleasure," replied our hero, who never gave way to exaggerated aristocratic ideas; and who besides did not wish to quarrel with his companion.

They both sat down to table. As the officer had promised, the breakfast was an excellent one. Tancrede eat like a convalescent of twenty.

"It is a fine thing to be young," said the official, looking at his charge with admiration. "What a charming appetite!" He had not exhibited a very poor one himself. "I was just like you at your age; only more lively, singing all day, as loud as I could, from morning till night, like a nightingale or a lark; but I always took care to sing other people's songs, not my own, no never! except it was with a friend like you, *tête-à-tête.* For you must know, I wrote some songs, not so good as yours, perhaps, but which nevertheless had their merits. Listen, now, here's one—

" Tonton, ton tempt est passe,
        Vieille coquette,
    Tonton, ton timbre est casse,
    Vieille pendule, tu repetes

A soixante ans
Le carillon de la clochette
Dans son printemps.
Mais à présent
Ton tocsin tintant
Ne réveille personne,
Quand sur le tendre ton
Ta grosse cloche sonne,
Non, non, non,
Si l'on t'entend,
Ce n'est qu'au son,
De ton argent comptant.

"Hem! what do you say to that, my chevalier?" said the officer, when he had finished and after he had given our hero time to appreciate his poetry.

"What I have to say, is," replied Tancrede, "that I think you are very imprudent to sing such songs."

"Why so?"

"I might inform against you."

"Bah! you would not be believed. I should say you only did it to revenge yourself upon me for my severity toward you, and it would all fall on your own back."

In the course of the following night they arrived at the Castle of Chalons-sur-Saone.

The chevalier was immediately conducted to the chamber destined for him; but as he was greatly fatigued with his long journey, and much weakened by his last wound, which was not yet quite healed, he threw himself on his bed, without even looking to see if there was anything in his chamber.

He only remarked that the room was lighted by a lamp suspended from the ceiling; and this attention gave him some satisfaction.

CHAPTER XXIX.

WHEN Tancrede first awoke, he saw the lamp was still burning; thinking it was not yet daylight, he turned his face to the wall, and went to sleep again.

But the second time he awoke, he was astonished to see that it was not yet daylight, for the lamp was still burning. He looked around him, and then the horrible truth flashed upon his mind; he was in an underground dungeon. This lamp, which he had welcomed as an extra attention, was

really his only sun. A turning cupboard contained his
breakfast; a sure sign that the day was already far advanced.

Strong-nerved as he was, this misfortune quite crushed
him. He seated himself on his bed, his arms hanging list-
lessly by his side, and asked himself what he had done
against God and man, that he should be thus forsaken by
the one, and maltreated by the other.

In this condition he passed a space of time, the duration
of which he could not measure. At length he heard a
sound in the wall; his cupboard made a turn and reappeared bearing his dinner, which replaced the breakfast
that he had left untasted.

Still, amid the profound misery that weighed upon him,
Nature, always exacting, would not be cheated, but sternly
demanded her rights! As he was both hungry and thirsty,
he mechanically approached the cupboard, and ate and
drank like a famished animal. Then he commenced pacing around the walls of his dungeon like a wild beast in its
cage.

It would have fared badly with Sylvandire, had she presented herself in this den at that moment.

The hours passed away without light or darkness indicating their progress. The days passed over without his
hearing any kind of sound. He was literally buried alive.
The only distraction he received was from the noise made
by his turning cupboard, when his meals were served, or
when the unseen attendant ascended to the ceiling to re-
plenish his lamp with oil, or put in a fresh wick.

But the hand that turned his cupboard or replenished
his lamp always remained invisible.

Two or three times, Tancrede addressed himself to the
unknown moving power, and inquired of him what day
and hour it was; not for the sake of knowing what the day
and the hour were, so much as to hear, at least, the sound
of a human voice. But he never obtained any response to
his questions, and the unhappy prisoner soon ceased to
renew attempts, the uselessness of which he fully recognized.

First, despair took possession of him; then, prostration
succeeded to despair. He sometimes slept twelve hours at
a stretch. He would roll on the floor like a brute, or remain for hours immovable as an idiot.

Sometimes he hoped he should become mad, and he welcomed the idea with shouts of the wildest laughter.

But even this happiness was denied him. As a stone thrown into a pool momentarily troubles the water, and causes the mud to rise to the surface; so, from the blow that had fallen upon his heart, had rage and despair mounted to his brain. But as, little by little, the water purifies itself again, so the mind of the prisoner became again calm; and, at the end of a month of this captivity, any one, looking at him, would have thought him tranquil, and almost restored to his accustomed serenity.

In this manner, the revenge that at first disturbed his reason subsided by degrees, and soured his heart to the bottom.

Then he appeared to become calm and resigned. He appeared to live as others lived; and his mind acquired activity through the repose of his body.

Compelled to review his situation, he imagined a thousand confused forms, the existence of which he never would have suspected, had he been at liberty in society and his mind distracted by external objects.

He examined his life, day by day, hour by hour, and almost minute by minute, from the moment he had become the husband of Sylvandire until the day he had been arrested on the Cours la Reine. He reviewed the temporary love that Sylvandire had appeared to feel toward him. He saw this factitious love gradually give way to indifference; then he perceived the development of the first symptoms of hatred, which Sylvandire had afterward so strongly manifested—these first symptoms had immediately followed the introduction of M. de Royancourt at the Hotel d'Anguilhem.

This hatred was soon strengthened by that which Sylvandire entertained against her husband's friends. Then commenced a strife between these two different natures, so unlike each other. Each one summoned to its aid its natural auxiliaries. Tancrede called Crette, D'Herbigny, Clos-Renaud, and the host of gentlemen of liberal hearts, who first advised their friend to make open and honest war, then a prudent retreat. Sylvandire had called in the Marquis de Royancourt, M. Bouteau, doubtless, and the Jesuit, Letellier. Perhaps they had had recourse to

tortuous maneuvers, hidden snares, nocturnal plots; and
they had succeeded.

Tancrede was now wholly in their power; tied hands and
feet; lying under an accusation which had no real connection with the cause of his arrest. This imprisonment would
continue just as long as the passion, love, or caprice of M.
de Royancourt existed for Sylvandire; perhaps even a little longer; for, to the fear of the recriminations of an injured husband, would succeed the fear of the vengeance of
the bruised prisoner. His imprisonment might then be
prolonged indefinitely; either by the love with which Sylvandire inspired the marquis resisting time, or by the fear
with which Tancrede inspired M. de Royancourt becoming
greater than his remorse.

Then our hero examined his own conduct toward her
with the same minuteness that he had examined that of
others; and he found a thousand ways, in such a case, of
avoiding all the misfortunes that happened to him.

"Yes," said he; "yes, I have been a great fool. I
should have done like so many husbands that I have known,
who are considerate and happy, and who, at this hour, walk
the streets of Paris in full liberty. I should have shut my
eyes; made love to some Poussette, as De Crette wittily advised. Most decidedly, all these men were men of sense.
I alone, the fool.

"Instead of being a poor prisoner, as I am, I should
have been a colonel in some fine regiment. I should have had
to fast three times a week, it is true; but on the other four
days of the week, in some little elegant quiet house in the
Faubourg Saint-Antoine, have feasted with my friends.
The king would have bestowed his blandest smile upon
me; and, once a week, I should have had the honor to kiss
the skinny hand of Madame de Maintenon. I should have
curried favor with Father Letellier, and been gazetted a
duke, and, perhaps, a peer of France.

"Yes, truly, I am a great fool!

"But, no! no! a hundred times, no! I have done what
I ought to have done, and what I would do again; for there
is but one sort of honor in this world, and but one way of
viewing it. Besides, I loved this woman, not with my
heart, for my heart was given to poor Constance, but I
loved her with pride; I loved her because she was beautiful; perhaps, also, because I had sacrificed so much for her;

perhaps, because she owed everything to me—but, whatever it was, I loved her. I ought not, I could not, suffer her to be lost.

"I have done, then, what I ought to have done; and it is not I who am the fool, but they who are infamous.

"But, again, some day I shall be free, and avenge myself. But when—when shall I be free? That is the question."

When at For-l'Eveque he had said, that if he was set at liberty, he would forgive everything. When in the Bastile, he had made some mental restrictions. At Chalons, he said that he was twenty-two, and the king was seventy-five, and that he would give the king ten years to live; that is to say, wait till he was eighty-five; which was as long as a crowned head could desire, however exacting he might be.

Now, if the king died the prisons would be opened. Our hero, then, looking at the worst side, would leave prison when he was thirty-two.

Tancrede next asked himself which he would prefer; to leave his prison at that moment and not revenge himself, or stay ten years longer in it, and then take his revenge at his leisure.

He decided that he would prefer to go out of prison ten years hence and revenge himself; but to revenge himself deeply and skillfully.

Thus, at the end of three months' isolation and seclusion, he had become a profound thinker, a consummate politician, a Machiavelli of the first order.

Could he have been seen, he would have presented himself seated upon a stool, his legs crossed, his elbow on his knee, resting his chin on his hand, with fixed eyes and a smile on his lips; and one would have thought that he was thinking of his father, or of his mother, or of Mlle. Constance de Beuzerie, of his happy childhood and youth, or some other sweet remembrance.

No: he was thinking of revenge!

Eleven months passed away in this manner; but the heart of the prisoner never despaired, nor did his courage ever fail him. Perhaps his complexion, deprived of the light of the sun, had grown paler during this long night; perhaps his herculean form had become reduced by his slender diet; but he had acquired a degree of elegance that would have been looked for in vain before. Tancrede con·

tinued strong and handsome; but he had become a stanch
hypocrite.

Every evening he prayed aloud for the health of the king
and Mme. de Maintenon; for he thought he might possibly
be watched, and his words listened to. It is true, that, at
the same moment, in his heart, he wished them both at the
devil; but that was in confidence with himself, and known
to no one but himself, and to God, to whom all things are
known.

One morning while he was putting his beautiful white
teeth into a piece of very brown bread, which served him
for breakfast, the door of his dungeon suddenly opened,
and a familiar voice fell upon his ears. Long accustomed
to the gloom and obscurity—for frequently his lamp was
not lighted for several days together—his eyes distinguished
a gentleman, magnificently attired, enter the cell, and pronounce his name.

It was M. de Royancourt, who advanced with open arms
to embrace him.

Tancrede was seated on his stool; he rose from it and
seized it by one of its legs with the intention of knocking
M. de Royancourt on the head. He was face to face with
his enemy. He had only to let his massive arm fall to
annihilate him; but he paused, threw the stool on his bed,
and ran to the Marquis de Royancourt with open arms.

In consequence of the darkness that prevailed, the marquis had not seen the threatening gesture.

These two men, who mortally hated each other, pressed
their hearts together as if they had been two friends, or two
brothers.

"You are here, then, my dear Anguilhem?" said the
marquis. "Oh! how long have we searched for you without finding you."

In spite of his presence of mind, our hero stood confounded at so much effrontery; but he dissimulated his
astonishment with a smile, and accepted the hand that M.
de Royancourt extended to him to lead him out of prison;
and warmly pressing his hand, he walked beside him into
the governor's apartments.

The chevalier, finding himself opposite a mirror, surveyed himself; but had some difficulty in recognizing the
Chevalier d'Anguilhem in the pale, bearded, tangled figure
before him, clothed in rags.

He smiled with the same sort of smile as that with which he had welcomed M. de Royancourt.

"You are free, my dear Monsieur d'Anguilhem," said the marquis. "But how is it that we have had no news of you for fifteen months? But we will talk about that by and by. Let us now attend to the most important."

"The most important, my dear liberator, my more than friend, my brother, will be, I think, to ascertain of the governor if I really am free, which at present I can not really credit."

"You are free, my dear chevalier, thanks to our intercession," replied the marquis.

"Believe me, I shall be grateful. The next most important thing I should say, my friend, will to obtain from the governor permission to take a bath, and to send for a barber and a tailor."

"Doubtless you can obtain everything that is necessary, my dear chevalier; the tailor, however, we can dispense with, as I have provided for your nakedness, and brought, in my chaise, some of your own clothes, which I obtained at your hotel; go and put them on—and, if you will accept of his services, my *valet-de-chambre* shall assist you."

"You are very kind, my dear marquis; I accept your offer."

Tancrede was conducted to a chamber, where a bath was brought to him; and while he was in the bath the marquis's valet shaved him and cut his hair.

Upon quitting the bath, the chevalier made his toilet. It was then that he first perceived how greatly he had altered. The only thing that he had ever been deficient in was that delicacy of form which constitutes a distinctive sign of race; this delicacy, grief, fasting, and perhaps reflection, had imparted to him. He was now the accomplished chevalier.

M. de Royancourt himself was astonished when he saw the matamorphosis. He had the air of a man of great power, which made the marquis tremble. He looked a man of firm resolve; and M. de Royancourt became, for the first time, aware of what he had to fear in having such a man for an enemy.

The governor wished to detain these gentlemen for breakfast; but our hero, smiling, replied, " that probably his excellency forgot that he had just served him with his when his friend De Royancourt arrived at his dungeon." The governor muttered some excuses, reflecting upon the severity of the rules of the establishment, which did not permit all the attention being paid to the inmates that was their due. Tancrede replied, with his fixed smile, "that he should be wrong to complain; he had been very well treated."

The chaise waited at the door, the post-horses were attached to it, M. de Royancourt and the chevalier got in and galloped off.

It was with the profoundest delight that our hero, oppressed for eleven months by the mephitic air of his dungeon, respired the pure and balmy air of a May morning. It was with inexpressible joy that he could run his eyes over extensive plains and distant mountains, with the blue sky. But all this joy and delight remained passive within him; he was as impenetrable in his joys as in his hate; and he viewed surrounding nature with the same fixed smile as that with which he had received this much-hated man.

Then, from time to time, he responded to the marquis's questions with an amicable gesture or friendly voice, and repeated his protestations of gratitude and devotion.

Thus far, the conversation had been maintained on the part of the marquis with a degree of embarrassment which he could not master; and on the part of Tancrede by an emotion which he had not strength enough entirely to suppress. Afterward it was carried on with more ease. At length, summoning up all his courage, he inquired about Sylvandire.

"Alas, poor lady!" replied M. de Royancourt, "you have been the cause of much unhappiness to her, and you have to atone for many injuires you have done her."

"Ah!" said our hero; "ah! indeed!"

"Doubtless you have," said M. de Royancourt. "When you threatened to leave her, she could not believe you would really go, but thought you only meant to frighten her; but when one day, two days, three days elapsed, without your coming back, she was obliged to believe it. Then she became almost crazy, did nothing but sigh and weep for a whole week. At last she consulted Monsieur d'Argensen, to discover where you were. All that Monsieur d'Argensen could tell her was, that you were not in

France. As you may well imagine, this news threw her into complete despair. One fine day, when her father called to see her, he learned that she had that morning set off in search of you, my dear chevalier. We never heard anything of her for three months, and could not imagine what had become of her. Poor lady! The king, who knows of everything that happens in his dominions, learned of this adventure. He said you were a bad husband, a bad subject, and a bad example, and ordered that you should be arrested."

" Good, wise, and excellent king," exclaimed the chevalier, in the most impressive manner.

" It was while searching your house as a state prisoner, that they found those unlucky songs that have caused all your misfortunes."

" Which I heartily repent of having preserved; they were not worth it. As for my being the author of them, of course you did not believe that I could be guilty of such base ingratitude—could you, marquis?"

" Oh! I never thought so, my dear chevalier. It was this conviction that impelled me to plead your cause."

" My liberator!" cried Tancrede, seizing the marquis's hands. " But pray, let us return to Sylvandire."

" Well, my dear chevalier, as I was going to say, Sylvandire followed you to London; when she arrived there, she learned that you had returned to Paris. At Dover she was just one day behind you, at Calais only two hours."

" Dear Sylvandire!" murmured her husband, in the most affectionate tones.

" At Calais she learned that you had just departed for Paris; and without losing a moment, without taking rest, of which she had so much need, she immediately set out in pursuit of you, fully hoping to overtake you on the road; but she was cruelly disappointed. Not overtaking you, she hoped to find you at home, and sat up all night expecting you; but you did not come. Imagine her grief."

" Ah! marquis! marquis! you tear my heart to pieces," cried Tancrede, wiping his tears with his handkerchief. " But go on! tell me the rest. And I to suspect such a fond wife! Ah, you are right, marquis, I am to blame! But tell me all."

" Well," said the marquis, deceived by the skill with which our hero played his part. " What more need I say?

She passed her days in the profoundest grief; for you never made your appearance, and we could not make out what had become of you."

"You did not know I was in prison, then? Well, on my word of honor I must say I had my doubts of it."

"Oh, *mon Dieu!* Yes, we were quite ignorant of it. Monsieur d'Argensen, in his fears for Madame d'Anguilhem, pressed by me, to whom he is indebted for his promotion, only informed us of your imprisonment a few days ago. Then, as you may suppose, Madame Sylvandire solicited all her friends for aid in procuring your release. Monsieur Bouteau and myself exerted ourselves to the utmost: we have prayed and entreated of Madame de Maintenon—we have implored the king; so that finally, we succeeded in obtaining your release. Ah! my dear D'Anguilhem," said the marquis, in a pathetic voice, "how much you must have suffered!"

"And I, during all this while, have been accusing you of coldness and indifference. Oh, miserable, ungrateful wretch that I am! You have forgiven me, my dear marquis? But do you think she ever will forgive me?"

"The heart of a woman is a fountain of tenderness," replied the marquis; "hope for the best, my dear chevalier."

"And now you have somewhat satisfied me on this point, my dear marquis, one word as to my parents. You know that conjugal love can not wholly extinguish filial love. The baron and baroness are in good health, I hope?"

"Yes, thank God. Your wife took the precaution of informing them that you were suddenly called away to take a long journey; for, like ourselves, they were ignorant of your captivity."

"Good Sylvandire! And our other friends, D'Herbigny, Clos-Renaud, Crette—"

Our hero let this last name escape him, rather than pronounce it.

The marquis observed this negligence.

"Why, as you very well know," he replied, "I see very little of your friends, who, at court, are considered as libertines, who haunt the Palais Royal. I believe, however, that they are very well, especially Monsieur de Crette with whom, I regret to say, I have had some misunderstanding. But, thank God! we are very good friends at present."

"Ah, really! You had some difference on account of Madame de Maintenon, doubtless. Crette is wrong not to admire that devout and worthy lady; but as you remarked, he is something of a libertine, and I think associates with De Broglie, Lafare and Canilhac."

"Unfortunate wretches, who risk their soul's welfare for the vanities of this world!" said M. de Royancourt, clasping his hands with an air of pity and compassion.

"Always supposing they have souls," said the chevalier.

M. de Royancourt made a sign of doubt; and for a time the conversation flagged.

Tancrede was enchanted with himself. He had put in action the precepts that fifteen months' imprisonment had developed within him. He saw that M. de Royancourt was completely duped, and he reveled in the hope that he should be able to deceive his wife as easily as he had deceived the marquis.

The rest of the journey was shortened by conversations of a similar nature, but slightly varied. They traveled day and night, stopping only at Auxerre and at Fontainebleau.

At length they arrived in Paris.

Our hero saw For-l'Eveque in the distance, and passed beneath the walls of the Bastile.

In ten minutes he was at the door of the Hotel d'Anguilhem.

He was evidently expected; everything betokened preparation and expectation. Upon entering the court-yard, the chevalier perceived the servants at the door, and his wife at the window.

He leaped from the coach, and ran toward the drawing-room. Sylvandire, followed by M. Bouteau, came to meet him. They met at the door of the room.

At this moment, and behind the hypocritical figure of his wife, Tancrede perceived through the door, the portraits of his father and mother, smiling from their frames. Although his heart had been greatly hardened by his fifteen months' captivity, the tears rushed to his eyes at beholding the images of the only friends a man can depend upon.

His emotion was so strong that he fainted.

Sylvandire had no doubt whatever that this emotion

arose from the chevalier's love for her; and that the joy of again seeing her had been too much for his shattered nerves.

CHAPTER XXX.

THREE days after the scene we have just described, the Hotel d'Anguilhem presented quite a patriarchal spectacle in the charming cordiality of Master Bouteau, the warm caresses of Sylvandire, the ardent expressions of friendship from M. de Royancourt, and the profound dissimulation of its owner.

All these good people had the aspect of loving each other in the most apostolic fashion.

Now, as in this world we can only see the surface of things, every one allows himself to be deceived by appearances, even those who have the greatest interest in penetrating the thoughts of another.

It was not the case with Tancrede, who, feeling himself, whichever way he turned, or extended his hand, surrounded with so much apparent affection, could not help feeling sometimes a doubt at the bottom of his heart.

Unfortunately Crette continued absent from Paris some eight or ten days. Tancrede presented himself *incog.*, at his house, and it was arranged with little Basque, that immediately his master returned, he would hasten to inform the chevalier.

During this time Sylvandire overwhelmed him with caresses; she inquired how he had passed his time in prison, and if he had ever thought of her while there.

He replied that a prison was one of the most agreeable places in the world, that the jailers were the politest and most obsequious of servants, and that he dined every day at the governor's table; that every afternoon he went out to ride with him in his coach, and that in the evening they played at cards or chess, after which he retired to rest in a neat comfortable little room, overlooking a beautiful garden; and the only thing that might be called disagreeable about it was, that the windows were barred, and the doors bolted at night.

Tancrede feared that if he had told Sylvandire what he had really suffered, she would have come to the conclusion that a man who had endured so much misery would indulge himself in a fearful revenge.

In reply to her inquiry whether he had thought of her, he vowed that from morning till night he could think of nothing else, and that while sleeping he dreamed only of her. Herein, he did not deceive her; we know that he told the exact truth.

Then Sylvandire assured him that she thought him greatly improved, and that his imprisonment had done him a vast deal of good.

One morning, little Basque came to inform Tancrede that the Marquis de Crette had returned half an hour ago.

The chevalier went out on foot, and hired a coach at the corner of the street, and drove to the Hotel Crette. The marquis was awaiting him; the two friends threw themselves into each other's arms.

Crette had heard a part of what had happened to his friend, particularly the details of his two escapes, and of the wounds he had received; but the marquis did not know of his solitary confinement in an underground dungeon, deprived of the light of the sun; nor of the tortures of the time that passed without the means of reckoning it, nor of the resolution our hero had taken to revenge himself on his wife, if, as he suspected, she had been the cause of his imprisonment.

Crette could only repeat what he had written to Tancrede at the Bastile; that is, of the disappearance of Sylvandire, and of his quarrel with M. de Royancourt, and the conviction, moral at least, if not material, that his wife had given up those unlucky songs which were, if not the pretext, the cause of his imprisonment.

As to Tancrede's release, it was due, as the prisoner suspected, to the interference of Crette, D'Herbigny and Chastellux; especially the latter, who was related to M. d'Argensen's wife—a relationship that he had never much valued till now, and only asserted in order to be useful to the chevalier. However, when M. Royancourt discovered that matters were very far advanced in our hero's favor, so that his imprisonment could not continue any longer, he improved the opportunity, and changed his character from vindictive persecutor to that of friendly advocate; and as he had much influence at court, he exercised it for the benefit of the prisoner, who obtained his liberty.

We know the rest.

Everything that Crette related to his friend accorded so perfectly with what he had frequently repeated to himself, that he could not for a moment doubt that he had arrived at a most exact appreciation of the causes, and at the greatest accuracy as to the results.

The two friends separated, after renewing their vows of eternal friendship, already sufficiently well proved for them fully to rely upon each other; but agreeing upon the necessity of meeting only on the most important occasions.

Although Tancrede was morally convinced, he wished, in order to satisfy his conscience, to obtain such material proofs as would leave him no room for doubt. For a voice sometimes whispered in his ear a word that made him falter,

" Perhaps!"

He had learned while in prison how to hold his tongue; and he had put this rare virtue into successful practice. No one could guess what was passing in his mind.

He now began to act.

He sought, in the first place, an interview with Breton.

Breton was a faithful servant, upon whose fidelity he could reckon.

When questioned as to M. de Royancourt, he replied, " that during the chevalier's absence from home the marquis came there every day; and that his visits had ceased only from the day that Madame d'Anguilhem disappeared."

Now it was evident to our hero, that if his dear wife had entertained the praiseworthy project of going in search of him, she would not have hesitated to inform all her servants of it, and to take some of them with her. M. de Royancourt had himself told him, that on setting out Sylvandire never mentioned to any one where she was going.

A month before her flight Mme. d'Anguilhem had dismissed her maid, who had been with her for ten years; this looked very suspicious in Tancrede's eyes, because Mlle. Clarisse was a very faithful servant, and very discreet, and would have been invaluable to her mistress in undertaking a fatiguing journey.

Our hero hoped to be able to draw something from Sylvandire herself; but when, hypocrite in love, he attempted to learn from his wife how she had employed her time during his long absence, she made all manner of frivolous excuses and evasions, so that it was utterly impossible to learn where she had been, or who she had stayed with. She would only confess to having spent two months in the convent of Filles-Dieu, which, it is true, was a convent renowned for the severity of its discipline; but where M. de Royancourt, as the friend of Mme. de Maintenon, could go in and out whenever he pleased; his sister being the superior, and his cousin the treasurer of the said convent.

To go to the convent of Filles-Dieu would be to betray his suspicions; so he assured his wife that he believed everything she had told him, and remarked, that her residence at the convent had very much improved her. Besides, he continued to conduct himself most amiably; calling M. Bouteau his " dear father " more frequently than ever, and receiving M. de Royancourt with the most affectionate politeness.

Those friends who did not know, as Crette did, that this tenderness covered some hidden, mysterious, and perhaps terrible fire, laughed not a little when the conversation turned upon this revival of love between the young couple, especially as in some circles they made merry at Mme. d'Anguilhem's expense—the virtuous Penelope, who, instead of waiting for her Ulysses, had set forth to seek him —but certainly not where she knew she could find him.

Meanwhile Tancrede had given the trusty Breton *carte blanche*, and had instructed him to bribe some of M. de Royancourt's servants, if he could. So one morning when Breton was dressing his master, he informed him that the marquis's coachman, who was about to quit his place, would open his mouth for a hundred louis. Breton invited the chevalier to profit by this man's discontent.

The chevalier took Breton's advice; and the same day was favored with an interview with the fellow, and was put in possession of the following very interesting facts.

Every night, from a date that coincided with that of Mme. Sylvandire's mysterious departure from home, M. de Royancourt betook himself after supper to the little village of Luzarches, sometimes on horseback and sometimes in his coach; that he stayed there four or five hours regularly every night; and at two o'clock, he returned to Paris where he arrived at four in the morning. He then went

to bed, and pretended he had not been out all night. For
greater precaution, his coach returned to his house at midnight, and all his servants supposed he came in it. Only
the coachman, who knew that he brought back only the
empty coach, and the valet, who waited up to let his master in at four o'clock in the morning, were in the secret,
and knew to the contrary.

Tancrede had now some clew. He promised himself he
would follow it up without loss of time. He at once betook himself to Luzarches.

It resulted from his inquiries, that he learned that a
young lady had taken a house there, where she dwelt alone,
attended only by a female servant. A man, whose name
was unknown, but who appeared to be a real gentleman,
came there every evening. They described Sylvandire so
that there was no possibility of doubting that it was she;
and a portrait of M. de Royancourt was still in the house,
and a very good likeness it was.

Any other person than our hero would have immediately
sent M. de Royancourt a challenge, or hired a couple of
bravos to assassinate him, or have made a great scandal.
But he knew that the scandal would lead him again to
For-l'Eveque; the duel, to the Bastile; and the assassina-
tion, to the wheel.

And, besides, this would not be revenge, as it would inflict more punishment upon him than he had already suffered. What he meditated was, a revenge that would leave
him happy and free, and still revenged!

Moreover, it was upon Sylvandire that all his hatred was
centered. Sylvandire had dishonored him—she, whom he
had loved; she, who had, for a time, made him happy—it
was Sylvandire that he hated so fearfully, that he feared he
would love her again.

From the moment that revenge appeared possible, our
hero determined what that revenge should be. He therefore cherished it carefully in one corner of his mind, and
quietly awaited the opportunity of putting it into execution.

Since he had left prison, his heart had become a stormy
sea, where the waves rolled in their immensity, to and fro,
unceasingly, obedient to the impulse of his ideas; and
where, from time to time, some good feelings came like
lightning-flashes, but were as soon lost in the gloom and
darkness of his soul.

To be once sure of being unhappy, to be once sure of having been deceived, is to feel strong and secure for the future.

It was first essential for Tancrede to be certain that he no longer loved this wicked woman, in order not to be checked by pity or remorse at the moment of putting his project of revenge into execution. We have said that he hated Sylvandire so much, that he was not quite sure that he did not still love her.

He therefore set himself to work to analyze one by one his feelings toward her.

When he saw her unexpectedly, it was like a dagger at his heart, a profound sorrow, an icy chill, something like the sensation we experience when the lancet first opens a vein. Notwithstanding the command he had over himself, all his blood rushed to his heart, and the next moment his heart, overcharged, sent all its blood to his extremities with so much violence that it made him feel ill. Yet amid all these convulsive and contradictory sensations, he could live as usual, talk indifferently, and even smile graciously. This was doubtless torture more cruel than even that of the prison of Chalons-sur-Saone.

Sometimes, in the middle of the night, disturbed by a dream, in which he still fancied himself prisoner in a foul dungeon, on a miserable truckle-bed, he would awake, his heart throbbing, his chest heaving, his hair on end, and find himself in a luxurious chamber, lighted by an alabaster lamp, softly couched on a bed with silk curtains, and beside him, sleeping tranquilly, that impassioned siren—that voluptuous enchantress—who, under so marvelous an exterior, concealed so hideous a reality. Then he would raise himself upon his elbow, and gaze at her with a fixed, deep, and fatal glance, and think of that hideous story of one who married a Ghoul, and who furtively watched her return to the conjugal bed, after her hideous repast in the cemetery.

Sylvandire was unconsciously dreaming a pleasant dream, murmuring some amorous complaint, and in a voluptuous smile displaying the enamel of her ivory teeth through her coral lips.

Then would her husband be seized with a ferocious desire to stifle this siren in a loving embrace, and receive her last sigh on his lips, so that, as her life had been given to another, she might at least owe her death to him; but he could accomplish only the first part of this project, he had not strength for the second.

As for Sylvandire, she felt so secure in her power over her husband, that her days were happy and her nights were tranquil. Never had it happened to her to open her eyes upon that wild look that would have fascinated her like a basilisk. But never by word or gesture did Tancrede betray himself.

M. de Royancourt continued his visits to the D'Anguilhems; but his attentions were visibly cooling.

"It must be so," said our hero, while watching the progress of the marquis's indifference as he had watched the progress of his love; "it must be so: possession brings with it indifference."

Then he redoubled his attentions to Sylvandire, who, feeling herself culpable, returned forced caresses to those of her husband. If Tancrede had not been possessed by the demon of revenge, he had, perhaps, been happy.

Sylvandire watched herself with the greatest vigilance; yet it happened one day, when, weary with having waited in vain for the coming of M. de Royancourt during a whole week, without his even deigning to send her a word of comfort, she seated herself at her writing-desk and penned a little note, full of tender reproaches; then rang the bell for the confidential page to carry it to the marquis.

But the confidential page was nowhere to be found. Breton, therefore, had answered madame's bell; and as she held the letter in her hand when he entered the room, she could not very well retain it until her page came in. In her confusion, she gave it to Breton, who assured her that the chevalier being out, he was perfectly at liberty, and could undertake her commission. To refuse his services would, she felt, give rise to suspicion. She handed him the note, saying, in a careless manner—

"Take this to the Marquis de Royancourt immediately."

As Breton was going out, he met his master in the hall. Upon the chevalier inquiring where he was going, he showed him the letter he had been sent with, and looked inquiringly into his face to know if he should proceed to deliver it.

Our hero was about to yield to the temptation, and take

it, when he heard behind a door the rustling of a satin robe. He guessed Sylvandire was playing the spy.

"A letter from madame for Monsieur de Royancourt," said Breton, promptly.

"Very good; take it immediately to its address," replied Tancrede; "and if you see the marquis, tell him from me, that it is unkind of him to neglect us as he does; it is eight days since I have seen him; that I complain very much of this indifference, and that I shall forgive him only on condition that he comes to-day and dines with us."

"But, sir," replied Breton.

"That will do, that will do; go and do as I have told you," continued our hero; "I shall not want you before you come back."

Then, to the great astonishment of Breton, he ascended to the salon where he found Sylvandire seated in great trepidation.

"It was very thoughtful of you, my dear Sylvandire," said he drawing off his ruffles and saluting her; "it was very thoughtful of you to send to Monsieur de Royancourt; I should be delighted if he would come and partake of the hare that my father has sent us from Anguilhem."

Sylvandire, who had become red, pale, and yellow by turns—Sylvandire, who in a second had put on all the colors of the rainbow, recovered all her presence of mind, and smiled.

"What a good husband I have got," thought Sylvandire, kissing him on both cheeks.

"What a weak master I have the misfortune to serve," said Breton; "who would believe that he was the same gentleman that gave Monsieur Kollinski such an ugly thrust, but a lucky hit for him though!"

At the dinner-hour M. de Royancourt was duly announced. The double invitation he had received, touched him no doubt; for he was delightfully amiable. As for Sylvandire, she was triumphant.

Tancrede quietly watched them both; he was witty without being sarcastic, gay without being affected.

During the dessert, he surprised some very significant glances passing between his wife and his guest.

Shortly afterward, when they rose from the table, and as they were passing into the *salon* to take coffee, he saw in a mirror the marquis, who conducted Sylvandire from

9

one room to the other, slip a note into her hand.   Sylvandire concealed it in her bosom.

"Shameless woman! impudent scoundrel!" murmured
the chevalier; "if I kill one, I ought to kill the other."

But he restrained himself, and vented his rage on his
ruffle, which he tore to pieces.

He must see that note; very difficult thing to do, but
very important.   He thought it over all the evening, and
at last hit upon a way, which he hoped might succeed.

It all depended upon what moment Sylvandire would
probably read this note.

"Doubtless, this evening, at her toilet," he replied to
himself.

During the whole evening he never lost sight of her for
a moment, to make sure that she had no opportunity of
reading the note.   When M. de Royancourt went away,
Tancrede contrived to conceal himself in the room adjoining Sylvandire's dressing-room.   He listened until he heard
her come in, and when he calculated that she had taken
out the note to read it, he deliberately set fire to the win-
dow-curtains.

"Fire!   Fire!" cried he, rushing into his wife's room.
"Save yourself, my dear Sylvandire!"

Sylvandire had M. de Royancourt's note in her hand,
and attempted to conceal it; but perceiving the volumes
of flame and smoke which filled the room, she uttered a
scream and fainted.

This was just what her husband wanted.   He opened
her hand, and while the room was blazing, hurriedly perused the following:

"Speak no more of the past, Sylvandire.   I often repent of what we have done; as for your proposal to fly
with me, and quit France together, it is madness, and I
reject it.   I begin to feel ashamed of deceiving so good a
man, who overwhelms me with his kindness and friendship.
If you believe me, Sylvandire, we shall part, and break all
connection.   You say you will die for love of me; live for
your poor husband, who adores you, that will be more
Christian."

"Ah! twice-damned wretch! Can I doubt now?"
groaned Tancrede.

He replaced the note in Sylvandire's hand, still cold and rigid, closed the door of the room, and rang for Breton.

The flames had consumed all the curtains, scorched the consoles, and blackened part of the wood-work, but did little further damage; for as soon as the alarm was given, and assistance arrived, a few pails of water, skillfully applied, extinguished the fire, and in ten minutes even the smoke had all disappeared.

When Sylvandire recovered her senses, she found herself alone, and in her boudoir, with the note crumbled, in her hand. She at once concluded that her husband had seen nothing, and quite joyful at having escaped all accident, proceeded to mingle with the workers.

The moment Tancrede perceived her, he ran to meet her.

"Oh, *mon Dieu!* my dear Sylvandire; what a misfortune has happened to you; see your pretty room all spoiled —and it was so bright and gay. The repairs will deprive you of the pleasure of receiving your friends for a month at least."

"Well, then, my love, let us go to Champigny," said Sylvandire, in the most tender tone.

"To Champigny?" replied Tancrede.

"Yes! do you dread the souvenirs the country will call to your remembrance?"

Tancrede opened his mouth to say:

"And why not to Luzarches?" But he restrained himself.

"Certainly not!" he replied aloud. You know how dear to my heart is every souvenir that I shall find in that house, which you have rendered so dear to me. But I think if you were as venturesome a wife as you are a lovable one, you would put a thousand pistoles in your purse, and say to your husband: 'Come, let us go, like two tender lovers, and visit that beautiful Provence, the music of which enchants you so much, when I sing their songs to my guitar.'"

"Oh, my love," said Sylvandire, making a pretty little mouth; "do you not think that would be a very long journey to make?"

"Well, well, my love, say no more about it; the thought came into my head, and it is gone again. Everything shall be as you wish."

But Sylvandire was too happy in not having been de-

tected to continue for any time to refuse her husband's
offer; besides, she thought that by going away, she would
wound M. de Royancourt's pride, and moreover, she wished
to revenge herself upon him for his infidelity in proposing
to her to be faithful to the chevalier.

"No, my love; no," said she. "I will not deprive
you, and I will not deny myself, this pleasure; besides, I
have promised always to consider your wishes before anything. Order, then, and I am ready to obey."

Tancrede could hardly conceal the joy he felt. He proceeded at once to make his preparations, and give his instructions to the servants; but, quick as he was, Sylvandire and M. de Royancourt found time to communicate
with each other.

One morning our hero was greatly surprised to hear the
marquis propose to accompany him and his wife to Provence.

This was not exactly what he had agreed for, nor altogether to his mind. Nevertheless, he pretended to receive
the proposal with much delight. But he delayed their departure under the pretext of having some important business in hand.

He hoped that, during the delay, something would happen to cause a rupture between the lovers.

He was not disappointed.

For he soon discovered a second note from M. de Royancourt, in which he announced to Sylvandire, that as, this
time, there was no probability of their being able to reconcile the difference that existed between them, he was going
to set out immediately for Utrecht.

Sylvandire vainly attempted to dissimulate her vexation;
her husband could trace every emotion of her heart by the
expression of her countenance. He held the master-key.

On the very day M. de Royancourt departed for Utrecht
she resumed the conversation about the proposed journey
to Provence.

"Upon my honor," said Tancrede to himself, "I am
playing a very ridiculous part, and a very degrading one
too; but, thank God, we shall soon arrive at the *dénoue-
ment*."

He therefore cordially seconded the overture his wife
made; and all the necessary preparations had been completed for some time; next day, which was the 1st of June,

1715, they set out from Paris apparently as loving as two turtle-doves.

CHAPTER XXXI.

OUR hero had played his part so well, that at the time of his departure there was nothing talked of so much as his love for his wife. Everybody had taken it seriously; even D'Herbigny, Clos-Renaud, and Chastellux; they remarked to every one that if the king could not reform Richelieu in the Bastile, the Castle of Chalons-sur-Saone had better seconded the matrimonial wishes of the great monarch with respect to the Chevalier d'Anguilhem.

Thus far, the chevalier had not duped his friend the Marquis de Crette, who had no faith in public rumor. He knew full well what a beautiful and persevering woman can do, and every time he saw Mlle. Poussette, he recommended her to study Mme. Sylvandire as a model for a perfect coquette.

"All your terrible projects of revenge appear to have miscarried," said he to Tancrede; "you wanted to kill everybody, but now you think better of it. It is perhaps wiser to do so; but certainly the example of the Chevalier d'Anguilhem will not make me renounce my liberty."

While everybody at Paris was discussing the subject of Tancrede's singular affection for his wife he was quietly wending his way to the south. Two days after their departure they passed through Chalons. The chevalier wished to study the effect produced upon his wife by the sight of the prison where he had been immured. Therefore he conducted her before the walls of the castle.

"Well," said Sylvandire, after seeing the castle two or three times; "why do you wish me to look at this horrible habitation?"

"Because I was buried there eleven months, while you were looking for me in every direction, dearest."

Sylvandire made a pretty little face, which was as to say—

"Well, however amiable the governor might be, you could not amuse yourself much there, I am sure."

"Yes, yes!" said her husband, in responding to the thoughts of his wife. "Yes, I suffered much in that place;

but more on account of being separated from you than from my imprisonment.''

"And we so little suspecting it!'' replied Sylvandire.

The *we* appeared charming to our hero.

Next day they reached Lyons, where they remained two or three days. In his constant attention to Sylvandire he would not permit her even to fatigue herself.

During these two or three days, Tancrede and Sylvandire made a pilgrimage to Notre-Dame de Fourvieres: the most renowned of all the Madonnas of France for strengthening domestic peace when it already existed in families, and for producing it in those where it did not prevail.

As may be supposed, this was an unnecessary precaution for our hero and his wife to take: they loved each other so well, they could entertain no fears that the good feelings they cherished for each other would ever diminish.

After a sojourn similar to that they had made at Chalons, the loving couple quitted the second capital of France, and proceeded to Valence, to Orange and to Avignon.

To Avignon specially. How pass Avignon without visiting the fountain of Vaucluse? That would have been an offense of *leze-poesie*.

At this date lovers were much more poetical and more pastoral than they are nowadays; they were fond of groves, villages, fountains, etc. For example, Astrea and Cleopatra.

They then made a pilgrimage to the fountain of Vaucluse, as they had made one to Notre-Dame de Fourvieres; and during the whole way Tancrede called Sylvandire nothing but his "dear Laura," and Sylvandire called our hero only her "beautiful Petrarch.''

The mendicants to whom they gave alms on the road shed tears at the sight of this beautiful couple.

Continuing their journey, they arrived at Arles. They wished to see the ruins of a city that disputed for a time with Byzantium the title of "Queen of the World.'' But for the maestral, as the learned assert, Arles would have been Constantinople.

But at this date they were much less occupied at Arles with what had happened there in times of old, than with what had occurred there within the previous fortnight.

A worthy citizen of Arles, who had been so unfortunate

as to marry a woman of a very different temper from his own, resolved to become a widower in order to get rid of domestic trials brought upon him by his wife's disposition. But to become a widower was of no avail, unless it were accomplished without subjecting himself to the rigor of the laws.

Now, the expedient by which he attempted to secure this object was as follows:

He had a pretty country-house on the banks of the Rhone, to which his wife was very partial, and to which he repaired with her every Sunday. The usual conveyance employed by the wife on these occasions was a charming little mule, beautifully caparisoned, and of which, as they say in this country, they took as much care as of the Pope. What did the murderer do? For the three day's preceding the Sunday's journey he kept the poor animal without water, so that on the Sunday morning the dame went on her usual trip, accompanied by her husband, who, on this occasion, cheerfully made one of the party, mounted on her mule, which looked for water everywhere. It no sooner perceived the Rhone, than it started at a gallop, and never stopped until it reached the river, into which it plunged headlong. Fortunately, or unfortunately, as the reader, husband or wife, will determine, the Rhone was very rapid at this place, so that the mule and the lady were carried away by the current, and soon disappeared beneath the waves. The husband, who witnessed the disaster, raised a great cry for help, in the hope that no one would hear him until it was too late to render assistance of any avail.

His hope was fully realized. The lady and the mule were drowned together. The husband mourned bitterly for—the mule; but under such circumstances we must be prepared to make great sacrifices.

But the affair made so great a noise that justice was roused; the husband was brought before the tribunals, but he appeared so distracted, and had shed so many tears over the death of the dear departed, that, in the absence of proof, he was acquitted.

Sylvandire greatly pitied the sad fate of the poor woman; and Tancrede in his indignation, declared that if this man had not been a low fellow, he would have called him to account for his infamous conduct.

They both hastened to quit this city of misfortune, and next day they reached Marseilles.

As this was the limit of their journey, they made arrangements at an hotel for a long residence. From the day of their arrival they promenaded upon the Cannebiere and in the Allees de Meillan, proclaiming their love everywhere by the most extravagant caresses; every one took them for a newly-married couple passing their honey-moon, and admired them.

In the hotel where they lodged, in the society where they were received, this favored couple were the theme of admiration.

"What a charming woman!" said the men; "and how her husband loves her!"

"What a nice gentleman! and how his wife doats upon him!" said the ladies.

Nothing was so much spoken of at Marseilles as Tancrede and Sylvandire.

One day our hero, who had gone out in the morning alone, returned to his hotel, and informed his wife that they were both going in the afternoon to visit a Sicilian merchant, with whom he could very advantageously place some funds for which he had no present use.

Sylvandire inquired what toilet it would be becoming in her to make; to which her husband replied:

"The most beautiful you have, my dear; for I wish, when this stranger returns to his own country, he may be able to say that he has seen no woman so beautiful as you."

This was a piece of that sort of advice which Sylvandire always followed with an exactness that did honor to her conjugal obedience.

Besides, her beauty, when heightened by the elegance of her laces and the brilliancy of her diamonds, was almost supernatural; and when she got into her sedan-chair, even the chairmen were dazzled and astonished.

The Sicilian merchant dwelt in the Rue de Paradis. He was a tall old man, with a gray pointed beard, like a portrait of the times of Cardinal Richelieu; the Jew, Greek, and Arab, all in one; and he spoke almost all languages. He seemed to have impatiently awaited his visitors, and presented himself before them with a very delighted countenance. The beauty of Sylvandire appeared to have surpassed all he had expected to find in her.

Nothing imparts confidence like success. Sylvandire saw the effect she produced, and was exuberant in grace and affability.

Tancrede, as a gallant husband, and to display the talents of his wife, turned the conversation upon a variety of topics, lively and serious.

Sylvandire sustained the proof indicated by the poet, and passed with equal success,

" 'From grave to gay, from lively to severe.''

Tancrede's bosom swelled with pride. From time to time he nodded his head to the Sicilian merchant, which might be interpreted to mean:

" You see I have told the truth.''

And the Sicilian merchant responded also by a sign which evidently meant:

" This is a woman such as we seldom meet with.''

Our hero begged Sylvandire to speak in Italian; and for half an hour she sustained a conversation in the Tuscan idiom and Roman accent.

He begged Sylvandire to sing; she sung a piece from the opera of " Orpheus,'' accompanying herself on the guitar.

This morceau was concluded amid much applause; and fresh signs and smiles were exchanged between the two auditors.

The Sicilian merchant whispered something in the ear of our hero.

" Oh! as for that,'' replied the chevalier, " it is impossible; however much I might try to persuade her, madame would never consent to that.''

" What is it, my love?'' inquired Sylvandire.

" Nothing,'' replied Tancrede.

" But what is it? What does your friend require?''

" He wants an impossibility.''

" But what is it?''

" Why, he says he has seen the gitanos of Spain, the almees of Egypt, and the bayaderes of India dance, but—''

" Well?''

" He pretends—''

" What?''

" He is quite sure you surpass them in grace, and he is certain that if you were to dance a minuet or a gavotte—''

"Oh!" said Sylvandire.

"I have told him, my love, that could not be."

"But, my love," said Sylvandire, not wishing to be backward in displaying her attractions, "if I had some one to figure with me, I would willingly dance a minuet."

"I will, if you will accept of me as a partner," said the old Sicilian.

"Well, then, and I will sing the tune," said Tancrede.

And then he commenced humming the air of a minuet of Exaudet's, while Sylvandire, with her grotesque partner, executed the figures with a charming grace and precision.

Sylvandire's success was triumphant.

"And what age is madame?" inquired the Sicilian merchant, in a tone that betrayed his admiration and astonishment.

"Nineteen years, seven months, and fifteen days," replied Tancrede, "not yet twenty, monsieur; not yet twenty!"

"Your praises are not exaggerated, my gentleman," replied the Sicilian merchant. "The description you gave of madame, though glowing, falls, I must say, far short of the reality."

"Oh, sir!" simpered Sylvandire, casting a look of gratitude upon her husband.

"No, on my honor!" replied the Sicilian, with a malicious laugh. "You are really the most beautiful and charming lady I have ever seen—a true oriental beauty—a pearl in a seraglio—a veritable houri—a matchless woman."

"It seems to me the gentleman courts me very gallantly in your presence, my dear," replied Sylvandire, affectedly.

"No, my love," replied Tancrede, "he only appreciates your charms at their full value; nothing more."

They then took their departure; and, in accompanying them to the door, the Sicilian invited them to breakfast with him on the morrow, on board a little bark lying in the harbor. "After breakfast," he said, "they would make up a little fishing party; the sardines were now abundant."

This novel fishing excursion delighted Sylvandire, who accepted the invitaton with eagerness; but seeing that her husband did not respond, she turned to him uneasily, and said to him.

" Why do you not speak? do you refuse the inv.tation?"

" No, my love; but I am afraid."

" Afraid! of what?"

" That you will not be able to bear the sea."

" Oh! there is no danger."

" You would like, then, to make one of this fishing party?"

" I should be delighted."

" It must be then just as you wish."

" You are a darling husband."

" Well, then, my dear sir! to-morrow."

" To-morrow," echoed Sylvandire.

" To-morrow," replied the Sicilian.

At the appointed hour on the morrow, they were at the Sicilian's house.

An elegant little boat awaited them near the custom-house steps, into which they stepped, and were immediately rowed to the bark, which was at anchor opposite the Château d'If.

It was a beautiful swift-sailing craft, that rode on the waves like a sea-bird. The captain was a man between thirty and thirty-five, remarkable for his oriental features and by his foreign costume. He only spoke Italian, which gave Sylvandire an opportunity of displaying her philological abilities. He had splendid eyes, a Grecian nose, and teeth like pearls.

They breakfasted with a good appetite, induced by the sea-air; and then watched the casting of the nets, which broke under the weight of the fish contained within them. It was then arranged that they should witness a night fishing, by torch-light, on the following evening.

Upon returning home, Sylvandire could talk of nothing but the handsome captain—how beautiful, noble, generous, and brave, he was; how well he expressed himself, how royally he had received them, and how his every word, gesture, and sign was obeyed as soon as made.

" Certainly, this man is above his position," said Sylvandire.

" Most certainly he is," replied her husband.

Next morning, our hero paid another visit to the Sicilian merchant. Upon returning home, he found his wife laughing and dancing to herself.

"Good," said he; "she is already in love with the captain."

The hour appointed for the evening's excursion was six o'clock. Sylvandire ran every ten minutes during the afternoon to see what o'clock it was; she would have put the hands forward could she have got at them. Tancrede smiled bitterly, and shook his head; but Sylvandire was too much occupied with her own pleasing anticipations to observe him.

The necessary permission from the harbor-master having arrived, they set out. The chevalier inquired of the merchant if he thought the weather would be fine.

"Splendid!" replied Sylvandire.

But the Sicilian merchant winked his eye in a very peculiar manner, as much as to say:

"Make yourself easy, we shall have just the sort of weather that would suit us."

They stepped into the boat, but as the wind was right ahead they made very little progress; the consequence was, it was growing dark before they reached the Isle of Pommegue.

Meanwhile, immense black clouds appeared in the horizon, advancing with the tide, and soon covered the moon, at first with light fleecy clouds, but which gradually thickened, and soon entirely veiled her light.

The sea, hitherto as calm as a lake, became ruffled, and struck with a sinister sound on the shore and the rocks: the foam, with its phosphorescent light, was as a sea of fire.

"*Mon Dieu!*" exclaimed Sylvandire, "it looks as if we were going to have a tempest."

"What do you think of the weather?" inquired Sylvandire of the Sicilian merchant.

"Fine weather for fishing—fine weather for fishing," replied the latter, with a mocking air, that surprised and alarmed Sylvandire.

"What does your friend mean, my love?" said she, clinging to Tancrede, who shuddered upon feeling the touch of this woman, whom he had loved so much, and whom he feared he might still love.

He shrunk from her mechanically.

"I am so frightened," said Sylvandire.

Tancrede did not reply; but buried his face in his hands.

The Sicilian merchant lighted a torch and waved it several times in the air, then extinguished it.

The wind howled dismally, like the sound of human wailings.

A vivid flash of lightning illuminated the sky; by its light they perceived the bark sailing down to them at a few yards' distance.

Next they perceived some dark object approaching through the gloom; it was a barge manned with five sailors.

Two of them rowed, two stood up in the fore part of the barge, and the other was at the helm.

By another flash of lightning, Sylvandire recognized in the helmsman the captain of the bark.

But now, that face which yesterday had appeared so handsome, wore a very sinister expression.

"Aboard!" cried the captain in Italian.

And the barge and the boat were soon alongside of each other.

"*Mon Dieu!*" cried Sylvandire. "Who are they? and what is going to happen?"

The physiognomy and expression of the new-comers appeared to her quite unlike what might be expected from a pleasure-party.

Scarcely had she pronounced these words, when the two rowers, and the other two men who were standing in the fore part of the barge, leaped into the boat; and while the two rowers seized Tancrede, and held him, or pretended to hold him, the other two men seized Sylvandire, lifted her in their arms, and carried her into the barge.

"Tancrede!" she screamed, " oh, Tancrede! help me! Tancrede, save me; oh, save me! Save your Sylvandire."

The chevalier instinctively made an effort to run to her; but the two men forcibly restrained him. It is quite true, however, that had he been inclined to exercise his strength, he could have taken one in each hand and pitched them into the sea.

Doubtless he thought this was not the proper moment to put forth his strength, so he satisfied himself with heaving a profound sigh, and putting his hand to his forehead.

Meanwhile Sylvandire, pale with terror, passed from the boat to the barge.

" Tancrede! Tancrede!" she cried again, " oh, save me!
I shall die!"

She then fainted.

But he remembered all the sufferings he had endured,
all the insults he had received, all the shame he had
suffered; and this recollection made him deaf to Sylvandire's appeal.

It was the hour of his revenge—and he counted the hours
as they struck.

" Away!" cried the Sicilian merchant.

The captain took Sylvandire in his arms from the men
who had lifted her from the boat, all fainting as she was,
and laid her in the stern, waving his hand to the merchant.

" Addio."

" Addio," replied the merchant, with his usual chuck-
ling laugh.

Tancrede had sat with his face buried in his hands. At
hearing the words of farewell, he raised his head to take a
last look at Sylvandire.

In the darkness that enveloped him he could just distinguish her white dress for a moment, and she vanished from
his sight.

The rowers seized their oars, and in a few moments the
barge was lost to view.

By a flash of lightning it could be seen that the barge
was alongside the bark and that Sylvandire was being
lifted into it.

The old merchant immediately seized the oars of his boat,
and began to row it toward the shore from whence he had
set out, and displayed a vigor of arm that no one would
have suspected from his meager feeble-looking frame.

" Well," said he to Tancrede, after a few moments'
silence, and slackening his oars. " Well, Monsieur le
Chevalier! you are free now. Have things been managed
as well as you desired, and are you satisfied with us?"

" Yes," replied the chevalier, gloomily. " I am free;
but by a crime."

" Bah! a crime!" replied the old man, " nonsense; you
must not view things in that light. Your lady will go
straight to Tunis: the captain has a commission from an
Indian prince to procure him a French lady, and you have
sent him yours. That is a capital arrangement for both of
you."

A sudden glimpse of the moon enabled Tancrede to see the white sails of the bark, which was scudding quickly away in the direction of Tunis.

"Now, then," said the old man, "we must arrange our business; for we shall soon be on shore. Make haste and tear your clothes, wet your head and feet, and break a plank or two in the side of the boat."

Tancrede did as he was instructed without uttering a word.

The wind had greatly increased in violence, and it was raging quite a storm, when they entered the harbor, at one o'clock in the morning.

As soon as the Sicilian merchant perceived the Round Tower, he began to shout and groan as loudly as he could.

This noise awoke Tancrede from his terrible dream.

"O povoro! ó malheureux! ó povoro marito!" cried the merchant. "Ohime! ohime!"

These cries repeated in various idioms soon brought all the officers out of the custom-house; and some belated citizens also grouped themselves among and around them.

"What's the matter?" inquired the supervisor.

"What's the matter? oh, she's gone! she's lost! the charming lady. O che peccato!"

And while the boat continued to approach the custom-house stairs, the merchant continued to utter his incoherent lamentations.

"But what has happened?" cried all the crowd.

As soon as the old man put his foot on shore, he related his story. "When the barge came to meet the chevalier and madame to take them to the fishery, she ran foul of their boat, broke their rudder, and damaged the side of the boat; the shock was so violent, that Mme. d'Anguilhem, who had risen up in the boat greatly alarmed, was knocked overboard and fell into the sea!

"Monsieur immediately jumped into the sea to save his wife," continued the old man; "but all in vain—the night was dark, and the sea was rough. The unfortunate lady was never seen again!"

This story was told with proper gesticulations and true Neapolitan pantomime. The Sicilian knew that it was necessary to adorn his story with all the amplifications of Italian rhetoric.

"Six times monsieur plunged into the sea. He had endeavored, but in vain, to hold him back by his clothes; but when he attempted to throw himself in for the seventh time, he had seized the chevalier, and held him by main force, and assured him that his wife had been saved by the people in the barge. The chevalier, quite overcome, had fainted; and while in this state, he, poor old man, had brought the boat back to port. As to the men in the barge, it was too dark to recognize them, and the violence of the winds and waves had soon driven them out of sight."

The good people on hearing this sad story, pitied D'Anguilhem; some, more tender-hearted than others, shed tears. He was quite cast down, dumb and motionless. His depression was taken for despair, almost for madness, and the interest he saw taken in his grief, increased it. Had he been poor, a collection would have been made on the spot, so sad appeared his condition, so real his grief, and so touching his despair.

Upon returning to his hotel, he shut himself up. The old man came thither, and spent the day in relating the sad story to every fresh batch of news-mongers. The chevalier had ordered that he might be left alone with his grief; so no one was admitted to his room but the Sicilian merchant, who at ten in the morning had come to inquire how the poor husband had passed the night.

They double-locked the door of the room. Then Tancrede counted out upon the table five hundred pistoles, which he handed to the Sicilian, receiving in exchange a report, signed by four respectable witnesses, which minutely described the nocturnal adventure that had caused the death of Mme. d'Anguilhem.

The chevalier sent this report to Master Bouteau, with a letter of condolence.

He also communicated the melancholy intelligence of the sudden loss of his beloved wife to his friends the Marquis de Crette, D'Herbigny, Clos-Renaud, and Chastellux.

This done, he took leave of the ill-fated city of Marseilles, and set out to seek consolation at D'Anguilhem, where he arrived twelve days after the loss of Sylvandire.

Now let us frankly confess one thing, which perhaps many of our readers have already guessed.

The Chevalier Tancrede d'Anguilhem had, purely and

simply, sold his wife to a Tunisian corsair, whose corre-
spondent in France was the *soi-disant* Sicilian merchant.

This was not so bad for a provincial.

CHAPTER XXXII.

THE Baron d'Anguilhem, as may be very well understood, from the love mingled with respect which he bore to
the home of his ancestors, had not attained to so great a
change of fortune without desiring to make some improvements in his property. Immediately after his son's marriage, and upon his arranging with him as to his share in
the inheritance, and returning to Anguilhem, he applied
himself to the great work which had for so long a time
occupied his mind, and which only the want of funds had
prevented him from undertaking.

The first among the alterations and improvements was
to plant a fine avenue of sycamore-trees in the front of his
residence. Since they had been transplanted thither, some
two years and a half, they had thriven wonderfully, and
already become quite imposing. Between the trunks of
these trees elder and hazel-trees had been planted. At the
end of this avenue, which was a quarter of a mile in length,
the manor of D'Anguilhem, now raised a story higher,
was conspicuous. The addition of a belvedere, the fashion
of which had just reached Loches, was a crowning ornament to the edifice.

But in all the architectural revolutions which had produced so pleasing a change in the ancestral home, the
famous Tower of Guerite had been religiously respected,
not a stone of it had been disturbed.

The buildings enlarged, the baron thought it necessary
to enlarge his estates. He bought the two leagues of
marsh, renowned as the scene of De Beuzerie's night adventure; it was useful only as a resort for wild ducks and
geese, but it increased the estate to its former extent as a
barony. Then, one by one, he acquired all the little
groves and woods which he had so long coveted; so that
the baron could now talk of " his woods," " his marshes,"
and " his plains;" but he never went so far, in speaking
of his vast possessions, as to make himself ridiculous.

Then the live stock had to be augmented.

He had two farm-laborers, instead of one as formerly;
three horses in his stable, among which Christopher figured; he had brought him from Paris when he returned
from Tancrede's wedding. Two female servants, Maria
and Gertrude, and the gamekeeper Lajeunesse, completed
the establishment.

We have not forgotten the Abbe Dubois, although he has
not been mentioned. Upon Tancrede's repairing to Paris,
the preceptor's occupation was gone; through the kind
offices of the baron, he was installed librarian at Loches,
and passed most of his time classifying and collating the
two hundred and forty dilapidated volumes of which the
public library was composed.

The Baron d'Anguilhem was now reckoned as the richest
landed proprietor of his locality. Men are generally considered to be richer or poorer than they really are. The
three hundred thousand francs he had reserved to himself
from the inheritance of M. de Bouzenois brought him more
than a million salutations a year, and the most distinguished
of their kind in all the province.

As for the baroness, to her credit be it said, she remained exactly the same: that is to say, the complete type
of a good wife and excellent mother. She had only added
to her modest wardrobe of six dresses the two she had
bought in Paris on the occasion of her son's wedding. On
all great rejoicings and similar occasions she continued, as
heretofore, to make the pastry, which was unrivaled.

We have brought Tancrede back to this place, because,
amid their change of fortune, the good father and tender
mother thought only of the dutiful son to whose self-sacri-
fice they were indebted for it. When they were alone together, which happened very frequently, the chevalier's
name was soon on the lips of one or the other, and wholly
engrossed their conversation. But nevertheless, it must
be confessed that there were times when the baron and the
baroness accused him of ingratitude.

The Baron and Baroness d'Anguilhem had never heard
of their son's long imprisonment. M. de Crette was fully
aware that the announcement of such a dreadful piece of
intelligence would have killed them. Confined to the
province, and having no influential friends at Paris, they
had no power to aid Tancrede's friends in their efforts to
obtain his release. Therefore, the marquis thought it as

well to draw upon his imagination for an excuse for the chevalier, in not communicating with his parents, and so spare them unnecessary pain. He wrote to them saying, that Tancrede had received a special mark of favor from his sovereign in being appointed to a secret mission to Holland; for which country he had departed so suddenly as to prevent him from communicating with his parents. As his residence in that country must be kept a profound secret from the world, he would be precluded from the pleasure of writing to his beloved parents until he was recalled to his native country; for the governments of each nation indulged themselves in the very reprehensible practice of opening any letters they pleased, with the very innocent intention of reading their contents and profiting by them.

Thus it happened that Tancrede's parents had received no news from him for nearly fifteen months; but, in consequence of the Marquis de Crette's foresight they had not been very uneasy.

Immediately after he was released from prison he wrote to his parents at Anguilhem. But, advised by Crette of the pious fraud he had practiced upon them, he did not undeceive them about his mission to The Hague. His letter, as may be supposed, was received with the greatest delight, and made the old folks very happy. But after so long an absence, they were particularly anxious to see himself. Invitations from his mother to come and spend a month at Anguilhem succeeded each other rapidly; but our hero had so serious and engrossing a matter in hand, that he had not been able to find time to gratify his parent's desire.

But after business comes pleasure.

Before setting out for Marseilles he wrote to the baroness to say that he was about taking a journey to Provence, and that on his return he should pass through Anguilhem, where he would spend a month or two.

On receipt of this intelligence immediate preparations were made at the castle to receive in a becoming manner the presumptive heir, and to *fête* the prodigal son. Workmen were put into the best rooms of the castle, and a large addition of furniture was procured from Loches, so that upon her arrival Mme. d'Anguilhem should want for nothing.

Thus it happened that when a chaise appeared at the end

of the avenue of sycamores, which now formed so pleasing
an approach to the castle, the cry of, "The chevalier! the
chevalier!" resounded throughout the building, and every
one ran to arms.

The chaise arrived at full gallop, and stopped at the
grand entrance. The porter flung open the gate wider
than it had swung for many a day, and in a moment Tancrede was fast locked in the embraces of his father and
mother, who shed tears of joy. From them he passed into
the arms of his old tutor, the Abbe Dubois.

The old domestics collected at a few paces behind the
principal characters, to evince their respect and affection;
the new-comers were attracted by curiosity to see the hope-
ful heir of the house of D'Anguilhem, of whose beauty and
prowess they had heard so much.

Old and new both found that their young master had become a very fine gentleman.

As for Castor, he barked furiously from his kennel; and
had not his chain been made of the best iron he would
doubtless have broken it.

After the first ebullition of joy was over, the baroness
remembered she had a daughter. She looked into the carriage, and seeing it empty, she said—

"And Madame d'Anguilhem, where is she?"

The color rushed into Tancrede's face, and his eyes filled
with tears: they were not hypocritical.

"Dear mother," said he, "I have met with a great misfortune. I have lost Madame d'Anguilhem— But let us
go in, and then I will tell you all about it."

It is impossible to describe the grief and astonishment
that prevailed in the drawing-room at the recital of the
catastrophe of Marseilles.

The baroness thought she must faint with grief: she kept
repeating—

"But what were they about in that barge?"

Nevertheless Tancrede soon succeeded in consoling his
mother, and to effect this miracle he had only to take her
aside and say these few words—

"God, who knows all things, dear mother, knows that
Madame d'Anguilhem did not make me very happy; and
unfortunately the world knows that she had not all the respect for our name that she owed to it; her misfortune is
truly a punishment."

The chevalier, forced to deceive in many things, upon this point at least did not deceive.

It was upward of three years since our hero had seen Anguilhem; but he had forgotten nothing during his long absence. His heart still warmly cherished the *souvenirs* of his youth, which all revolved around his love for Mlle. de Beuzerie. Anterior *souvenirs* he had none; it seemed to him that he only commenced to live from the day he had first seen Constance.

The baroness, as we have said, had prepared the best bed-chamber for the chevalier and his wife; but Tancrede preferred to sleep in his own little chamber. It was there, he remembered, the young girl he believed to be dead, had appeared to him to tell him to live. He went to the picture representing the Crucifixion, and knelt before it, as was his practice in those happy days, and attempted to repeat one of his childish prayers. But at that period, when he was young, pure-minded, full of hope and expectation, he had not done anything which could be regarded as a crime.

He retired to bed; but his head rested a long time on the pillow before he could go to sleep. But sleep came at last, and with sleep came dreams. He thought that the picture moved as of yore; but this time it was not Constance that appeared to him—it was Sylvandire who descended from the pedestal, and who, icy cold, came and laid herself beside him.

Three times Tancrede awoke, and three times he composed himself to sleep again, to dream again the same dream.

In the morning he rose at break of day, and went to the stable and saddled Christopher. And as he had need to chase away the morbid remembrance of Sylvandire by a more tender remembrance, he took the road to a certain place where, on a certain Easter-eve, he had found the coach of M. de Beuzerie upset in the marsh, and had brought home Constance in triumph on the back of this same Christopher, which, after the lapse of six years, was now pursuing the same road.

He recognized the place; it seemed to him as if that important event had only happened the night before, and that everything which had occurred to him since that night was only a dream.

At breakfast-time he returned to the castle, with a more

calm and tranquil mind. The remembrances of the morning had chased away the dreams of the night. Constance had vanquished Sylvandire.

During breakfast he inquired of his parents the news of all the neighborhood; but, according to the habit of people who think too much of one person, it was of this very person they dared not utter a word. He constantly hoped that his father or his mother would pronounce the name of Mlle. de Beuzerie; but her name never passed their lips.

It must be admitted that he waited with an impatience amounting to anxiety. At every moment he expected to hear the baron, among other genealogical enumerations of the province, say these fatal words—

"Apropos, Mademoiselle Constance de Beuzerie has married the Marquis de Croisey, or somebody else."

But to the great astonishment of the chevalier nothing of the sort was said by the baron, and neither he nor the baroness ever once named Constance.

After breakfast, Tancrede mounted Christopher, who set out in a very bad humor. He had not forgotten the chevalier's old habits, nor his amorous eccentricities, which he suspected were now going to be repeated. Now Christopher had grown older like all the other personages of this history—Christopher was, in fact, six years older.

This time Tancrede took the road to a place very well known to his poor steed. It was to Chapelle Saint-Hippolyte, whither he and Constance had flown to get married, and where the good old curate so piously betrayed them to their parents.

He hoped that the curate would recognize him, and speak to him about Constance.

Alas! the curate was dead, and a stranger occupied his place: he had come from Lorient, and knew nothing of local affairs.

The new pastor had never heard of Constance; it was therefore not very probable that he should speak about her.

Even the curate's housekeeper was also a stranger; she too had come from Lorient. The chevalier had therefore no better chance with her than with her master. Besides, she spoke only the low Breton dialect, a tongue with which the chevalier was not very familiar, although the learned have since discovered that it is the ancient Celtic

Tancrede returned to the castle as ignorant as when he left it.

At dinner the same silence prevailed; the chevalier was mute and thoughtful. He kept revolving in his mind what he could say that might lead the conversation to the subject of his cherished Constance. At length, after a thousand hints, which were entirely lost upon his parents, he boldly asked—

"And our old quarrel with the Beuzeries," said he, attempting to smile, "you have not said anything about that."

"It is quite smoothed over," replied the baron, "and we are cruelly avenged."

"Ah! how so?" cried Tancrede, trembling from head to foot, and thinking that perhaps Constance was dead, or unhappily married.

"Just imagine," replied the baron, while the baroness regarded her son with much uneasiness—"Just imagine that Constance has never got married, and not likely to be."

A convulsive trembling seized upon Tancrede. He blushed and grew pale by turns. He attempted to rise from his chair, but fell back into it, unable to stand. Then the tears filled his eyes, his head sunk on his breast, and he heaved a profound sigh.

"Yes," said the baroness; "she retired some time ago to the convent of Loches; and it is not quite certain, although her friends are greatly opposed to it, that she will not take the veil!"

"Not married! not married!" thought the chevalier, "and perhaps still loves me!"

"She who was once so proud, too," said the baron, ignorant of what was passing at this moment in his son's heart.

"You mean whose parents were so proud," observed the baroness; "dear Constance, God knows, is a good and pious girl, whom I love as a mother."

Tancrede thanked his mother by an affectionate glance.

"And—and what did she say to—to—to—my marriage?"

"Upon my word, we do not know," replied the baron with an air of embarrassment; "for we have not seen the Beuzeries since your departure."

The conversation ceased. The chevalier became even
more pensive than usual, and rose from the table without
uttering another word.

After dinner he unchained Castor, shouldered his gun,
and took his old ramble to the warren. But three years!
how the time passes away; and in that time, what events
had happened! At every step of the road, he had a regret
or a remorse. He expected to see Sylvandire start from
behind every bush; he wept because he did not meet Constance.

Tancrede's arrival was the occasion of festivals throughout all the country round. The grief occasioned by the
death of the young baroness was not of long continuance.
She was scarcely known to any one there.

Besides, there was another reason why the effect produced by the accident Tancrede had related to his mother,
and which his mother communicated to everybody, produced only a brief impression. Tancrede, in becoming a
widower, had become free to marry again; and he was only
twenty-two and handsomer than ever—even when he
used to be called "handsome or pretty Tancrede." Besides, he was rich; for, without reckoning what would come
to him at the death of his parents, that is to say, " his expectations," to use a hideous phrase, he possessed, in his
own right, an income of fifty thousand a year.

Therefore his appearance in the various circles in which
he visited, caused quite a flutter among managing mothers
and marriageable maids.

He was the hero of the chase, of balls, and of other festivals; but, alas! a very dismal hero. Yet at these meetings he sometimes encountered a figure more sad even than
his own—it was that of Viscount de Beuzerie. The chevalier could not endure the sight of him; for the thought
that his obstinate pride had been the cause of all his misfortunes and unhappiness, made him feel quite ill, and
called up a host of bitter reflections.

One day, while hunting, he encountered the viscount
near that same warren where, nearly three years previously,
they had had such a sharp altercation, and where afterward, setting out full of hope and expectation, he had
taken farewell of Constance.

M. de Beuzerie, who had leaped through a piece of lucern

to avoid the presence of the chevalier, suddenly changed his mind, and found himself face to face with him.

"Monsieur d'Anguilhem," said the baron, "have the goodness to tell me yourself, in order that I may be satisfied from your own mouth, whether you are married or whether you are not."

"I am a widower," replied our hero, trembling.

"Then come with me, sir," replied the viscount, "and you will save all my family from despair. My daughter has shut herself up in a convent; she never wishes to hear from us; she says that we have deceived her, and insists that you are still a bachelor, and that you have not released her from her promise, and therefore that she belongs only to you or to God. And then, perhaps she is a little unsettled in her mind, poor dear child, for during these two years past, her mother and myself have been quite unable to comprehend her conduct."

Tancrede, in his astonishment at this intelligence, let his gun fall, and looked vacantly at the baron.

"Alas! alas!" said the old man, moved to tears; "it has all come back upon us, Monsieur d'Anguilhem, and we are truly very unhappy."

"Oh! Monsieur le Vicomte," cried he; "pardon me, pardon Constance. But I begin to perceive the true state of the matter. Before going with you, allow me to go to Anguilhem. I have a word or two of explanation to ask of my father; then I am at your service. At what hour to-morrow do you desire me to come to Beuzerie?"

"Wait for me, then, Monsieur le Chevalier," replied the viscount. I will call upon you in passing."

"I will wait for you."

"But do not think this is an engagement, in the way you might take it, Monsieur d'Anguilhem. I may reckon upon you, may I not?" replied he, with some earnestness, for he was not quite sure that the remembrance of the old offense he had given to his young neighbor was yet effaced.

The chevalier responded by an affirmative gesture, and immediately took the road to Anguilhem. After proceeding about a hundred yards, he turned his head, and saw the old gentleman seated on a bank, motionless, and with his head inclined on his bosom, like a statue of resignation.

In two hours' time Tancrede was at Anguilhem.

He went in search of his father, and found him gathering apricots in his orchard.

"Father," said he, "did you ever give to Mademoiselle Constance de Beuzerie the letter containing the announcement of my marriage, which I intrusted you to deliver into her own hands?"

M. d'Anguilhem, taken thus by surprise, hesitated a moment, and blushed.

This expression of shame on the part of a parent he so dearly loved was a bitter reproach to Tancrede's feelings. So, taking the baron's hand into his own,

"Never mind, dear father," said he; "whatever you have thought proper to do must be for the best."

"No, my dear son," said the baron; "I have not given it to her; you did not tell me what the contents of this letter were; and I was afraid, I must confess, that under the very difficult circumstances in which we were placed, this unhappy letter might only complicate matters, and make bad worse."

"Then the letter is—"

"Upstairs, in my strong box."

The baron, followed by Tancrede, entered the house, and went upstairs to his room. He opened his old oak chest and took from it the letter, still unsealed, and handed it to his son.

"Ah! I understand it all now," exclaimed the youth. "I told Constance to believe nothing she heard about me only in my own words or writing; she has not believed; she has waited all this time for me to release her from her engagement. And she would have waited all her life, noble girl! How she has loved me!"

Tancrede took the letter and proceeded to his own room, there to reflect at his leisure upon past occurrences, and perhaps, also, to speculate upon future events.

CHAPTER XXXIII.

TANCREDE passed a very agitated night. He dreamed again of the moving picture; this time it was Constance who appeared—but at the moment she touched the door of his chamber to approach his bedside, Sylvandire came between them with a menacing air; so that whatever efforts the young lovers made to embrace each other, they were frustrated by their evil genius.

However little faith the chevalier might have in dreams, this, under present circumstances, seemed very significant, and even looked prophetic. It left a very gloomy impression on his mind, which was not entirely dissipated when, at eight in the morning, M. de Beuzerie was announced.

The old gentleman was on horseback. Tancrede at once comprehended what errand he was upon, so he ordered Christopher to be saddled immediately. He understood that the viscount was on the way to Loches, and that he expected the chevalier to accompany him.

They both set out on their road to that city.

As they proceeded along, Tancrede's mind was entirely engrossed with the thoughts of again seeing Constance. His emotion became so great that the viscount looked at him with much anxiety. As soon as he perceived he was the object of M. de Beuzerie's scrutiny, he roused all his energies to compose himself.

Loches soon appeared in sight. The chevalier could scarcely understand that one among that mass of houses contained his beloved Constance; he could scarcely believe that in half an hour, in a quarter of an hour, even in five minutes, he might be face to face with her whom he had not seen for three years, and from whom during all those three years, he had thought himself separated forever.

They entered the city, they arrived at the street; they knocked at the convent gate; it was opened by the attendant.

M. de Beuzerie asked permission to see his daughter, and the attendant quietly replied:

"Very good, monsieur le vicomte; step into the parlor, and I will go and inform mademoiselle you are here."

This response, simple and natural as it was, gave the chevalier a sort of ague-fit. He fully expected to hear, instead, that Mlle. Constance had left the convent, and gone no one knew whither; or, as he had heard at Chinon, that Constance was dead.

The viscount and the chevalier were introduced into the parlor, while the attendant went to seek Constance.

Neither the viscount nor our hero exchanged a word; the father approached the grating, while the young man remained partly concealed in the shadow of the walls of the room.

In a few minutes the door opened, and Constance, dressed all in white, made her appearance, and advanced with slow and silent steps toward the grating.

She looked pale and thin, but more beautiful and graceful than ever. It might have been said that her every earthly feeling had been consumed by the flame of her love; and that of the suffering woman of this world there remained only the happy angel awaiting her summons to heaven.

Suddenly, in glancing from her father, Constance caught a glimpse of Tancrede; their eyes met; she uttered a scream and staggered against the grating. Her lover, thinking she was going to fall, rushed toward the grating, and put his arms through the railings to save her.

"Oh, Constance, Constance!" said he; "you are an angel; but so perfect as you are, can you ever forgive me?"

"'Tis he!" cried Constance, "'tis he indeed!" She clasped her hands, and raising her eyes to heaven, she exclaimed, "Oh, *mon Dieu!* I thank thee. I have done well to believe; I have done right to hope. He has come back to me again!"

"But it is not the less true that he married," said the Viscount de Beuzerie, desirous of proving to his daughter that he had not deceived her.

"Married!" gasped Constance, "married! Oh, Tancrede! can that be true?"

"Alas!" replied he, "I was obliged to yield to a stern necessity; and see here is the letter in which I informed you of that fatal event, but which my father, heaven-inspired doubtless, never gave to you."

"Then why do you come here?"

"To tell you that I am again—free—and to thank you for your generous devotion."

"You are free? Do you say you are free?"

"Yes!" murmured he, almost inaudibly.

"Dear father," exclaimed Constance, "take me out of this place immediately. Oh, *mon Dieu! mon Dieu!* I who have so wished to die. Oh! now!—oh! Heaven!—I wish only to live; for my Tancrede is free."

Every word of tenderness the young girl uttered struck like a dagger deep into the heart of the chevalier.

Turning to M. de Beuzerie, he begged him to leave him for a moment with Constance.

The old man was so delighted at the change he perceived in his daughter, whom he believed lost to him forever, that he at once acceded to Tancrede's request, and retired from the parlor, leaving them alone.

No sooner was the door shut than Tancrede seized Constance by the hand and covered it with kisses.

"Oh! Constance," said he, "you see that I was impelled by circumstances which I could not control; tell me do you really pardon me—can you forgive me?"

"I freely forgive you; and I love you more than ever." Then suddenly checking herself, and concealing her face in her hands, she said, "I have spoken to you of my happiness, dear Tancrede, but I forgot the poor deceased one, whom I insult, and whose spirit will perhaps curse me."

Tancrede felt a cold chill creep over him, and sighed deeply.

"You will mourn for her," said Constance; "for doubtless she was beautiful, more beautiful than ever I was. Oh! much more than I can ever be. But, oh! she could never have loved you as I do—of that I am very sure."

"No, Constance," replied he; "but I must nevertheless conform to custom, and mourn for her the appointed time."

"Oh, yes, my love; yes, no doubt. To wait with hope is nothing; to wait in despair is worse than death. Now you have returned to me, after three years, I am sure of you."

And she held out her hand to him with that angelic confidence, which made her, unconsciously, a sublime picture of resignation and devotion.

At this moment M. de Beuzerie re-entered the parlor. The young people looked at him smiling. They had said all they desired to say, although three long years had elapsed since they had seen each other.

But everything they desired to say was comprised in two words.

"I *love you*." And when these were spoken everything had been said.

"Well, Constance," said the old man, "are you ready to come with us?"

Constance looked at Tancrede as if to ask him, once more, if it were true, that she might venture to leave her convent.

"Yes, sir," said the chevalier to the Viscount de Beuzerie. "Yes; mademoiselle consents to restore to you all the pleasure and happiness her absence has deprived you of."

Constance pressed her hands upon her heart. Her beautiful eyes beamed with emotion; a flush of joy suffused her cheeks with color, and she appeared as beautiful and as radiant as an angel.

But M. de Beuzerie and Constance could not leave the convent abruptly; it would have appeared so strange. On the other hand, Tancrede could not remain.

He therefore retired, after saluting M. de Beuzerie and kissing Mlle. Constance's hand. And while the father and his daughter were making their arrangements with the lady superior, preparatory to Constance's departure, our hero torn with anguish, and choking with grief, took his solitary way to Anguilhem.

Upon his return, his mother saw his troubled aspect. She followed him on tiptoe to his chamber, and listening at the door, heard him giving vent to his grief in sighs and sobs.

The good lady retired shaking her head mournfully, apprehending misfortune, without knowing what these misfortunes might be; and because her son wept, she wept also. A report was soon circulated throughout the province that the Viscount de Beuzerie and the Chevalier d'Anguilhem had gone together to the convent of Loches to pay a visit to Mlle. Constance de Beuzerie, and that the result of this visit was, that the novice had renounced her intention of taking the veil, and returned home in company with her father.

Everybody fancied they saw in this unexpected return of the young lady to more worldly ideas, a prompt solution of the difficulties that had existed between the two families, and which our hero's first marriage had rendered more acrimonious than ever.

Constance herself had no doubt of her future happiness; she had faith in her lover while absent, how could she doubt when he had returned to her after three years as loving as ever?

Amid all the *souvenirs* of his youth he had returned to his first and only love. The feeling he had experienced for Sylvandire, which he understood better now that he had returned to Constance, was a material love—a delirium of the senses, the fascination of her beauty, if we may say so. Besides, this love, which reposed upon no elevated feeling, had always been a love full of uneasiness and jealousy; the feeling he experienced for Constance was pure happiness, calm and serene.

But this happiness was cruelly disturbed by the catastrophe at Marseilles. Sometimes Tancrede succeeded for a time in forgetting that terrible night, and then his countenance was illumined by the brightest joy. A smile beaming with happiness played around his mouth till a thought crossed his mind. Then he would suddenly become pale as death; his brow would become suffused with a cold perspiration, and every hair of his head seemed to stand on end.

To his mind's eye there appeared the vision of the bark flying through the mist toward the coast of Tunis.

As we have said, Tancrede had expressed to Constance his desire to mourn for a year, and Constance had approved of his conformity to conventionality. He had not said a word about marriage; but Constance had remained faithful to him in spite of his infidelity, and seeing him returned to her, did not think there was any necessity for speaking of a union which had been long ago contracted in the eyes of God. Therefore, when Tancrede, who hoped that the distractions to be obtained by a residence in Paris would chase away the horrors that tormented his mind—when he spoke of the necessity for his going to the capital, under the pretext of looking after his affairs so long neglected, Constance raised no objection, but merely asked when she might expect him to return.

" As soon as I possibly can," replied he.

This reply was sufficient to satisfy the mind of the confiding girl.

Once more Tancrede bade adieu to the Castle of Anguilhem, to the baron and baroness, to the Abbe Dubois, to Christopher, and to Castor. He wrote to the Marquis de Crette, informing him that he hoped to have the pleasure of seeing him in Paris in the course of a week; and he then

set out upon his journey, which he performed by short
stages.

But on the third day of his journey, he found his slow
progress unendurable; as it left him too much time to
think of things he was particularly anxious to forget. He
then took post-horses, and arrived in Paris on the fourth
night after his departure from Anguilhem.

There was yet a terrible moment to come for him. It
was that when he re-entered alone the house he had departed
from in the company of Sylvandire. He scarcely ventured
to raise his eyes, for fear of seeing his wife's apartments
lighted up; and he fully expected a servant to come and
say to him,

"Madame has returned during the absence of Monsieur
le Chevalier; and begs Monsieur le Chevalier to wait upon
her in her boudoir."

But her apartments were dark and silent, and no voice
spoke to him of Sylvandire.

Breton undressed his master. Tancrede trembled in
the presence of this old confidant of his jealousy. It seemed
to him that Breton, who knew of all the trouble and sorrow Sylvandire had caused him, looked at him, as much
as to say—

"Well, we have taken our revenge, then?"

But another trial awaited him, the most terrible of all.
It was when he waited upon his father-in-law, the President Bouteau. Master Bouteau cast a very scrutinizing
glance upon him. He was not a judge for nothing. But
Tancrede had collected all his strength for this moment,
and he sustained the glance without flinching. The president had not loved his daughter; during the nineteen
years she had been on his hands, he had had ample opportunity of appreciating her character. But as a judge, he
had a habit of questioning, and he would not have been
sorry to have found, even in his own family, a little crimi-
nal affair to exercise his talents upon. Only this time the
opportunity was wanting. For how could he read the
thoughts of this clever dissimulator, who, moreover, never
claimed his wife's dowry?

The result was, that Master Bouteau condoled with his
son-in-law for the loss they had _both_ sustained. But Master
Bouteau mourned in so moderate a fashion, that he continued to dine with Tancrede frequently, and they were

better friends than ever. Then the world more than ever admired the love that the chevalier bore to his wife, because even after her death it was still extended to her family.

This intimacy continued during three months, to the great edification of the circle that could appreciate it. But one fine morning, replying angrily to an advocate who had offended him, Master Bouteau, who was very irritable, and who had a short, fat neck, fell down in a fit of apoplexy, and died, without for a moment recovering his consciousness.

This melancholy event was by no means displeasing to our hero—at which his best friends need not be shocked; for if they had only found themselves for twenty-four hours in the chevalier's position, they would then have fully comprehended how the most excellent father-in-law may become, sometimes, also a very fastidious one.

At the first news of this occurrence, the housekeeper who had served Master Bouteau for fifteen years, hastened to Tancrede, who quickly repaired to the residence of his father-in-law; but, as we have said, the respected president was in a state of insensibility.

Upon opening Master Bouteau's will, it was found that he had left three hundred thousand francs to his son-in-law; fifty thousand to Mlle. Fanchon, his housekeeper, and a hundred thousand in legacies to different churches and hospitals.

As for the ready money, there was no trouble about that, for not a single crown was found anywhere. Mlle. Fanchon had the reputation of being a very orderly methodical person.

Master Bouteau was interred, with all the honors due to his elevated social position, in the cemetery of Pere la Chaise, which was becoming the fashionable burying-place at that epoch.

The three hundred thousand francs bequeathed to Tancrede by his father-in-law embarrassed him very much; this money oppressed him singularly; it was Sylvandire's inheritance. But how could he convey that money to her? there was the hitch. Besides, with this money Sylvandire could purchase her freedom and return to France. This idea made him shudder.

He resolved, nevertheless, to hold this money always ready for disposal in the shape of bonds.

Let us now pass from Master Bouteau, with whom we have done forever, to the Marquis de Crette, with whom we have not yet done.

If Master Bouteau had possessed a germ of suspicion, M. de Crette had pushed his germ to its fullest development. But he was at the same time a courtier and delicate-minded—a very rare thing. Besides, he loved the chevalier as if he had been his own brother. Therefore he asked him no questions about his wife; only he remarked one day in conversation, by way of parenthesis —

"Apropos, my friend, you know I had an old account to settle with that Royancourt?"

"Yes," replied Tancrede.

"Well, he can do you no more injury now. I followed him to Utrecht; and there, in full court, I trod upon his toes so as to make it necessary for him to demand satisfaction."

"And—?" inquired the chevalier.

"And I gave him a gentle hint with the point of my sword in the—"

"You killed him, then?"

"No, not exactly; he is now under the hands of an excellent surgeon. But, however, as the wound was rather serious, he may not get through the winter. Do not let it seriously disturb you, if at any moment you hear that he has taken his departure for another and better world."

One morning shortly after this conversation, there appeared in the "Gazette de Hollande" of the 14th March, 1716, the following paragraph:

"*Amsterdam.*—The Marquis de Royancourt died this morning from the effects of a wound he received while hunting. This nobleman had been among us eight months, charged with an important mission from his most Christian majesty."

"So, so," thought the chevalier, "it appears that there is a Providence over us all, and it relieves me of all my persecutors one after another."

It is a true proverb that says—"Help yourself, and Heaven will help you."

This necrological gazette was brought to the chevalier by his friend Crette.

"Now your imprisonment is settled for," said the marquis to the chevalier, when he had read the article in question. "I took care of the one, and you took care of—"

But Tancrede became suddenly so pale, that the marquis stopped before he had finished his sentence. Extending his hand to his friend, he said—

"Pardon, my dear chevalier. I do not ask for your secrets; only, you know, if these secrets are of a nature calculated to compromise you some day, you will find me in the future as you have found me in the past."

Tancrede pressed the hand of the marquis, and heaved a great sigh; but did not reply.

By this the marquis understood that his secret was a very grave affair.

To dissipate the chevalier's melancholy, the marquis constantly advised dissipation. But Tancrede as constantly replied, that his griefs were too deep to be healed by such expedients.

Crette saw that he must wait for what time would bring forth.

But as time brought no change in the melancholy that overwhelmed his friend, but which on the contrary became more and more intense, Crette and his friends endeavored, from time to time, to make him enter into their amusements, in spite of himself, so to speak. But these distractions always produced the very opposite result from that which this excellent friend intended they should.

On one occasion, D'Herbigny had enticed our hero to take a ride with him to Saint Cloud. D'Herbigny, convinced that his moroseness was caused by the death of his wife, upon seeing a lady pass by in an open carriage, said—

"Ah! how much that lady resembles poor Sylvandire." He then turned his head to observe the effect produced on Tancrede by these consolatory words; but to his surprise, he saw him clinging to the saddle, with his hair on end, haggard eyes, and pale as death.

"He is very weak about that woman," said D'Herbigny to himself, shaking his head. "It's of no use. He will never be cured." And he brought the chevalier home more dead than alive.

Upon another occasion, when Tancrede, D'Herbigny, Crette, and Chastellux dined together, Chastellux proposed to his friends that they should go to the Comedie Francaise, which he frequented very much on account of his admira-tion for Mlle. Poussette. Crette and D'Herbigny accepted the offer with a view of amusing their friend, who agreed to go without knowing what was proposed.

The play was "Phedre," which was becoming quite popular; and M. de Pourceaugnac enjoyed then, as at the present day, the privilege of exciting in the highest degree the hilarity of the audience. Tancrede, who was always buried in his own reflections, listened to "Phedre" with-out hearing it. But he undertook to speak slightingly of the comedy, when the scene occurred, when the two law-yers sing to the unhappy husband, accused of having mar-ried two wives:

> "Polygamy is a hanging offense."

Now this scene, which extorted the greatest mirth from the audience, produced quite an opposite effect upon D'Anguilhem. He uttered a suppressed cry, which his friends supposed was his way of laughing, then threw him-self back, and fell fainting into the arms of De Crette. He was carried home in a very bad condition, and during the night became delirious.

Crette never quitted his side; but took the precaution of keeping everybody out of the room while the raving fit was on, and watched by him alone.

Next day, the Marquis de Crette appeared almost as anx-ious and full of care as his friend, who soon recovered from this critical attack, but still remained oppressed with his melancholy, which seemed to increase day by day

---

CHAPTER XXXIV.

What rendered Tancrede more and more sad was, that the time seemed to pass on with the most frightful rapid-ity: and that out of the year he had required for mourn-ing, nine months had already elapsed.

Strictly speaking, as we have shown, he had promised nothing to Constance; but it was evident that Constance had not required promises from him, in order to induce her to believe her union with him as a thing decided upon.

From the moment that Tancrede had visited her at the convent, and prayed her to quit it, and she had consented to return to her home, it was with the tacit understanding that she should become his wife. Everybody thought the same: the viscount and viscountess thought so, and so did the baron and baroness, and all the neighbors around Anguilhem and Beuzerie; in fact, all those who had heard of the old loves of Tancrede and Constance, and those who had heard their new engagement spoken of.

Then again he loved Constance more than ever he had done before. Every other day he received a letter from her, and each of these letters was a fresh leaf from the book of her heart, in which he read the promise of inexpressible joys. His situation was fearful. Impelled by love, restrained by fear. His union with Constance had two aspects; the one smiling with happiness, the other weeping in despair.

Twenty times he was on the point of setting out for Anguilhem and confessing everything to his father and to Constance; but his good genius held him back, as Achilles was withheld by Minerva.

Finally, upon the urgent entreaties of all his friends, driven from his last intrenchments, losing his senses after a fresh delay of six months, he gave his word for the beginning of December, 1716. When that time arrived, he pretended to fall ill, hoping to die: then he promised definitely for the month of February, 1717.

Constance submitted with angelic resignation to all these delays, without even inquiring the cause of them. Meanwhile she had lost her mother, and was herself obliged to demand a period for mourning.

It was decided that the marriage should be celebrated in Paris. Eight days before that appointed for it to take place, the baron and baroness came and established themselves at the Hotel d'Anguilhem, while the Viscount de Beuzerie and his daughter occupied a neighboring house which had been taken and prepared for them by the chevalier.

The Hotel d'Anguilhem had been entirely renovated; everything had been changed; furniture, hangings, pictures, and mirrors. The chevalier would have considered it as a profanation to make use of anything that had belonged to Sylvandire.

It will be remembered that, upon taking possession of
M. de Bouzenois' inheritance, he had sent to his mother
the diamonds and jewels which he found in the caskets.
A portion of these formed the *cadeau* from the baroness to
her daughter-in-law.

The approaching marriage of the Chevalier d'Anguilhem
made a great noise in the fashionable world. It was the
only subject of gossip at the date of the arrival of the Persian embassador, Mehemet Riza-Beg, who, as we have
said, arrived at the capital bearing presents from his sovereign to Louis the Fourteenth. The embassador held
audience every day; to the ladies in the evenings, and to
the gentlemen in the mornings.

We have a few words to say respecting this singular personage, who subsequently figures in our history, and who
merits our special attention.

Mehemet Riza-Beg was, for the moment, the personage
who, next to the Chevalier d'Anguilhem, most occupied
public attention. We must, however, avow, with that
modesty of which we have given so many proofs in the
course of this authentic history, that the chevalier occupied
the attention of only a small section of the Parisian world,
while the Persian embassador, Mehemet Riza-Beg, occupied the attention of all France.

In fact, since Abdalla, who, in the year 807, had been
sent as embassador by Aaron, King of Persia, to Charlemagne, Emperor of the West, and who had brought from
his master a live elephant, which was considered as a great
wonder; the succeeding sovereigns of France had never received a direct message from the country of the "Thousand and One Nights." When, in the middle of the year
1716, the rumor spread abroad that Ussein, the Shah of
Persia, grandson of the great Sephi, and son of the Sultan
Solyman, having heard, even in remote Ispahan, his capital, of the merits of the great King Louis the Fourteenth,
he had resolved to send an embassador with presents. This
news, as yet uncertain, appeared singularly to flatter the
pride of the conqueror of Flanders; and as if, at the moment of showing him the nothingness of human greatness,
Heaven had wished to give his vanity some compensation,
they soon learned that Mehemet Riza-Beg had disembarked
at Marseilles.

The arrival of this embassador was great news for Versailles. The old king, constantly surrounded by his bastards, and tormented by them, struck by the hand of Heaven in the person of his sons, and of his grandsons, became more and more peevish, so that even Mme. de Maintenon, a woman of great resources, complained to her friends of the terrible task she had undertaken, to amuse the king, the most unamusable person, not only in France and Navarre, but in the whole of Europe.

Mehemet Riza-Beg arrived then, as we see, to galvanize, as we should say nowadays, that great sepulcher they call Versailles, and that great corpse they called Louis the Fourteenth.

There were people who whispered that Mehemet Riza-Beg was not the embassador of Ussein, Shah of Persia, but of Mme. de Maintenon, anonymous Queen of France.

Whoever he was, and wherever he came from, Mehemet Riza-Beg was received with the greatest honors.

No sooner was his landing at Marseilles become known, than the king sent M. de Saint-Olon, his embassador at the Court of Morocco, to meet him. In fact, the honors due to extraordinary envoys were lavished upon Mehemet Riza-Beg, who arrived at Charenton on the 26th of January, and made his entry into the capital on the 7th of February following, and was received at solemn audience on the 19th of the same month.

Now, as we have said, the embassador was the sun of the day; nothing was so much spoken of as his magnificence, his singularities, and the torments of his capricious whims, to which he subjected Baron Breteuil, who was charged by the great king with receiving this embassador extraordinary whom his brother of Persia had sent to him.

It was, therefore, quite natural that, after seeing Versailles and Paris, M. de Beuzerie and his daughter should desire to see the embassador.

Tancrede, who expanded at the approach of his new happiness, believed it to be his duty not to refuse this little gratification to his affianced bride.

It was, therefore, arranged that as the nuptial benediction would be pronounced at midday, and that as nothing is more tiresome to the newly-married than the wedding-day, during which they are obliged to receive the congratulations of their relations. and friends—it was then arranged, I say, that between the benediction and the wed-

ding-dinner, they should go and pay the proposed visit to
the embassador.

The 26th of February was the day fixed for the union of
Constance and the chevalier. Forced to face this moment,
solemn to every one, but terrible to our hero, he had ended,
not by forgetting the situation in which this second marriage placed him, but by diverting his thoughts from it.

In fine, he was like those men who, having made a sacrifice of their lives, know that from one moment to another
this life may be taken from them; but who, while expecting the blow, wish to pass their few remaining days as
gayly as possible.

Tancrede, since he rose in the morning, was intoxicated
with the happiness of seeing Constance, and he forgot
everything in looking at her.

Upon leaving the Church of Saint-Roch, where they
were married, the ladies carried off Constance with them
to disrobe her; while he and the Marquis de Crette proceeded to the embassy to see Mehemet Riza-Beg. As we
have stated, the gentlemen were admitted in the morning
and the ladies in the evening. The Marquis de Crette was
acquainted with the Baron de Breteuil, and had obtained
tickets from him.

The chevalier and the marquis were duly ushered into
the presence of his excellency. There was a great crowd,
who passed in, four at a time, before the embassador, who
was seated on a mat in the middle of his salon, gravely
saluting the gentlemen as they passed. The visitors were
announced as they entered the room.

When it came to the turn of the two friends, they were
announced like the others, as—

"The Marquis de Crette and the Chevalier d'Anguilhem."

At this moment, Mehemet Riza-Beg was occupied in
smoking his hookah; or, rather, a female slave on her
knees before him was preparing to light his pipe.

The two gentlemen advanced four or five paces into the
salon, when they suddenly stopped, and stared, livid and
motionless, as if the head of this slave, like that of Medusa,
had changed them into marble; then, after a moment's
stupefaction, they took each other by the hand and retreated from the salon, without having even seen the embassador.

"Oh! Tancrede," said the marquis, on arriving in the ante-chamber, "what a resemblance!"

"Crette," replied our hero, "it is not a resemblance, it is Sylvandire herself, and I am lost."

Then in a few words, he briefly related his history to his friend, who, however, had very little to learn. During his night's delirium he had told nearly everything.

"In that case," said Crette, "you must fly immediately; take at once all you can, gold, diamonds, jewels, and set out for Flanders, Holland, or England. Go to the end of the world—anywhere, but go."

Tancrede never stirred.

"But how happens it that she is come with that animal of an embassador?" said Crette.

"Who can fathom the designs of Heaven?" replied D'Anguilhem.

"Come now, no theology," cried the marquis, dragging him away; "lose not a second; send for a post-chaise, jump into it, and start."

"Go, without Constance? Never! never!"

"But, my dear friend, do you know to what danger you are exposed?"

"To death. I know it; but what signifies death to me, provided that I live only till to-morrow?"

"Permit me to say that your reasoning is perfectly absurd. To-morrow, my friend, you will be, I hope, still less desirous of dying than to-day. You must live, *morbleu!* and live a long time: so, set out to-day—this moment, even! Tell me only where you go, and to-morrow, nay, this evening, I will send your wife to you, or I will bring her myself if you wish it, and once together, you will forget the embassador, you will forget Sylvandire, you will forget the universe."

"No, Crette; leave me, abandon me to my fate. You see well that I am born to misfortunes."

"Oh! if you lose your senses, chevalier, you will be truly insupportable; but do you wish to become the laughing-stock of all France? Do you desire that—*diable!* remember the gallows of Monsieur de Pourceaugnac. Apropos, that was why—"

"Alas! yet, my friend."

"Poor boy! But I repeat to you, decide, and decide at once: the king does not joke on such matters. Peste!

Think of For-l'Eveque, of the Bastile, of Chalons-sur-
Saone.   Fifteen months' imprisonment for having neglected your wife, what will be your punishment for having sold
her?''

While thus discoursing, they had returned to the Hotel
d'Anguilhem.   Constance, in her turn, had gone out with
her friends and the baroness to pay a visit to the embassador.

Crette availed himself of this moment to urge his friend
to take his resolution.   Tancrede had nearly thirty thousand francs ready money in hand, and diamonds worth
two hundred thousand francs, which was more than necessary for present wants.   He had pretty well decided to fly,
when suddenly the ladies returned.   The doors of the embassy, by one of the numerous caprices of the embassador,
had been suddenly closed, and the reception postponed
until five o'clock in the evening.

The sight of Constance produced its effect.   Tancrede
had no longer the strength to fly, nor the courage to tell
the truth.

Dinner was announced.

The chevalier followed the guests mechanically, and
seated himself at the table with an air of absent-mindedness
that was remarked by everybody.

But on a wedding-day, the head of a newly-married man
may be a prey to thoughts of a very opposite nature, and
yet no one would be so indiscreet as to ask him what he is
thinking of.   Constance, however, looked at him from
time to time with anxiety.   The least noise made De Crette
and D'Anguilhem tremble, and look toward the door.

Things passed on quietly and the dessert was served.
The chevalier and Crette began to gain courage.   Our
hero smiled upon his wife and she gave him new life with
her smiles.   Crette, with that charming aristocratic talent
which so few gentlemen have preserved to the present day,
related some of those anecdotes which no one nowadays
thinks of repeating, when suddenly a very ugly-looking
negro made his appearance at the door, and requested to
see the Baron d'Anguilhem.

The baron rose from the table, when Tancrede, understanding that he was the person the messenger addressed,
made a sign to his father to reseat himself; then, pale as
death, followed the negro.

Tancrede descended the staircase without having the courage to put a single question to his guide. Besides, if he had entertained any doubts as to the object of his mission, they were quickly dispelled. In the court-yard he saw a double sedan-chair, and inside was seated the young slave he had recognized in the morning, and the recognition of whom had produced such a terrible effect upon him.

The slave made a sign to him to enter the chair, and pointed to him to take the vacant seat opposite to her. Tancrede obeyed mechanically, without uttering a word, and seated himself on the front seat. The negro closed the door of the chair, and the loving couple found themselves *tête-à-tête*.

"So," said Sylvandire, "I see you once again, my dear Tancrede, thank God! but it has cost me a deal of trouble."

Tancrede bowed.

"You did not expect to see me to-day, I suppose, did you?" continued Sylvandire, evidently taking the pleasure that a cat enjoys with a mouse before devouring it.

"No! I must admit I did not," replied he.

"Ah! you thought I was at Constantinople, or Cairo, or at least at Tripoli; but I love you so much, dear Tancrede, that I could no longer endure being separated from you; so I gladly embraced the first opportunity that offered itself of returning to Europe."

"You are very good," murmured her husband.

"But how am I recompensed for my love? When I arrived I inquired for you, and I was told you were about taking another wife, and to-day, even this very day, you have married her. Do you not know I am jealous, you ungrateful wretch?"

Every word chilled the heart of the chevalier. After a moment's silence, during which Sylvandire never took her eyes off him.

"Well, what do you want?" inquired he.

"I wish to know at what price you sold me, in order to add the amount to the little bill of claims I have against you."

"Upon my word," said Tancrede. "as for that, I had a good right to sell a wife who had caused me a long imprisonment."

"I could have done worse than that, you rascal," replied Sylvandire, in a most caressing tone.

"Had me killed, I suppose? Ah, madame, if you had done that, you would, I must confess, have conferred upon me a very deep obligation."

"Listen," said Sylvandire; "no jesting, if you please; let us talk of business."

"Gladly," replied Tancrede; "but I beg to assure you on my part that I am in no humor for jesting, and have no thoughts of it. Speak, then, as seriously as you please, I am all attention."

"Tancrede," replied Sylvandire, "do you know that you have made me happy without your intending it? I met Mehemet Riza-Beg, I wept to him, and he married me."

"What?" cried our hero, at this ray of hope, "and have you married again, also?"

"I have, but in the Mohammedan fashion, which is, perhaps, a very good fashion in that country, but goes for nothing in this. The consequence is, that I have really only one husband; but you, you have two wives. Now, you know, my dear love, that polygamy is—"

"Yes! yes! I know," said the chevalier.

"You are then completely caught, completely in my power, for I only waited till the thing was done, you understand why; at all events, as you would not politely make me a visit this morning, you receive mine this evening."

"Do you wish, then, to ruin me?" cried Tancrede.

"You are mad. What good would it be for me to ruin you? No, no, *dear* Tancrede, I first wish to obtain from you the hundred thousand crowns you inherited from my poor father."

"Oh!" cried he, "that is quite fair. I have the money in good bonds, all ready to be sent to you."

And he made a movement to go out of the chair and fetch his portfolio.

But Sylvandire checked him.

"Stop! stop! that is not all. You are not going to get off so easily," cried Sylvandire.

"I am waiting," said our hero.

"There is the hundred thousand crowns, my dowry."

"What! your dowry! You know very well that I never received that hundred thousand."

"I know that they are specified in my marriage settlement, and that I can not cheat my second husband out of them; his proceedings, you will understand, are very different from yours, as he has bought me, and as for you —you *sold* me."

"Well, well," said Tancrede, "all in good time. I will give you the hundred thousand crowns also, to save words."

"Then—" continued Sylvandire.

"What? is there anything else?" cried Tancrede.

"To be sure there is—the price of my body for which you sold me. The deuce, my dear Tancrede! if I was not of age, I was at least emancipated, and could dispose of myself. Now the daughter of a jurisconsul must be worth a very good price."

"As for that," said he, "I give you my word of honor that I never touched a sou, but even—even—gave five hundred pistoles into the bargain."

"Oh! it is not very complimentary to tell me that, sir," replied Sylvandire, simpering; "but as you are a man of honor, and as you give me your word, I suppose I must believe you; then there will be, if you please, six hundred thousand francs to pay me."

"When do you want them?" inquired Tancrede.

"I have a good mind still," continued Sylvandire, without replying to his question, "I have a good mind to make my appearance in your dining-room, instead of sitting here in the court, and get honest Breton to announce me—you still have Breton?"

The chevalier bowed affirmatively.

"And make honest Breton announce 'Madame d'Anguilhem,' in order to see how you would look between your two wives, Turk that you are? But I prefer another kind of satisfaction. You will give me, as I have told you, the six hundred thousand francs first—and then we shall see."

"Where do you wish this money sent to?" inquired the chevalier.

"To the embassy," replied Sylvandire. "You will ask for the favorite slave of his excellency, Mehemet Riza Beg. I shall know what that means, and will respond to the invitation."

"And when will you expect to receive this six hundred thousand francs?" inquired her husband, repeating the question, which had remained unanswered.

"In two hours."

"In two hours!" cried he, "you might as well ask me to blow my brains out. How do you suppose I can collect a hundred thousand crowns in two hours?"

"But you have diamonds, sell them; you have friends, use them—make an appeal to their purses. I am sorry to be so exacting, but we are going away directly, my dear Tancrede. His excellency, Mehemet Riza-Beg, has only stayed thus long at my earnest entreaty that we should stay until your marriage was celebrated."

"In two hours! In two hours!" cried Tancrede—"impossible at this time of night! at least wait till to-morrow morning."

"I can not wait a minute longer than the two hours."

"Then you must do what you please."

"What I please! Oh, mon Dieu! that is a very simple affair. I shall enter your house, ascend into your chamber, go to bed, and wait till you come— Angola," continued Sylvandire, addressing the negro, and making a sign for him to open the door of the chair, "open, I wish to come out."

The negro placed his hand on the button of the door. Tancrede stopped Sylvandire.

"But think of the consequences."

"The consequences are nothing to me, they are everything to you. Mehemet has no right to me except in having bought me; and I doubt if the sale would be considered legal in France. Besides, it is you who sold me, and it would very ill become you to reproach me with anything that has occurred to me during the time I have been in the possession of my purchaser."

"But, madame—"

"Listen," said Sylvandire, "I have said that I would give you two hours; and as I mean what I say, I still give them to you. But if, at the expiration of two hours—pay attention to what I say—"

"I do not lose one word," replied he, with a sigh.

"If, in the two hours, the six hundred thousand francs are not at the embassy—"

"What then?" inquired Tancrede anxiously.

"What then, my dear?" replied Sylvandire, "except to

hear Madame d'Anguilhem announced, and to see me make my appearance."

Upon this, Sylvandire saluted her husband with a charming movement of the head, and a malicious smile. Then, making a sign to the negro, Angola, the door of the chair was opened, and the chevalier stepped out.

"Mind you are punctual," said Sylvandire.

"*Au revoir.*"

The chair was immediately carried off by the negroes; but at the outside gate, Sylvandire put her head out of the window, and again saluted Tancrede by waving her handkerchief.

CHAPTER XXXV.

TANCREDE found the Marquis de Crette waiting for him at the top of the staircase.

"Well?"

"Ah, well! indeed, my friend. It was she."

"So I supposed. What does she want?"

"Impossibilities."

"What are they?"

"Six hundred thousand francs in two hours."

"Six hundred thousand francs in two hours!" repeated Crette. "Good!"

"How, good? when I have only three hundred thousand upon which I can put my hand; and here, in two hours, if I do not find three hundred thousand others, which is utterly impossible—"

"Well; if you do not find them, what will she do then?"

"She will come to this house, and publicly announce herself under the name of Madame d'Anguilhem."

"She will not do it."

"Why not?"

"I do not know why; but if she would dare to do it at all, she would have done so already."

"Ah! my friend."

"Listen; they want your money—she does not demand her rights; she conceals herself. There is something beneath the surface."

"But, my friend, she does not conceal herself, for in two hours, as she has told me, she will come here and proclaim herself my wife."

"Yes, I know it very well; and it is not a very pleasant prospect," said Crette.

"My friend, I shall go and blow out my brains," cried Tancrede.

"There is always time enough for that. Leave the business to *me*."

"What will you do?"

"I do not know; but I will try and save you."

"Ah, my friend—my only friend; my dear Crette!" cried Tancrede, throwing himself into the arms of the marquis.

"Ah, well; yes—I know all that," replied Crette; "but we must not lose our time in this way."

"What can I do? I leave my fate in your hands. Order, and I obey."

"Return to the company in the salon—it is now half-past eight; there is plenty of time—put on the best face you can. I do not expect too much from you, my friend. Place Breton at the door, and let him prevent any one entering the saloon without your permission."

"I will put a guard at the outer gate."

"Now give me three hundred thousand in bonds, all the jewels you have, and as much cash as you can spare. I will run to my notary, and make use of his purse. The deuce is in it, if we can not make up the amount."

"Oh, yes, Crette; do find the money—sell everything, and serve your poor friend."

The chevalier took the bonds for three hundred thousand from his portfolio, and all the diamonds and jewels he had just given to Constance. With these Crette jumped into his coach, which had been ordered meanwhile, and set off at full gallop to his notary's.

Tancrede returned to the saloon, and, in obedience to his friend Crette's advice, put on as cheerful a face as he possibly could.

Meanwhile Crette was busy. He hastened home, and got twenty-five thousand francs—from his notary he got fifty thousand. All this, with the thirty thousand ready cash given him by Tancrede, and the diamonds pledged nearly at their full value, almost made up the six hundred thousand francs demanded.

This business had taken up an hour and a half in the execution; therefore, there was no time to lose.

Upon leaving his notary, Crette ordered his coach to be driven to the Persian Embassy.

In five minutes he was at the door.

He ascended the staircase. In consequence of the change in the hour of reception, the ladies were descending it in little groups.

The marquis encountered Mlle. Pousette on the stairs. She seemed to be greatly diverted with something, and was convulsed with laughter. The marquis wished to avoid her, for he feared she might detain him. But mademoiselle quickly perceived him, and rushed into his arms.

"What amuses you so greatly?" asked Crette. "What are you laughing at, mademoiselle?"

"Oh, my dear marquis! you will never believe it. The most unheard of thing, the most unexpected, the most wonderful, the most fabulous, the most romantic, the most mythological, the most—oh! oh! oh! dear me."

"Mon Dieu!" thought De Crette, "can it be possible she has recognized Sylvandire?"

"Such an adventure is never found but in romances, in fairy-tales, in the 'Thousand and One Nights.' Such an adventure—who could believe it?"

"Yes! yes!" cried Crette, "I will believe it, every word, if you do, my charmer; but make haste and tell me, for I am in a great hurry."

"Are you going to see the embassador?"

"Yes, and I fear I shall be too late."

"Well, then, do you look at him; look between his eyes, as I look at you now: then imagine his great black beard and his mustaches removed, and satisfy your curiosity. Then come to me to-morrow morning, or this evening, if you please, monsieur le marquis, and we will talk the matter over."

Then smiling a roguish smile, and pressing the marquis's hand, she prepared to descend the staircase.

"But what does all this mean?" said Crette; "I am to look the embassador hard in the face, between his eyes, remove his beard and mustaches— Why, my charming Poussette, do you happen to know his excellency the Persian ambassador?"

"Do I know him? Do I know you? Do I know D'Herbigny, or Chastellux? As I might have known your friend Tancrede if he had not been so cruel."

" Poussette, my dear girl," cried the marquis, " you can save the life of—"

" Yours, marquis?"

" Not mine, exactly, but that of my best friend—which amounts to the same thing—of the chevalier."

" What must I do for that?"

" Tell me who this embassador is? His name, Poussette, his name! Twenty thousand francs and the best thanks of the handsomest gentleman in Paris are yours. I pledge myself to obtain them for you: if he will not pay, I will. Poussette, my dearest friend, what is the name of this embassador?"

" Ah! for shame. You think I am mercenary, marquis; you deserve to be—"

" Poussette, dear, his name, and before midnight I will bring you the twenty thousand. Expect me."

" Well, marquis, it is—but I am sure you will not believe me."

" I do believe you. Go on. I always believe everything the ladies say."

" It is—"

" Poussette, you torture me."

" Well, then, it is the Indian!"

" What Indian?"

" Why, my yellow admirer."

" What! the Malay, Tancrede's adversary, Monsieur Afghano?"

" The very same."

" Ah, Poussette, darling of my heart, let me kiss you!"

" Fy! marquis!"

And Crette saluted the young lady without concerning himself at being the object of attraction to all the company descending the staircase.

" But are you quite sure of it?" continued the marquis, scarcely able to believe the welcome news, which he feared was too good to be true.

" I tell you that I recognized him in spite of his disguise of thick beard and mustache, in spite of his teeth dyed black, in spite of his finger-nails dyed red, although he pretended not to see me, the ungrateful wretch. Ah, marquis, marquis, how ungrateful you men are!"

" My dear Poussette," said Crette, " I wish to prove to you the contrary. Wait supper for me, I shall be with you before twelve. Adieu, my little Venus, if what you tell me is true, you have done me a great service, which I shall never forget as long as I live."

Mlle. Poussette proceeded to her chair, and Crette ascended the staircase four steps at a time.

At the door of the embassador's salon the negro stopped him.

"What do you want?" said he to the marquis; "the hour for the reception of gentlemen has passed long ago. His excellency has retired."

"It is not his excellency that I want," replied the marquis, "but his favorite slave."

"Then you come from—"

"From the Chevalier d'Anguilhem."

"In that case enter."

And the negro introduced the marquis into a room furnished in the oriental fashion, where he left him alone, while, as he said, he went to inform the person for whom the marquis inquired. Five minutes afterward Sylvandire entered the room.

"Ah! it is you, is it, marquis? I had a presentiment that I should have the pleasure of seeing you. This pleasing anticipation is realized. Have you brought the six hundred thousand francs?"

"No!" replied the marquis, boldly.

"No? then what have you come for?"

"To speak to your master, his excellency Mehemet Riza-Beg."

"What about?"

"About Monsieur d'Argensen, lieutenant-general of police of this kingdom."

Sylvandire turned pale. Crette remarked the effect produced by his words, and took courage.

"His excellency can not receive you now, he is fatigued, and has retired to his bed."

"Well, then, I must go and fetch some one who will wake him up."

"Wait a minute," said Sylvandire, "while I go and see if his excellency is visible."

"Excuse me, madame," said Crette, "but I have my reasons for accompanying you, or I—"

And he made a step toward the door.

"You can enter," said Sylvandire.

And she opened a door which led to a corridor.

The marquis followed her, and entered into the embassador's reception-room. Mehemet Riza-Beg was seated on his mat, and giving himself most ridiculous airs.

" Stay while I call the interpreter," said Sylvandire.

" That is quite unnecessary," said Crette.

" Can you speak Persian, then, marquis?"

" No, I can not; but his excellency will have the goodness to speak French."

" He can not; he does not know our language."

" You believe so, do you?" cried Crette.

And he approached the embassador, looking as Mlle. Poussette had directed him to do.

" You will oblige me, will you not, Monsieur Afghano, by speaking French? You have not forgotten our beautiful tongue, have you?" said the marquis, slapping him on the shoulder.

The embassador uncrossed his legs, and, raising himself on his hands, looked aghast at the marquis.

" Oh, la!" said Crette, " my good fellow, if I had thought that the sight of an old acquaintance would have produced this effect I should have instructed madame to forewarn you."

" What do you want with me?" said Afghano.

" There now," said the marquis, laughing, and turning to Sylvandire, " I told you his excellency would make an exception in my favor."

" What I wish, my dear Monsieur Afghano," continued Crette, turning to the sham embassador; " what I wish to do, is to inform you that the king, whom you have mystified, will know in one hour that he has been your dupe. That is what I wish."

The Malay gnashed his teeth, and seized the handle of his dagger.

" None of that nonsense, if you please," said Crette. " No tragedy, I beg; it will not help you at all. For, I warn you, that I have a second who knows your pedigree as well as I do, and who will set out for Versailles in an hour, if I do not return to prevent him. Still, my dear friend, that need not stop you: kill me, if it is agreeable to you. I shall never be famous; and to die by your hand would render me immortal. Only think! the Marquis de Crette killed by the hand of his excellency Mehemet Riza-Beg, embassador extraordinary from the very sublime Emperor of Persia. Diable! I should be only too fortunate. No, no, put up your weapon; and show more peaceable intentions."

"Well, well! be it so; I am a well-disposed prince. I wish as you wish. Let us speak of business;" saying which, the embassador rose up, and went and bolted the door himself.

"Yes," continued Crette. "I understand you have bought madame; and you have made a good bargain, for madame is a very charming lady; then, you have become acquainted, that is quite natural; and, becoming acquainted, you find, upon comparing notes, that you both have a grievance, and against the same man, our poor Tancrede. Is it not so?"

"Just so."

"Well, then you said, 'We have a common hatred, let us revenge ourselves together.' Meanwhile, you have heard that no one knew how to amuse the king, and, as you are a man of imagination, you improvised this little embassy for his special amusement. Bravo! my friend, bravo! There was everything to be gained, nothing to lose. You pocket the presents which his most Christian majesty has bestowed upon you in exchange for the baubles that you have presented him in the name of your sovereign, whom you have made appear like a rascal.

"As for madame, she thought to herself—I will go and take the inheritance left me by my father, which was quite just; and my dowry, which was much less just, seeing that madame never had a dowry. Upon this, you both came to Paris, and fortune favored you beyond your wildest expectations. You ascertained that Monsieur d'Anguilhem was about to marry again, and you waited until the marriage was celebrated. Then, when the thing was done, and could not be gainsaid, you set yourselves to work immediately to open the mine of gold that you saw at your feet. So you began by extorting from your victim six hundred thousand francs through his fear of the rope that hangs suspended over the heads of bigamists. But this was not all. After this demand had been met, you would have been ready with another; and so, exaction after exaction. You would have lived for the rest of your lives under the shadow of this lucky tyranny, extorting from

the chevalier, little by little, the whole of his inheritance
from Monsieur de Bouzenois, and put it into the hands of
Monsieur Afghano.

"I believe I have hit it aright, have I not, sir? have I
not, madame?" said Crette, casting upon each in their
turn, a look, half-scornful, half-menacing. "The deuce!
We are French, and therefore not spiteful, as Monsieur
Boileau Despreaux says, whom, doubtless, madame has
read in her youth."

Sylvandire and Afghano appeared annihilated and
crushed before Crette, like two criminals before their
judge.

"And now," said Crette, "as the position of each is
clear, as the chevalier can be hanged for bigamy, and as
Monsieur Afghano can be hanged, drawn and quartered
for forgery, and as Madame Sylvandire can be sent to
Saint-Lazare as a strumpet, why, let us talk politics.

"You have put your hand upon nearly a million from
the King of France, my dear Monsieur Afghano. You
have three hundred thousand crowns left you by your father, in this portfolio, my dear Madame d'Anguilhem.
You have nearly two millions besides, Monsieur Afghano,
making altogether, if I reckon rightly, three millions three
hundred thousand francs. That is a very pretty little sum
upon which a man may retire to Tripoli, or Constantinople, or Cairo, and enjoy the life of a sultan. I shall
make no obstacles."

"Monsieur le marquis," said Afghano, "I will go to-
morrow. I swear it."

"One moment. One moment, if you please; you will
go, I wish it, but there are two little conditions I must
make."

"What are they, monsieur? I will listen to them."

"You must swear you will never return to Paris again."

"I swear it."

"I can believe you; for your oath is guaranteed by the
fear that your villainy will be discovered. I ask, then, for
no better guaranty than your word. I am quite sure I
shall never see you here again."

The Malay bowed.

"But it is not the same with madame; if she happens to
part from you, or you from her; and if it happens that I
can no longer prove that you are an impostor, and that

she is your accomplice; it is just possible that she might take it into her head to wish to resume her seat at the conjugal fireside, which would embarrass us greatly, as there is only room for two. I can not therefore trust to madame's word, but madame will write me a little note, which I will dictate myself; and when I shall have this letter in my hands, why, then, madame will be at liberty to follow you to the end of the world."

Sylvandire uttered an exclamation of dissent.

"It must be done," said Crette. "The terms are rather hard, I confess, to obey laws rather than to dictate them; but it is a condition, *sine quâ non.*"

"And suppose I refuse?" said Sylvandire.

"Well! when I leave this place, I go straight to the lieutenant of police; I report to him the little game you are both playing, and in half an hour you are both in the Bastile, but—in separate apartments!"

"But," said Sylvandire, "do not suppose we are isolated here; we have not come without taking proper precautions. We have very powerful friends and protectors."

"Of course you do not include Monsieur de Royancourt among them, for I have had the honor of passing my sword through his corrupt body. I presume the powerful friends you allude to are—the Jesuits."

"Perhaps so."

"Alas! my dear Madame d'Anguilhem, although you have cultivated the acquaintance of those gentlemen a little in former days, you do not know them yet. You would outrageously compromise them in calling upon them for aid in your present difficulty, and they would spare no pains to sacrifice you both mercilessly. They are not fools."

"That is true, it is but too true," murmured Afghano.

"In that case," said Sylvandire, "I must then do—"

"What the marquis requires, my dear friend," replied the Malay; "believe me it is the most prudent course."

"But if I give you this letter, will you promise to let us leave France with what we have got, goods and money, without molestation?"

"I engage to do so, on my honor. I, Alphonso, Marquis de Crette."

"I am ready, sir," replied Sylvandire, seating herself at a writing-table, and preparing a sheet of paper, "dictate. I will write."

"Allow me first to examine the sheet of paper upon which you propose to write," said the marquis, holding up the paper before the candle. The examination proving satisfactory, he said:

"Write."

"AT TUNIS, 11*th October*, 1715.

"MONSIEUR D'ANGUILHEM,—Mourn no longer for my death with that deep grief, which, as I am informed, you have ever exhibited for my loss. I live; and if I fell into the sea, and feigned to be drowned, it was only an artifice to enable me to escape from the dominion of a husband who, in spite of all his kindness and affection for me, I felt I could never love, to pass into the arms of a man I adore. To-day, sir, I am become his wife, under other laws, divine and human, and never will you see me again. Dead to you, I wish still to be kind to you. Consider yourself, then, from this moment, as completely widowed, and also perfectly free.

"May you be as happy as I am happy: this is the last wish for you from her who once was,

"SYLVANDIRE dame D'ANGUILHEM.

"P.S.—This letter will be delivered to you by a trusty messenger whom my husband sends to France."

"What use will you make of this letter?" inquired Sylvandire, after addressing and sealing it, and handing it to the marquis.

"You will know, madame, if in breaking your promise, you compel me to make use of it."

Saluting Afghano and Sylvandire, the marquis made his way the door; upon opening it, he said, loud enough to be heard by all the attendants,

"Condescend, your excellency, to accept or my profound respects."

Afghano remained, as it were, transfixed; astounded at the scene he had passed through.

Triumph, exultation, defiance, terror, humiliation, hope, congratulation!

Sylvandire followed De Crette.

"Marquis," said she, in a low voice, as they passed through the ante-chamber—"is his wife handsome?"

"Not so beautiful as you, madame, but she loves him more."

" As you please," replied Sylvandire. " I prefer to be a princess."

" Another marriage like the last, madame," replied Crette, " and you will attain your aim; you are already an embaasadress."

Sylvandire heaved a profound sigh, and returned to the salon.

CONCLUSION.

CRETTE returned to his coach, and immediately proceeded with all speed to the Hotel d'Anguilhem.

He found Constance, who, in a little salon, sat alone and unhappy, weeping to see her husband so dull and thoughtful.

" Honor compelled him to keep his word with me," said she; " but it is very evident that he no longer loves me."

At this moment Crette opened the door; she supposed it was her husband coming to seek her; she rose quickly to run to him, but seeing it was the marquis, she sunk back into her chair.

Crette understood what it was that troubled the heart of the young bride, and went to her, to cheer her up.

"Come, come," said he; " dry up your tears, wipe those lovely eyes, dear lady, and let us go into the drawing-room together. In a quarter of an hour Tancrede will be so much improved that you will have no cause to complain. I will be answerable for the future."

Then taking her by the hand, he proceeded to the drawing-room.

Breton guarded the door, as he had been ordered to do. The marquis beckoned to Breton to come to him. Breton obeyed.

" My friend," said De Crette, " throw open the doors, and announce in your best voice, solemnly,

" ' Madame Tancrede d'Anguilhem!' "

Breton, who could see no reason why he should not admit the bride of his master, and his best friend, instantly obeyed; and inflating his lungs to the utmost, he threw open the folding-doors, and made the place resound with that name, so terrible to the ears of the chevalier:

" MADAME TANCREDE D'ANGUILHEM!"

Tancrede was engaged in conversation with D'Herbigny

and Monsieur de Beuzerie in a remote corner of the room. He no sooner heard the terrible announcement than he felt the room going round. Attempting to rise, his legs gave way under him, and, sinking upon a couch, he buried his face in his hands.

Constance entered radiant with smiles and happiness. Crette gave her his arm.

They proceeded to where Tancrede was sitting, who, hearing the noise of their footsteps, dared not look up, but sat secretly hoping that the earth would open and swallow him.

"Well, my friend!" said Crette, slapping him on the shoulder. The touch of his hand made the chevalier shudder, and almost froze the marrow in his bones— "What ails you? Here's Constance."

Tancrede raised his head, and fixed upon his friend a pair of haggard eyes.

"Ah! Crette!—ah! Constance! I thought—Pardon!"

"What did you think? See, here is Madame d'Anguilhem come to look for you, and you look as if you were afraid of her," said the marquis giving his hand to Tancrede, and at the same time slipping him Sylvandire's letter. "It is eleven o'clock, chevalier, take your wife away."

"Oh, yes! yes!" cried Tancrede, "to the end of the world, if need be."

"No, not so far as that," replied Crette; "it is not necessary now."

Then, while the bride and bridegroom passed down the room, the marquis said aloud:

"Have you heard the news, ladies and gentlemen? The Persian embassador departs to-morrow, with all his suite. I have promised to see him off. He will embark at Chaillot."

"We shall not go, shall we?" said Constance, opening their chamber door.

"Oh, no!" replied Tancrede, shutting it.

Next day Crette communicated to his friend the two engagements he had entered into with Mlle. Poussette. The first of which, the remittance of the twenty thousand francs, had been scrupulously fulfilled the evening before by the marquis.

As the chevalier was a man of honor, and incapable of

deceiving his friends, we do not doubt that in time the second engagement was kept with the same fidelity.

It is scarcely necessary to say, that Constance and Tancrede are still quoted as a model of domestic felicity, not at Paris, where good examples are quickly forgotten, but at Loches and its environs.

THE END.